"The queer teen historical you didn't know was missing from your life." **—TEEN VOGUE**

"A warm and joyous romp of a book, with a beautifully constructed romance and a thoughtful examination of intersectional privilege. And it's possibly the most purely fun book I've encountered in ages." **—CONSTANCE GRADY, VOX.COM**

"A rollicking ride that also turns a keen eye to issues like class, racism, homosexuality, and identity." **—BRIGHTLY.COM**

"Lee's rip-roaring, genre-trampling, beautifully affirmative novel absolutely lives up to the hype, whisking readers off on a breathless and refreshingly unique adventure. . . . Her wholly unique voice provides a raucous, funny and devastatingly moving tale of defiant originality, self-acceptance, and love in all its wonderful and unpredictable forms."
—RT BOOK REVIEWS

"Careening from fete to fiasco on a Grand Tour of eighteenth century Europe, *The Gentlemen's Guide to Vice And Virtue* is a dizzying, dazzling, and roguishly romantic romp. This book makes me want to unrequite my own love so I can requite him all over again."
—HEIDI HEILIG, AUTHOR OF *THE GIRL FROM EVERYWHERE*

"Don't read this book unless you like adventure, hijinks, and forbidden romance, and if you do, then read it twice."
—STACEY LEE, AUTHOR OF
THE SECRET OF A HEART NOTE* AND *UNDER A PAINTED SKY

"An outrageously fun, witty, fascinating, and romantic adventure, starring a memorable trio I'd happily travel with for ages. Lee is a definite force in diverse historical YA."

—DAHLIA ADLER, FOUNDER OF LGBTQ READS
AND AUTHOR OF *UNDER THE LIGHTS*

"*The Gentleman's Guide to Vice and Virtue* is a Grand Tour all its own. Hilarious and romantic, adventurous and scandalous, Monty's adventures are just as delightful as Monty himself. I adored this book!"

—RACHEL HAWKINS,
AUTHOR OF THE REBEL BELLE SERIES

"Sweet, smart, and powerful, *The Gentleman's Guide to Vice and Virtue* tackles timely topics that will resonate profoundly with readers—all wrapped up in a truly epic road trip. Prepare to laugh, gasp, swoon, and cheer."

—CLAIRE LEGRAND, AUTHOR OF THE WINTERSPELL SERIES

"A delightful romp of a road trip through eighteenth century Europe, packed with witty dialogue, razor-sharp pacing, and the perfect amount of swoon. You should abso-bloody-lutely read this book." —ERIN BOWMAN, AUTHOR OF *VENGEANCE ROAD*

Also by Mackenzi Lee
This Monstrous Thing
The Lady's Guide to Petticoats and Piracy

The Gentleman's Guide to Vice and Virtue

Mackenzi Lee

KATHERINE TEGEN BOOKS

An Imprint of HarperCollins Publishers

FOR BRIANA AND BETH

L'AMOUR PEUT SOULEVER DES
MONTAGNES.

Katherine Tegen Books is an imprint of HarperCollins Publishers.

The Gentleman's Guide to Vice and Virtue
Copyright © 2017 by Mackenzie Van Engelenhoven
All rights reserved. Printed in the United States of America. No part of
this book may be used or reproduced in any manner whatsoever without
written permission except in the case of brief quotations embodied in
critical articles and reviews. For information address HarperCollins
Children's Books, a division of HarperCollins Publishers,
195 Broadway, New York, NY 10007.
www.epicreads.com

Library of Congress Control Number: 2016949692
ISBN 978-0-06-238281-8

Typography by Carla Weise
Map by David Curtis
18 19 20 21 22   PC/LSCH   10 9 8 7 6 5 4 3 2 1
❖
First paperback edition, 2018

He saunter'd Europe round,
And gather'd ev'ry vice on Christian ground; . . .
The Stews and Palace equally explored,
Intrigued with glory, and with spirit whored;

. . . .
. . . .

Tried all hors-d'œuvres, all liqueurs defined,
Judicious drank, and greatly daring dined.
—Alexander Pope, *The Dunciad*

Let me put it like this. In this place, whoever looks
seriously about him and has eyes to see is bound to become
a stronger character.
—Goethe, *Italian Journey*

Our Grand Tour

Reasons I am looking
forward to our Tour:

No Father ✓
Gambling ✓
Parties ✓
A year with Percy ♡

Au revoir,
England

Cheshire,
England

Paris

What a
disaster!

Barcelona   Marseilles

Beware pirates!

The Netherlands?
Percy is NOT
going to school here.
I refuse to
believe it.

Venice Attractive people
abound!

Oia, Santorini

A surprise
detour

Why is Felicity
still with us?!

Cheshire, England

17—

1

On the morning we are to leave for our Grand Tour of the Continent, I wake in bed beside Percy. For a disorienting moment, it's unclear whether we've *slept together* or simply slept together.

Percy's still got all his clothes on from the night before, albeit most in neither the state nor the location they were in when originally donned, and while the bedcovers are a bit roughed up, there's no sign of any strumming. So although I've got nothing on but my waistcoat—by some sorcery now buttoned back to front—and one shoe, it seems safe to assume we both kept our bits to ourselves.

Which is a strange sort of relief, because I'd like to be sober the first time we're together. If there ever is a first time. Which it's starting to seem like there won't be.

Beside me, Percy rolls over, narrowly avoiding thwacking me across the nose when he tosses his arm over his head. His face settles into the crook of my elbow as he tugs far more than his share of the bedclothes to his side without waking. His hair stinks of cigars and his breath is rancid, though judging by the taste rolling around the back of my throat—a virulent tincture of baptized gin and a stranger's perfume—mine's worse.

From the other side of the room, there's the snap of drapes being pulled back, and sunlight assaults me. I throw my hands over my face. Percy flails awake with a caw like a raven's. He tries to roll over, finds me in his path, keeps rolling anyway, and ends up on top of me. My bladder protests soundly to this. We must have drunk an extraordinary amount last night if it's hanging this heavily over me. And here I was starting to feel rather smug about my ability to get foxed out of my mind most nights and then be a functioning human by the next afternoon, provided that the afternoon in question is a late one.

Which is when I realize why I am both utterly wrecked and still a little drunk—it isn't the afternoon, when I'm accustomed to rising. It's quite early in the morning, because Percy and I are leaving for the Continent today.

"Good morning, gentlemen," Sinclair says from the other side of the room. I can only make out his silhouette against the window—he's still torturing us with the goddamned sunlight. "My lord," he continues, with a brow inclined in my direction, "your mother sent me to wake you. Your carriage is scheduled to leave within the hour, and Mr. Powell and his wife are taking tea in the dining room."

From somewhere near my navel, Percy makes an affirming noise in response to his uncle and aunt's presence—a noise that resembles no human language.

"And your father arrived from London last night, my lord," Sinclair adds to me. "He wishes to see you before you depart."

Neither Percy nor I move. The lone shoe still clinging to my foot surrenders and hits the floor with a hollow *thunk* of wooden heel on Oriental carpet.

"Should I give you both a moment to recover your senses?" Sinclair asks.

"Yes," Percy and I say in unison.

Sinclair leaves—I hear the door latch behind him. Outside the window, I can hear carriage wheels crackling against the gravel drive and the calls of the grooms as they yoke the horses.

Then Percy lets out a grisly moan and I start to laugh for no reason.

He takes a swipe at me and misses. "What?"

"You sound like a bear."

"Well, you smell like a barroom floor." He slides headfirst off the bed, gets tangled in the sheets, and ends up doing a sort of bent-waist headstand with his cheek against the carpeting. His foot rams me in the stomach, a little too low for comfort, and my laugh turns into a grunt. "Steady on, there, darling."

The urge to relieve myself is too strong to ignore any longer, and I drag myself up with one hand on the hangings. A few of the stays pop. Bending down to find the chamber pot under the bed seems likely to result in my demise, or at least a premature emptying of my bladder, so I throw open the French doors and piss into the hedges instead.

When I turn back, Percy's still on the floor, upside down with his feet propped on the bed. His hair came undone from its ribboned queue while we slept and it edges his face in a wild black cloud. I pour a glass of sherry from the decanter on the sideboard and down it in two swallows. Hardly any flavor manages to kick its way through the taste of whatever crawled into my mouth and died during the night, but the hum will get me through a send-off with my parents. And days in a carriage with Felicity. Lord, give me strength.

"How did we get home last night?" Percy asks.

"Where were we last night? It's all a bit woolly after the third hand of piquet."

"I think you won that hand."

"I'm not entirely certain I was playing that hand. If we're being honest, I had a few drinks."

"And if we're truly being honest, it wasn't just a few."

"I wasn't *that* drunk, was I?"

"Monty. You tried to take your stockings off over your shoes."

I scoop a handful of water from the basin Sinclair left, toss it across my face, then slap myself a few times— a feeble attempt to rally for the day. There's a *flump* behind me as Percy rolls the rest of the way onto the rug.

I wrangle my waistcoat off over my head and drop it onto the floor. From his back, Percy points at my stomach. "You've something peculiar down there."

"What?" I look down. There's a smear of bright red rouge below my navel. "Look at that."

"How do you suppose that got there?" Percy asks with a smirk as I spit on my hand and scrub at it.

"A gentleman doesn't tell."

"Was it a gentleman?"

"Swear to God, Perce, if I remembered, I'd tell you." I take another swallow of sherry straight out of the decanter and set it down on the sideboard, nearly missing. It lands a little harder than I meant. "It's a burden, you know."

"What is?"

"Being this good-looking. Not a soul can keep their hands off me."

He laughs, closemouthed. "Poor Monty, such a cross."

"Cross? What cross?"

"Everyone falls in immediate, passionate love with you."

"They can hardly be blamed. I'd fall in love with me, if I met me." And then I flash him a smile that is equal parts rapscallion and boyish dimples so deep you could pour tea into them.

"As modest as you are handsome." He arches his back—an exaggerated stretch with his head pressed into the rug and fingers woven together above him. Percy's showy about so few things, but he's a damned opera in the mornings. "Are you ready for today?"

"I suppose? I haven't much been involved in the planning, my father's done it all. And if everything wasn't prepared, he wouldn't be sending us off."

"Has Felicity stopped screaming about school?"

"I don't have a notion where Felicity's mind's at. I still don't see why we have to take her along."

"Only as far as Marseilles."

"After two goddamned months in Paris."

"You'll survive one more summer with your sister."

Above us, the baby kicks up his crying—the floorboards aren't near enough to stifle it—followed by the sound of the nursemaid's heels as she dashes to his call, a clack like horses' hooves on cobbles.

Percy and I both flick our eyes to the ceiling.

"The Goblin's awake," I say lightly. Muted as it is, his wailing stokes the ache pulsing in my head.

"Try not to sound too happy about his existence."

I've seen very little of my baby brother since he

arrived three months previous, just enough to marvel at, firstly, how strange and shriveled he looks, like a tomato that's been left out in the sun for the summer, and, secondly, how someone so tiny has such huge potential to ruin my entire bloody life.

I suck a drop of sherry from my thumb. "What a menace he is."

"He can't be that much of a menace, he's only about this big." Percy holds his hands up in demonstration.

"He shows up out of nowhere—"

"Not sure you can claim *out of nowhere*—"

"—and then cries all the while and wakes us and takes up space."

"The nerve."

"You're not being very sympathetic."

"You're not giving me many reasons to be."

I throw a pillow at him, which he's still too sleepy to bat away in time, so it hits him straight in the face. He gives it a halfhearted toss back at me as I flop across the bed, lying on my stomach with my head hanging over the edge and my face above his.

He raises his eyebrows. "That's a very serious face. Are you making plans to sell the Goblin off to a roving troupe of players in hopes they'll raise him as one of their own? You failed with Felicity, but the second time might be the charm."

In truth, I am thinking how this tousle-haired,

bit-off-his-guard, morning-after Percy is my absolute favorite Percy. I am thinking that if Percy and I have this last junket together on the Continent, I intend to fill it with as many mornings like this as possible. I am thinking how I am going to spend the next year ignoring the fact that there will be any year beyond it—I will get wildly drunk whenever possible, dally with pretty girls who have foreign accents, and wake up beside Percy, savoring the pleasant kick of my heartbeat whenever I'm near him.

I reach down and touch his lips with my ring finger. I think about winking as well, which is, admittedly, a tad excessive, but I've always been of the mind that subtlety is a waste of time. Fortune favors the flirtatious.

And by now, if Percy doesn't know how I feel, it's his own damn fault for being thick.

"I am thinking that today we are leaving on our Grand Tour," I reply, "and I'm not going to waste any of it."

2

Breakfast is laid out in the dining room when we arrive and the staff have already made themselves scarce. The French doors are flung wide so the hazy morning sunshine flutters in across the veranda, curtains billowing inward when the wind catches them. The gold inlay along the scrollwork glows dewy and warm in the light.

Mother looks like she's already been up for hours, in a blue Jesuit with her lovely dark hair swept back in a neat chignon. I ruffle my fingers through mine, trying to work it into that deliberately rumpled look I usually favor, handsome in the *it looked like this when I woke* sort of way. Across the table from her, Percy's aunt and uncle are straight-faced and unspeaking. There's food enough for a militia spread before the three of them, but Mother's poking at a single boiled egg in a delftware cup—she's been making a valiant effort to reclaim her figure since the Goblin wreaked havoc upon it—and neither of Percy's guardians is having more than coffee. Percy and I are unlikely to make any noticeable impact either—my stomach's still precarious, and Percy's finicky about food. He stopped eating meat a year ago, like some sort of extended Lent, claiming it's for his health, but he's still sick in bed far more often than I am. It's hard to be sympathetic when I've told him ever since he adopted it that unless he gives me a better explanation, I think his diet is absurd.

Percy's aunt reaches out when we enter, and he takes her hand. They have the same soft features—thin nosed and fine boned—as Percy's father has in portraits, though Percy's got thick black hair that grows in coarse curls and defies wigs, queues, and anything fashionable. Percy's lived with his aunt and uncle all his life, ever since his father returned from the family estate in Barbados with a jungle fever, his French violin, and an infant son with skin the color of sandalwood, then expired. Lucky for Percy, his aunt and uncle took him in. Lucky for me as well, or else we might never have met, and then what would have been the point of my life?

My mother looks up as we enter and smooths the wrinkles around the corners of her eyes like they're creases in a tablecloth. "And the gentlemen arise."

"Good morning, Mother."

Percy gives her a little bow before he sits, like he's a

proper guest. It's a ridiculous pretense from a lad I know better than either of my actual siblings. And also like a fair amount more.

The actual sibling present doesn't acknowledge our arrival. She has one of her amatory novels propped against a crystal jam pot, a serving fork wedged between the pages to hold it open. "That'll melt your brain, Felicity," I say as I drop into the seat beside her.

"Not as fast as gin will," she replies without looking up.

My father—thank God—is absent.

"Felicity," my mother hisses down to her. "Perhaps you should remove your spectacles at the table."

"I need them for reading," Felicity says, eyes still fixed upon her smut.

"You shouldn't be reading at all. We have guests."

Felicity licks her finger and turns the page. Mother glowers down at the cutlery. I help myself to a piece of toast from a silver rack and settle in to watch them volley. It's always pleasant when it's Felicity being needled instead of me.

Mother glances across the table at Percy—his aunt is plucking at the rather distinct cigar burn on the braided cuff of his coat—then says to me in a confidential tone, "One of my maids found a pair of your breeches in the harpsichord this morning. I believe they were the same ones you left the house in last night."

"That's . . . odd," I say—I thought I'd lost them long before we got home. I have a sudden memory of stripping off my clothes as Percy and I staggered through the parlor in the wee dawn hours, scattering them behind me like fallen trees. "Didn't happen to find a shoe as well, did she?"

"Did you want them packed?"

"I'm sure I've plenty."

"I wish you had at least looked through what was sent."

"What for? I can send for anything I've left behind, and we'll be getting new duds in Paris."

"It makes me anxious to think of sending your fine things to some unknown French flat with a strange staff."

"Father arranged the flat, and the staff. Take it up with him if you're skittish."

"I'm skittish about you two boys on your own on the Continent for a year."

"Well, you should have raised that concern a bit earlier than the day we leave."

My mother purses her lips and goes back to poking at her egg.

Like a summoned demon, my father appears suddenly in the doorway to the dining room. My pulse rocks, and I tuck into my toast, like food might disguise me as his gaze roams the table. His golden hair is slicked back into a tidy queue, the way mine might have a prayer of looking if it didn't spend most of its life getting raked through by the fingers of interested parties.

I can tell he's come for me, but he casts his attention first upon my mother, just long enough to kiss her on the top of the head, before it snags upon my sister. "Felicity, get those goddamn spectacles off your face."

"I need them for reading," she replies without looking up.

"You shouldn't be reading at the breakfast table."

"Father—"

"Remove them at once or I'll snap them in half. Henry, I'd like a word."

My Christian name from my father's mouth jars me so badly I actually wince. We share that ghastly *Henry*, and every time he says it, there's a bit of a grit-toothed grimace, like he deeply regrets my christening. I half expected him and Mother to call the Goblin "Henry" as well, in hopes of bequeathing the name to someone who still has a chance of proving worthy of it.

"Why don't you sit and have some breakfast with us?" Mother says. Father has his hands on her shoulders, and she places one of hers overtop, trying to drag him into the empty chair on her other side, but he pulls away.

"I need a private word with Henry." He nods at Percy's aunt and uncle with hardly a glance—proper salutations aren't for lower members of the peerage.

"The boys are leaving today," Mother tries again.

"I know that. Why else would I wish to speak to Henry?" He lobs a frown in my direction. "Now, if you don't mind."

I toss my napkin onto the table and follow him from the room. As I pass Percy, he looks up at me and his mouth curls into a sympathetic smile. The faint freckles he's got splattered below his eyes twist up. I give him an affectionate flick on the back of the head as I go by.

I follow my father into his sitting room. The windows are thrown open, lace drapes casting lattice shadows over the floor and the sickly perfume of spring blossoms dying on the vine blowing in from the yard. Father sits down at his desk and shuffles through the papers stacked there. For a moment, I think he's going to start back in on his work and leave me to sit and stare at him like an imbecile. I take a calculated risk and reach for the brandy on the sideboard, but Father says, "Henry," and I stop.

"Yes, sir."

"Do you remember Mr. Lockwood?"

I look up and realize there's a scholarly swell already standing beside the fire. He's redheaded and ruddy cheeked, with a patchy beard decorating his chin. I had been so intent on my father, I'd failed to notice him.

Mr. Lockwood gives me a short bow, spectacles slipping down his nose. "My lord. I'm sure we'll become better acquainted in the coming months, as we travel together."

I'd like to throw up on his buckled shoes, but I refrain. I hadn't wanted a bear-leader, primarily because I'm not interested in any of the scholarly things a bear-leader is meant to teach his charges. But a guardian presence of their selection had been one of my parents' conditions for my touring, and as I had very few chips to wager in that game, I had agreed.

Father laces the papers he was mucking with into a leather skin and extends it to Lockwood. "Preliminary documents. Passports, letters of credit, bills of health, introductions to my acquaintances in France." Lockwood tucks the papers into his coat, and Father twists around to face me, one elbow resting on his desk. I slide my hands between my legs and the sofa.

"Sit up straight," he snaps. "You're small enough without slumping."

With more effort than it should take, I pull back my shoulders and look him in the eye. He frowns, and I nearly sink straight back down.

"What do you think I wish to speak about, Henry?" he says.

"I don't know, sir."

"Well, take a guess." I look down, which I know is a mistake but I can't help it. "Look at me when I'm speaking to you."

I raise my eyes, staring at a spot over his head so I don't have to look straight at him. "Did you want to discuss my Tour?"

He rolls his eyes, a short flick skyward that's just long enough to make me feel like a bleeding simpleton, and my temper flares—why ask such an obvious question if he was just going to mock me when I answered?—but I keep silent. A lecture is gathering in the air like a thunderstorm.

"I want to be certain you're clear on the conditions of this Tour before you depart," he says. "I still believe your mother and I are foolish to indulge you a single inch further than we already have since your expulsion from Eton. But, against my better judgment, I am giving you this one year to get ahold of yourself. Do you understand me?"

"Yes, sir."

"Mr. Lockwood and I have discussed what we think is the best course of action for your time abroad."

"Course of action?" I repeat, looking between them. Up until this moment, I'd thought we all understood that this year was for Percy and me to do as we pleased, with a bear-leader along to arrange the annoying things like lodging and food and provide an obligatory parental eye that, like any good parental eye, would be frequently blind to youthful iniquities.

Mr. Lockwood clears his throat rather grandly, stepping into the light from the window, then back out at once, blinking the sun from his eyes. "Your father and I have discussed your situation and determined that you will be best served with some restraints placed upon your activities while on the Continent."

I look between him and my father, like one of them will crack and confess this is a jest, because restraints were certainly not part of the understanding I came to with my parents when this Tour was first agreed upon.

"Under my watch," Lockwood says, "there will be no gambling, limited tobacco, and absolutely no cigars."

Well, this is turning a bit not good.

"No visitations to any dens of iniquity," he goes on, "or sordid establishments of any kind. No caterwauling, no inappropriate relations with the opposite sex. No fornication. No slothfulness, or excessive sleeping late."

It's beginning to feel like he's shuffling his way through the seven deadly sins, in ascending order of my favorites.

"And," he says, rust on the razor's edge, "spirits in moderation only."

I'm ready to protest loudly to this until I catch my father's hard stare. "And I defer entirely to Mr. Lockwood's judgment," he says. "While you travel, he speaks for me."

Which is exactly the last thing I need accompanying me to the Continent—a surrogate of my father.

"When you and I next see each other," he continues, "I expect you to be sober and stable and"—he casts a look at Lockwood, like he's unsure how to tactfully phrase this—"discreet, at the very least. Your ridiculous little cries for attention are to cease, and you'll begin working at my side on the management of the estate and the peerage."

I would rather have my eyes gouged out with sucket forks and fed back to me, but it seems best not to tell him so.

"I have set your itinerary with your father," Lockwood says, withdrawing a small pad from his pocket and consulting it with a squint. "We begin in Paris for the summer—"

"I have some colleagues I'd like you to call on there," Father interrupts. "Acquaintances it will be important for you to maintain once you're over the estate. And I've arranged for you to accompany our friend Lord Ambassador Robert Worthington and his wife to a ball at Versailles. You will not embarrass me."

"When have I ever embarrassed you?" I murmur.

As soon as I say it, I can feel us both riffle through our mental libraries for each incident in which I shamed my father. It's an extensive catalogue. Neither of us says any of it aloud, though. Not with Mr. Lockwood here.

Lockwood chooses to take a clumsy hack through the awkward silence by pretending it doesn't exist. "From Paris, we continue on to Marseilles, where we will deliver your sister, Miss Montague, for school. I have accommodation arranged as far as there. We will winter in Italy—I have suggested Venice, Florence, and Rome, and your father concurs—then either Geneva or Berlin, depending upon the snowfall in the Alps. On our return, we will collect your sister, and the two of you will be home for the summer. Mr. Newton will make his own way to Holland for school."

The air in the room is hot, and it's making me feel petulant. Or perhaps I'm entitled to a little petulance because this whole lecture seems a bit of a sour send-off and I'm still rather panicked over the fact that at the end of all this, Percy's going to bloody law school in bloody Holland and I'm going to be properly apart from him for the first time in my life.

But then Father gives me a frostbitten look, and I drop my gaze. "Fine."

"Excuse me?"

"Yes, sir."

Father stares hard at me, his hands folded before him. For a moment, none of us speaks. Outside on the drive, one of the footmen scolds a groom to step lively. A mare nickers.

"Mr. Lockwood," Father says, "may I have a moment alone with my son?"

As one, my muscles all clench in anticipation.

On his way to the door, Mr. Lockwood pauses at my side and gives me a short clap on the shoulder that's so firm it makes me start. I was expecting a swing to come from entirely the opposite direction and be significantly less friendly. "We're going to have an excellent time, my lord," he says. "You will hear poetry and symphonies and see the finest treasures the world has to offer. It will be a cultural experience that will shape the remainder of your life."

Dear. Lord. Fortune has well and truly vomited down my front in the form of Mr. Lockwood.

As Lockwood closes the door, Father reaches toward me and I flinch, but he's only going for the brandy on the sideboard, moving it out of my grasp. God, I've got to get my head on straight.

"This is the *last chance* I'm giving you, Henry," he says, a bit of the old French accent peeping through, as it always does when his temper is rising. Those soft edges on his vowels are usually my first warning, and I almost put my hands up preemptively. "When you return home, we'll start in on the estate work. Together. You'll come to London with me and observe the duties of a lord there. And if you can't return to us mature enough for that, then don't come back at all. There'll be no place left for you in this family or any of our finances. You'll be out."

Right on schedule, the disinheritance rears its ugly head. But after years of holding it over me—*clean up, sober up, stop letting lads climb in through your bedroom window at night or else*—for the first time, we both know he means it. Because until a few months ago, if it wasn't me who got the estate, he'd have had no one to pass it to that would keep it in the family.

Upstairs, the Goblin begins to wail.

"Indicate that you understand me, Henry," Father snaps, and I force myself to meet his eyes again.

"Yes, sir. I understand you."

He lets loose a long sigh, paired with the thin-lipped disappointment of a man who's just seen the unrecognizable results of a commissioned portrait of himself. "I hope you one day have a son that's as much of a leech as you are. Now, you've a coach waiting."

I fly to my feet, ready to be rid of this sweltering room. But before I get far, he calls, "One final thing." I turn back with the hope we might speak from a distance, but he crooks a finger until I consent to return to his side. He casts a glance at the door, though Lockwood is long gone, then says to me in a low voice, "If I catch even a whiff of you mucking around with boys, while you're away or once you return, you'll be cut off. Permanently. No further conversation about it."

And that is our farewell in its entirety.

Out of doors, the sun still feels like a personal affront. The air is steamy, a ferric storm beginning to conspire at the horizon. The hedges along our drive sparkle where the dew sits, leaves turned to the light and shivering when the wind runs through them. The gravel crunches as the horses paw at it, harnessed and anxious to depart.

Percy is already at the carriage, his back to the house, which allows me an unobserved moment of staring at his arse—not that it's particularly noteworthy arse, but it's Percy's, which is what makes it very much worth the noting. He's directing one of the porters loading the last of our luggage that wasn't sent ahead. "I'll keep it with me," he's saying, his arms extended.

"There's room to stow it, sir."

"I know. I'd rather have it with me is all."

The porter surrenders and hands Percy his fiddle case, the only relic left him by his father, which he cuddles like he was concerned they'd never see each other again.

"Have your aunt and uncle gone?" I call as I cross the drive toward him and he looks up from stroking his fiddle case.

"Yes, we had a chaste farewell. What did your father want?"

"Oh, the usual. Told me not to break too many hearts." I rub my temples. A headache is building to a boil behind my eyes. "Christ, it's bright. Are we off soon?"

"There's your mother and Felicity." Percy nods in the direction of the front steps, where the pair of them are silhouetted against the white stone like they're fashioned from cut paper. "You'd best say good-bye."

"Kiss for good luck?"

I lean in, but Percy puts the fiddle case between us with a laugh. "Good try, Monty."

Hard not to let that pinch.

Felicity is looking sour and unattractive as usual, with her face scrunched up against the sun. She's got the bridge specs tucked down the front of her Brunswick—Mother might not have noticed, but I can see the imprint of the chain through the fabric. Barely five and ten and she already looks like a spinster.

"Please," Mother is saying to her, though Felicity's staring into the sun like she's more interested in going blind than in taking maternal counsel. "I don't want letters from the school about you."

The finishing school has been a long time coming, but Felicity is still so scowly about it you'd think she hadn't spent all her born days proving to my parents that if one of their children needed civilizing, it was she. Contrary thing that she is, she's begged for an education for years, and now that it's finally handed to her, she's dug in her heels like a stubborn mule.

Mother opens her arms. "Felicity, come kiss me good-bye."

"I'd rather not," Felicity replies, and stalks down the steps toward the carriage.

My mother sighs through her nose, but lets her go. Then she turns to me. "You'll write."

"Of course."

"Don't drink too much."

"Could I get an absolute value on *too much*?"

"Henry," she says, the same sigh behind her voice as when Felicity stormed away. The *what are we to do with you?* sort.

"Right. Yes. I won't."

"Try to behave. And don't torment Felicity."

"Mother. I'm the victim. She torments *me*."

"She's fifteen."

"The most vicious age."

"Try to be a gentleman, Henry. Just try." She kisses me on the cheek, then gives my arm a pat like she might a dog. Her skirts rasp against the stone as she turns back into the house and I go the opposite way down the drive, one hand rising to shield my face from the sun.

I swing myself into the carriage, and the footman shuts the door behind me. Percy's got his fiddle case balanced on his knees and he's playing with the latches. Felicity's scrunched up in one corner, like she's trying to get as far from us as possible. She's already reading.

I slide into the seat beside Percy and pull my pipe from my coat.

Felicity executes an eye roll that must give her a spectacular view of the inside of her skull. "Please, brother, we haven't even left the county, don't smoke yet."

"Nice to have you along, Felicity." I clamp the pipe

26

between my teeth and fish about in my pocket for the flint. "Remind me again where we're permitted to drop you by the side of the road."

"Keen to make more room in the carriage for your harem of boys?"

I scowl, and she tucks back into her novel, looking a bit smugger than before.

The coach door opens, and Mr. Lockwood clambers up beside Felicity, knocking his head on the frame as he goes. She slinks a little farther into the corner.

"Now, gentlemen. Lady." He polishes his spectacles on the tails of his coat, replaces them, and offers us what I think is meant to be a smile, but he's so toothy the effect is a bit like that of an embarrassed shark. "I believe we're ready to depart."

There's a whistle from the footman, then the axles creak as the coach gives a sudden lurch forward. Percy catches himself on my knee.

And like that, we are off.

The great tragic love story of Percy and me is neither great nor truly a love story, and is tragic only for its single-sidedness. It is also not an epic monolith that has plagued me since boyhood, as might be expected. Rather, it is simply the tale of how two people can be important to each other their whole lives, and then, one morning, quite without meaning to, one of them wakes to find that importance has been magnified into a sudden and intense desire to put his tongue in the other's mouth.

A long, slow slide, then a sudden impact.

Though the story of Percy and me—the account sans love and tragedy—is forever. As far back as I can remember, Percy has been in my life. We've ridden and hunted and sunbathed and reveled together since we were barely old enough to walk, fought and made up and run amok across the countryside. We've shared all our firsts—first lost tooth, first broken bone, first school day, the first time we were ever sweet on a girl (though I have always been more vocal about and passionate in my infatuations than Percy). First time drunk, when we were reading at our parsonage's Easter service but got foxed on nicked wine before. We were just sober enough to think we were subtle about it and just tipsy enough that we were likely as subtle as a symphony.

Even the first kiss I ever had, though disappointingly not with Percy, still involved him, in a roundabout way. I'd kissed Richard Peele at my father's Christmas party the year I turned thirteen, and though I thought it was quite a fine kiss, as far as first ones go, he got cold feet about it and blabbed to his parents and the other Cheshire lads and everyone who would listen that I was perverted and had forced myself on him, which was untrue, for I would like it to be noted that I have never forced myself on anyone. (I'd also like it noted that every time since then that Richard Peele and I have had a shag, it's always been at his volition. I am but a willing stander-by.) My father made me apologize to the Peeles, while he gave them the *lots of boys mess around at that age* speech—which he's gotten a lot of use out of over the years, though the *at that age* part is becoming less and less relevant—then, after they'd left, he hit me so hard my vision went spotty.

So I had walked around for weeks wearing an ugly

bruise and mottled shame, with everyone eyeing me sideways and making spiteful remarks within my earshot, and I began to feel certain I had turned all my friends against me for something I couldn't help. But the next time the boys played billiards in town, Percy bashed Richard in the side of the face with his cue so hard that he lost a tooth. Percy apologized, like it was an accident, but it was fairly transparent vengeance. Percy had avenged me when no one else would look me in the eyes.

The truth is that Percy has always been important to me, long before I fell so hard for him there was an audible *crash*. It's only lately that his knee bumping mine under a narrow pub table leaves me fumbling for words. A small shift in the gravity between us and suddenly all my stars are out of alignment, planets knocked from their orbits, and I'm left stumbling, without map or heading, through the bewildering territory of being in love with your best friend.

If the whole of England were sinking into the sea and I had the only boat with a seat for a single person more, I'd save Percy. And if he'd already drowned, I probably wouldn't save anyone. Probably there wouldn't be much point in me going forward either. Though I would hang on because I'd likely wash up in France, and from what I remember from the summer my family spent there when Felicity and I were young, there are some lovely women in France. Some handsome boys as well, many of whom wear their breeches very tight, though I wasn't clear where I stood on that when I was eleven.

As we sail across the Channel toward Calais, this is what I'm thinking of—Percy and me and England sinking into the sea behind us, and also French lads and their tight breeches and, zounds, I can't wait to get to Paris. I am also maybe a tiny bit drunk. I nicked a bottle of gin from a bar before we left Dover, and Percy and I have been passing it between us for the last hour. There are still a few swallows left.

I haven't seen Felicity since we boarded the packet, nor much of Lockwood either—he spent most of our time in Dover as we waited for a storm to pass fussing over luggage and customs and correspondence. Then, once the boat left the harbor, our bear-leader became occupied with being sick over the rail, and we became occupied with avoiding him, and those two activities were perfectly compatible.

Beyond the prow of the packet, the water and the sky are the same ghostly gray, but through the fog I can make out the first signs of the port winking at us—a link of golden lights gilding the invisible coastline like a chain. The waves are rough, and side by side, with our elbows upon the rail, Percy and I keep bumping shoulders. When we strike a rough patch and he nearly loses his footing, I seize the chance to grab him by the hand and haul him upright again. I have become a veritable scholar in seemingly innocent ploys to get his skin against mine.

It's the first time we've been properly alone together since Cheshire, and I've spent the whole while filling him in on the tyrannical restraints placed upon us by Lockwood and my father. Percy listens with his fists stacked atop each other on the railing and his chin resting upon them. When I'm finished, he wordlessly hands me the gin bottle. I snatch it with the plan to drain it, only to find he's beat me to it. "Bastard." He laughs, and I pitch the bottle into the gray water, where it bobs for a moment before the bow of the packet sucks it under. "How is it that we've landed the only bear-leader for hire who's entirely opposed to the true purpose of the Tour?"

"Which is . . . remind me."

"Strong spirits and loose women."

"Sounds instead like it's going to be weak wine with dinner and handling yourself in your bedroom after."

"No shame in that. If the Good Lord didn't want men to play with themselves, we'd have hooks for hands. Still, I'd rather not be keeping myself company from now until next September. God, this is going to be a disaster." I look to him, hoping for some sort of despair that is at least on a comparable level with mine—I thought we were all operating under the same understanding that this year was to be for Percy and me to do as we pleased before he goes to school and I load stones in my pockets and throw myself into the ocean—but instead he's looking aggravatingly pleased. "Hold on, are you keen on all this cultural shite?"

"I'm not . . . *not* keen." And then he gives me a smile that I think is supposed to be apologetic but instead looks very, *very* keen.

"No, no, no, you have to be on my side about this! Lockwood is tyranny and oppression and all that! Don't be seduced away by his promises of poetry and symphonies and—Dear Lord, am I to be subjected to *music* for the entirety of our Tour?"

"Absolutely you will. And the only thing you will hate more than listening to Lockwood's selected music will be listening to me talk about said music. Sometimes I'll talk to Lockwood *about* music and you will *hate* it. You're going to have to listen to me *and* Lockwood using words like *atonal* and *chromatic scale* and *cadenza*."

"*Et tu?*"

"Aw, look at you using your Latin vocabulary. Eton wasn't a waste in its entirety."

"That was Latin *and* history, so take that—I'm highly educated." I turn my face to his—or, more accurately, up to his. Percy's taller than most, and I'm unencumbered with excessive stature, so though I swear there was a time we were the same height, it's ancient history—he's got the aerial advantage over me these days. Most men do, and some ladies as well—Felicity's nearly as tall as I am, which is mortifying.

Percy tucks a piece of my collar that's been blown asunder back into place, his fingers brushing the bare skin along my neck for a second. "What did you think this year was going to be? Gambling halls and cathouses the whole while? You will grow weary of that, you know. Fornication with strangers in piss-rank alleyways loses its bittersweet charm with time."

"I suppose I thought it was going to be you and me."

"Fornicating in alleyways?"

"No, you dunce, but . . . the two of us. Doing what we wanted." Perfecting my phrasing without betraying my heart is starting to feel like a complicated dance. "Together."

"Still will be."

"Yes, but I mean, the last year before you go to law school and I start working with my father and we won't be seeing each other so much."

"Yes. Law school." Percy turns his face to the coastline again, a thin-fingered breeze rising off the water and pulling a few strands free from the ribbon tying off his queue. He's been talking for months about cutting his hair short so it's easier to get under a wig, but I've made it clear I will murder him if he does, for I quite adore that unruly mop of his.

I press my face into his shoulder to make him pay attention to me again and give a theatrical moan. "But bloody Lockwood and his bloody cultural outings have wrecked that."

Percy twists a lock of my hair between his fingers, a soft smile teasing his lips. My heart kicks again, so hard I have to catch my breath. It's unfair that I can nearly always tell when someone's making eyes at me, except when it comes to Percy, as we've always been rather hands-on with each other. Impossible now, after so long, to ask him not to be without admitting why. Can't seal up a conversation with a casual *Oh, by the way, could you perhaps not touch me the way you always have because each time it puts fresh splinters in my heart?* Particularly when what I'd really like to say is *Oh, by the way, could you please keep touching me, and perhaps do it all the time, and while we're at it, would you like to take off all your clothes and climb in bed?* They're both weighted alike.

He gives a tug on my hair. "I have an idea of how we will survive the year. We shall pretend that we are pirates—"

"Oh, I love this."

"—storming some sort of city fortress. Sacking it for gold. Like we used to."

"Remind me of your pirate alias."

"Captain Two Tooth the Terrible."

"Threatening."

"I was six, I only had about two teeth at the time. And it's *Captain*. *Captain* Two Tooth the Terrible."

"Pardon me, Captain."

"So insubordinate. I should have you locked in the brig."

As the packet skips forward with its nose to France, we talk for a while, and then we don't, and then we do again, and I am reminded of how exquisitely easy friendship with Percy is, equal parts comfortable silence and never lacking things to say to each other.

Or rather it *was* easy, until I ruined it by losing my bleeding mind every time he does that thing where he tips his head to the side when he smiles.

We're still there, holding court at the prow, when the sailors begin to scamper about the deck and, high above us, the bell peals, a low, somber note in continuum. Passengers emerge from below and cluster at the rails, moths drawn to the fool's gold shine of the approaching coastline.

Percy rests his chin on top of my head, his hands on my shoulders as we too turn our faces to the shore. "Did you know—" he says.

"Oh, are we playing the *did you know* game?"

"Did you know this year is not going to be a disaster?"

"I don't believe it."

"It is not going to be a disaster," he repeats overtop of me, "because it is you and I and the Continent and not even Lockwood or your father can wreck it completely. I promise."

He nudges the side of my head with his nose until I consent to look up at him, then does that tipped-head smile again, and I swear to God it's so adorable I forget my own damn name.

"France on the horizon, Captain," I say.

"Steel thyself, mate," he replies.

Paris

Before the end of our first month in Paris, the violent biblical deaths we are seeing immortalized in paintings and hung in an endless procession of private collections are beginning to look rather appealing.

In spite of Percy's assurance otherwise, the days are a succession of dull disasters. I have lived most of my life as a devotee of the philosophy that a man should not see two sevens in one day, but most mornings Lockwood sends Sinclair in to wake me hours before I want to be woken. I am then stuffed into suitable attire and shoved into the dining room of our French apartments, where I'm forced to sit through a civilized breakfast and not put my head down on my eggs or stab my bear-leader in the eye with the cutlery.

While Felicity stays behind at the apartments, Lockwood takes Percy and me out most afternoons, sometimes for meaningless strolls to soak up the city like a stain, sometimes for formal gatherings, sometimes for visits to various sites that are meant to be intellectually stimulating and instead have me considering feigning some sort of debilitating illness just to be allowed to withdraw. The galleries all start to look the same—even the Louvre Palace, still full of art the French royal family left there when they abandoned it for Versailles, doesn't hold my attention for long. The collectors themselves are the worst—most of them my father's friends, all rich men and variations on him. Conversing with them makes me tense and twitchy, waiting for someone to mock me if I say the wrong thing.

Even Paris itself is a cruel mistress—it's a shithole of a place, with more people crammed into it than seems possible and truly incredible traffic. Twice as many carriages and handcarts and sedans crowd the streets as in London, and there are no footpaths to speak of. The buildings are taller than in London as well, the lanes weaving them together narrow, their stones weathered and slick. Sewage falls from the windows as chamber pots are tossed, and the gutters fester with it, great mastiff dogs roaming feral through them.

But Lockwood is aggravatingly delighted by the filthy enchantment of it all, and everyone else in our little band seems to be enjoying themselves with all this art and culture and the seeing of historical sights, and I start to wonder if perhaps I'm just too stupid to do the same.

Three weeks in, Percy and I still haven't managed to escape the eye of our tyrant cicerone for a night out on our own. There's hardly an evening we aren't dragged to readings and concerts and even the goddamn opera (though not the theater, which Lockwood tells us is breeding ground for sodomites and fops, and as such sounds more to my taste), which, paired with the early mornings, leave me too worn down to work up much excitement for midnight outings. The first nocturnal excursion we're blessedly excused from is a scientific lecture Lockwood badgers us to attend, entitled "The Synthetic Panacea: An Alchemical Hypothesis," but Percy pleads an afternoon headache and I plead being entirely occupied with watching him have said headache, and Lockwood seems to trust Percy's word over mine.

Instead of our usual communal meal in the dining room, we all sup at intervals. Percy and I take the meal in his room and then lie tangled upon his bed, drowsy and languid as the sky turns bruise-colored with sunset and smoke. The first time I rise all evening is to see if I can bully one of the staff into giving me some whiskey for his ague and my enjoyment. The lanterns haven't been lit yet, and the hallway is so shadowy that I nearly smash into Felicity, who is pressed up against the wall with her shoes in her hand, wearing a plain Brunswick with the hood pulled up, like a bandit come to lift the silver.

I've done enough sneaking out in my lifetime to know precisely what she's up to.

She starts when she sees me, and clutches her boots to her chest. "What are you doing?" she hisses.

"I could ask you the same," I reply, far louder than is needed, and she flails a hand. In the sitting room, I hear Lockwood clear his throat. "Trying to escape undetected, are we?"

"Please don't tell."

"Are you meeting a boy? Or perhaps a *man*? Or have you been passing your nights as one of those dancing girls with the scarlet garters?"

"If you say one word to Lockwood," she says, her face scrunched up, "I'll tell him it was you who drank that bottle of port that he missed last week."

Now it's my turn to scrunch up my face, which isn't a good look for me. Felicity crosses her arms, and I cross mine, and we regard each other through the shadows, stalemated. Blackmail is aggravating in normal circumstances, but far worse when it's coming from a younger sister.

"Fine, I'll keep quiet," I say.

Felicity smiles, eyebrows sloping to a positively nefarious angle. "Lovely. Now be a good lad and go distract

Lockwood for me so he won't hear the door. Perhaps ask him to tell you something long and loud about Gothic architecture."

"They're going to throw you out of school if you behave this way."

"Well, it took Eton years to catch on to your larks, and I'm a fair amount cleverer, so I'm not concerned." She smiles again, and in that moment, all my childhood instincts come out, for I'd like nothing better than to give her hair a good tug. "Enjoy your evening," she says, then glides to the door, stocking-footed on the stone so she hardly needs lift her feet.

Lockwood is settled in an armchair before the fireplace, unwigged, with a banyan loose over his waistcoat. He looks up when I enter and his brow creases, as though the sight of me alone is cause for consternation. "My lord. May I help you?"

Out in the hallway, I hear the soft click of the front latch.

And if Felicity is sneaking out, it's about damn time Percy and I did so as well. "I think we'll be attending that lecture tonight after all," I say.

"Oh. Oh!" He sits up. "You and Mr. Newton both?"

"Yes," I say, offering Percy an internal apology in case his headache was real. "We'll get a coach to Montparnasse, so you needn't come—you're nearly dressed for bed. And we might have some supper after. So don't wait up."

And bless his little cotton socks, he must truly believe in the transformative power travel can have over a young man, because he swallows it.

As it turns out, it's hardly even a lie—we *do* get a coach to Montparnasse, and we *do* have supper. It consists of a pint of baptized beer downed standing up in the corner of a smoky boxing ring, then spirits at a music hall after.

The boxing is my choice, the music hall Percy's—his condition for coming out with me in spite of the headache that was apparently very much real was that at least half of the evening would be spent somewhere men weren't brutalizing one another and we can hear each other without shouting. But the music hall is packed and nearly as loud as the fights. The walls are plastered in moldering velvet and golden fringe, the ceiling painted with an elaborate mural of cherubs frolicking with naked women in foamy clouds—the cherubs seem to be there purely to keep it from being pornographic. Candles on the tables—sheathed in red glass—rouge the light.

We spend our fights' winnings on one of the private boxes in the top gallery, looking down upon the crowd and above the haze of pipe smoke. Tournaments of backgammon and faro are being played all about, shouts going up over piquet and lottery, but Percy and I keep only each other's company. It's bleeding hot with so many people packed so tight, and the box is private enough that we both shuck down to our shirtsleeves.

We finish near a Scotch pint of spirits between us before the interlude—Percy's drinking more than he usually does and it's making him giggly. I'm feeling it too—giddy and bold, coquettish at being out and alone in Paris with him and sitting on a belly of gin and warm whiskey.

Percy leans over from his chair to rest his chin upon my shoulder, one of his feet brushing my shin as it bounces in time to the music. "Having fun?"

I give a nip at his ear—meant to just lean in, but I misjudge the distance and decide halfway there to commit to it. He yelps in surprise. "No, but you are."

Music is not an art I claim to understand or enjoy, but Percy looks so happy in that moment that I feel happy too, a sudden swell of delight to be alive and here with him. Though snatching at the heels of that is the thought of the hourglass attached to these last days before Percy and I part. Our Tour suddenly seems like an impossibly short time.

For a moment, I toy with the idea that, at the end of it all, I could *not* go home. Run away to Holland with Percy. Or perhaps just run. Which would leave me stuck with nothing. No money and no skills to earn it. I'm too useless to make a life on my own, no matter how odious the one selected for me is. I'm well shackled to my father, no way to escape or want things for myself.

And what would you want even if you could? says a small voice in my head.

I've no answer, which sets off a flare of panic inside me. I suddenly feel myself to be drifting, out of even my own control.

What do you want?

The musicians take a recess and a man comes onto the stage to do a recitation of a poetical nature. A few people in the crowd boo. Percy knocks his shoulder into mine when I join them. "Stop that."

"He deserves it."

"Why? Poor thing, he's just a poet."

"Is more reason needed?" I kick my feet up on the table, misjudging the distance and catching my toe on the edge. Our empty glasses wobble. "Poetry is the most embarrassing art form. I can sort of understand why all the poets off themselves."

"It's not so easy."

"Course it is. Here, attend." I whack him on the back of the head to make him pay attention to me instead of the stage. "I'm going to write a poem about you. 'There once was a fellow named Percy,'" I start, then falter. "'Who . . .' Damn, what rhymes with *Percy*?"

"Thought you said it was easy."

"*Blercy*? That's a word, isn't it?"

Percy sips at his whiskey, then sets his glass upon

48

the rail and says with a lilt, "There was a young fellow I knew / Named Henry Montague."

"Well, that's unfair. Everything rhymes with my surname. *Blue. Chew. Mutton stew.*"

"He drinks lots of liquor / And never gets sick-er." He pauses for fullest effect, then finishes, "And he's four inches longer than you."

I burst out laughing. Percy drops his head over the back of the chair, with a grin. He looks very pleased with himself. Nothing delights me more than filthy things born from Percy's tongue. Most who know him wouldn't believe that such a quiet, polite lad has told me stories that would color a sailor's cheeks.

"Oh, Perce. That was beautiful."

"You're welcome."

"I should share it with Lockwood."

His head shoots up. "Don't you dare."

"Or at least write it down, for posterity—"

"I swear to God, I shall never speak to you again."

"Perhaps I'll say it back to myself as I'm falling asleep tonight."

He kicks the leg of my chair, and I'm nearly unseated. "Goose."

I laugh, and it comes out a tipsy giggle. "Do another one."

Percy gives me a smile, then leans forward with his

elbows on his knees like he's thinking hard. "Monty often smells of piss."

"Well, I like this one significantly less."

"But plays a wicked hand of whist."

"Better."

"Though Lockwood may doubt him, / There's something about him / That everyone just wants to . . ." And then he stops, a bright flush creeping into his cheeks.

The corners of my mouth begin to turn up. "Go on, Percy."

"What?"

"Finish it."

"Finish what?"

"Your poem."

"My what?"

"The rhyme, half-wit."

"Does it rhyme? I didn't realize. Oh, wait. . . ." He feigns reviewing the verse in his head. "I hear it now."

I lean in to him. "Come now, what were you going to say?"

"Nothing. I don't remember."

"Yes, you do. Go on." He makes a humming noise with his lips closed. "Do you want to finish it, or do you want me to keep pestering you?"

"Ah. Bit of a tough choice."

I press my foot into his shin. His stocking has slipped from his garter and is bunched up around his ankle.

"That everyone just wants to what, Percy? What is it exactly that everyone wants to do to me?"

"Fine." Now he's really blushing, poor boy. He's not so dark skinned that he can't still go fantastically red when sufficient cause arises. He blows a short breath, then scrunches up his nose. It looks like he's working rather hard not to smile. "Though Lockwood may doubt him, / There's something about him / That everyone just wants to kiss."

That single word sends a pulse up my spine like a struck lightning rod. Percy laughs and ducks his chin, suddenly shy. I mean to sit back and say something coy so we can play it off as a laugh—I swear to God, I do. But then he licks his lips, and his eyes flit to my mouth in a way that seems a little out of his control.

And I want to. So badly, I do. Just thinking about it makes all the blood leave my head. And the drink has just enough of a hold on me that the part of my brain that usually steps in the path of terrible ideas and halts them with a sensible *Steady on there, lad, let's think this one through* seems to have taken the night off. So in spite of being in possession of a full understanding of what a terrible decision it is to do so, I lean in and kiss Percy on the mouth.

I truly intend to make it a peck, just a small one, like it's only because of the rhyme and not because I've been going mad with wanting him for two years. But before

I can pull away, Percy puts his hand on the back of my neck and presses me to him and suddenly it's not me kissing Percy, it's Percy kissing me.

For perhaps a full minute, I'm so stunned that the only thing I can think is, *Dear Lord, this is actually happening*. Percy is kissing me. *Really* kissing me. Neither of us is sober, or even sober-adjacent, but at least I'm still seeing straight. And, damnation, it feels *so good*. As good as I've always imagined it would be. It makes every other kiss I've ever had turn to smoke and disappear.

And then it's not just Percy kissing me—we're kissing each other.

I can't decide if I'd rather keep my hands in his hair or do something about getting his shirt out of the way— I'm feeling frantic and scrambly, unable to commit to a single place to put my hands because I want to touch him abso-bloody-lutely *everywhere*. Then he slips his tongue into my mouth, and I am momentarily distracted by the way the entirety of my being spills over with that feeling. It's like being set aflame. More than that—it's like stars exploding, heavens on fire. Kissing Percy is an incendiary thing.

I tug his bottom lip between my teeth and work it gently, and he lets go a bright, weighted breath as he slides from his chair onto my lap. His hands go under my shirt, tearing it out of the waistband of my breeches in handfuls, then his arms slide all the way around me, and I'm struggling to stay soft, trying to think of the least arousing things possible, and it just isn't working because Percy's got his legs on either side of my lap and his mouth is open against mine and I can feel his palms up and down my back.

I run my tongue down his jawline, so enthusiastic that my teeth scrape him, at the same time working my fingers against the buttons of his breeches until the essential one pops. He inhales softly with his head tipped skyward when my fingers meet his skin. His nails dig into my spine, my shirt rucked up in his fists. I know we should be careful—it's a private box, but not *that* private, and if anyone saw us like this, we might get in real trouble—but I don't care. Not about who might be lingering nearby or the pillory for sodomites or my father's threat of what will happen if I'm caught with a lad. Nothing matters right then but him.

"Monty," he says, my name punching its way through a gasp. I don't reply because I'm far more interested in sucking on his neck than in doing any talking, but he takes my face in his hands and raises it to his. "Wait. Stop."

I stop. It may be the hardest thing I've ever had to do, though it should be noted I have not had a very hard life. "What is it?" It's ridiculous how winded I am, like I've been running.

Percy looks me dead in the eyes. I've still got one

hand spread like a starburst on his chest, and his heart is pounding against my fingertips. "Is this just a laugh to you?"

"No," I say before I can think it through. Then, when his eyes widen a little, I pin on hastily, "Yes. I dunno. What do you want me to say?"

"I want . . . Nothing. Forget it."

"Well, why'd you stop, you goose?" I think we'll take up where we left off, so I lean in again, but he ducks out of the way and I freeze, my hand hovering between us.

Then he says, very quietly, "Don't."

Which is not a particularly fine thing to hear when I've still got one hand down his trousers.

I don't move right away—give him a moment to change his mind and come back to me, though it's clear from his expression that I'm fooling myself in thinking he will. It's a fight to keep my face straight, pretend I don't have years' worth of wanting attached to this excellent kiss with the most gorgeous boy I know, but I manage to say, "Fine," without giving away how much that single word feels like the trapdoor of a scaffold falling out from under me.

Percy looks up. "Really? *Fine*?" he repeats. "That's all you have to say?"

"Fine by me." I shove him off my lap, which is what I think I would probably do if this were a laugh, but it's harder than I mean to and he falls. "You started it. You and your daft poem."

"Right, of course." Suddenly he sounds angry. He's fiddling with the buttons of his breeches, refastening them with more force than necessary. "This is my fault."

"I didn't say it was your fault, Perce, I said you started it."

"Well, you wanted it too."

"*Too*? I wanted it *too*?"

"You know what I mean."

"I really don't. And I really don't care. God, it was just a kiss!"

"Right, I forgot you'll kiss anything with a mouth." Percy picks himself up with a bit of a stumble and winces.

I reach out, even though I'm too far away to help. "You all right?"

"You just shoved me and now you're asking if I'm all right?"

"I'm trying to be decent."

"I think you missed that chance a long while ago."

"God, Perce, why are you being such a prick?"

"Let's go home."

"Fine," I say. "Let's go."

And so we conclude what might have been a fireworks-and-poetry sort of evening with the most uncomfortable walk home ever shared by any two people in history.

5

I do a valiant job of ignoring Percy for the next few days. He keeps his distance as well—I can't decide if he's avoiding me or just giving me space to cool off—though not so far that I don't notice the rather telling mark on his neck that his collars aren't quite high enough to cover. It's a fine reminder of the most mortifying thing I've ever done.

I don't claim a perfect record when it comes to romantic advances, but Percy's rejection stings like salt in an open wound. It plays in my head for days, over and over no matter how hard I try to shake it off or console myself with the memory of how good it felt before it all fell apart. My attempts to scrub it out with whiskey lifted from our kitchen do no good either. I keep hearing that single word—*don't*—and reliving the moment he pushed me away.

Lots of boys mess around at that age. I can still hear my father saying it, and it feels like a kick in the teeth every time. *Lots of boys mess around. Especially when it's late and they're mauled and far from home.*

I stay comfortably drunk for the next few days, perhaps toeing the line between comfortably and deliriously, for I forget entirely that my father arranged for us to accompany Lord Ambassador Worthington to Versailles for a summer ball until Lockwood announces it over breakfast in a voice that implies I'm an imbecile for forgetting. But it is, however temporary, a distraction from thinking of Percy. And Lockwood won't be coming, so it might be a properly good evening.

Felicity seems to be laboring under the delusion that she will not be required to attend, in spite of the fact that she shopped for outfitting alongside Percy and me when we first arrived. She gives an unconvincing performance of nondescript unwellness, and seems shocked when Lockwood is unmoved. When she finally agrees to dress, she emerges from her room looking as though she's put the least effort possible into it. She's in the French gown tailored for her, which was rather matronly to begin with, but no cosmetics and her hair is in the same twisted plait she's worn it in all day. She hasn't even washed the ink off her fingers—the remnants of some scribblings she's been doing in the margins of her novel. Her maid follows, looking cowed.

Lockwood gives a dramatic sucking-in of the cheeks, paired with an equally dramatic tapping of the foot, as he surveys her. Felicity folds her arms and surveys him straight back. She's a fierce, stubborn creature when she wants to be, and, I begrudgingly allow, it can be glorious.

"It seems," Lockwood says at last, "that the three of you all lack an understanding of the reality of your positions."

"The reality is, I don't see the point in me being made to attend tonight," Felicity says. "I've asked to go to see the galleries with you and Monty and Percy and hear the lectures, but you—"

"Well, for a start, I must say I find it inappropriate how informal you are with each other," Lockwood interrupts. "From now on, I'd like to hear you address one another properly—no given names, please, or these pet names of which you seem fond."

I nearly burst out laughing at that. I can't imagine calling Percy *Mr. Newton* with a straight face, nor can I see Felicity doing the same—Percy's around so often they might as well be siblings. They certainly get on better than she and I do. Though I'm rather cheered by the thought of Felicity being made to address me as *my lord*.

Lockwood catches my grin before I can pocket it and pivots his sights. "And you. Such blatant disregard for one's own privilege, I have never witnessed. Do you know what I was doing when I was your age? I joined the navy, risking my life for king and country. I did not have the chance or the means to take a tour of the Continent, and here you are handed that opportunity at no personal sacrifice and you squander it."

Well, this situation certainly got away from me. I don't see why it's me getting the lecture when it's only Felicity being belligerent.

"And"—Lockwood turns to Percy, seems to decide there's nothing about him that's really worth getting worked up over, and moves back to a collective address— "be forewarned that I will have very little patience for further antics from any of you. Am I understood?"

"We're late" is all Felicity says in reply—which we are. Lockwood is immediately flustered, calling for our footman and ushering us to the door, our departure so hasty that Felicity isn't made to clean up. Which is unfair.

"You'll be the talk of the evening in that rig," I say to her as I offer her my hand into the carriage. "Tell me, is that actual sackcloth, or simply plain muslin?"

"Well, you've enough frills for the both of us," she replies, ignoring my hand. "You'll put the ladies to shame."

I resist the urge to rip some of the ruched trim off the mint-colored coat I had until this moment thought was quite handsome. My little sister has inherited from my father the knack for making me a self-conscious fool about everything.

"I think you look nice," Percy tells me, which makes me want to throw something at him. He's got on an indigo coat with a flowered brocade along the cuffs and velvet breeches to match. It isn't fair that we're quarreling and he still looks so goddamn fantastic.

We meet the lord ambassador and his wife at the palace gates. He's a tall fellow with a gray buckle-rolled wig, and he has a sword hanging from his belt. His wife is short and stout, though her hair makes her nearly as tall as he is. She's powdered pale as milk, a distinct rim at her hairline that the cone missed, with too much rouge overtop and a pox patch beneath each eye. In their poor imitation of French fashion, they look like pastries in a bakery window at the end of the day, trying a bit too hard to be beautiful as they wilt.

"Lord Disley." The lord ambassador gives me a firm handshake when we meet, with one hand on my elbow like he's trying to buckle me to his side. It's a bit of an effort to pry my way out. "Well met, my lord, very well met. I've heard . . . so much about you from your father."

Which starts the evening off on a remarkably sour note.

The lord ambassador ignores Percy when he gives his hand, instead offering up a critical and not at all subtle up-and-down before he turns to Felicity. "And Miss Montague. You look so very like your mother. Such a lovely woman. You'll be so lovely someday."

Felicity frowns, like she's trying to work out whether or not what he said was a jab. I'm not certain either, though that frown is doing nothing for the case of her current loveliness.

"Oh, stop that, Robert, she's already gorgeous," his wife says, which seems to make Felicity even more uncomfortable. Lady Worthington takes her by the arm and makes her spin once, which Felicity executes with halting steps, like she isn't entirely certain what is happening but is quite certain she doesn't like it. "What an interesting dress," the lord ambassador's wife remarks, and I can't resist a snort at that one. Worthington frowns at me. So does Percy, which is far more annoying.

As one lady coos and the other reluctantly allows herself to be cooed at, the lord ambassador takes me aside and says in a confidential whisper, "Your . . . Who is that, precisely?" He nods to Percy, who is doing a rather obvious pantomime of not eavesdropping.

"My friend," I reply flatly. "He's my friend."

"Does your father know? He didn't mention you'd be bringing . . ."

"Percy's traveling with me," I say. "We're touring together."

"Oh. Oh, of course. Mr. Newton." The note of surprise in his voice is as blatant as a battle-ax as he turns to Percy. "I know your uncle."

"Do you?" Percy asks.

"Yes, old friends. He had just been appointed to the admiralty court when I was still a merchant out of Liverpool. He never mentioned he had a ward that was . . ." He drifts off, pumping his hand in a circle like he might waft an appropriate ending to that sentence our way, then instead says, "You've been in Paris since May, have you? How do you find it?"

When I don't answer, Percy steps in. "Very interesting."

"Such a fine, fine city, Paris. Though we find the food to be rather less than to our taste. The food is better in London."

"But the beds are better in Paris," I say.

"Shall we go in?" Percy says quickly.

The lord ambassador's eyes narrow a bit at me, then he claps my shoulder before leading us up the drive. I jog to catch him up before Percy can fall into step beside me.

Versailles is a delirious fantasy of a place. We cross through a card room and into the mirrored hall where the king receives his court, every surface not covered with a looking glass gilded in gold or frescoed in jewel tones. Wax drips in hot, sticky threads from the chandeliers. The light is pyrite, with snowflakes of color refracted through the crystals splattering the walls.

The party spills into the gardens, the air hot and hazy with pollen rising from the flowers in golden bursts when they're brushed. Hedges line the walks, carved into a menagerie of shapes, roses bursting between them. The stars are stifled by the furious light from the palace, and the candelabra lining the stairs are reflected like glittering coins against the bright silk everyone is wearing. People mill along the paths and beneath the open dome at the center of the Orangerie, foamy blossoms and soft-tongued orchids pressing their leaves against the glass like hands. The women are stuffed into skirts supported by panniers that make them as wide as they are tall, and everyone's hair is powdered and curled and pasted into sculptural rigidity. Percy and I are two of the only men who aren't wigged. My hair grows so thick and dark and ruffles so handsomely that I refuse to cover it until it ceases to be all or any of those things.

No one takes notice of our announcement. The atmosphere is already far too feverish.

The ambassador's wife peels Felicity away from us, leaving Percy and me to her husband. I try to wander away to secure both a drink and someone to make eyes at across the crowd that I can promise will end with someone's trousers off. But Worthington sticks closer to me than I would like, making introductions to a parade of nobles who all look the same in their wigs and powder and forcing me to be a spectator to polite conversation about the poet Voltaire's exile to England, whether bachelors should be made to pay higher taxes, the broken-off engagement between the boy king of France and the Spanish infanta and what that means for relations between the houses of Hapsburg and Bourbon.

This is going to be the rest of your life, says a small voice in the back of my head.

I've never been good at feigning sincerity, or pretending to be keen on things I'm not, and I haven't a clue what to say to these people. I'm accustomed to spending parties like this either mucking about with Percy or drinking until I've found someone else to muck about with, but Percy's being annoying and the lord ambassador has a nasty habit of waving servers with the wine and champagne away. I finally manage to get my hand around a glass, but when I try to have it refilled, he puts his hand over the top, never breaking eye contact with the lady he's speaking to. I survive the rest of the conversation by imagining taking my empty coupe and shoving it either down his throat or up his arse.

"I hear you have a bit of a problem," he says to me as the other half of his conversation wafts away. "Excess is not flattering, young man."

I'd take sloppy drunk over dull and restrained any day, though saying that aloud doesn't seem likely to aid in the refilling of my glass.

Percy stays with us, though a bit apart—his desire to keep post-kiss distance from me seems to be doing battle with his desire to not be alone in this crowd. If I'm riding on the coattails of my father's connections in being here, he's clinging to the seams, with no title, a gentry family, and the darkest skin of anyone who isn't minding the refreshments. Most people we meet either gape openly like he's fine art on display or pretend he doesn't exist. One woman actually claps her hands in delight when she spots him, like she's just witnessed a soft-eared puppy perform a trick.

"You know, I'm very involved in your cause," she keeps saying to him as her husband natters on to Worthington and me, until Percy finally asks, "What cause?"

She looks shocked he had to ask. "The abolition of the slave trade, of course. My club has been boycotting slave-grown sugarcane since the winter."

"That's not really my cause," Percy replies.

"Where are you headed next?" her husband asks, and it's a moment before I realize he's addressing me. I'm caught between wanting to smack the pox patches off this woman's face and to smack Percy because I'm still angry about our kiss. Perhaps I could get them both with a wide swing.

"Marseilles at the end of summer, didn't you say, Disley?" Worthington prompts.

"Yes," I reply. "Then east to Venice, Florence, and Rome. Perhaps Geneva."

"How long since you came from Africa?" the woman asks, and Percy replies, his tone remarkably gentle for what a jilt she's being, "I was raised in England, madam."

"You should speak to my club before you leave Paris," she says, bobbing toward him like a top about to tip.

"I don't think—"

"We were in Venice earlier this year," her husband says, dragging me back into his conversation. "Quite a place. You should see Saint Bartolomeo's while you're there—the frescoes are better than at Saint Mark's, and the friars will walk you up to the bell tower if you're willing to part with some coinage. Avoid the Carnevale—it's all hedonism and masquerades. Oh, and there's an island off the coast, with a chapel—can't remember the name, but it's been sinking into the Lagoon. It'll be underwater by the end of summer."

"My club meets Thursday evenings," the woman is saying, and Percy is replying, "I don't think I'd have anything to say."

But she pushes on. "To have been raised the way you were! In a wealthy household, with natural children . . ."

I can feel waves of secondhand embarrassment wafting off Percy like I'm standing too close to an oven, and the gentleman is tapping the bowl of his clay pipe against the back of his hand out of time with the music, and I want a drink so badly I can hardly think straight.

"It's a dramatic sight, crumbling and half sunk into the sea." His pipe knocks into his ring with a clatter that sets my teeth on edge. "We took a boat out, though they only let you get so close—"

"Well, doesn't that just sound like the most fun thing I can imagine," I interrupt, louder than I mean to though I don't retreat from it.

"I beg your pardon?"

"Sitting in a boat and watching an island sink slowly into the sea," I say. "What a thrill. Perhaps while we're a thousand miles from home, we'll also take in an eyeful of tea boiling."

The gentleman is so shocked he takes an actual step backward from me, which is a tad dramatic. "Merely a suggestion, my lord. I thought you might enjoy—"

"I can't imagine I would," I reply, stone-faced.

"Well, then. I'm sorry to have wasted your time. Excuse us."

He takes his wife's arm, and as he leads her away, I hear her say, "Negroes are so standoffish." A fitting end to a conversation that was essentially prolonged mortification for all parties involved.

The ambassador looks as though he's about to scold me, but he's distracted when his wig catches on a passing woman's and they're both nearly uncoiffed. I look over at Percy, hoping he might thank me for saving him from conversing further with that cow, and then we'll conspire about how bloody awful this night has turned out to be. But he's frowning at me with nearly the same enthusiasm as the ambassador. "What's wrong with you?" I ask.

He blows a sharp sigh through his nose. "Must you be an ass to everyone you meet?"

"He was the one giving daft travel advice."

"You're being obnoxious."

"Zounds, Perce. Be a bit gentle, why don't you?"

"Can't you put in some effort? Please? Even if you don't give a whit what anyone has to say, these are important people. People who could be good for you to know. And even if they weren't, you should at least try to be kind."

God, I would cut off my own feet for my champagne glass to magically refill itself in this moment. I'm craning my neck for a passing server. "I really don't care who anyone here is."

Percy grabs me by the sleeve, pulling me around so we're face-to-face. The back of his hand brushes mine, and we shy from each other like spooked horses. That goddamn kiss is ruining my life. "Well, you should."

"Why does it matter to you?" I snap, shoving my fists into my pockets. His cravat has slipped, and I can see my teethmarks crawling up his neck, which is just bloody aggravating.

"Because we can't all have the luxury of not caring what people think of us."

I scowl. "Leave me alone. Go speak to someone else."

"Who am I meant to speak to?"

"Fine, go serve the drinks, then," I snap, and

immediately wish I hadn't. I reach out before he can say anything and take hold of his arm. "Wait, I'm sorry—"

He shrugs off my grip. "Thanks for that, Monty."

"I didn't mean—"

"But you did," he says, then stalks away. All the righteous indignation I've been nursing for days wilts like butter in the sun.

Worthington reappears suddenly at my side, scraping a hand along his wig. A small blossom of starchy powder blooms from its strands. "Where's Mr. Newton gone?"

"Don't know," I reply, resisting the urge to toss back my coupe one more time to make certain there isn't a last swallow clinging to the bottom.

"Come here, you should be introduced to the Duke of Bourbon," he says, fastening my arm in a surprisingly strong grip, and I am pivoted to face a man coming toward us. He's a stocky and ungenial-looking fellow in a red-and-gold justacorps, with a curled wig enveloping his head like a horned cyclone. "Do try and be civil. This is the young king's former prime minister—he's just been dismissed for unknown reasons. Still a touchy subject."

"I really don't care," I reply, though in the back of my head I can hear Percy's admonition to try and be kinder like the echo of a cymbal. A stab of guilt goes through me, and I think, perhaps, it might be novel to give this society-manners thing a bit of an effort.

"Good evening, my lord." The ambassador darts into

the path of the duke, who looked ready to pass us by, and offers a short bow.

"*Bonsoir, ambassadeur*," the duke replies, hardly bothering to make eye contact. "You look well."

"Always a pleasure. A fine evening, as is usually had here. How good to see you. Not that it's a surprise. Of course you're here." Bourbon looks as though he'd like to sidle away from this conversation, though the ambassador seems equally as desperate to keep him anchored. "Will His Majesty be in attendance?"

"His Majesty remains indisposed," the duke replies.

"A shame. We all pray for his swift recovery, as always. May I present Lord Henry Montague, Viscount of Disley, recently arrived from England?"

Just try, says Percy's voice in my head. I give the duke the most sincere smile I can muster, dimples employed for fullest effect, and offer him the same small bow the ambassador did. It feels like a strange imitation, a stage version of the way I've seen other men behave. "It's a pleasure."

"The pleasure is mine," he says, his tone noticeably absent of any pleasure as he wraps me in a stare that could pin a man to the wall. "You're Henri Montague's eldest?"

Always a hideous place to start, but I keep that luminous smile fixed. "Yes."

"Henry is touring," the ambassador says, like that might somehow open a conversational door, but the duke ignores him and keeps that calculating gaze fixed upon me. It raises the hairs on the back of my neck. He's not a tall fellow, but he's solid, and I'm neither of those things. In that steel-tipped stare of his, I feel significantly smaller than usual.

"How fares your father of late?" he asks.

"Ah, yes." The ambassador gives a fluttery laugh. He's fiddling with his sleeve links. "Your father is French, isn't he, Disley? I'd forgotten."

"Are the two of you close?" the duke asks.

I can feel fat drops of sweat, sticky with my hair pomade, rolling down the back of my neck. "I wouldn't say close."

"Do you see much of him?"

"Well, not lately, as we've the English Channel between us." I give myself a bit of a hat-tip for that—clever, but not impertinent. I might not be as terrible at this as I thought.

The duke doesn't smile. "Are you mocking me?"

Worthington makes a sound that's rather like choking.

"No," I say quickly. "No, not at all. It was a jest—"

"At my expense."

"It was the way you said it—"

"Is there something wrong with the way I speak?"

"No, I . . ." I look between them. The ambassador is staring at me with his jaw unhinged. "Would you like me to explain it?"

The duke's frown goes deeper. "Do you think I'm an imbecile?"

Dear God, what is happening? This conversation is suddenly a wriggling fish between my fingers and I'm losing my grip. "I think we've misstepped somewhere," I say, offering my best apologetic smile. "You were asking about my father."

The duke doesn't return it. "I'm afraid I've lost the thread."

I slump a few inches nearer to the ground. "Sorry."

"Your father has a pointed sense of humor. Clearly you take after him."

"Do I?" I look between him and the ambassador again, though neither seems willing to come to my rescue. "What do you mean, pointed sense of humor?"

"Would you like me to explain it?" the duke replies, a bitter mimic.

The best strategy seems to be fleeing back to the summit of this tangential peak and pretending we never scaled it, so I say, "I was seeing a great deal of my father before I left for the Continent. My mother's just had a child and that's kept him at home."

"Ah." The duke fishes a silver vinaigrette from his pocket and takes a grand sniff. "The last I heard, he was staying more at his estate to keep an eye upon a delinquent son who enjoyed drinking and boys more than he did his studies at Eton."

All the color drains out of my face. A few people glance our way, key phrases in his statement catching gossip-hungry ears. The duke gives me a cool expression, and I'm quite ready to either overturn a table or do a dramatic collapse to the ground. Perhaps both in quick succession. *Look, see!* I would shout at Percy if he were here beside me. *This is what happens when I try.*

Ambassador Worthington makes a verbal hurdle between us. "This is Henri Montague's son," he offers, as though there's been some kind of mistake.

"Yes, I know," the duke replies. Then, back to me, he says, "And by all reports I've heard, he's a scoundrel."

"Well, at least I've not been dismissed from my position as lapdog to an invalidic puppet of a king," I snap.

The duke's smugness slips like a poorly laced mask. For the first time since the start of our egregious interaction, he seems to be considering something other than making me look a fool, though this thing seems to be whether it would be appropriate to strangle me with his bare hands in the middle of mixed company. "Watch that tongue, Montague," he says, his voice low and coiled, a poisonous snake lurking in the tall grass. Then he snaps his vinaigrette shut and stalks away, leaving the ambassador and me both staring after him like wax figures of ourselves.

My ears are still ringing—I'm unsure whether my father is going out of his way to speak badly of me to all his intimates and make a real meal of my humiliation, or whether I've such a foul reputation that the stench has preceded me here. And what's worse, I'm not sure which of those options is preferable.

Worthington's face is still stuck in its mask of polite society when he turns to me, but the steam coming out his ears is nearly palpable. I expect a stuttered second-hand apology, some sort of gasping and fawning and *poor Monty, I'm so terribly sorry he said such hateful things to you*.

Instead he says to me, very calmly, "How dare you speak to him like that."

Which is when I realize he isn't on my side either.

"Did you hear what he said to me?" I demand.

"He is your better."

"I don't care if he's the bleeding king, he insulted—"

Worthington reaches suddenly for me, and my hands fly up, an involuntary defense. But all he does is place his palm upon my arm in an almost pitying way and say, "When your father wrote to request I make your introductions, I had it in my head he was exaggerating about your lack of moral fortitude, but I see he's been rather astute in his assessment. Now, I believe your father to be a first-rate fellow, so I place no responsibility upon him. He's no doubt done the best he could, yet sometimes the tares fall among the wheat. But this devil-may-care attitude you believe so charming, tossing your social connections into the fire and instead choosing to associate with colored men such as your Mr. Newton—"

"Let's get something straight," I interrupt, jerking my arm out of his grip with such force that I nearly knock out the woman standing behind me. "You are not my father, I am not your responsibility, and I did not come here to have a list of my faults related from him or be condemned for who I associate with—not by you or that damned duke. So while it's been a jolly good time, being treated like a child all evening, I think I've just about had enough and I can make my own way from here."

And then I turn on my heel and march off, snatching a glass from the tray of a passing server as I go, draining it, and replacing it before he's even noticed me. If my father is so keen on telling everyone what a rake I am, I'm happy to live up to my reputation. Wouldn't want to disappoint him.

It's an impressive performance as far as dramatic storm-offs go, but as soon as I've left Worthington I realize I've got nowhere to storm off to. I look around for Percy—I'm ready to surrender our standoff just for the sake of company and perhaps a bit of sympathy as well. I spot him over near the dance floor, and start to weave through the crowd, but then I realize he's talking to someone—a lad in a blond wig who looks a bit older than us, with such stark freckles I can see them under his powder. He's got on a fine suit of ribbed gray silk with ruffles at the collar that swing when he leans in to Percy so that whatever he's saying can be heard over the music. Percy says something in return and the lad laughs, openmouthed, with his head thrown back. Percy gives him a shy smile, and the freckled little shit touches him on the arm and then leaves his damn hand there for far longer than is really necessary. I've never wanted so badly to knock someone's teeth in as I do right then. Knock those stupid freckles straight off his face.

The freckled buck flags one of the servers for champagne—one for him and Percy each—and I whip around and go in the opposite direction.

Felicity is on the veranda, valiantly holding up a wall between two Venetian windows, and I swallow my pride and join her, snagging another coupe along the way.

"You're looking jaded," I say as I lean in to the stone.

"And you're looking angry. Are you and Percy still quarreling?"

"Is it that obvious?"

"Well, considering that you're barely looking at each other, it seemed logical. Where's the ambassador got to?"

"Don't know. I'm hiding from him."

"And I'm hiding from his wife. Cheers to being no good at parties."

"I'm usually very good at parties. I think it's the party's fault."

A knot of people pushes past us, the woman in the lead carrying a wineglass in one hand and a chocolate entremets aloft in the other. The train of her dress scrapes over our feet as she passes, and Felicity and I both press closer to the wall. "Who were you and he speaking to?" she asks. "The solid fellow."

"The Duke of Bourbon, I think his title is. He's the charm of an aging Genghis Khan."

To my great surprise, Felicity gives a rather genuine snort of laughter. It catches us both off guard—her hand flies to her mouth and we go wide-eyed at each other. Then she shakes her head, with a rueful chuckle. "*Aging Genghis Khan.* You do make me laugh sometimes."

I swallow a mouthful of champagne. The bubbles are making my tongue feel like woven cloth. "Former prime minister to the king, though apparently that *former* part is still touchy, so don't go bringing it up. Learned that the hard way."

"Is the king here? Isn't this his party?"

"He's ill. Nearly perpetually, from the sound of it." It strikes me suddenly how very backward it feels to be skirting the edges of a party with my sister while Percy is somewhere on the other side. I take another drink, then ask, just for something to say, "So, where were you sneaking off to the other night?"

Felicity tips her head back to the wall so she's staring up at the scrollwork overhanging us. "Nowhere."

"You were meeting a boy, weren't you?"

"When would I have had time to meet a boy? I've hardly been allowed to leave the apartments since we arrived. Lockwood makes me sit still and stitch and play the harpsichord all day and night while you and Percy are traipsing around the city."

"Oh, *traipse* is hardly the word I'd use. *Shuffle like prisoners*, perhaps?"

"Well, you're seeing far more of Paris than I've been permitted to."

"So, is that where you were? Seeing the sights in the dead of night?"

"If you must know, I was at that lecture."

"What lecture?"

"The alchemical one. The one you told Lockwood you attended."

"Oh." I had forgotten everything that happened that night except the kiss. I almost look around for Percy again. "Are you . . . interested in alchemy?"

"Not particularly. I'm disinclined to superstition on the whole, but the idea of creating synthetic panaceas from existing organic substances by altering their resting chemical state . . . I'm sorry, am I boring you?"

"No, I stopped listening a while ago." I mean for it to

be glib and silly, something that might make her laugh again, but instead a look of rather sincere hurt flits across her face before she covers it with a frown.

I'm about to apologize, but then she snaps, "If you aren't interested, don't ask."

My own temper, still raw from Worthington's telling-off, flares again. "Fine. In future, I'll refrain." I raise my glass, which is somehow empty. "Have a good time here by yourself."

"Enjoy avoiding the ambassador," she replies, and I wander off before I can decide whether she was being mean.

As much as I like crowds and champagne and dancing, I feel like I'm starting to sink into this party and be swallowed by it. A strange panic spawned from all the filigree is sitting right at the edge of my mind. It's the sort of feeling I would usually combat by sneaking away with Percy and a bottle of gin. But Percy is off somewhere having his arm touched by that lad whose freckles look like a pox, so instead I wander along the veranda, losing tally of how much I've had to drink. I stop and rest my elbows upon the rail, surrounded on all sides by rustling satin and a language I can hardly speak and feeling very, very alone.

Then, from beside me, someone says, "You look lost."

I turn. A startlingly pretty young woman is standing

behind me, her wide skirt fanned between us like the pages of a book. She has large, dark eyes with a patch in one corner, and skin powdered almost white but for the poppy of rouge upon each cheek. Her stiff blond wig is arranged around sprigs of juniper and an ornament in the likeness of a fox, its ears tipped in the same inky black that lines her lashes. She's got the most incredible neck I've ever seen, and directly below it a truly fantastic set of breasts.

"Not at all," I reply, ruffling my hair on instinct. "Simply making a careful choice of the best company. Though I think the search is ended now that you're here."

She laughs, a tiny, pretty sound like a bell that doesn't strike me as entirely genuine but I'm quite certain I don't care. "I come highly recommended. Are you on your Tour?"

"And here I thought I was blending in rather well."

"Your scholarly study of the party sets you apart, my lord. Your thinking face is very handsome."

And then she touches my arm lightly, same as that lad put his hand on Percy. I fight a sudden urge to look around for him in the crowd, and instead shift my weight along the rail so the entirety of my attention is devoted to this lovely creature who seems very interested in me.

"Have you a name, my foxy lady?" I ask.

"Have you?" she counters.

"Henry Montague."

"How simple," she says, and I realize my error in omitting my title. I'm a bit drunker than I thought if I'm making such careless mistakes. "Your father must be French."

"*Oui*, though you wouldn't know it from how ghastly my French is."

"Should we make things easier?" she says in English, words silk-trimmed by her accent. "Now we'll understand each other better. So, shall I call you Henry? If we are forgoing formality, you may call me Jeanne." She tips down her chin and gives me a look through the veil of her eyelashes. *Oh dear*, it says, *now I'm shy*. "Acceptable?"

"Divine."

She smiles, then flicks open the ivory fan hanging from her wrist and begins to work it up and down. The breeze flutters the single ringlet trailing down the back of that neck of hers that swans would envy. I have been mentally patting myself on the head for keeping my eyes on her face the whole time we've been speaking, but then the bastards betray me suddenly and dive straight down the front of her dress.

I think for a moment she may not have noticed, but then her mouth twists up and I know she's seen. But instead of slapping me or calling me a boor and storming off, she says, "My lord, would you like to see . . ." Telling pause. Eyelash flutter. "More of Versailles?"

"You know, I believe that I would. Though I'm short a guide."

"Perhaps you'll allow me."

"But this party seemed to be just picking up speed. I'd hate to drag you away."

"Life is filled with sacrifices."

"Am I a sacrifice?"

"One I'm happy to make."

Zounds, this girl is fun. And right now, I need a bit of fun. Get my mind off Worthington and the damned duke and Percy and that handsome bastard with the freckles putting his hands all over him. I offer her my arm. "Lead the way, my lady."

Jeanne puts her small, perfect hand on my elbow and steers me toward a set of French doors opening into the hall. As we cross the threshold, I let slip my resolution for a single second and, like Lott's wife turned to salt, glance over my shoulder to see if I can spot Percy. He's right where he was before—on the fringes of the dance floor, but alone now, and looking at me in a way that suggests he's been doing it for a while. When I catch his eye, he starts and gives a self-conscious tug on his jacket collar. Then he offers me a bit of a disappointed smile, an *I'd expect no more from you* sort that strikes flint inside me.

My mind plays a quick roulette of what variety of look in return will most affect him. Perhaps pleading eyes—*Save me from this girl dragging me away against my will*—and then he'll come rushing to my rescue. Or perhaps a curled-lip sneer—*Jealous? Well, you had your chance with me and you missed it.*

I settle on a shrug paired with an indifferent smirk. *That's fine*, it says. *You have your fun and I'll have mine.* And perhaps a smidge of *I am not even a bit thinking of what transpired between us at the music hall last week.*

And Percy looks away.

Jeanne knows her way through the gilded labyrinth that is the interior of Versailles, and she drifts along like a cloud of perfume. Every room we wander through is filled with people, and though I enjoy the crowds and the noise and the frescoes the colors of a bowl of ripe fruit, I would much rather find a quiet place to be alone with this winsome girl and her excellent breasts.

She leads me to a deserted wing I'm certain we aren't meant to be in, then stops before a painted door and slides her hand into the pocket slit of her skirt, with-drawing a gold key on a black ribbon.

"Now, where did you get that?" I ask, leaning in as she unlocks the door like I'm interested in it, but really it's to get a better angle down that dress.

She smiles. "My position comes with privileges."

The room she leads me into looks like a private parlor, the antechamber to someone's bedroom. Three crystal chandeliers cast a golden glow across the rich red walls and mahogany furnishings. There's a fireplace so large that it seems rather a small room that can be safely set on fire, and an Oriental rug so thick it makes me feel wobbly in my heels. The window is open onto the grounds, and the music and bright chatter of the party waft in, though they sound muted and far away.

Jeanne slips her fan from her wrist, then spreads her hands across the felt-topped card table before the fireplace. "This is quieter, *non*? Versailles can be overwhelming."

"Oh, I find it rather whelming." She laughs, and I give her what I know from experience is a knee-weakening smile. "Quite a scandal to bring a gentleman unaccompanied to your apartments, madam."

"How fortunate that these aren't my apartments. Though you flatter me in thinking I've rooms this grand. A friend of mine," she says, enough of a lilt on *friend* that I can make the inference. "Louis Henri."

"Louis the king?"

"There is more than one Louis in all of France, you know. This one's the Duke of Bourbon."

"Oh, him."

"You sound as though you've met."

"Yes, we had words." I don't mention the particulars of the incident, though the thought of it makes me feel small and shriveled-up again.

But now here I am in his apartments.

Retaliation is calling my name.

My first idea is to piss in his desk drawers, but there's a

lady present. Thievery seems a better choice—something easy enough to get away with but not so obvious as to tie me to the crime. The task is to pick something that will annoy the shit out of him when he finds it missing, but not incite an international incident.

I wander around the salon, making a show of inventorying the place, a casual thief. I can feel Jeanne watching me, so I keep my chin tipped up, waiting for her to look away so that I can pocket something. Though I'm rather hard to look away from—I'm giving her my finest angle, the sort that belongs on a coin.

Atop the desk, there's a set of ivory dice that I consider, and a scent-and-patch case with a clear glass facet and silver screw top. Fine movables—everything here is fine—but too ordinary to achieve the desired level of annoyance. At the writing desk, I flirt briefly with the notion of nicking the inkstand, until I realize it would be beastly inconvenient to carry around for the rest of the night, as it's full of ink.

But beside the inkstand there's a small trinket box, made of slick ebony and a little larger than my fist. The top is set with six opal dials, each inscribed with the alphabet in sequence. When I run my finger along them, they turn, the letters shifting.

"All right, you've seen the room," Jeanne calls. There's a rustle of skirts as she settles herself. "Come pay attention to me now."

I glance up to see if she's watching, but she's already seated at the card table with her back to me.

Vengeance *and* a pretty girl—the pair is turning this initially disastrous evening into one of the better parties we've been to in Paris. *If only Percy and I weren't quarreling*, I think, then squash that thought like a spider underfoot.

I slip the box into my pocket—consider leaving a ransom note as well, or not so much a ransom note as a three-word statement: *You're a bastard*—then slide into the chair across the table from Jeanne. "Are we playing?" I ask as she flicks a deck of cards between her hands.

Her eyes dart to mine. "What do you play?"

"Everything. Anything. What do *you* play, madam?"

"Well, I find myself partial to a game in which each player is dealt two cards, adds their numbers, and whichever pair is a sum closer to ten and three wins."

"Why ten and three?"

"It's my lucky number."

"I've not heard of this game."

"That is because, my good lord, I have just now made it up."

"And is there to be a wager? Or a consequence for the player with cards less close?"

"They must sacrifice an article of clothing."

Good. Lord. I deserve some sort of medal for the

effort it takes not to look down her dress when she says that.

Jeanne purses her lips, smearing the scarlet paint upon them. "Do you care to play?"

"Deal me in." I whip off my coat and toss it onto the sofa.

"Hold on, we've not started yet."

"I know. I don't want to make it too hard for you. I'd hate for you to lose your dignity."

"Don't count on that, my lord."

It is an incredibly stupid game. We both know it. We also both know that the true game is not in the cards, but in the coquettish removal of each subsequent article of clothing. Jeanne slides off one of her many rings; I remove my shoes in what can only be described as the most sensual display any man has ever made with his footwear. I'm more liberal with the undressing—by the time I'm in nothing but my breeches, she's still peeling off jewelry one excruciating piece at a time. Under her powder, her cheeks are pink, but she's keeping her wits about her admirably. Were our situations reversed, I would have lost my mind by now.

The lead-up is fun, but I'm starting to grow restless to be done with this, like downing a sour drink fast, which is not the sentiment I'm accustomed to accompanying earthly delights of this variety. Out on the veranda, a bit of a romp seemed like an unbearably magnificent idea, but as I wait for Jeanne to make a theatrical show of flipping her next pair of cards, my mind is stuck on the image of Percy and that lad standing beside the dance floor and wondering what it was that Percy said that made him laugh. And then I am thinking about Percy's fingers threading through my hair as I leaned in to him and him pressing our mouths together. The flutter of his breath passed between us, a feeling like a pulse point, and I'll be damned if one stupid kiss with Percy has ruined me.

The next time Jeanne loses, she removes a single pearl-drop earring and sets it on the table, but I place my hand over hers before she can deal again. "One moment, my lady. Earrings come in pairs."

"So?"

"So they come off in pairs too. No protesting, I took my shoes off together."

"I'm beginning to think it doesn't take much to get your clothes off."

"Well, I don't want to deprive you."

"Thank you, my lord. You are indeed a fine specimen."

She touches her top lip with the tip of her tongue and a soft shiver of desire goes through me, chased with relief that Percy has not wrecked me after all. Perhaps this can still be exactly what I intended when I followed her from the gardens, and it is with that hope buoyant in my heart that I lean toward her. "Here, let me help you with that other earring."

I reach out. She leans in. Time turns slow and delicious, seconds rolling forward like sun-warmed honey. I put my mouth much closer to her skin than it needs to be as I unclasp the pearl. My fingers trail down her neck—the ghost of a touch—then I waft my lips across her jawline.

And, as I knew would come to pass, she puts a finger beneath my chin, tips my mouth toward hers, and kisses me.

But my first thought is not how absolutely gorgeous it is to have this pretty thing at last putting her lips upon mine. It is how much better it was the week previous when it was Percy doing the same.

I nearly swat the air, like that might clear Percy from my head as though he were a gnat. Instead, I put my hands on those two magnificent breasts that have been staring me down the whole evening and distract myself with the business of freeing them from their casings, and I am not thinking about Percy, not even a bit.

Aristocratic ladies, it should be noted, wear a beastly lot of clothing. Particularly at parties. I could strip to nothing in twenty seconds if given adequate motivation, and she's more than adequate. But undressing Jeanne is not as easy as it was when I imagined it every time she removed another piece of jewelry. My mouth is still on hers as we stagger to our feet, so I haven't even got a good view of what it is I'm meant to be ripping off. I take a guess and tear at the laces until something snaps and the stomacher falls away, which at least pops her breasts from their breast prison. But then there's a ghastly cage around her waist, with petticoats and corsets and a chemise and I swear to God there's another corset under that and then a whole creative other layer of who-knows-what but I'm certain it's there simply to keep me from her skin. Perhaps fashion is just a reinforcement of a lady's chastity, in hopes that the interested party may lose interest and abandon any deflowering attempts simply for all the clothing in the way.

In contrast, Jeanne only needs undo four buttons on the flap of my breeches and then slide them down my hips, which is just unfair. Her fingers wend their way up my spine, and I'm shocked suddenly from the moment by the memory of Percy's hands there, his palms parentheses around my rib cage and a touch that made me feel hungry and breakable. His legs wrapped around me. The sound of his short, sharp breath when I put my lips to his neck.

Goddammit, Percy.

I let go of Jeanne just long enough to unfasten the buttons at my knees and get my breeches around my ankles, then I kick them onto the sofa in a high arc. She traces my lips with the tip of her tongue, talc from her skin coating my mouth, and, hellfire and damnation, I am not thinking about Percy. I put my arms all the way around her, jerking her toward me.

Then, from behind us, the door latch snaps and someone says, "What's going on?"

I whip my hands out of Jeanne's dress, nearly losing a finger in the process since somehow I've gotten tangled in the back lacings of her corsets. The Duke of Bourbon fills the doorway to the room, two more lordly-looking gentlemen at his sides, all of them with their mouths gaping, like beached fish.

I let fly a choice four-letter word and try to shield myself with the massive cage Jeanne has strapped to her waist.

The duke squints at me. "God, Disley?"

"Um, yes. Evening! Bourbon, wasn't it?"

His face sets. "What the devil are you doing here?"

"To be clear . . . ," I say, edging toward the sofa where my clothes are piled and cursing myself for having made such a dramatic show of flinging them away. I have to drag Jeanne with me to be certain I stay concealed. "*Here* as in Versailles? Because I was certainly invited."

"In my apartments. What are you doing in my damned apartments?"

"Oh, you mean here as in *here*."

"You vile little rake, just like your—" His face is

going red and I brace myself, but his attention is commandeered by Jeanne, still standing bare-breasted at my side. "Mademoiselle Le Brey, cover yourself, for God's sake," he snaps.

Jeanne starts tugging at her corset, which does less to cover her and more to emphasize the fact that she's not. The two other men are gaping at her chest and Bourbon looks like he's about to commit homicide upon anyone within an arm's distance and I am well versed in seizing the moment, so I snatch my clothes off the sofa and make my escape straight out the open window.

Which is how I come to be running through the gardens of the Palace of Versailles, dressed only as Nature intended.

I round a hedgerow flanking the Orangerie, realizing that beyond actually fleeing the scene, I have no exit strategy. I have a strong sense I'm being chased and I haven't time to stop on the lawn and re-dress. I try to pull my breeches back on as I go and nearly lurch face-first into the shrubbery, so I choose to keep my clothing bundled up in front of my most vulnerable parts and continue my flight.

I skirt the wall of the palace, trying to avoid the windows and stay between the topiaries. There isn't an empty room—nowhere I could dart in and hide or re-robe myself. I'm disoriented and distracted, and go farther than I intend to. When I round the next corner, I find I am in the courtyard, partygoers spilling down the stairs and into the bright lights. I stop dead, which is a fatal miscalculation on my part because a woman sees me and shrieks.

And then everyone turns to stare at me, the Viscount of Disley, standing in the courtyard, with his hair askew and a woman's powder smeared across his face like flour. And, also, without a stitch of clothing on.

And then, because Fortune is a heartless bitch, I hear someone behind me say, "Monty?"

And, of course, there is Percy, standing beside Felicity, who for the first time in all of her born days seems too shocked to be smirking, and with them, the lord ambassador and his wife. We all gape at each other. Or rather, they gape at me.

There's really nothing to do but pretend I'm fully clothed and in control of the situation. So I walk up to Percy and say, "There you are. I think we should be going."

They're all staring at me. The whole courtyard is staring at me, but it's Percy and Felicity that I feel the most. Felicity's got her fish mouth in place but Percy's shock is starting to fade and he looks . . . embarrassed—of me or for me, it's hard to say.

"My lord," the ambassador says, and I turn, still trying to play dead casual. His wife squeaks.

"Yes, sir?"

His face is scarlet. "Have you . . . any possible explanation for your current state of dress?"

"Undress," I correct him. "And thank you so much for a lovely evening; it's been quite . . . revealing. But we're expected home, so we'll hear from you soon? We should have you for supper before we move south. Percy? Felicity?" I would take their arms but my hands are otherwise occupied, so I tip my chin up and begin to walk away and hope to God they will follow me. They both do, though neither says a word.

When we are at last installed again in our carriage by some rather wide-eyed attendants, I drop my shield and start to shuffle back into my breeches. Felicity throws up her hands with a shriek. "Dear God, Monty, my eyes."

I arch my back, trying to wriggle in without striking my head on one of the hanging lanterns. "Shame you haven't your attractive specs on."

"What were you doing?"

"Look at what I'm wearing and make an educated guess." I fasten my breeches, then look over at Percy, who is staring forward, stone-faced. "What's the matter with you?"

His mouth tightens. "Are you drunk?"

"Excuse me?"

"Are you drunk?" he repeats.

"Have you ever seen him sober?" Felicity says under her breath.

94

Percy's still staring away from me, though that stare is turning into a glare. "Can't you control yourself? *Ever?*"

"I'm sorry, are you getting on me to behave? You aren't exactly a saintly enough candidate to be delivering a morality lecture, darling."

"Do you think I could *ever* act the way you do and get away with it?"

"What does that mean?"

"Look at me and take a guess."

"Really? You want to have *that* conversation right now? You let everyone walk all over you because you're skin's a bit dark—"

"Oh dear God, Monty, stop," Felicity says.

"—but if you'd grow a spine, I wouldn't have to stand up for you because you'd do it yourself."

He looks, for a moment, too astonished to speak. Felicity's gaping at me too, and I have a deep sense I have said something very wrong, but then Percy tips his chin up. "If that was me—caught naked with some . . . person at the palace—I wouldn't have been permitted to walk away from that garden the way you just did."

I start to say something, but he interrupts, his voice slicing, "Aren't you tired of this—aren't you tired of being this person? You look like a drunken ass all the time, *all the bloody time*, and it's getting . . ."

"It's getting what, Percy?" He's not going to say it,

so I offer the word up for him. "Embarrassing? Are you embarrassed of me?"

He doesn't reply, which is answer enough. I wait for defiance to filter through me, but instead I'm filled with it too, that hot, rancid shame rising like a fetid tide.

"Who was she?" Felicity demands. "It was a she, wasn't it?"

I pull my shirt over my head with a bit more force than is needed. The collar snags my hair. "A girl I met."

"And what happened to her?"

"I don't know, I bolted."

"You were caught with a woman and then you left her there? Monty, you tomcat!"

"She'll be fine. They didn't chase me down."

"Because you're a man."

"So?"

"It's different for women. No one condemns a man for that sort of thing, but she'll carry that with her."

"It won't matter, she's someone's mistress. She's just a whore!"

Felicity's hands fist around her dress, and for a moment I think she may slap me, but the carriage strikes a rut and we're all three nearly unseated. She catches herself on the window treatments, then glares at me again. "Don't you dare," she says, her voice low and tight, "say anything like that ever again. This is your fault, *Henry*. No one else's."

I look to Percy, but he's staring out the window now with his face still stone, and I realize what a stupid mistake it was to think Percy gave half a damn what I was doing with a French courtier in a back room. I slink down in my seat and hate them both intensely. I've been betrayed—Felicity's never been on my side, but I thought I could count on Percy. Though now it seems the whole world has been scrambled up.

I intend to sleep the next morning until I can sleep no more, but Sinclair wakes me early—the sky outside my window is still opaline with the sunrise. It takes me a while to rally myself to get out of bed. Partly because I'm wrung out and partly because I'm absolutely writhing at the thought of looking Percy and Felicity in the eyes. Mostly Percy. I'm also feeling worse than I expected—I didn't think I had drunk that much, thanks to the lord ambassador's blockade, but my stomach won't sit still, and my whole body feels as though it's been dragged behind a carriage.

I roll from bed after at least a half of an hour and scrub water from the basin in the corner across my face. I'm light-headed and wobbly when I raise my head to the glass, and I stagger sideways, stepping directly onto my balled-up coat from the night previous. A sharp stab of pain goes through my foot and I sit down hard with a yelp.

I've stepped upon the box I picked up in the duke's apartments; it's still in the pocket of my coat, with its edges snagged in the stitchery. It's stranger in the daylight and away from the delirious shine of the party. I spin the dials round, spelling out the first few letters of my name. In the wake of my grand exit, I forgot I took it, though now the same sort of savage pleasure I got the night before at pocketing it comes back, which is the only good thing about the morning thus far. I tuck the box into my coat pocket, a reminder that I am somewhat clever and not everything is terrible.

When I finally drag myself from my room, I find that we are packing. The servants have trunks open and spread out across the sitting room. A few are being hauled below stairs. Felicity is at the breakfast table, staring at her novel with too much determination to be natural, and Lockwood is beside her, a damask banyan over his suit and his eyes fixed upon my bedroom door—waiting for me. The news of my display has most certainly reached him. Nothing travels quite so swiftly as gossip.

Mr. Lockwood stands up and fastens his banyan as furiously as I've ever seen anyone fasten anything. "I see I have been too lax in my discipline."

"*Discipline*?" I repeat. All the banging luggage has got a headache throbbing against my eyes. "We're on our

Tour. We're meant to be having a good time."

"A good time, yes, but this, my lord, is unacceptable. You shamed your hosts, who were kind enough to bring you to a social event you should have been grateful to attend. You debased your father's good name before his friends. Each one of your foolish actions reflects as much upon him as it does upon you. You," he says, his voice pinched up as tight as his forehead, "are an embarrassment."

Several hours from now, I will certainly think of a retort to this, a perfect combination of wit and defiance that would leave him stumbling. But in that moment, I can't think of a damn thing, so I stand there, struck dumb, and let him scold me like a child.

"I did warn you," Lockwood says, "as did your father, that inappropriate behavior would not be tolerated. So you and I will be returning to England forthwith."

I swear the floor drops out from beneath me at the thought of seeing my father again so much quicker than I anticipated and under such grim circumstances.

"However," Mr. Lockwood continues, "as I'm responsible for seeing your sister to school, we'll be departing for Marseilles this morning to deliver her before we return."

At the table, Felicity winces a little, but Lockwood takes no notice. "Once Miss Montague has been installed, Mr. Newton will go north to Holland and you and I will leave for England, where you will take responsibility before your father for your actions."

Don't come back at all. I can still hear him say it.

"I don't want to go home," I say, and my feeble attempt to varnish over my panic turns the words far more petulant than I intend. "It wasn't that bad."

"My lord, your behavior was disgraceful. Doubly so since you deny the impropriety. You are a shame to yourself, and to your family name." He's brandy-faced and reckless now, and even as he speaks again I can see that he doesn't mean to say it, but it doesn't matter, because he does. "No wonder your father doesn't want you around."

I want to knock his nose flat for saying that. Instead I throw up on his slippers, which is only slightly less satisfying.

Our journey to Marseilles is uncomfortable, in both the literal and the more abstract senses of the word. Lockwood clearly chose to flee the burning remains of my reputation in Paris before anyone had time to properly smell the smoke, so arrangements for our flight are cobbled together. Sinclair is sent ahead for lodging in Marseilles, but inns along the way are scarce, and we often find ourselves scrambling for housing. It would be easier, but we've got Felicity, and most places don't take ladies—or Negroes either, and Percy's just dark enough that we're sometimes barred because of him.

Our progress is slow. The roads are rougher than those from Calais to Paris, and we break an axletree outside of Lyon, which delays us almost half a day. We left our Parisian staff and a good deal of luggage to follow us later—we travel with only a valet and a coachman—so I'm doing far more of my own upkeep than I'm accustomed to. We wake each morning to a blistering sun, and I'm soaked in sweat before noonday.

None of us are speaking to each other. Felicity keeps her nose tucked into her novel, finishes it by the end of the first day, then immediately begins it again. Lockwood makes a study of Lassels's *The Voyage of Italy*, which seems like simply a means of reminding me of the places we won't see because of the damage I've wrought. Percy looks everywhere but at me, and when we stop to lodge on the first night, he asks Lockwood to get us separate rooms, which is the most openly spiteful gesture I've ever received from him.

On the fifth day of the most uncomfortable breed of silence I've ever endured, we shift from pastured countryside into woodlands, crackled trees with bare, slim trunks sheltering the rutted road from the summer heat. Their branches scrape against the carriage roof like fingers as we pass beneath them.

We've seen few other travelers in the forest, so the sounds of horses, then men's voices, startle us all. Felicity even looks up from her book. Lockwood twitches back the drapes for a view of the road.

Our carriage flails to a halt, so abrupt that Lockwood nearly pitches out the window. I catch myself on Felicity, who shoulders me off.

"Why've we stopped?" Percy asks.

The voices get louder—angry and persistent French I can't understand. The carriage dips as our coachman climbs down.

"Out!" a voice barks. "Tell your passengers to disembark or they will be made to." The carriage bounces again, then there's a *crack*. A moment later, one of our trunks drops past the window and smashes against the ground.

"What's going on?" Felicity says quietly.

"Out, now!" someone shouts.

Lockwood peers through the gap in the drapes, then snaps back into his seat. His face is white. "Highwaymen," he says under his breath.

"Highwaymen?" I cry, loud as he was soft. "Are we actually being robbed by honest-to-God highwaymen?"

"Don't panic," Lockwood instructs, though he looks panicked. "I've read what to do."

"You've *read*?" I repeat. I half expect Felicity to leap to the defense of reading, but she's got her mouth clamped shut. Her knuckles are white around the spine of her book.

"We will comply with all their demands," Lockwood

says. "Most highwaymen are simply looking for easy money and to get away quickly. Things can be replaced." There's a loud *thwack* on the side of the carriage like someone's slapped it. We all jump. Percy's hand fastens around my knee. Lockwood blanches, then straightens his coat. "I shall reason with them. Do not leave this carriage unless I instruct you to do so."

And into the breach he goes.

The three of us stay statued inside, the silence between us a very loud thing. The carriage shakes as the highwaymen unfasten the rest of our trunks from the roof. It won't take them long to go through the little luggage we have with us and pick out the shiny things. Then they'll let us go. And we will proceed to Marseilles with a bit less baggage and an excellent war story that will impress all the lads back home. That is what I tell myself in my head, though the brash instructions from outside seem to say otherwise.

Then the carriage door bangs open and the business end of a hunting knife is thrust in. "Out!" a man yells in French. "*Sortez!* Get out!"

I'm shaking like mad but I've got my wits about me enough to obey. Outside, I count five men, though I think there may be more on the other side. They're all dressed in greatcoats and spatterdashes, their faces covered with black kerchiefs, and they're armed with an impressive array of weaponry, though most look fancier than I would have expected from bandits. If the situation weren't so dire, I'd comment on how quintessentially highwayman-ish they look, as though they borrowed the outfits from the theater.

Across from the carriage door, Lockwood is on his knees with his hands on his head, one of the well-costumed highwaymen holding a pistol to the base of his skull. Our coachman is spread-eagled in the ditch, the soil around his head dark. I'm not sure if he's dead or just insensible, but the sight stops me in my tracks.

"On the ground!" a highwayman shouts at me. I have a history of reacting poorly when shouted at, particularly by men with French accents, and I freeze, stuck halfway out of the carriage, until Percy presses his fingers into my spine from behind. I stumble forward and fall to my knees, hands rising without my meaning them to.

Our luggage has all been gutted and the contents are strewn across the ground like a down of autumn leaves. I spot Lockwood's toilet case, drawers all wrenched open and bottles smashed into glittering sand. Pieces of our backgammon board are scattered amid stockings and garters and snarled neckwear. One of the men kicks a pile of Felicity's petticoats and they blossom like upside-down tulips.

One of the highwaymen shoves Percy to his knees at my side, Felicity on the other. Another ducks into the cab where we were just sitting. I hear him clattering around, then the toothy snap of a knife splitting upholstery, before he emerges with nothing but Percy's fiddle case, which he tosses onto the ground and kicks open.

"Please, it's only a fiddle!" Percy cries, reaching out like he might stop the man. I can see his hand trembling.

The highwayman handles the instrument gently, even as he shucks out the felt and tears open the rosin drawer like he's looking for something. *"Rien!"* he calls to the man behind me.

"Please put it back," Percy says quietly. *"S'il vous plaît, remettez-le en place."* And, to my great surprise, the highwayman does. Either he's the most respectful bandit of all time, or he wants to keep it in good shape for when he pawns it.

There's one man standing in the middle of it all who seems to be in charge, with a pistol hanging loosely at his side and the other men frantic around him. A gold signet ring on his finger catches the light. It's large enough that, even from a distance, I can see it's inscribed with a crest bearing the fleur-de-lis in triplicate. He's staring hard at me, and above his kerchief his eyes narrow. I flinch. Someone grabs the collar of my coat from behind and hauls me up, but the leader calls, *"Attends, ne les tue pas tout de suite."*

Don't kill them yet.

YET? I want to shout back at him. *What do you mean, yet, like our murder is the inevitable ending to this scene?*

We're all more than willing to cooperate if they'd just take our things and let us be.

The leader jerks his pistol in my direction and all the fight in me evaporates. *"Où est-ce?"*

Felicity has her head down, fingers knit behind her head, but she glances over at me. I can't make my brain remember a word of French after the declaration of our impending death, so I stammer, "What?"

"La boîte. Ce que vous avez volé. Rendez-le."

I translate a few words this time. "Where's what? *Où est-ce quoi?"* I've no idea what *volé* is.

"La boîte volée."

"What?" I look wildly to Felicity for some sort of linguistic assistance. Her face is white.

"Il n'y a rien!" one of the men calls from the other side of the carriage.

The man holding me flings me to the ground so I'm on my back, looking up. The sunlight blots as the highwaymen's leader steps over me, pistol swinging lazily at his side. My panic is a living thing. *"C'est où?"*

"I don't know what you're saying!" I cry.

He takes a step forward, his heavy black boot landing straight on my hand and easing down. My bones start to protest. "Do you understand me now, my lord?" he says in English.

And I wish in that moment that I were brave. I wish to God I were. But I'm shaking and terrified and out of the corner of my eye I can see our coachman's body on the ground, blood seeping from his forehead, and I don't want to die or get my fingers broken off like dry tree limbs. I haven't a courageous bone in my body—if I knew what they were looking for, short of it being my own damn sister, I would have handed it over without a thought. But I'm clueless and helpless, and as the highwayman presses his foot down on my fingers, all I can think is, *Nothing bad has ever happened to me before. Nothing bad has ever happened in my whole life.*

"Stop it, we don't know what you're talking about!" Felicity cries. *"Nous n'avons rien volé."*

The highwayman steps off my hand, but he keeps addressing me as he walks backward to Felicity. "What if I rip her fingers off? Perhaps you'll tell me then."

He jerks a knife out of his belt, but suddenly, in a feat of unexpected heroics straight out of an adventure novel, Percy grabs his fiddle case from the ground and swings it like a brickbat. It connects with the skull of the leader and he topples to the ground. Felicity seems to take her cue from this, for she snatches up one of her petticoats from the soil, flings it in the face of the man with his gun on her, then slams her elbow between his legs, so he's down for the count. I scramble to my feet and start to stagger away, not certain where I'm going other than getting the holy hell away from here, but one of the highwaymen grabs a handful of my coat and jerks me backward. I choke as my collar cinches around my neck. My first instinct is to faint with fear, but everyone else is being brave, and that makes me feel courageous too, so instead I whip around and throw my first-ever punch straight at his chin.

And it bloody well hurts. No one warns you that knocking a man across the jaw probably hurts you as much as it does whoever's getting your fist to their face. He and I both cuss at the same time, and I double over, just as a gun fires and a bullet goes flying over my head. I feel the whistle against the back of my neck. So perhaps throwing an incredibly inept punch saved my life.

"Run!" I hear Lockwood shout, and Percy grabs me by the wrist and drags me off the road and into the trees, Felicity on our heels. She's got a fistful of her skirt hoisted nearly to her waist, and I get a view of a good deal more of my sister's legs than I ever wished to see. There's the crack of another gunshot, and something knocks me hard in the back of the head. I think for a minute I've been shot, but then I realize it was Percy swinging his violin case around to use like a shield.

Behind us, I hear the horses scream, then the clatter of the coach wheels. I don't dare look to see if Lockwood and our company are making their escape as well—I'm too afraid of catching my foot on something and falling, and I can hear the bandits chasing us. The underbrush is crashing and there's another gunshot, but we keep running. I don't know how long we can go for. I am somehow feeling both as though I could sprint all the way to Marseilles fed only by fear, and as though my pounding heart is getting in the way of my lungs, making it hard to breathe deep enough. My throat is starting to feel raw.

"Here, here, here!" Felicity cries, and pulls me over a ridge slick with leaves. I lose my footing and sit down hard, tripping Percy so that we both tumble down the slope like demented mountain goats, simultaneously trying to regain our footing and keep moving forward.

"Over here," Felicity hisses, and we clamber after her, behind a great rock jutting from the roots of a massive ash tree, and press ourselves up against its back side. I hear the highwaymen crash by us. Their shouts waft behind them, fading to echoes like birdcalls flitting between the trees.

We sit for a long time, all of us gasping and trying to make no noise beyond that. We're breathing so hard it seems a miracle that that alone doesn't give us away. I can feel Felicity shaking next to me and I realize suddenly that she's clutching my hand. I can't remember the last time I held hands with my sister.

We hear the highwaymen retreat, then come back in our direction, but never close enough to be a threat. Eventually, the noise of them fades into silence, and the forest is nothing but the crackle of the trees.

The rush is starting to fade and a swell of pain goes through my palm. I peel my fingers from between Felicity's and shake my hand out a few times, wincing. "I think I broke my hand."

"You've not broken your hand," Felicity says.

"I should know, it's my hand."

"Let me see it."

I pull it up against my stomach. "No."

"Let me see." Felicity grabs me around the wrist, then mashes her fingers into my palm. I yelp.

"It's not broken," she says.

"How do you know?"

"Because it's hardly swollen, and I can feel that the bones are all still intact."

I don't know how Felicity knows what bones are meant to feel like.

"But don't tuck your thumb into your fist next time you punch someone," she adds.

I'm also not clear how Felicity knows the best way to throw a punch.

I look over at Percy. He's got his violin case pressed to his stomach, two fingers stuck into the pair of bullet holes now etched into the edges, as though he's plugging a leak. "What do we do now?" he asks.

"Go back to the carriage," I say. It seems so obvious.

Felicity's brow puckers. "Do you think we could find it again? We'll get lost. Or ambushed."

"They're highwaymen," I say. "They want money and then they run. They'll be long gone by now."

"I don't think those were highwaymen. They were looking for something. Something they thought we had, and they seemed rather determined to murder us for its possession."

"Is that what they were saying? I was sort of . . . panicking."

"Do we have it?" Percy asks.

"Have what?" I say. "We don't know what they're after."

Felicity flicks a leaf off the hem of her dress, then says, "If any of us is smuggling, now would be the time to come forward."

And then they both look to me.

"What?" I protest.

"Well, out of all of us you seem the most likely to have picked up something," she replies. "Did anyone drop something in your pocket while she had her tongue down your throat?"

I am about to complain, but, rake that I am, that tasteful phrasing on Felicity's part pricks a sudden vein of memory. One hand strays to my pocket, tented around the outline of the trinket box I took from the Duke of Bourbon. I had forgotten entirely that it was there. "Oh no."

Percy looks sideways at me. "Oh no what?"

I swallow. "I'd first like it to be noted that I am most certainly not a smuggler."

"Monty . . . ," he says, my name sopping with dread.

"And," I continue overtop him, "I'd like you to both remember just how much you adore me and how dull your lives would be without me in them."

"What did you do?"

I pull the box from my pocket and hold it flat on my palm for them to see. "Stole this."

"From where?"

"Ah . . . Versailles."

Felicity snatches the box from my palm, dials clacking together like teeth when her fingers close around them. "Henry Montague, I'm going to murder you in your sleep!"

"This can't be what they were looking for. It's puny— it's just a trinket box!"

"This"—Felicity waggles it before my face—"is not an ordinary trinket box."

"Then what is it?"

"It's some sort of puzzle, right?" Percy says, taking the box from Felicity. "When you put the letters in the correct alignment, it opens. There's a word or cipher you have to spell." He spins the dials a few times, then makes a trial of the latch, like his first guess might be right. Nothing happens. "Obviously it's meant to hide something or keep it safe."

"And so Monty thought that might be the best thing to take—something clearly valuable," Felicity says.

"It wasn't *clearly valuable*," I protest. "It looked plain in comparison to everything else there."

"It was in the palace! Why were you stealing from the king at all?"

"It wasn't the king's! We were in someone else's apartments."

"You stole from someone important."

"Yes, but why would highwaymen be after something belonging to a duke?"

"Enough," Percy interrupts. He presses the box back into my palm, then says, "Monty took this. Nothing we can do about that now, so we should try to find the road and join back up with our company, if they got away." That *if* hangs very heavy. It makes me squirm to think that if those highwaymen truly were after the box and if any of our company didn't escape them, that would be on my shoulders. "How far do you think we are from Marseilles?"

He looks to me, but I can't remember, so I just stare back blankly.

"Lockwood said it would take a week," Felicity offers. "We've been traveling for five days, so we must be close. I think our best strategy would be to find the road, start toward Marseilles, and hope Lockwood escaped and we can join up with him."

"How?" I ask. "We don't know where the road is."

"Monty, why don't you worry about making certain your hand isn't broken?" Felicity says. It's the verbal equivalent of tossing me something shiny to hold my attention while the adults talk. I glower at her, though she's gone swivel-eyed through the trees and doesn't notice.

"We go south." Percy traces the sun's path across the sky with his finger, then points. "Toward the sea. The road was heading south."

"So," Felicity says, "we walk south until we find a road, then see if we meet up with Lockwood, or else find a carriage or a wagon that will take us the rest of the way. Our equipage will be in Marseilles soon—unless Lockwood and our men didn't . . . didn't make it." She swallows, then scrubs a hand under her nose. "I think it's best to assume they did, and plan for any eventualities only if we find evidence to the contrary."

Percy nods, and they both seem so certain about it that I feel like the stupidest person there.

"Well, then," I say, like I was a critical part of the planning, "that's decided." I try to rise, but I'm shakier than I expected and my legs go straight out from under me. I end up slumping forward into the brush, soaking my knees in the damp soil.

"Don't stand so fast," Felicity instructs from behind me. "And take a deep breath or you're going to faint."

I think about arguing, but she actually seems to know what she's talking about. I roll onto my back and stare up at the sky, wide and open above us like a tossed picnic blanket shaken from its folds.

"At least Percy saved his violin," I say, and Percy lets out a grateful, breathy laugh.

We walk without seeing any sign of our carriage or an end to the trees or even a sliver of road until the sun is nearly set, and then it's an empty road that we find, not a light or a house in sight. Percy is the first to suggest what we are all thinking, which is stopping to sleep, since it doesn't seem likely we'll find anywhere to stay before we collapse. Summer is peaking like whipped meringue, and the night is thick-aired and damp. Crickets strum from the underbrush.

"This is altogether a different sort of evening than I was hoping for," I say as we spread ourselves in the warm shadow of a white-barked poplar tree.

"Disappointed?" Percy asks.

I'm gasping for a drink—it's all I've been thinking of for the last several hours, trying to calculate the best-case scenario for getting alcohol in me fast. But I just laugh.

Percy stretches out beside me, which makes my skin stand on end until he puts his violin case deliberately between us. I take that as my sign to stay away. Felicity lies down on my other side and curls up with her hands pillowed under her head. "If you keep rubbing your hand like that," she says to me, "you might actually break it."

I hadn't realized I was. "It bloody hurts!"

"Should have been better at punching."

"How was I supposed to know there was a correct way to do it? On that subject, how do *you* know?"

"How do you *not* know?" she counters. "That can't be the first time you've hit someone."

"With any degree of seriousness, yes."

"You hit me once at the pond," Percy says.

"Yes, but we were boys. And it was more of a smack. And you were teasing me because I wouldn't put my head under the water, so you deserved it."

"What about when you came home all black-and-blue from Eton?" Felicity asks.

I try to laugh, but my throat closes up around the sound and it comes out a bit more like I'm drowning. "That wasn't from a fight."

"That's what Mother told me."

"Yes, well. Parents lie."

"Why would she lie about that?"

"Hm."

"I think you're lying to me."

"I'm not."

"I think you got in a fight and that's why they expelled you. You came home so bashed up—"

"I remember."

"—you must have done something nasty enough to get one of the other boys to put his fist in your face."

"No."

"You're not one to start fights, but I assumed you'd at least have swung back."

"It wasn't another boy, it was Father."

Silence drops upon us like wet wool. The trees whisper as the wind rakes through them, leaves moon-stained and glittering. Between the branches, I can see the stars, so bright and thick that the sky looks sugared.

Then Felicity says, "Oh."

My eyes are starting to pinch, and I screw up my face against it. "Good old Father."

"I didn't know that. I swear, Mother told me—"

"Why are we talking about this?" I laugh again, because I don't know what else to do. I want a drink so badly I'm ready to sprint to the next town for it. I press my fists against my eyes and suck in a sharp breath as pain shoots down my wrist. "My hand is absolutely broken."

"It's not broken," Felicity says, and the exasperation behind her voice makes me feel better.

"I think it might be."

"It's not."

"We should sleep," Percy says.

"Right." I turn onto my side and find myself face-to-face with him. In the moonlight, his skin looks like polished stone. He smiles at me, so sympathetic it makes me shrivel up. *Poor Monty*, it says, and I want to die when I think of him pitying me.

Poor Monty, with a father who beats you until you bleed.

Poor Monty, with a fortune to inherit and an estate to run.

Poor Monty, who's useless and embarrassing.

"Good night," Percy says, then rolls over, away from me.

Poor Monty, in love with your best friend.

As it happens, there is no way to get comfortable on the ground, as it's primarily composed of dirt and rocks and other sharp things that there's a reason no one stuffs their mattresses with. I'm bone weary from the day, an ache left over from the panic still lingering in my limbs, but I lie for a long time on my back, then my side, then my other side, trying to cozy up and fall asleep and think about something that isn't how hard it is to be stone-cold sober or my father beating the shit out of me after I was expelled from school. It's running circles in my mind, all the vicious details of that week—my father's face as the headmaster explained what had happened. The way that, after a while, he'd been hitting me for long enough that I heard more than felt the blows landing. The exquisite discomfort of the carriage ride home, my ribs rattling around in my chest every time we hit a rut and my head packed up tight, like it was full of cotton. All the things he called me that I'll never forget.

I had woken at home the next morning in the worst pain of my life, so sore I could hardly get out of bed, but my father made me come to breakfast and sit beside him. My mother didn't say a word about why I'd arrived home looking like I'd run face-first into a stone wall at top speed, and the idea of Father being the reason I was swollen and bruised would have been so absurd to Felicity it apparently never crossed her mind.

Halfway through breakfast, I excused myself to go vomit in the back garden, and when no one came after me, I stayed there, lying on the lawn beside the pond with no strength to get up. It was the same sort of day as when we left for our Tour—gray and stifling, the air sweating from a storm the night before and the sky threatening to tear open again. Patches of the garden path were still dark, and the grass was so damp that I was wet to the skin in minutes. But I didn't move. I lay flat on my back, staring at the clouds and waiting for rain, shame rattling around inside me like a marble in a jar.

After a time, a shadow fell across my face, and when I opened my eyes, there was Percy, silhouetted against the bright sky as he peered down at me. "Christ."

"Hallo there, darling." My voice broke on the final word, because of course I needed this moment to be more humiliating than it already was. "How was your term?"

"Jesus Christ. What happened?"

"Eton threw me out."

"I heard. That's not what I'm concerned about right now."

"Oh, this?" I waved a hand vaguely at my face, trying not to wince as I felt the pull in my ribs like the tightening of a violin string. "Don't I look dashing?"

"Monty."

"*Piratical* is perhaps a better word."

"Please be serious."

"Took a dozen men to bring me down."

"Who did this?"

"Who do you think?"

Percy didn't say anything to that. Instead he lay down next to me, our faces side by side but our bodies pointing in opposite directions. A bird swooped low above us, chittering merrily. "So why'd they toss you out?" he asked.

"Well. I had a bit of a gambling enthusiasm."

"Everyone at Eton has a gambling enthusiasm. It's

not enough to expel you."

"It was enough for them to search my rooms. And there was found some incriminating correspondence between myself and that lad I wrote to tell you about. Which was rather enough."

"Oh God."

"In my defense, he was very handsome."

"And they told your father about them, did they?"

"Oh, he got to read them all. And then throw them back at me. Literally. Some of them he read aloud to punctuate . . ." I swiped a hand across the side of my face that felt less like an open wound. Percy pretended not to see. "So now he's going to be home more, to keep an eye on me. Not so much time away in London, and that's entirely my fault. I'm going to have to see him all the time and be around him—all the bleeding time, and it's not going to change *anything*."

"I know."

"If he could beat this out of me, I would have let him long ago."

The clouds shifted and churned above us, spreading like blood across the sky. At the edge of the lawn, the pond tested its shores. Harpsichord music drifted through the parlor windows, heavy-handed scales played at top speed. Felicity practicing with great indignance.

"I wish I were dead," I said, then closed my eyes—or

rather eye, one being out of commission—so I wouldn't have to see Percy look at me, but I felt the grass prickle my neck as he shifted.

"Do you mean that?"

It wasn't the first time I'd thought it—wouldn't be the last either, though I didn't know that then—but it was the first time I'd said it aloud, to anyone. It's a strange thing, to want to die. Stranger still when you don't feel you deserve to get away so easily. I should have fought myself harder, kept it all better penned. Shouldn't have wanted to act on my unnatural instincts. Shouldn't have felt so grateful and relieved and not alone for the first time in my life when Sinjon Westfall kissed me behind the dormitories on Saint Mark's Eve, and so certain no one could ever make me ashamed for it. Not the headmaster, or my friends back home, or the other boys in my year. The whole while between being found out and waiting to be collected, I'd felt so defiant and righteous, unshakable in my surety that I'd done nothing wrong, but my father had knocked that straight out of me.

"I don't know," I said. "Yes. Maybe."

"Well, don't . . . don't do that. Don't want to be dead. Here." Percy nudged me with his shoulder until I opened my eyes. He had his arm extended straight above us, fingers splayed wide. "Here are five reasons not to be dead. Number one, because your birthday is next month and I already have something really excellent for you and you don't want to die before I give it to you." I laughed a little at that, but I was so near tears it ended up sounding less like a laugh and more like a slurp. Percy didn't comment. "Number two"—he was ticking them off on his fingers as he went—"if you weren't around there'd be no one who's worse than me at billiards. You are so rubbish at billiards it makes me look quite a bit better than I actually am. Number three, I wouldn't have anyone who would hate Richard Peele with me."

"I hate Richard Peele," I said quietly.

"*WE HATE RICHARD PEELE!*" Percy seconded, so loud that a bird took flight from the hedgerow. I laughed again, and it sounded more human this time. "Number four, we still have never managed to slide all the way down the staircase at my house on a serving tray, and without you there, the inevitable victory will be hollow. And five"—he folded his thumb into his fist and pressed it up to the sky—"if you weren't here, everything would be the worst. Abso-bloody-lutely awful. It'd be dull and lonely and just . . . don't, all right? Don't be dead. I'm sorry you were expelled and I'm sorry about your father but I'm so glad you're home and I . . . really need you right now. So don't wish you were dead because I'm so glad that you're not." Silence for a moment. Then Percy said, "All right?"

And I said, "All right."

Percy climbed to his feet and offered me a hand. He

was gentle about it, but I still winced as he pulled me up, and he had to steady me with a soft touch to my elbow. He'd gotten taller since I'd seen him at Christmas—somehow he suddenly had a good five inches on me—and he'd broadened out a bit as well, not so lanky and knobby and ninety percent knees like he'd always been, growing up. His limbs didn't seem too long for his body anymore.

When I look back on it now, I realize that must have been the first time, in all the while we'd known each other, it occurred to me that Percy might actually be rather handsome.

Perspective is a goddamn son of a bitch.

Marseilles

8

We are three days on the road, sleeping in sheltered groves and hitching rides on farmers' carts through fields of close-fisted sunflowers and blooming lavender. We reach Marseilles in the late evening—the linkboys are already out trimming the lantern wicks. It's a sprawling, shining city, cleaner and brighter than Paris. Notre-Dame de la Garde sits high on the hill above the sea, its white stone reflecting back the sunset as it caramelizes across the breakers, turning the waves gold. The streets of the Panier are narrow and high, wet washing strung between the windows catching the sunlight and flashing like glass.

The banks are all shut up for the day, and as our plan was to find Father's bank and see if a message from Lockwood or Sinclair has been left for us, we're rather foiled. It seems we're condemned to spend another night exposed to the elements unless we go knocking on doors at random, which makes me want to throw myself into the sea. I'm sore head to toe from the walking and the sleeping on hard ground, and my stomach is scratching against my spine. We've been eating a mixture of thieved and charitable scraps for days, and the meager breakfast swapped for Felicity's earrings this morning left me long ago.

As we wander down the main road, toward the fort guarding the harbor, we stumble upon a fair set up along the water, red-and-white-striped tents with ribbons knotted to their ropes and fluttering in the breeze. Paper garlands are strung over the walkways, and the air smells of boiling oil and the mealy tang of beer. Carts of food are lined up between the tents, piled with cheeses rolled in wax, greased turkey legs, skillets filled with candied almonds, and sweet rolls domed with liquefied sugar and berry coulis. It seems the most nickable supper we are going to find.

Felicity takes charge of the thievery, so Percy and I find a table on the pier to wait for her, looking out across the syrupy water and the flocks of ships moored there, gulls flailing between them like snowflakes riding the wind. We sit on either side, Percy's fiddle case between us. The wood grain is rough and weathered by years of being chewed at by the spray kicked up from the sea.

I'm so tired I put my head down and close my

eyes. "Never thought I'd say this, but I'll be glad to see Lockwood."

Percy laughs wearily. "Are you getting sentimental?"

"God no—he's got our banknotes. I want a real drink and a real bed and real food—I could ravish a plate of cakes right now." When Percy doesn't reply, I sit up. He's got his head balanced on his fists, and he looks weary. More than weary, verging on ill—clammy and absent, though I'm likely in an equally sorry state. "You look poorly."

He doesn't answer for a moment, then glances up, like he only just realized I spoke. "What?"

"You don't look well."

He shakes his head a few times to rouse himself. "I'm tired."

"So am I. We should be stronger than this. Though I suppose we did just walk across France."

"We didn't walk across France," Felicity says as she flops down on the bench beside me. She's got a gibassier bun in each hand, fine grains of aniseed from the filling dusting her fingers.

We eat with the sound of the sea and the tinkling melody of fair music underscoring our silence. I finish much faster than Percy or Felicity, who both seem to be trying to savor theirs while I opted for the method of gentlemanly inhalation. I suck the flakes of pastry off my fingers, then wipe my hands on my coattails, leaving oily tracks behind. My wrist knocks against the box in my pocket, and I pull it out and spin the dials.

Felicity watches me, a thin strand of candied orange peel pinched between her thumb and forefinger. "Describe for us what brilliant logic it was that led you to think stealing from the French king was a good idea."

"It wasn't the king. It was his minister."

"I believe stealing from a minister to the king is still a capital offense. You're going to have to return it, you know."

"Why? It's just a trinket box."

"Because firstly, we are being pursued for it."

"Allegedly."

She rolls her eyes. "Secondly, because it is not yours. And thirdly, because it was an incredibly childish thing to do."

"You're going to make a very fine governess someday with that enthusiasm for rule following," I say, with a scowl. "That finishing school will have nothing to teach you."

She sticks the pad of her thumb in her mouth and sucks at a spot of glaze. "Perhaps I don't want to go to school."

"Course you do. You've been whining for years about how badly you want schooling, and now you can stop being obnoxious because you're finally going."

Her mouth puckers. "You know, saying things like

that might be the reason most people find you insuffer-able."

"People find me insufferable?"

"When you use that sort of phraseology, yes, it's a word I'd use."

"I'm just being honest!"

"Be a little less honest and a little more tactful."

"You've put up such a fuss—"

"Yes, for education. An *actual* education, not finishing school—they're going to squeeze me into corsets and bully me into silence."

It's true—Felicity's not a broken horse. A finishing school will kick the spirit straight out of her, and while I've never been particularly fond of my sister, the thought of a quiet, simpering, cross-stitching, tea-sipping Felicity feels like a slash through a painting.

I almost begin to feel a bit sorry for her, but then she wrecks that with a sour "Do you know how horrid it feels to watch my brother get tossed out of the best boarding school in England, then get to travel the Continent as a reward, while I'm stuck behind, not permitted to study the same things or read the same books or even visit the same places while we're abroad, just because I had the bad luck to be born a girl?"

"Reward?" My temper is starting to rise to match hers. "You think this Tour is a *reward*? This is a last meal before my execution."

"Oh, how tragic, you have to run an estate and be a lord and have a good, rich, cozy life on your own terms."

I gape at her—mostly because I thought we had developed some understanding between us, after what I had confessed to her the night of the highwaymen's attack, that there is nothing cozy about the life I'll be walking back to at the end of this year, but here she is spitting in my face like a mouthful of melon seeds.

"Leave him alone, Felicity," Percy says quietly.

Felicity flicks a pastry flake from her thumb with the tip of her finger, then says, with an upturned nose, "How lucky we would all be to have the problems of Henry Montague."

I stand up, because Felicity learned to be mean from our father, and with each snide comment the shade of him is filtering through darker and darker.

"Where are you going?" Percy calls.

"To wash all this damn sap off my hands," I say, though it's fairly transparent I'm storming off because of my sister.

I walk for a minute, directionless, my head fuzzy with anger and also a lot of wanting for a drink, before I realize I have no clue where I'm going and I've got to be able to find my way back to Percy and Felicity. I stop. A group of children skate by me, their hands linked and their hair flying behind them, angling toward a man setting up a projector for a magic lantern show. A woman outside a viciously green tent shouts in my direction, "Look into my eye for a sight of your own death! Only a sou for a glance!" A pair of acrobats balance on their hands over the edge of the pier, to applause from a sparse audience.

"*Vos pieds sont douloureux*," someone says behind me, and I turn.

A wooden stand with a purple awning is set up against the edge of the pier, the word *Apothicaire* stenciled over a slop of red paint on the front. A man with coarse graying hair, a leather apron thrown over his patchy coat, is behind the counter, leaning against it on his elbows. Behind him, shelves are stuffed with an assortment of bottles and vials, labels peeling away like dead skin and the monikers of their tinctures sketched in spidery handwriting across them. A gallery of maladies.

"*Pardon?*" I say when I realize he's addressing me. "Sorry?"

"*Vos pieds.* Your feet. You have sore feet."

"How do you know that?"

"You're walking on them strangely, like they're hurting you. You need an ointment."

"Bet you say that to everyone who passes."

"I don't always mean it. You—I'm worried for your feet."

"I'm walking fine."

"Then something else. You're too stiff to be without pain. A mistake of the young, maybe? A venereal pox?"

"What? No. Definitely not that."

He waggles a finger at me. "You're not well. I can tell it."

I try to edge away, but he keeps talking, his voice getting louder the farther I go, and I don't want some randy medicine man shouting across the pier that I've got something festering on my bits, so I snap at him, more peevish than I intend, "I'm not unwell, I'm unhappy."

He seems unmoved. "Is there much of a difference? I have tonics for your feet, and metrical charms my grand-mothers can concoct for your ill humor." He taps his finger at a row of witch bottles on a low shelf, their con-tents tarlike and frothing.

"Well, I'm not interested. Even if I had coins to spare, they wouldn't be spent on you and your daft charms." I start to walk away again before he can say anything more about whatever I've got wrong with my head or my feet or my bits, so hasty I sideswipe a cart of oranges behind me, sending a tower of them collapsing in all directions. The cart man starts to shout at me, and I'm so flustered that I immediately forget every word I know in French.

"Sorry," I say in English. "Sorry. *Désolé*." I start scooping oranges off the path before they get stepped on or kicked into the harbor. Two get away from me and plop into the water. I want to sit down where I stand and scream.

One of the oranges rolls down the planking, and a man stops it with the toe of his boot. I'm about to scramble forward and grab it when he reaches down and I catch the flash of a gold signet ring on his finger. The same ring the highwayman was wearing when he and his gang laid siege.

The highwaymen have found us. By some impossible coincidence, we've been Dick Turpined and then tracked down. Or perhaps there's nothing coincidental about it— perhaps Felicity was right and they were looking for us after all. They've come for the box.

The man with the gold ring is moving to put the orange back on the cart from the other side, so I scramble out of the way before he can see me and hide in the only place available, which is behind the counter of the apothecary's stall.

The apothecary doesn't look down, but his lips pull into a taut smile. "Friends of yours?" he says, and though his eyes are elsewhere, it's clear he's addressing me.

"Please, don't say anything to them," I hiss.

"Can I help you gentlemen?" he calls. "That's quite a bruise, sir. How did you come by it?"

"That's not your concern." It's the same voice from the forest, confirmed when the man's fingers curl over the counter—that ring is unmistakable. He's leaning over, squinting at the labels on the bottles as the apothecary runs his fingers over them. *Don't look down*, I think.

Dear God, please don't look down.

"If I knew the cause, I could better treat it," the apothecary says. "A bleeding beneath the skin takes a different salve than a slip and fall—"

"I was struck in the head with a fiddle case," the highwayman snaps, his disdain palpable. "Does that help your diagnosis, mountebank?"

Definitely our assailants, unless there is a rash of tourists using instruments to fend off toby-gills of late.

"Where'd that boy go?" I hear the man with the orange cart shout. My heart's really sitting on my lungs—it's getting hard to breathe around it.

"The balm of Gilead, then, applied twice daily, will take down the swelling." The apothecary almost trips over me as he turns back to the counter. The tin lands a little harder than is natural, but the highwayman must not notice. I hear the chink of coins on the counter, then the men's boots as they retreat.

The apothecary keeps his face up, but after a moment says to me, "They've gone around back toward the city. You'd best go the other way if you're avoiding them."

I pull myself up with one hand on the shelves. The bottles tremble against each other. "Thank you."

The apothecary shrugs. "They look fierce and you look helpless. Do you owe them money?"

"They think I owe them something." I check to make

certain the highwaymen are truly gone—the man with the orange cart has been blessedly distracted by the start of the magic lantern show—then bolt in the other direction, my shoes slapping the damp planking with an empty *thwack*.

Percy and Felicity are, thank God, right where I left them, still at the table with Percy's fiddle between them. Somehow Felicity still has a bite of her gibassier left gummed to her thumb and she's nibbling at it. Percy's got his head in his hands and is massaging his temples. He doesn't raise his head, even when I skid up beside them and proclaim, "They found us."

"Who?" Felicity asks. "Mr. Lockwood?"

"No, the highwaymen. The men who attacked us. They're here."

"How do you know it's them?"

"I saw them. One of them has this ring—I remember it."

Felicity is already on her feet. "Do you think they're looking for us?"

"Why else would they be here? You think the group of bandits who attacked us just happen to be strolling through a fair at the same time we are?"

"We need to go, we need to see if Lockwood's arrived and find where our company is."

"No, we need to find out if they're actually after

this"—and here I snatch up the puzzle box from where it's still sitting on the table between them—"and return it so they'll let us alone."

"You think we should go looking for the men who were ready to kill us?" Felicity asks. "They're not going to let us walk away after we give them what they want. We need to get out of here. Percy, are you certain you're well?"

Percy looks far less well than he did when I left. He keeps squinting, like the light is too bright, and he's sweating and doesn't look quite *here*. I can't think of another way to describe it. But he stands up, shouldering his fiddle case. "I'm fine. Let's go."

"How are we going to find Lockwood?" I ask as we weave through the crowd, Felicity in the lead.

"Do you know where he meant for us to stay?" she asks.

"No, he sent Sinclair."

"Well, do you know Father's bank here? We could ask them if they've accepted any letters in his name or if Sinclair left word about accommodation."

"No. Maybe? It's the Bank of England, I think."

"You *think*?"

"Yes, it is. Wait . . . yes."

"Do you ever listen, Henry, or is everything just sweet nothings in your ear?"

I look up as we round a corner and catch a glimpse of exactly the troop of men we are trying to avoid, down the path ahead of us and coming our way. I grab Felicity's arm and jerk her backward between two of the tents, nearly tripping myself when my shin catches one of the ropes tying them off. Percy dodges next to me, his fiddle case clutched to his chest. "They're right there," I hiss. Felicity peers out from between the tents, then ducks back to my side.

"You're certain that's them?"

"I'm certain that one of them is wearing the same ring as the man who attacked us."

"That's not a whole lot of certainty, is it?"

"He's also got the imprint of Percy's fiddle case carved into his forehead, so how much more would you like?"

Shadows stretch along the pier, preceding their casters, and we all sink back. I try to think small and invisible thoughts, willing them to not look at us, not see us, not turn as they pass. I'd gladly toss the puzzle box at their heads as they go by, but Felicity's logic makes more sense than mine—they planned to kill us in the forest and I can't imagine they'd let us go with a *Thanks, chums* and a pat on the back now. I haven't yet a plan of what to do beyond *don't get murdered at a seaside fair*, but for now, that requires staying out of sight.

The highwaymen file past us, the one with the gold ring in the lead. He's got his hand over his face, rubbing his temples, but as it drops, I catch a glimpse of his profile and recognition dawns suddenly upon me.

I know him. And he's most certainly not a highwayman—it's the Duke of Bourbon.

He starts to turn his head toward us, livid bruise coming into view, and my heart nearly throws itself to its death. But at the same minute, a firework explodes overhead, turning the navy sky bright red. The highwaymen all look up, and Percy, Felicity, and I, seemingly of the same mind on the subject of not getting murdered, duck the rest of the way down the row, then around the corner and out of sight.

We stop between two tents, canvas shielding us on all sides from the crowds gathered along the pier. The ground is peppered with stakes wedged into the planks and straining against the ropes strung taut between them. It's a narrow corridor to walk.

"I know him," I hiss.

"What?" Felicity replies. She's got one hand pressed to her chest, breathing hard.

"The man, the highwayman, I saw his face. I know him."

"Monty," Percy says from behind me.

I press on. I'm so sure of it and so desperate to finally be useful and right about something that I won't be interrupted. "It's the Duke of Bourbon, the French king's prime minister. I met him at Versailles."

"Monty." Percy shifts to my side, his hand brushing my elbow.

"The box came from his apartments."

"Monty."

"What is it, Perce?"

"Take this." He's trying to press his violin case into my hands.

"Why?"

"Because I think I'm going to faint."

And then he does.

God bless Percy for the warning, but I'm not as quick on my feet as that. I haven't got a firm hold on the fiddle case when he collapses, and I sacrifice my grip on it to catch him before he hits the ground. It bounces along the boards, one of the latches popping open with a metallic *ping*.

Catching him sends me to my knees and we sink down together, my arms under his and his face pressed into my chest. I expect him to be limp as cloth but instead he's gone rigid. His body's twisted up and stiff, a contorted sculpture of himself, and it doesn't look like he's breathing. The muscles in his chest feel like they're pulled up too tight to let in any air, and I can hear his teeth squeak as they grind together.

"Percy." I lay him on the ground and shake him lightly. "Hey, Perce, come on, wake up." I don't know why I'm talking to him. It feels like the only thing I can do. His back arches, veins in his neck straining against his skin, and I think maybe he's coming around, but then he starts to shake. Not just shake—convulse, frightening and out of control. His limbs look like they're trying to pull away from his body, head kicking at the planking.

And I don't know what do. I've never felt so stupid and helpless and afraid in my life. *Do something*, I think, because my best friend is writhing on the ground, in obvious pain, but I am absolutely stuck. I can't think of a thing to do to help him. I can't even move.

Suddenly Felicity is kneeling beside me. "Get out of the way," she snaps, and I come back to myself enough to follow orders. She takes my place, grabbing two fist-fuls of Percy's coat and hauling him onto his side so there's less chance of him slamming into one of the tent stakes as he convulses. "Percy," she says, leaning over him. "Percy, can you hear me?" He doesn't respond—I'm not sure if he'd be able to even if he heard. Felicity puts one hand on his shoulder, like she's keeping him steady on his side, and kicks the fiddle case out of his way. Then she sits back and does nothing but hold him in that place.

"What are you doing?" I cry. I've got my hands pressed to either side of my face—a farcical gesture of horror. "We've got to help him!"

"There's nothing to be done," she replies, and she sounds so calm it feeds my panic.

"He needs help!"

"It should be over in a minute. We have to wait."

"You can't—"

I start to crawl forward without any plan of what I'm about to do, but Felicity whips around and skewers me with a glare. "Unless you know what you're talking about, please stay out of the way and keep quiet."

I can't watch it. I can't watch Felicity being so calm and Percy's body wrenching and distorted, and me sitting on the ground feeling so goddamn helpless.

It seems like it lasts forever, as though we've spent days here, waiting, spectators to what I'm certain is Percy dying slowly in intense agony. His breathing sounds labored and gravelly, and his lips are tinged faintly blue. When Felicity tips him farther on his side, spittle pinked with blood froths at the corner of his mouth. "He's coming out of it," she says quietly. She has one hand hovering near the back of his head, as a cushion between his arched neck and the iron tent stakes.

Percy's body gives a final pull, knees coiling up to his chest; then he vomits. Felicity keeps a good hold on him so that when his muscles loosen, he stays on his side. His eyes are still closed.

Wake up, Perce, I think. *Come on, wake up and be alive and be all right. Please be all right.*

"We need to get him somewhere close by," Felicity says, brushing his hair away from where it's stuck to his lips with a soft touch. That's either too subtle or I'm not thinking straight, because she looks over at me and snaps, "If you want to help, now would be the time for that."

I stagger to my feet, so shaky I nearly keel straight back over, and stumble down the path between the tents. I don't know where to go—there's nothing nearby but the fair stands, and the highwaymen are probably still prowling, searching for us.

I look down into the slat of sea visible between the planks, just as an orange bobs past, its rind slick and glittering with beads of seawater.

I sprint back the way I went before, shouldering through the crowds all stopped and staring up at the fireworks, until I find the apothecary's stand again. He's stepped out from under its awning and is watching the show too, but he turns when he sees me coming. "You return."

"My friend needs help," I blurt.

"I'm sorry to hear that."

"Can you help him?"

"In what way?"

"You're a doctor."

"I'm an apothecary."

"But you know . . . You can . . ." I'm so winded I can hardly get words out. My chest feels corked. "Please, I don't know what's wrong with him!"

The apothecary is sizing me up, all the mirth gone from his face. "I think you're trouble."

"We're not trouble, we're *in* trouble," I say. "We're travelers and we've nowhere to go and he needs help and . . . Please, he's had some kind of fit and he was shaking and he won't wake and I don't know what's wrong. *Please.*"

My voice gets properly pitchy on that last bit, which must make me sound sufficiently pathetic, or at least sincere, for he takes me by the elbow and says, "Show me where he is."

I nearly throw my arms around him for that.

I want to run, but the apothecary seems insistent on a brisk walk and I'm forced to match it or else lose him in the crowd. As we clamber through the people with their faces turned to the sky, he asks me to recount what happened, and I give him a tongue-tied version that brings the panic in me back up to a boil. I'm such a wreck I can hardly remember where I've come from. All the tents look the same. I'm about to tell him I'm afraid I won't be able to find Percy and Felicity again when I spot her silhouette, black against the brackish canvas. "Here," I say, and I lead him between the tents. Another firework pops over our heads.

Percy's still insensible, but he's starting to stir. Felicity's kneeling over him, one of his hands in hers, speaking to him though he doesn't seem to hear. A watery ribbon of blood and spittle slips from the corner of his mouth and down his cheek. Felicity pulls her sleeve over her thumb and wipes it away. She looks up as we approach, casting a wary eye at the stranger.

"He's an apothecary," I explain. "He can help."

The apothecary doesn't say a word to Felicity as she shuffles out of his way and he adopts her place, taking Percy's face in his hands and peering at it, then checking his pulse, then his eyes and inside his mouth. He too swipes his thumb at the blood.

"He's bleeding," I murmur, not realizing I've spoken aloud until Felicity replies, "He bit his tongue, that's all."

The apothecary takes a waxed envelope of smelling salts from the pocket of his coat and slips his finger under the flap, all the while speaking to Percy in a language I don't recognize. His voice is very gentle. "*Obre els ulls. Has passat una nit difícil, veritat? Em pots mirar? Mira'm.* Look at me."

Percy opens his eyes, and I let go a sigh of relief, even though it seems to take him a tremendous effort. His gaze is a long way off from us.

"*Molt bé, molt bé,*" the apothecary murmurs. "Do you know where you are?" Percy blinks twice, slowly, then his eyes slide closed again and his head tips sideways. The apothecary catches it before his face smacks the ground. "He needs rest."

"We've nowhere to go," Felicity replies.

"I have a boat moored in the canal where you may bring him. I'll see what more can be done for him there."

I nod, waiting for someone to do something useful, until Felicity snaps at me, "He's not going to walk it off, Monty. You have to carry him."

"Oh. Right." The apothecary slides out of the way, and I hoist Percy over my shoulder. My feet stumble for purchase on the ground and I almost fall, but Felicity pushes me straight, and we follow the apothecary between the tents.

Beyond the pier, our guide leads us, sure-footed, down a thin, sandy path past the sailing ships and along the riverbank, until we reach a tar-caked dock where a fleet of brightly painted canal boats are moored, neat as harpsichord keys. My arms are starting to shake. My whole body feels like it's shaking, inside and out.

The apothecary jumps aboard one of the boats, taking up a lantern from the prow before he grabs me by the arm and hauls me after him. Felicity follows with a light step.

The canal boat has a narrow deck with a covered cabin in the center, and I follow him into it. It's a trick maneuvering both Percy and I through the small door without knocking either of us out cold, and once we're inside, my head nearly brushes the ceiling. The apothecary leads me to a built-in box bed covered in pieced quilts and a handful of thin pillows. Hanging earthenware lanterns decorate the walls in diamond shards of light that bob and sway as the boat bounces in the water.

"Here." The apothecary pulls back the blankets on the bed, and I ease Percy down onto it.

I didn't realize he had woken, but he grabs onto me, like he thinks he's falling. "Monty!"

"Right here, Perce." I'm trying to keep the shudder out of my voice, and failing. "I'm right here, it's . . ." I've got no clue what I'm supposed to say. "It's all right." God, I sound so daft.

"It's bright," he murmurs. His voice is muzzy and slurred—he hardly sounds like himself—and his eyes still aren't focused. Seems he's having a hard time keeping them open at all—he keeps squinting like he's looking into the sun. His hands are clamped around my coat, so tight his knuckles are blotched, and when I sit him upon the bed, he clutches me tighter, his voice pitching. "Don't leave me!"

"I won't."

He seems so distressed that I don't want to peel him off, so I stoop there, my hands around his, trying to convince him to lie down, with my voice shaking. His shoulders slump suddenly, head falling forward against my chest, and I think he's going to let me go, but then his fingers go tight and he tries to stand again. "I need my violin. Where is it? Where's my violin? I need it now."

"I've got it, Percy." Felicity appears at my side, prying Percy's fingers off my coat and guiding him down onto the bed. "Try to relax, it's all right. You're safe now, relax." On the other side of the cabin, the apothecary pulls a medicine chest from a shelf and begins rummaging through its drawers, bottles clinking together in a soft chorus from inside.

I can tell that I'm useless, so I slink backward, onto the deck and into the cool night air. Above the water, the stars are spread in smudgy handfuls across the twilight. I can still hear the music of the fair, and closer by a slow tune plucked out upon a mandolin, one lonely string at a time. On the bank, crickets are purring. I sit down with my back to the railing, turning my face to the sky and letting the shaky fatigue settle through me.

Turns out, panic is rather exhausting, and I fall asleep without meaning to, my head tipped back against the railing of the boat, before anyone has come out.

It feels like I've hardly closed my eyes when Felicity is shaking me awake. Sunrise is a spilled glass of wine across the horizon, stars fading back into imaginary things. Someone put a blanket over me while I slept and my knees are aching after so long folded up to my chest.

In spite of the night we've had, Felicity looks very awake. Her eyes are wide and alert, and she's undone the pins from her hair and woven it into a plait that swings over her shoulder as she leans toward me. I, in contrast, feel like a washed-up carcass of myself. My eyes are crusty, and a thin line of spittle has run down my chin while I slept. I swipe it away. I haven't shaved in a week and I'm starting to get fuzzy.

"Are you well?" Felicity asks.

"What—me? Yes. How's Percy?"

She looks down at the deck and my heart seizes up.

"Sore and weary. He's trying to rest but he's been too agitated to stay asleep for long. He's going to be fine," she adds, for I must look stricken. "Only a matter of time."

"Sorry, I should have . . . I should have stayed up with him. With you."

"You were tired. And there wasn't much to be done. Pascal bled him and he took some mugwort, so we'll see if that has any effect."

"Pascal?"

"The apothecary. The man you found."

"Does he know what's wrong with Percy?"

Felicity slides to her knees in front of me, one hand on the rail. "I think you'd best speak to Percy."

"What do I need to speak to him about?" I ask, dread creeping around me and tightening like a noose.

"He's got something to tell you and I don't want to be the go-between."

"Oh. Right. Well, I should probably go speak to Percy, then," I say, like it was my idea, and pull myself up. Felicity doesn't reply. She takes my spot on the deck as I descend the few steps into the belly of the boat.

The cabin is still dark, but they've lit a few more lanterns and the shadows sway as the current rocks us. It feels like being drunk, a little tipsy and unsteady, but with none of the warm, comfortable buzz. The air smells of incense and seawater, and there's a cup of tea resting on the floor beside the bed, steam rising from the surface and threading its fingers with dust motes drifting through the pale light.

Percy is curled up in the corner of the box bed, stripped down to only rumpled breeches and a clean shirt, the translucent material clinging to his skin with sweat. There's a violet bruise beneath his eye like a crack in a glass windowpane, and a thread of bandage tied off in the crook of one elbow. A small blush of blood has seeped through it. He looks more tired than I've ever seen him. His hair is undone from its queue, and it falls in long coils around his face.

I ease myself down on the opposite corner of the bed, one leg pulled up under me, and Percy opens his eyes. "Morning," I say quietly. Percy doesn't reply. The sound of the sea kicking against the side of the boat fills the silence.

I'm swallowing the urge to say something daft because I hate this taut band between us. It feels like the walls are closing in. *Say something, Monty. Be a friend, be a gentleman, be a human being. It's Percy, your best friend, Percy who you've gotten foxed with, who plays you his violin, who used to spit apple seeds at you from high up in the orchard treetops. Percy who you kissed in Paris, who looks so damn beautiful, even now. Say something kind. Something that will make him stop looking so alone and afraid.* But I can't come up with a damn thing. All I want to do is dash out of reach of whatever it is he's about to say.

Percy presses his forehead to the wall. "I'm sorry," he murmurs. His voice has a drowsy tint to it.

"For what?"

"For what happened."

"It wasn't your fault, Perce. You couldn't have done—"

"It's epilepsy," he says, and I stop.

"What?"

"Epilepsy," he repeats, then covers his face with his hands so it comes out muffled when he says it again. "I have epilepsy."

I don't know what to say to that, so I blurt, "Well, so long as that's all it is."

I hope it might make him laugh, but instead he lets out a tense sigh through his teeth. "Can you please not be yourself right now?"

I look down at the bed, my hands worrying the worn stitching of the blanket. "So you . . . you're ill."

"Yes."

"Epilepsy."

"Yes."

I know almost nothing about epilepsy. Devils and possession and insanity, those are the sorts of things I've heard of, but they're the stuff of horror stories that end with the moral "Thank God each day for your health." And besides, this is Percy, the best lad I know. None of those things can be right.

"And there isn't . . ." I halt, and I swear I'm so rotten at this that even the silence winces. I'm not sure what I'm allowed to ask and what I shouldn't and what questions I'm comfortable hearing the answers to.

Is it contagious?

Does it hurt?

When will you be well again?

Are you going to die?

Are you going to die?

Are you going to die?

I wish we could go back to the moment before he told me and I could just keep not knowing. "Is there a cure? Or treatment, or anything?"

"No. No cure. None of the treatments have worked."

"Oh. Well, that's . . . too bad." His mouth pulls tight, like he's going to say something to correct me, but then he just nods, and I want to turn to sand and slip between the boards. "So you, um, you have these . . ."

"Fits."

"Yes. All right, yes. That."

"You can say it."

I really don't think I can. "How long have they . . . ? How long has this been happening?"

"Every few months—"

"No, I mean, when did it start?"

Percy is still turned to the wall, and before he answers, he twists even farther from me. His face is almost out of sight. "Right before you came home from Eton."

"Eton?" I gape at him. "Percy, that was two years ago. You've been ill for *two years* and you never said anything to me about it?"

"No one knows, all right? Only my family and some of our staff."

"When were you going to tell me?"

"I was sort of hoping I'd never have to. I've been lucky so far."

"Lucky?" I've shifted from meek to spitting-with-fury on the other side of a second. "You kept this secret from me for two years, Percy, two goddamn years. How could you not tell me?"

At last, he raises his head. "Are you really trying to make this about you?"

"I want to know!"

"I'm telling you now, aren't I?"

"Yes, because you have to. Because I had to watch—"

"Well, I'm sorry you *had to watch*." The venom rises in his voice suddenly. "How hard for you to *have to watch*."

"Why didn't you tell me?"

He clenches his hands into fists around the blankets, face set, then says, "Fine, you want to know why? Because at the end of this year, I'm not going to law school, I'm going into an asylum."

We stare at each other. It takes a long moment for

me to grasp what he's said—it's so horrid and utterly unbelievable that I'm certain I must have heard wrong. "You're . . . what?"

"There's a place in Holland. A sanatorium. For the . . ." He squeezes his eyes tight and finishes very carefully. "For the insane."

I don't know what to say. I've heard stories of Bedlam in London—black, poisonous rumors no one speaks of in polite company. Asylums aren't hospitals or spas, they aren't somewhere you go to get well. They're somewhere you go after everything else has been tried. Somewhere you're hidden away and forgotten, bound to your bed and starved and emptied of your blood. They're somewhere you go to die. If Percy goes into a sanatorium, he'll never come home. We won't see each other again.

My chest is so tight I can hardly get words out. "But you're not insane" is all I manage to say.

"Perhaps I am. This isn't ordinary, is it?" He tips his chin, staring down with his cheeks sucked in.

"Is that what you want? Go to Holland and die in a madhouse?"

He winces a bit, and I wish at once I hadn't spoken so bluntly, but I don't retreat from it.

"Of course not."

"Is this your uncle, then? Is it his idea to send you away?" I am starting to speak so fast I can hardly understand myself, grasping frantically at any thread of a way to fix this. *You can't,* I am thinking. *You can't be ill because I need you and you can't go away to die in some asylum because what am I supposed to do without you?* "You have to tell them no. Tell them you won't. You can't go. Just tell them you won't!"

"I haven't got a choice. My family won't care for me any longer."

"Then go somewhere else—anywhere!"

"How?" he snaps. "And how could you possibly understand any of this? If anyone found out, my whole family would suffer for it, and I'm not going to weigh them down any more than I already have." He's kneading the blanket against his legs, veins in his hands standing out like bright threads beneath his skin. "My aunt thinks that this is God's way of punishing me. The family's bastard Negro boy has convulsive fits—it's appropriate. She still won't be disabused of the notion that I'm possessed by the devil, and my uncle keeps telling me that I need to stop being hysterical and overcome it."

He tips his head backward, and when the lantern light catches his eyes, I realize he's crying. Or rather, he's trying very hard not to cry, which is even worse. I don't have a clue of what to do. I feel like a loon for sitting still and not doing anything to comfort him, but my limbs hardly feel as though they belong to me. I can't remember how to touch him.

Percy keeps talking, his face skyward. "My little

cousin still won't sit near me because he thinks it's catching. He's got to be coaxed into being in the same room. It took a year to find a valet who was willing to stay on after he knew he'd have to serve a dark-skinned boy who had convulsions without warning. I have been cupped by savage barbers and exorcised and blessed and I haven't eaten meat in a year and a bloody half and it's not going away, so I have to. Monty, are you listening to me?"

I am, but I'm not hearing it. Or it's not going through my brain. I'm hearing without understanding a word. This feels like a nightmare, a dream of being buried alive that I thrash against but can't wake from, and everything he says is another spadeful of dirt pressing down on my chest. All this pain in him I've never noticed.

"Monty."

"Yes," I say faintly. "Yes, I'm listening."

He takes a long breath, one hand pressed to his forehead. "So let's find Lockwood and see if we can convince him to let us keep traveling. We'll see the Continent and have all the good times we planned and then I'll go to Holland and—"

I stand up, so fast my foot catches on the blanket and I stumble. "No. No, just . . . just stop, Percy, stop." He looks up at me, his mouth tight to stop the trembling. I feel like crying too—feel like falling down into the bed next to him and sobbing. I'm shaking and dizzy, emotion distilled into physical symptoms, and all

I manage to say is "Why didn't you tell me?"

"Because you're a wreck! Complete shambles. I've spent years chasing you around, making certain you didn't drink yourself to death or pass out in a gutter or slit your own wrists—"

I'm right there on the edge of tears. I can feel them round and hot and clogging my throat, but I am not going to cry.

"—and I know you've had a rough go, with your father and being thrown out of school, but you've not been yourself. Not for a while. And I couldn't have you making this worse. I'm sorry, I just couldn't."

Another spade of earth hits me. "But you didn't even give me a chance," I say. My voice comes out very, very small. "I thought we told each other everything."

"This isn't about us."

"It's always going to be about us."

"No, you want this to be about *you*. You care about what happens to me because of what that would mean for you. *You* are the only thing that matters to you."

I can't think of anything to say, so I settle for the second-best thing to a witty retort and storm out. But even that gets botched when the boat suddenly tips and I'm pitched into the wall.

I straighten myself out, stomp to the door, and don't look back.

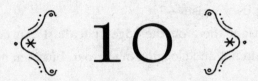

10

Felicity is still on the deck when I return, her chin to her chest and her eyes closed, but she looks up as I slump beside her. If she were Percy, I'd bury my head in her shoulder and moan, but she's not, she's Felicity, and the only person I want to talk to about my fight with Percy is Percy. Which just seems unfair.

"So, what did you two talk about?" Felicity asks lightly.

"Percy's ill."

"Yes."

"Epilepsy."

"He told me."

"When? Two years ago when he first found out?"

"No. About an hour ago, before you woke up."

"He's . . ." I mash my fingers into my forehead. I'm not certain if he told her about the sanatorium, and I'm afraid that giving voice to it is going to make it feel even more sickening and real than it already does, so I say, "He's not possessed."

"No, he's not," she says, and the firmness in her voice surprises me. "And his doctors are backward quacks if any of them told him so. If they've been keeping up with any recent research, they should know it's been proven that epilepsy is nothing to do with demonic possession. That's all dark ages nonsense."

"So, what causes it?"

"The Boerhaave School published a pamphlet—"

"The what?"

"Never mind."

"No, tell me. The—that thing you said. The school thing. What does it say?"

She lets out a little sigh through her nose. "It simply claims there are many reasons someone might develop epilepsy, but no one truly understands any of them. It's all speculation."

"Can it be cured?" Because if there's a cure, if there is anything that could possibly make him well, he won't be sent to Holland and I won't lose him.

But Felicity shakes her head, and my lifeline slips out to sea.

I press my face into my knees. The first rays of the sun are starting to creep across the back of my neck. It's maddening that the world is so quiet and still and completely unchanged from the moment before I stepped into the cabin of the boat.

Percy's ill.

It's seeping through me like a poison, leaving me jumbled up and numb. *Percy's ill and will never be well again and is being sent away to die in a sanatorium because of it.* And, close on its heels, a second thought that leaves me nearly as cold—*Percy didn't trust me enough to tell me so.*

"Felicity, am I a good person?"

She looks sideways at me, one eyebrow ascending. "Why? Are you having some sort of crisis?"

"No. Yes." I scrub my fingers through my hair. "Percy didn't tell me."

"I know. That wasn't very good of him, but I sort of understand it."

"Why? What's so wrong with me that you both seem to think I couldn't handle knowing?"

"Well . . . you're a bit of a rake."

"Thanks for that."

"You can't behave the way you do and then be surprised when someone tells you so." She massages her temples with the tips of her fingers, her mouth pulling into a frown. "I do not pretend to understand the passionate friendship you and Percy have always sustained—you're important to each other, there's no questioning that. But I don't think you can blame him for not telling you. Your attention is usually elsewhere, and when hard things

164

come up, you . . . drink, you sleep around. You run away."

I want to run away right then but there's just Percy in the cabin and water on either side, and the person I most want to run away from is me.

Instead I say, "I'm glad you were there. For Percy. If it had been just me he probably would have died."

"He wouldn't have died."

"You seem to be underestimating my incompetence."

"Epileptic fits aren't fatal, unless some outside force comes into play. If he'd struck his head, or fallen into the sea—"

"Please stop," I say, and she lapses into silence.

I muss my fingers through my hair again. For the first time in a long while, I feel compelled to do something about someone's pain besides my own, but the press is blunted by knowing there's not a damn thing to be done for him. Nor can I undo these past two years. He's had no one, not even his family, on his side for this. I'd always thought it was Percy and me against the world, but the truth was, I marooned him long ago and never realized it.

"How did you know what was happening to him?" I ask.

She shrugs. "I didn't, but I had a guess."

"And about . . . that school you were talking about."

"The Boerhaave School? It's not a literal school. It's

a school of scientific thought. I've read about it some."

"I thought you read . . . What exactly is in those books of yours?"

She crosses her arms and blows a tight sigh through her nose. "If I tell you something, you can't mock me for it. And I don't only mean now. You can't whip this out and mock me for it at some later date when you're feeling peevish."

"I'm not going to mock you."

She takes another huffy breath, nostrils flaring, then says, "I've been studying medicine."

"Medicine? Since when have you been interested in that?"

"Since my whole life."

"Where do you learn about medicine?"

"I read. I've been stripping the covers off amatory novels and swapping them with medical textbooks for years so Father wouldn't find out. He'd rather I read those trampy Eliza Haywoods than study almanacs on surgery and anatomy."

I burst out laughing. "Feli, you glorious little shit. That's the most devious thing I've ever heard."

She laughs too, and I remember suddenly we've got matching sets of dimples. It's so rare that I see Felicity smile I'd forgotten we both inherited them from our father. "I'd rather study medicine than go to finishing school. That's what I wanted. But they don't let girls into universities. Girls go to finishing school and boys go to medical school."

"Not me. I'm supposed to run the estate."

I laugh, like it isn't excruciating to be the punch line of your own joke, but Felicity's face softens. "I didn't know Father was so rough on you."

"Every father is rough on his sons. I'm not the only one."

"Doesn't make it easier."

"I survived it, didn't I?"

"Did you?" She touches her forehead lightly to my shoulder, then sits up straight again. "What are you smiling at?"

"Nothing," I say, though said smile breaks into a sudden laugh. "Only, I think it's quite amusing that our respectable parents raised two contrary children."

Felicity grins at me in return, and then she laughs as well—a loud and distinctly unladylike sound, and I love it all the more for that. "Two contrary children," she repeats. "Our new little brother doesn't have a chance."

Pascal finds Felicity and me for breakfast—a blissfully full and not-thieved meal, satisfying in spite of the fact that it contains a fair amount more rice and beans than I'm generally inclined to. We eat crouched on the deck of the canal boat around a smoking iron stove, tin plates cupped between our hands and no utensils but bread.

The fair, Pascal tells us, is a traveling one. The merchants load their tents into boats and float up and down the Rhône, stopping in towns they come to and mixing with the local tradesmen until they've recruited enough to set up stalls.

As the dawn breaks, muddy and pink across the water, women spread laundry along the rails and jump between the decks to speak to each other. Children run along the banks. Men play cards and smoke pipes, the gauzy threads that rise from their lips mingling with the early-morning mist off the water. They seem complete unto themselves, a small, floating kingdom along the fringes of the sea and, remarkably, ordinary to themselves. Perhaps this is what the Grand Tour is meant to do—show me the way other people live, in lives that are not like my own. It's a strange feeling, realizing that other people you don't know have their own full lives that don't touch yours.

I try to watch without staring, until Felicity kicks me. "You needn't look at them like they're on display."

"I'm interested."

"You're gawking. Monty, we're guests."

Pascal slides a piece of bread around the rim of his plate, two fingers propping the crust. "You should take some food to Mr. Newton."

"I don't think he'll eat," Felicity replies. "I tried earlier but he couldn't keep anything down."

Pascal chews for a moment, looking to the cabin where Percy's lying, then says, "Where is it you come from?"

"England," I reply. "We're touring."

"You seem to be running."

"Well, that's what we're currently doing, but we were once touring."

"The men you were running from—are they traveling with you?"

"No, they attacked us on the road from Paris. We think they're looking for . . ." I glance at Felicity. She gives me a little shrug, as if to say, *Why not?* I pull the puzzle box out of my pocket and hand it to Pascal. "We think they're after this."

He turns it over in his hands, spinning the dials a few times. "A box."

"That's the extent of what we know about it."

"Why do they want it?"

"We don't know," Felicity says. "And we're afraid if we hand it over, we'll be killed for taking it."

"Ah, so you stole it?"

"Yes, but not from them." Then I remember the highwayman was the duke from Versailles, in whose apartments I was caught with a bare-breasted French girl. "Perhaps sort of from them."

"It looks quite old." He hands the puzzle box back to me and I stash it in my coat. "There are two women who travel in our company who made their living in antiques. They deal mostly in trinkets now—little things that sell at carnivals. But they may know something about it, if you let me show them."

I look over at Felicity, like we might consult on this, but she says, "Yes, absolutely. If they could tell us anything, that would be so appreciated."

"They may be at the fair already. I'll see if I can fetch them. Stay here."

As Pascal picks his way across the deck, I murmur to Felicity, "You think this is a good idea?"

"I think I'd like to know why we're being hunted," she says. "And what we can do to stop it." She pokes at the pocket of my coat harboring the puzzle box. "This is your fault, Henry. At least try to fix things."

I would like very much to punch her in the nose for saying that, even though she's right.

Pascal returns half an hour later with a woman on each arm, both old and bent and dressed head-to-toe in black, complete with thick veils like they're in mourning. He climbs onto the boat first, then helps them each across. Felicity and I both stand.

"*Senyorete*s Ernesta Herrera"—he inclines toward the taller of the two—"*i* Eva Davila. They are the grandmothers to our company—*les nostres àvies*." He smiles fondly at the two when he says it. "I told them about your situation and they believe they might be able to help."

I start to pull the puzzle box out of my pocket, but the taller woman's hand—Ernesta's—shoots out much faster than her pace led me to believe it was capable of and closes around my wrist. "Not here," she hisses in accented French.

"Why not here?"

"If people are after it," she says, "do not wave it around."

We follow the grandmothers into the cabin of the boat. Ernesta laughs softly when she sees Percy in bed and says over her shoulder to Pascal, "You have a menagerie of these unfortunates, *mijo*."

As we shuffle in, I try to look anywhere but at Percy, but that's a bit of a trick in a room that's barely eight foot square. I do manage to only do it out of the corner of my eye, not straight on, which is a bit coyer and conveys that I'm still mad as hell at him. He looks well pathetic, curled up on his side, face turned to the pillow as pale sunlight wafts through the cabin door. His hair is matted on one side where he's been lying on it, and his skin looks slick and waxy.

But I refuse to be moved.

Pascal stays out on deck, while Ernesta and Eva settle themselves on cushions tossed across the floor. Felicity perches on the end of the box bed and says something to Percy, too quietly for me to hear. He shakes his head, face turned away from hers.

There's nowhere else to sit unless I want to cuddle up with Percy, so I stand sort of awkwardly in the center of it all, trying to get my sea legs and not knock my head on the hanging lamps.

"Could we perhaps speak elsewhere?" Felicity says, but Percy opens his eyes and pushes himself up on an elbow. The neck of his shirt slips down over his shoulder, revealing the sharp course of his collarbone.

"No, I want to hear this."

Ernesta holds out a hand to me. "Let us see."

I surrender the puzzle box. She turns it over in her hands, then passes it to Eva. "You have stolen this."

Felicity and Percy both look at me, and there's no point denying it, so I nod.

"You must return it."

"The men I took it from are trying to kill us," I say.

"Not to them." She waves a hand. "It does not belong to them."

"How do you know?"

"This is a Baseggio puzzle box. They are expensive and rare. And they are not used to hold things of worldly value, like money or jewelry or the wants of common thieves." She spins one of the dials with the tip of her finger. It makes a soft ticking sound, like a clock winding.

"These boxes were designed to carry alchemical compounds over long distances and keep them safe if stolen."

Eva taps the end of the box and says something in a language I don't understand. Ernesta translates. "The name of the owner is carved here, on the rim." She holds it up and points to the thin band of enameling along the hinge, inscribed with gold letters that I hadn't noticed before. "Professor Mateu Robles."

"I know him," Felicity says. Then she adds, when we all look to her, "Not personally. I attended a lecture on his work in Paris. He studies panaceas."

"What's a panacea?" Percy asks.

"A cure-all," Felicity explains. "An item or a compound that is a remedy for mutiple ailments, like a bezoar or ginseng."

"Robles is well known in Spain," Ernesta says. "One of the last great alchemists in the court before the crown changed hands, though of late better known for killing his wife."

Felicity lets out a small squeak at that.

"He killed his wife?" Percy says hoarsely.

"An experiment gone wrong," Ernesta says. "An accident, but she died by his hand all the same."

"But the box didn't come from Mateu Robles," I say. "I stole it from the king of France."

"You stole it from the Duke of Bourbon," Felicity corrects, though the detail seems a bit irrelevant—I think she just enjoys rubbing it in that I'm a thief. "He's the one who's after us."

"What's in it?" Percy asks. He's sitting up now, arms folded around his knees and leaning forward for a better look, like the box has changed since last he held it.

"Something with alchemical properties most likely, which makes it valuable," Ernesta replies. "Or dangerous. Or both." She shakes the box lightly beside her ear, like it might announce its own name. "Not a compound, though. It sounds to be a single item."

"Couldn't someone break the box open?" Felicity asks. "It doesn't look very sturdy."

"The boxes are often lined with vials of acid, or some other corrosive substance. If the box is broken, the object inside is destroyed." Eva says something, and Ernesta nods. "She says that it must be returned to its owner."

And then they both look at me.

"By who?" I ask. "Us?"

"You are the thieves."

"Monty's the thief," Felicity says.

"No, I am the second thief. Which I think cancels out my thievery."

"This box carries cargo likely more precious than you can imagine. It must be returned to Mateu Robles."

"Then you take it. You know more about it than we do."

Ernesta shakes her head. "We have been expelled

from Spain. We indulge in practices outlawed by the crown, and we cannot return without consequences."

"You're Spanish?"

I can feel Felicity resisting the urge to roll her eyes. She's practically vibrating with the effort.

Ernesta, for her part, does not roll her eyes at me. "We're Catalonian," she says.

I'm not sure of the distinction, but for fear of outright mockery from my sister, I move forward like that makes sense. "And you think this professor is in Spain?"

"The Robleses are an old Catalonian family. They were in the court at the same time as we were, but they were expelled when the House of Bourbon won the throne, and they returned to Barcelona."

"And you want us to take it to them there?" I ask.

"Absolutely not," Felicity interrupts, shaking her head so vehemently her plait whips the bedpost behind her. "I'm sorry, but we can't. We need to find our company and see that this is returned to the king of France."

"It doesn't belong to him," Ernesta says. "It must be returned to the professor alone—no one but him."

"But surely there's a reason the king had it," Felicity argues. "And we can't travel! We've no money and our cicerone is waiting for us here and Percy's been taken ill—we can't go anywhere if he's unwell."

Percy stares down at the quilts, tugging at a loose thread between the patches, and for a moment I think he'll protest, but he keeps silent.

Felicity opens her mouth, like she's got more reasons we can't ferry alchemical compounds south queued up, but she's interrupted by a sharp rap at the cabin door, followed by Pascal flinging it open. He's flush-faced and breathing hard, like he's been running. "Soldiers," he pants. "Marco ran down—they tore apart the fair and they're headed this way."

My heartbeat stutters. It's rather clear who in this room they're after.

The thought occurs to me that if they are the king's men, and if they are truly after us, and if they are being led by the duke, this might all be resolved by giving them the box. Though there seems to be equal odds they'll slit our throats and drop our bodies in the sea, and I'm not risking that. But more than that—alchemy and panaceas and cure-alls are knocking around in my mind. If there's anyone who can help Percy—perhaps even keep him from the asylum—it may be this family and their mad little box. And I'm not handing that over.

"We can't give it to them," I blurt out.

Felicity and Percy both look to me. So do the grandmothers, Ernesta wearing an expression that conveys this was such an obvious statement it's redundant.

"They might kill us for stealing it," I say quickly, "and if it doesn't belong to the king and it contains something that could be dangerous in the wrong hands . . . I

think we should wait."

"We'll hide you," Pascal says.

Outside the cabin, I can hear the guards' boots slapping the dock. "Come out, now!" a familiar voice yells. The duke is definitely here. "All of you. Empty the boats."

"I think Monty's right," Percy says. "We don't give them the box."

I turn to Felicity, who looks as though she thoroughly disagrees, but throws up her hands in surrender. "Fine!"

Neither Ernesta nor Eva seems particularly troubled by the hordes of soldiers boarding the boat. Which is good because I'm short on a plan but have an abundance of panic.

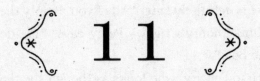

11

The king's guard boards our boat—I can hear their shouted instructions through the walls, and the floor pitches each time one of them climbs aboard. Pascal is out on the deck attempting reason, but it doesn't sound like they're particularly keen on hearing it. The word *fugitives* gets tossed around a few times, and *harboring*, which I have a strong sense is not in reference to the boats. I pray they'll bypass the cabin altogether and we won't have to test our disguise, but then I hear the stairs creak and a moment later the door is tossed open.

"You were instructed to disembark." The Duke of Bourbon strides in, decked in livery of the king's guard, with a rapier at his side that looks like it could do a fair amount of damage if swung about. He's distinctly more ruffled looking than he was when I saw him at the palace, his nose burnt by days in the sun and his head unwigged. His hair is a short, coarse gray that curls in the back.

"Apologies, gentlemen." Pascal darts through the soldiers to Bourbon's side. "But these women are not permitted to go onto the deck."

Zounds, it is beastly hot under this veil. The air is smoky with the incense Ernesta lit, making it hard to see and harder to breathe, and the clothes we stripped off the bed were not meant to double as skirts—the fabric is slick, and I've got one hand on my back like I'm a hunched-over old woman when really I'm just trying to keep the damn rug swathed around my waist from becoming both indecent and incriminating.

"Why?" Bourbon taps his foot in the direction of Felicity, who's wrapped up in what a few moments ago was a wall hanging and has a cushion cover over her head like a veil. "Woman, show us your face."

"They cannot, *senyor*," Pascal says.

"We will hear no protestations," Bourbon snaps. "She will show me her face or be made to. They all will."

"They cannot because they are poxed!" Pascal cries.

Bourbon, who had been reaching for the edge of the cushion cover currently doubling as Felicity's veil, draws back. "Poxed?"

Beside me, Percy, similarly swathed in bed trimmings, sways on his feet, though I'm not certain if he's playacting or sincerely faint. I want to reach out to him, but I'm afraid of drawing the duke's eye and exposing my distinctly mannish and unpoxed hands.

"A strain from the Portuguese seas," Pascal goes on. "We have quarantined them for the safety of the city. So long as they keep their faces covered and the scabs unexposed, there is no danger."

Percy's definitely falling—he reaches out for me and I grab him, trying to keep him on his feet. The swaddling over my head starts to slip. The duke turns in our direction, but on the other side of the cabin Ernesta lets out a high-pitched wail and he whirls around. She seems to be really going for the theatrics, for she falls to her knees before Bourbon and clutches his boots, which successfully diverts his attention from Percy's sincere collapse. Eva follows her lead, face pressed to the ground as she pleads to him in keening Catalan.

Bourbon shakes them off, then signals to his men. They're tripping over themselves in their haste to get back into the open air.

In the doorway, we hear him say to Pascal, "You Spaniards are to be cleared out of here by tomorrow morning or you'll be arrested. We will not have you cluttering up the river with your filth. And if we find you're hiding these criminals, the punishment will be severe."

Pascal bows his head. "Yes, sir. We want no trouble."

As soon as they're gone, Felicity is at Percy's other elbow, and together we help him to the bed. He sits down hard on the bare mattress, then slumps onto his side and pulls his legs up to his chest. "Are you well?" Felicity asks, then asks again when he doesn't respond, and for a cold, clenched-up moment, I think he's going to have another fit and I almost take a step back. I'm not certain I'm stout enough to witness it again.

But he's nodding, though he's breathing hard. "Yes. Yes, just faint."

I'm ready to strip this damn dress off as soon as the king's men have gone, but no one else moves to do the same, so I suffer and sweat a while longer. When Pascal returns to tell us the soldiers have gone, I whip the veil off my face and take a gasping breath that's mostly incense and immediately start to cough. Felicity slides off her headpiece and crumples it between her hands, shoulders quavering. "I'm so sorry," she's saying to Pascal, "I'm so sorry, your fair, your whole company, because of us, we're so sorry." And Pascal is trying to reassure her, though he looks pained.

Someone puts a hand on my arm, and I look around to find Eva standing beside me. *"Vosaltres passeu la nit amb nosaltres. Nosaltres farem la nostra pel matí."*

"You stay the night with us," Ernesta translates. "We go our own ways in the morning."

The grandmothers and Pascal go with some of the others from their company to clean up the mess of the fair.

Felicity offers to help, but they decline in case any of Bourbon's men spot us. It hadn't occurred to me to ask.

They return at dusk, and we have supper on the boat, the five of us on the deck while Percy sleeps in the cabin. He's still ill and unsteady, and I'm starting to wonder how we're going to move on if he can't stand straight. Maybe we should stay in Marseilles and find Lockwood and forget all this nonsense after all.

Some people from the other boats come join us, and we eat gathered around the iron stove at the prow. The lantern light pebbled throughout the line of canal boats glitters on the water, reflections the color of a daffodil cone bobbing amid the waves. After supper, Felicity excuses herself to see to Percy, leaving me sitting like a boulder displacing a stream in the midst of all these people who speak a language I don't understand and live a life I understand even less.

After a time, Ernesta comes and sits beside me. Her joints crack as she moves. "Would you like me to read for you?"

I don't understand what she's asking until she slides a deck of tarot cards from a velvet bag slung at her hip. I almost laugh. "Don't take this wrong," I say, "but I think all that tarot-tea-leaves what-have-you is nonsense."

She shuffles the cards, and they make a sound like wind slithering through tall grass. "That does not answer my question." She holds out the deck, and it feels like an invitation I can't turn away, the calling card of a traveler far from home. Against my better judgment, I take the deck. "Shuffle," she instructs, and I do, with significantly less grace than she, then return them. She fans the cards on the ground between us. "Choose your first."

I make a show of letting my fingers walk over the cards like they're a pathway. To my great surprise, a warm hum quavers in my fingertips, and I stop, without quite knowing why, and touch one. "Five cards," she prompts, and I select the rest of my set.

Ernesta eases them ahead of the others. "The first is a representation of you," she explains as she flips it. "The King of Cups. Emotional balance, stability, and generosity." That sounds quite good until she pins on: "But, as you've drawn it upside down, you are the inverse. Emotional and volatile, a man whose heart rules his life. Confusion in love and relationships. A lack of control and balance."

Which is less good.

She flips the second card, which is thankfully right side up so there's no chance of her pulling that bait-and-switch again. "The four of cups," she says. "A dissatisfaction with life." She turns the next and clicks her tongue. "So many cups."

"What does that mean?" I ask, a bit more anxious than I mean to sound.

"Cups are the suit of passion and love. The heart suit. Here, the eight of cups means leaving things behind. The heavy things that cling to us and weigh us down, but we grow accustomed to familiar weights and cannot let them go."

Ernesta turns the next card over. The lantern light jumps, glancing off the sketch of a skeletal head, upside down. "Death reversed," she says.

In spite of not believing in any of this, I've gotten rather wrapped up in it, and seeing that staring back at me is downright spooky. "Does that mean—"

"You're not going to die," she says, like she read my mind, though I suppose it's a common question when the specter is flipped. "Death reversed is a transformation. A new life, or a new view on the one you have." She peels my last card from the deck without looking at it and sets it so it overlaps with the King of Cups. The King of Wands. The two drawings seem to look at each other, their eyes turned inward.

She doesn't explain the second king. Just stares at the pair with a scrutiny that deepens the wrinkles in her forehead. "In the east," she says after a time, her gaze still downcast, "there is a tradition known as *kintsukuroi*. It is the practice of mending broken ceramic pottery using lacquer dusted with gold and silver and other precious metals. It is meant to symbolize that things can be more beautiful for having been broken."

"Why are you telling me this?" I ask.

At last she looks up at me. Her irises are polished obsidian in the moonlight. "Because I want you to know," she says, "that there is life after survival."

I don't know what to say to that. My throat feels suddenly swollen, so I simply nod.

Ernesta gathers up her cards and leaves me alone to mull the reading while I drink some sharp-edged spirits Pascal gave me that's so acidic it's likely meant to be medicinal. I tip my head back against the railing and look up at the stars. A firefly drifts from the bank of the river and lands on my knee, throbbing golden like it fell from the sky.

Someone sits beside me, and when I look over, there's Percy, his shoulder right up against mine. He pulls his knees up to his chest, a little stiff, like he's still hurting, then glances over at me with his chin tucked. His lashes cast spiderwebs upon his cheeks.

"How are you feeling?" I ask, before the silence has a chance to turn uncomfortable or I say something infinitely stupider.

One of his hands strays absently to the spot on his arm where the fleam went in for the bloodletting. "Better."

"Good. That's . . . good." My own hand slips into my pocket and closes around the alchemical puzzle box. The dials shuffle beneath my fingertips. "I don't want to fight with you."

He looks over at me. "I don't want you to fight with me either."

I laugh—a short, sincere burst that catches even me off guard—and the moment feels so adjacent to ordinary that I loosen. Or maybe that's the spirits, though I haven't had much. I hold the bottle out to him. "Do you want a drink?" He shakes his head. I take another swallow for courage, but all I can think of is, *Percy is ill, Percy is going to an asylum at the end of this Tour, and he didn't trust you enough to tell you so.*

"I think we should go to Barcelona," I say before I've really thought it out.

"You want to return the box?"

"Well, yes, but I was thinking about what Felicity said, and the grandmothers, about Mateu Robles. If he does work with alchemy and healing and . . . whatever that other word was."

"Panacea."

"Yes. That."

He's there before I have to explain the rest of my reasoning. "I've tried alchemical treatments before."

"What if this is different? He may be able to cure you. I think it's daft not to try, at least."

"Monty, I've been promised so many cures by so many doctors—"

"But if you can find a way to be rid of your . . . illness, you won't have to go to Holland. You can come home with me. We can go back."

He scrapes at his bottom lip with his teeth, staring up at the stars, and I can't fathom why he isn't meeting me with an enthusiastic *yes yes yes let's go to Barcelona and find someone who can make me well and keep me from an asylum*. "I'd rather . . ." He trails off, pressing his thumb into his chin.

"Please," I say. His strange silence is feeding my desperation. *Let me help you!* I want to shout at him. *I have failed you on this front for years without knowing it, so let me help you now!* "What do we have to lose?"

Before he can reply, Felicity slides down on my other side, her skirts puffed for a moment before they settle on the planking. "So," she says, like we're in the middle of a conversation already, "tomorrow we begin the search for Lockwood. Or at least attempt to secure some sort of lodging. If we can show them a promise from the bank, even if we can't withdraw actual funds—"

"I think we should go to Barcelona," I interrupt.

Felicity pivots to face me, executing an eyebrow arch so precise it looks penciled on. "Excuse me?"

"Apparently it's very important this box is returned."

"And how will we travel? We've no supplies and no transport and no money."

"We could try and get to some of Father's."

Felicity is already shaking her head. "No, absolutely not. We've nothing to do with this box or the Robleses or any of it. We need to find our company and see that the box is returned to the king."

"It doesn't belong to the king," I say.

"Yes, but there's probably a good reason he had it. Perhaps it was given to him."

"Why give something to him in a box he couldn't open? What sort of bastard does that? He stole the box and we should return it to its owner. And if we return it to Mateu Robles, we'll be rid of it. Get the duke off our tail—we're no good to him if we haven't got it. Besides, if we find Lockwood now, we'll be made to go home."

"Perhaps not," she says. "You made rather a mess of yourself at Versailles, but if we rejoin him here, he might be so impressed by our resourcefulness and so glad we survived the highwaymen that he'll let you carry on. Which will absolutely not happen if we go gallivanting to Spain alone. That's going to put you on his not list for certain."

I hadn't considered that. Bolting naked from the French palace seems like something my father might consider a permanent black mark upon my record—good news for the Goblin—but if Lockwood would consent to let us keep traveling, going home at the end of the allotted year with Versailles as a small side note to an otherwise successful Tour would significantly bolster my chances of holding on to my inheritance as opposed to being sent home because of it. Or at least I could work the *look at the horrors we went through please don't disinherit me after such an ordeal* angle.

But traveling for the rest of the year isn't going to do a damn thing for Percy. He'd still be heading off to Holland at the end of it.

"The man who owns this box is an alchemist," I say. "And if he studies the cure-all side of it, like you heard at that lecture, he might know something that could help cure Percy. If we take him his box, maybe we could trade it for that information."

Her brow knits, and she looks to Percy. "Is that what you want?"

Percy has this thumb to his mouth, chewing at the pad like he's thinking hard. My heart seizes up a bit, mostly from the frustration that he isn't entirely on my side about this. But then he says, "I think Monty's right—we should take the box to Mateu Robles. It belongs to him."

I nearly throw my arms around him at those words, but instead I turn to my sister. "If you don't want to come, we'd be happy to drop you at the school. Term hasn't started yet—you won't even miss the first day of your social conversation class."

She ignores me and instead says to Percy, "Are you sure this would be a good idea for you?"

"I think it's—" I start, but she snaps, "I wasn't addressing you, Henry." Then, again to Percy, she says, "Are you well enough to travel?"

And I feel like an insensitive rake again for not thinking of that from the start.

But Percy nods. "I'm all right."

Felicity sighs so hard her nostrils flare, like his wellness has ruined her plans. "Can we all agree that if we can't secure some funds, we shouldn't go? It's already an absurd journey, but to undertake it with nothing is downright foolish. We'll hardly be able to get out of the city unless we have coinage."

"Agreed," Percy says, then looks at me. I was hoping the question of money might be something we three could collaborate on rather than a condition of our departure, but I nod.

Felicity stretches her arms behind her head, then stands. "I want you to both know that in spite of the fact that I am going along, I think this is a terrible idea."

"Don't pretend you aren't interested in all this," I say. "Alchemy seems right up your street."

"Medicine and alchemy are unrelated fields," she says, thought she doesn't do a particularly good job of concealing said interest.

"Fine. Then consider your opinion noted."

"Fine." She winds her hair into a knot. "I'm going to get some sleep before we go. Percy, do you want a hand?"

"No, I think I'll stay out," he says.

"Good night, then. Let me know if you need anything."

As Felicity disappears, picking her way across the narrow deck to the cabin, I look over at Percy again. He's still looking up at the stars, the silvery light from the moon slithering across the water and stitching his skin. In the glow of it, he looks pearled and fine, a boy fashioned from precious stones and the insides of seashells.

"I think we're doing the right thing," I say, sort of to Percy and sort of to myself.

"At least we'll know what's in the box," he says with a half smile. "Felicity's right about Lockwood, though. If we go to Spain, he'll probably send us packing as soon as we're reunited."

"But maybe Mateu Robles will have something to help you and you can come home."

"And maybe he won't. You might be giving up your Tour for me."

"Worth it, that." I scrub my hands through my hair. "Though I think . . . it's mostly my fault we were being sent home early. So . . . I'm sorry. For that. Sorry about the box as well. That I picked it up."

"I'm sorry I didn't tell you I'm ill."

"I really wish you had."

He nods. I take another drink.

"You're my best mate, Monty," he says suddenly. "And I don't want to ruin that. Especially not now. I didn't tell you I was ill because I didn't want to scare you away, and if I didn't have you—if I hadn't had you for these past few years, I think I'd have lost my mind. So if things can't be the same between us, can they at least not be terrible? You're not permitted to be strange and uncomfortable around me now."

"So long as you don't go falling in love with me."

I don't know why I say it. Call it battlements around my helpless heart. Percy looks away from me fast, shoulders curling up. It almost looks like a flinch. But then he says, "I'll try my best."

He seems like he wants to touch me, but we've both lost any sense of how men who haven't kissed each other do that. He finally taps my knee, open-palmed and short, the way we used to try and hold our hands to candle flames without being burned when we were boys, and I wonder if there will ever again be a day when it doesn't feel as though he might fly to pieces between my hands.

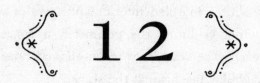

12

We part ways with Pascal and the grandmothers the next morning as the sun rises. Their fair has disappeared from the pier, and the first of the boats have already kicked off from their moorings and are drifting up the river, a flock of colored swans riding the current.

Percy, Felicity, and I wander the city, searching for the French partner institution to the Bank of England. It's hardly morning but the sun is already beginning to cook the stones. The heat rises from them in shimmering waves. Shops have their signs flipped and their fronts open onto the pavement, displays of produce and flowers and tailored clothes spreading out. A sharp gunpowder smell rolls from a blacksmith shop, along with the bell-clang of the hammer. A shoeblack with a stained rag stuffed into his breeches and a ball of sticky polish rolling between his palms wolf-whistles at Felicity from his perch on a coffeehouse stoop. I extend a tasteful finger to him as we pass.

We find the bank on the high street. It's a classical building with a marbled interior and rows of wooden-barred windows lining the perimeter, a wigged clerk behind each. The sounds of red heels and brass-tipped canes click like dice against the stone.

"If we don't act soon, they're going to think we're scouting the place for a robbery," Felicity says after we've spent a half of an hour in the lobby, doing what can only be termed *lurking*.

"We could tell them the truth," Percy suggests.

"Yes, but we've only one chance," she replies, "and the truth is a bit too preposterous to be convincing. Alchemical puzzle boxes and all that."

I'm hardly listening to them—I've spent most of the while we've been loitering watching the clerk at the window nearest to the door, and after close scrutiny of his last few interactions, I'm fairly certain he and I have a big thing in common.

When you are a lad who enjoys getting other lads in bed, you have to develop a rather fastidious sense for who plays the same instrument or there's a chance you'll find yourself at the business end of a hangman's knot. And if this fellow and I had met at a bar, I would have already bought him a drink and put his fingers in my mouth. It's a great risk—I'm not so much jumping to a conclusion as vaulting haphazardly to it—but, somehow, I know.

"Stay here," I say.

"What are you doing?" Felicity hisses at me as I start across the lobby.

"Helping." I check myself in one of the mirrors lining the hall, ruffle my hair for good measure, then stride from the atrium and straight up to the man's window. Not even a man, he's just a boy—apprenticeship age, even younger than me. He looks up when I approach, and I give him a big eyeful of the dimples that have launched a thousand ships. "Um, *bonjour. Parlez-vous anglais?*"

"*Oui*," he replies. "May I help you?"

"I've a bit of an unorthodox query." I let out a shy laugh, flit my eyes down to the floor, then back to him through my lashes. His neck goes a little red. Fan-bloody-tastic. "You see, I'm touring."

"I assumed."

"Oh, am I so obvious?"

"Well, the English."

"Of course." I laugh again. "The English. God, I'm so awful at French. I can only say about three things. *When is supper? Can you help me?* and *You have lovely eyes— Tes yeux sont magnifiques.* Was that right?"

"Very well done. Is the last one to impress all the French girls?"

"Well, I was saying it to you just then. They're quite something."

I give him a moment of intense eye contact with my head tipped a little to the side. The corners of his mouth turn up and he shuffles the papers in front of him. "You had a question."

"Oh, yes. Sorry, you're . . ." Shy smile. Telling pause. "Distracting." Now he's really blushing. *Poor, sweet thing*, I think as I lean forward on the counter and he looks very directly at my lips. *Wait until you fall for the boy who can't love you back.* "So I'm on my Tour and . . . Sorry, it's so queer. On the way down from Paris, we were robbed."

"Good heavens."

"Yes, it was rather harrowing. We didn't have much on us, thank God, but they took all the letters of credit my father sent with me. I know this is his bank, but I haven't got the actual papers."

He gets ahead of me a moment before I explain it. "You want to make a withdrawal against your father's name without a letter of credit."

"I told you it was an unorthodox question."

"I was expecting much worse." He cracks a shy smile. "I thought you were going to ask me to dinner."

"I still might. Though you'd have to pay." He laughs and I bring the dimples out to play again.

"I'm sorry, but I don't—"

I know that as soon as the word *no* makes its appearance, I will have lost irreclaimable ground, so, in what can only be described as a Hannibalistic maneuver, I cut him off at the pass. "I'll give you my father's name, and his address in England. He should be in your ledgers, but if there's a problem, you can write to him and he'll send funds, I know it. I'm so sorry, but I'm in such a tight spot and I'm a long way from home and it'll take months before my parents can send any money and I've nowhere to go. I hardly even speak French." I pitch my voice a little, not quite pathetic, but sympathetic, and his whole face melts like butter. I am not good at much, but what I do, I do well. "Sorry, this all sounds strange."

"No," he says quickly. "I'm so sorry you're having a hard time."

I run my thumb along my bottom lip. "I've been standing in the lobby for the last half of an hour trying to get up my courage to come in and ask, I was so afraid I'd be turned down. Honestly, I came to you because you looked the nicest. I mean the kindest. I mean, not that you're not . . . You're very nice looking. I promise, I'm not a scoundrel. I just don't know what else there is to be done. I've nothing else left."

He sucks in his cheeks, then glances down the row of clerks. "Give me your father's name and address," he says quietly. "I can't give you much, but I'll do what I can."

I could have kissed him for that. Were we not in distinctly upright society, I would have. He disappears behind the counter, then returns with a small stack of bills. "There was a note with the account," he says as I sign the receipt, then slides a scrap of paper across the counter to me. At the top is written an address, then below it, in a hasty scrawl:

> *We have secured lodging at this location and,*
> *God willing, you will meet us here.*

Beneath is Lockwood's signature.

As sour as I am on our bear-leader, it's a relief to know that he survived the highwaymen's attack. Not only that, but he's *here*—we could find him by the afternoon and be back on schedule. Might not even be made to go home, if Felicity's theory is correct. Instead I'm looking at weeks of rough travel with little money and none of the comforts to which I'm accustomed, and an unknown destination waiting for us at the end of it.

But also maybe something that could keep Percy from an asylum.

The clerk stamps the receipt, then asks, "Is everything all right?"

"Fine." I fold the note in half and slide it back across the counter. "Could you dispose of that for me, please?" I give him another smile, and when he hands me the bills, I let our fingers overlap on purpose. He looks ready to burst with pleasure.

"How did you do that?" Felicity asks as I rejoin them on the other side of the lobby and show off my spoils.

"Simple," I reply, and flash her my most roguish smile. "You have your skills and I have mine."

13

We hire horses from a man in Marseilles and start along the seaside toward Spain. I am somehow stuck with an obstinate mount that resembles less a horse and more a leggy sausage, and seems fond of ingesting my commands and then ignoring them in their entirety. He's also the hungriest horse for miles—he's far more interested in pulling up leaves along the road than walking it.

I'm a good rider, but I'm not accustomed to being on a horse for much longer than the length of a hunting trip, and the roads are rough, often nothing but thin paths winding through the scrub. By our third day, I'm so bow-legged and sore that I can hardly get up at night to piss. Percy's as bad off as I, though his legs are a fair amount longer, which I'm convinced makes a difference.

Felicity rides sidesaddle, so she's spared some of the pain, though having her with us limits our lodging options. The number of public houses and inns along the road thins the closer we get to the border, and most take only male lodgers. One night we're so desperate that we sneak her into the room after everyone else is abed. And while I'm not a particularly attentive elder brother, that has even me concerned for my sister's modesty. But she sleeps soundly between Percy and me, the blanket all the way over her head, and I'm grateful for something to fill the space that would have been there anyway.

The heat is brutal, especially up against the coast, where the sunlight sits on the ocean and festers into a haze. Felicity soaks her petticoats in the sea to keep cool, and Percy and I do the same to our shirts, though they dry before we're properly chilled. I try to wet my hair once as well, but I have never in my life liked putting my head all the way under and Percy knows it, so as soon as I get as far into the water as I intend to, he takes it upon himself to dunk me the rest of the way. When I surface, spluttering and indignant and far more put out than a nearly grown man should be over being made to go under the water, Percy's laughing like a fool. He also seems braced for retaliation, for, as soon as I'm back on my feet, he bolts, kicking up the sea as he runs. I'm ready to chase him down and shove him in, but I stop. Percy stops too, when he realizes I'm not after him, and looks back at me—a gaze that feels partly like a challenge and partly like a question, and I wish I had a better answer.

I can tell it's writ all over me—the way that, the week previous, I would have tackled him straight into the sea for a laugh and had no concern. Percy must know what I'm thinking, because he gives me a sad smile and turns for the shore, and I know I've just proved he was right for not telling me he was ill.

Somehow nothing's changed, and everything has.

The coastal road turns so rough and mountainous that we reach Spain without realizing it until we come upon the same sort of packed customs house we fought our way through in Calais. This one is considerably more of a pain in the arse, since none of us speaks any helpful language or has a passport, which isn't a dead end, but it's certainly a hindrance. In addition, we're fairly vagrant looking, closing in on two weeks unwashed, unshaven, and in the same clothes as when we were ambushed outside Marseilles. We've made a few feeble attempts to clean up as we went, but we're still ripe.

It will be days before we can get new documents issued, so we take up residence at a border inn for travelers waiting to cross into Catalonia. The wealthy have rooms abovestairs, and since we, with our few remaining sous and no Spanish coinage, are not among that number, we sleep on straw bedrolls on the common room floor. It's crowded and noisy, mostly men but a few families with children screaming their bloody lungs out. I hope sincerely that when we make it home—*if* we make it home—the Goblin will have grown out of his wailing years.

Percy and I leave Felicity in the common room with a book borrowed from a spinster she's befriended and together climb up onto the roof of the livery stable in the yard. The shingles have a good slant to them, and I have to wedge my feet into the gutter and pull my knees up to my chest to sit straight. Percy lies down flat, his legs dangling over the edge as he stares up at the sky. Beneath us, on the other side of the slate, I can hear the horses nickering at each other, the fresh post mares keening to be off.

We don't speak for a while. Percy seems lost in his thoughts and I'm busy trying to roll tobacco in a scrap of Bible page torn from a manhandled copy I dug up in the common room. I could snort it straight, but to my great shame, I've never been able to take snuff without sneezing, and as futile as this effort is beginning to seem, I'd rather smoke. Once my makeshift cigar is assembled, I have to lean a rather dangerous distance over the edge of the roof to catch the tip in the grease lamp hanging above the livery door. Percy grabs the tail of my coat to keep me from falling.

"What happened to your pipe?" he asks as I take the first drag and the whole damn thing nearly collapses between my fingers.

I tip my head back and blow out the smoke in a long,

precious stream before I answer. "Somewhere with Lock-wood and our carriage back in France. Ah, look here, I can read the scripture as I go."

"Let it never be said that you aren't resourceful."

I hold out the rolled tobacco to him. "Careful—it's a bit fragile." Instead of taking it, Percy puts his mouth to my fingers and takes a pull. His lips brush my skin, and a tremor goes through me, like a shadow passed over the moon, so absolute I almost shiver. Instead of doing the foolish thing it makes me want to do, which is lean in until those selfsame lips are upon mine, I catch his chin in my hand and scrub at the stubble starting to pebble it. "You're getting rather scruffy, darling."

Percy blows the smoke straight into my face and I reel back, coughing. He laughs. "And you're well freckled."

"No! Really? God. That'll wreck my complexion."

It's a petty complaint, considering how roughed up we've become over the last few weeks. We're all of us sun-burnt and wind-scraped, and I know I've lost weight—my waistcoat sat snug against me when we I got it tailored in Paris and now I have to fold an inch of material to make it tight. I've got fleabites from our dodgy lodgings up and down my back, and I'm beginning to suspect some lice have taken up residence as well. The dust from traveling is starting to feel like a second skin.

I hold out the tobacco again, but Percy shakes his head. "Have some more."

"I don't want any."

"Go on. Tobacco's good for your health."

It's not the worst thing I could have said to him, but it's certainly a contender, and I feel like an ass the moment it leaves my mouth.

Percy sucks in his cheeks and looks back up at the sky. "And you're worried for my health, are you?"

"Should I not be?"

His mouth puckers, and I feel like I've said the wrong thing yet again for no reason.

I shuffle my knees on the slate, casting about for something to say that won't do any further damage to us. Percy closes his eyes and takes a deep breath, hands folded over his stomach. His black eye is starting to fade. In the darkness, it's no more than a shadow. *Nothing's different*, I tell myself, but I can't quite believe it. We feel like changeling versions of ourselves lying here, brittle likenesses doing a mimic of the way they have seen us behave before.

What if it happens again? It rises through my thoughts like shipwreck flotsam when I look at him. *What if it happens right now?*

"Are you feeling well?" I ask him before I really think it through.

He doesn't open his eyes. "Don't ask if you don't care."

"God, Perce, of course I care."

"If you want me to say I'm fine so you'll feel better—"

"I—" *Definitely was hoping that would happen*, I realize, and my stomach twists. I take another long pull, then say as the smoke slips out, "Give me a chance."

Percy scrubs his hands along his breeches. "Fine. I feel horrid. I'm tired and I'm sore all over and the riding is making it worse, but if I say something, Felicity will get protective and we won't be moving for days. I'm mortified you both had to see me like that. I haven't been sleeping well, and sometimes when I don't sleep it brings on fits, so I'm worried it's going to happen again and every time I feel the least bit odd I get panicked it's coming on and then we'll have to hold everything on my account." He turns to me, his chin tipped up. "*That's* how I'm feeling. Aren't you glad you asked?"

I can feel him shoving me away, but I hold my ground. "Yes."

Percy's face softens, then he turns away from me, his fingers working over his knuckles until they crack. "Sorry."

I draw another lungful of smoke, so deep I feel like my ribs are about to pop. "Does it hurt? When it happens."

"I don't know. I never remember it. Thank God. It's awful afterward, though. And the head examinations and cold baths and the bloodletting and whatever else the doctors feel the need to do. God, it's miserable. My uncle hired a man to drill holes in my head to let the demons out, though that got squashed when he showed up to the house drunk."

"Christ. And none of it's helped?"

"Not a thing." He laughs, then nudges me with his elbow. "Here, you'll enjoy this—my uncle's physician told us I was having convulsive fits because I was playing with myself. That was an uncomfortable conversation." When I don't reply, he says, "You can laugh. I thought it was amusing."

"Please don't go to Holland," I say.

His mouth tightens, and he turns away from me again. Against the sky, the stars crown him, marking the edges of his silhouette like he is a constellation of himself. "What am I supposed to do, Monty?"

"Just . . . just don't! Go back home and tell your aunt and uncle you won't. Or run away—stay abroad or go to university and get a town house in Manchester and forget them."

"That wouldn't—"

"Why wouldn't that work? Why can't you just go?"

"Well, think it through. My uncle won't fund a life beyond an institution. And the way I look, most places won't employ me without his reference. And I can't live alone for . . . obvious reasons. Running isn't an option. Not alone, anyway." He looks over at me quickly, then away again.

The smoldering end of my cigar crumbles, a fleet of

falling stars between my fingers before they're extin-
guished against the slate. "I think Mateu Robles is going
to have something that will help stop your . . . You just
haven't found it yet! But we will, and then you'll be better, and then you won't have to leave. Don't you want
that?"

"I'd rather it didn't matter. It's not good, being ill,
but I live with it. I wish my family cared for me enough
to love me still. Not in spite of it. Or only if it went away.
Maybe if they hadn't already had to deal with me being
dark-skinned . . ." He presses his fingers into his chin,
then shakes his head a few times. "I don't know, doesn't
matter. Can't change it. Any of it."

"I could say something to your uncle."

"No."

"Why not? If he won't listen to you—"

"I know you think you're being helpful when you say
things like that, and when you defend me, and I appreci-
ate it, I really do, but please, don't. I don't need you to
stand up for me—I can do that."

"But you don't—"

"You're right, sometimes I don't, because I'm not the
light-skinned son of an earl so I haven't the luxury of
talking back to everyone who speaks ill of me. But I
don't need you to rescue me."

"I'm sorry." It comes out soft and meek, like the
bleat of a lamb.

Percy looks over at me, his face veiled by the twilight and impossible to read. Then he folds his hand into a fist and presses it against my knee, like a slowed-down punch. "Come here."

"I'm here," I say, so quiet I almost don't hear myself.

"Lie down with me."

My heart hurtles, beating like frantic wings against the base of my throat. I stub out my rolled tobacco and toss it off the roof, then stretch out beside him. My knees crack rather spectacularly as I go. The tiles are still sun-warmed, and I can feel the heat through my coat, all the way to my skin.

My head's higher than his, but we're close enough that I can see the freckles beneath his eyes. If I had to pick a favorite part of Percy's face—which would be impossible, really, but if held at gunpoint and forced to make a selection—it would be that small star-map across his skin. A part of him it feels as though no one else but me is ever close enough to see.

Percy shifts his weight on the tiles, sliding toward me in a way that I will myself not to be fooled into thinking is intentional. "Maybe someday you will be able to look at me and the first thing you think of won't be watching me have a convulsive fit."

"I don't think of that," I say, though that's a lie.

He must know it too, because he says, "It's all right. I suspect it's a hard thing to forget."

I press my head backward against the shingles, arching my neck. "At least you'll never have to run an estate." I realize what I've said as soon as it's left my mouth, and I fumble. "Wait. No, I'm sorry, that was . . . Damnation. Sorry. That was a horrible thing to say."

"Is managing your father's estate truly the worst thing that could happen to you?"

"Aside from the obvious things like famine and pestilence and losing my looks? Yes."

"So maybe it doesn't seem like the best thing right now, fine. But someday you're going to want to settle down, and when you do, you'll have a home. And income and a title. You won't want for much."

"That's not really what troubles me about it."

"So, what is it?"

I feel suddenly like an even greater ass than before for all the while I've spent moaning to him about my champagne problems while he's being shipped off to a sanatorium, and yet here he is, lying beside me and pretending our futures are comparable. "Nothing. You're right, I'm very lucky."

"I didn't say *lucky*. I said you won't want."

When I look over at him, he's still got his eyes on the sky. We're the inverse of each other, I realize, Percy desperately wanting to go home and not feeling he can, me wanting to be anywhere else but with nowhere to go. Perhaps he can't understand it, the way that house will always be haunted for me, even if my father were gone from it. I can't imagine living in it for the rest of my life, throwing parties in its parlors and filling the cabinets with my papers, all the while ignoring the dark spot on the dining room floor that's never washed away, where I tore my chin open when my father knocked me to the ground with a single well-swung fist; or the hearth that chipped my tooth when I was thrown into it. There are bodies buried beneath the flagstones of my parents' estate, and some graves never green.

I flick a scale of tobacco off my breeches. "Lucky me. Someday I will have everything my father does. Perhaps I'll even have a son of my own I can beat the shit out of."

"If I ever see your father again, I swear to God, I'm going to knock him out."

"Aw, Perce, that's the sweetest thing you've ever said to me."

"I mean it."

"Hypothetically defending my honor. I'm touched." I close my eyes and press the heels of my hands against them until my vision spots. "I shouldn't complain."

"You aren't complaining." He lets his head tip sideways so it brushes my shoulder. Not quite resting there. But not quite not, either. "You aren't like your father. You know that, don't you?"

"Course I am. A more imbecilic and disappointing version."

"Don't say that."

"All boys are their fathers. Looking at your parents is akin to seeing the future, isn't it?"

"Is it?" He smiles. "Perhaps that's how I'll know mine someday, then."

"Better than a fiddle."

He raises his head. "You're nothing like your father, Monty. For a start, you're far more decent than he is."

I'm not sure how, after all the terrible things I've done, he can possibly mean that. "You might be the only person left on earth who thinks me decent."

Between us, I feel his knuckles brush mine. Perhaps it's by chance, but it feels more like a question, and when I spread my fingers in answer, his hand slides into mine. "Then everyone else doesn't know you."

Barcelona

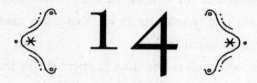

14

Barcelona is a walled city, lean streets and tall houses interspersed with the skeletons of Roman ruins. A massive citadel sits along the marina, more ominous than the guardian presence of Notre-Dame in Marseilles.

There isn't the traffic of Paris, but it's certainly a loud place, and a bright one. The sun on the water is dazzling and the streets seem reflective, cobblestones flecked with muscovite that shines like glass. The shop fronts and awnings and even the ladies' dresses seem a brighter hue than we've seen elsewhere. It's not gilt like the finery in Paris, but it's vibrant, fresh-cut flowers rather than wax ones.

We arrive on a sweltering day, the sun livid and the sky the hazy yellow of melted butter. The heat seems to pack tight between the walls and cradle the stones. Most of the people we come across speak French, mixed in with Catalan, which I recognize from the fair. Felicity does most of the talking. Pascal's grandmothers weren't wrong in their assessment that the Robleses are a known family—we only have to inquire after them twice before we're directed to their house in the Barri Gòtic, the old quarter of the city with medieval structures masquerading behind classical facades.

The house itself is less than I expected. For the manor of an old court family, the front is unimpressive—gray with no adornment, and so narrow it seems to have been squashed between the buildings on either side, with the excess oozing out the top. The portico is a mosaic of stone and brick, stunted balconies sprouting beneath the windows and the railings chewed with rust. All the curtains are drawn.

When I pull the bell cord, the waxed door smothers the echo of the chimes. Felicity looks up at the house, fine strands of hair stuck to the sweat glistening upon her neck. "We're rather off the edge of the map now, aren't we?"

"Don't be so dramatic." I look over at Percy. He's staring up too, though his gaze isn't as high as Felicity's. I follow his eyes and notice a death's-head carved above the door frame, thin, choppy lines intertwining into a bare skull flanked with feathery wings.

Bolting suddenly presents itself as a very promising option. But I run my fingers along the edges of the box in my pocket and root myself on that stoop.

"I don't think anyone's—" Percy starts, but the door swings suddenly open and I am face-to-face with a woman probably a decade older than us. Long, glossy black hair hangs loose around her shoulders, framing her face, and her olive skin is stretched taut over a pointed chin and high cheekbones. Also a tight dress and fantastic figure—it's rather hard not to notice. I ruffle my hair on reflex. It must be a sight.

"*Bona dia*," she says, stiff as starched sheets. She's hardly got the door open wide enough for us to see her. "*Us puc ajudar?*"

I was expecting French, and I fumble. "Um . . . English?"

She shakes her head and suddenly she's speaking aggressive Catalan at me. I haven't a clue what she's saying, but I take it it's not friendly.

"Wait," Felicity says behind me in French. "Please, we only need a moment."

The woman starts to shut the door, but I thrust my foot out and catch it. She gives that no heed and keeps trying to slam it, which about folds my foot in half, but I manage to whip the puzzle box out of my pocket and thrust it into the narrow space between us.

She freezes, her eyes widening. "Where did you get that?" she says, this time in English.

It's hard not to be petulant to a woman who nearly

217

amputated my toes with her entryway, so I say, a bit bolder than is likely wise, "Oh, that's odd, I didn't think you spoke English."

I feel someone poke me in the back—whether Percy or Felicity, it's difficult to say.

"Where?" the woman demands.

"Unwedge my foot from beneath your door and we shall tell you."

"We were told to give it to Professor Mateu Robles," Percy says from behind me. "Could we see him?"

"He isn't here," the woman replies.

"Will he be back soon?" Felicity asks. "And could you let Monty's foot go?"

"I'll take the box for him."

Felicity gives me a nod, like that's my cue to hand it over, but I don't let go. I'm a bit nervous the woman will slam the door in our faces as soon as it's in her grip and we'll have no chance to speak to Robles. "We were told to give it to the professor. And we were hoping to speak to him. About some of his work with alchemy—"

"I don't know anything about that," she says.

"Well, yes, so if we could speak to *him*—"

"He's dead."

Which is just the rancid icing on a crumbling cake. I resist doing a rather dramatic flail of despair onto the doorstep. "Well. I am certainly glad we came all this way to find that out." I try to yank my foot out from under the door but the little bastard is really under there. I swear the woman is pressing harder to keep me pinned.

"But if you'd like to speak to my brother," she says, "he's here. Mateu was our father—I'm Helena Robles. The box belongs to my brother Dante now."

"Yes," Felicity pipes up. "That would be good, thank you."

Helena opens the door fully, then turns on her heel and starts through the house, beckoning us after.

I prop myself up on the frame so I can get a grip on my foot and try to rub the pain out. "I think she broke my toes."

"She didn't break your toes," Felicity says.

I stamp my foot hard against the ground a few times, then start to follow Helena, but Felicity makes a snatch at my arm. "Monty, wait—"

Her expression alone says *This is not a good idea.* Percy's says it too. He must have been backing up the whole time we were arguing because he's nearly to the street, his fiddle case held before him like a shield.

"We found him, didn't we?" I say. "The professor. Or, we found out he's kicked it. We're supposed to give it to him, and he's not here, so we should talk to the son. It makes sense."

Percy looks over my shoulder into the house. "Yes, but—"

Helena appears again suddenly, like an apparition.

We all three jump. "Are you coming?"

I look back at the pair of them. They're both still staring at me like I've finally lost my mind. "Well, are you?" I ask.

Felicity follows me. Then, with slightly more hesitation, Percy does too.

The house is dark and narrow, thick drapes blotting out all the windows and giving the room an angled, smoky light. I was hoping for some relief from the heat, but the house is stifling. It's like stepping from the smithy into the forge.

Helena leads us down the hallway, past a pair of armless classical statues, bodies wound into the twist of a swan's neck, then stops before a door at the end, another death's-head etched into the baseboard. She reaches for the latch, then stops and turns back to us. She's eyeing the box in my hand rather intently, fingers coiling at her side like she'd like to get hold of it. "My brother does not do well with strangers."

I'm not sure what we're supposed to say in reply. It's not as though we're an imposition—we've brought the damn box back to them, after all, and at great personal risk, I'd like to add. They should be throwing gratitude and kindness and cream puffs at us, though I'd settle for just the cream puffs.

"Is there something you'd like us to do about that?"

I ask flatly. Felicity kicks the back of my foot.

Helena puts a hand to her brow, then shakes her head. "I'm sorry. You simply . . . You've startled me."

"We're sorry to intrude," Felicity offers.

"No, you've done us a favor. We didn't think we'd see it again, once it was . . . stolen. But don't be put off by Dante."

She cracks the handle, and we file through the door after her. My foot catches on a loose floorcloth near the threshold and I nearly pitch forward into her backside, which would make for a rather ungentlemanly impression upon our gracious hosts. Percy clearly doesn't learn from my error, for three seconds after I right myself, I hear him stumble.

Beyond the door, we are enveloped by a thick incense smell that makes me want to bat at the air. The maroon-papered walls are almost entirely blotted out by *things*—there's no other word for it. Three walls are shelves stuffed with books, interrupted by bell jars sheltering funguses, canopic urns and gold-leafed death masks, and a stone trefoil knot that looks like it was recently dug up from some ancient ruins, red clay still clinging to its crevices. On one wall is a papyrus scroll bearing an etching of a dragon coiled in a circle, swallowing its own tail. Someone's scribbled Eastern-looking characters in paint along a panel of the wainscoting, and an actual tombstone is resting against the desk. A heart-shaped locket hanging from its curlicues at first glance appears carved from obsidian but upon closer inspection proves to be transparent glass filled with blood.

Wedged into one corner of the room behind a crystallophone so large it nearly obstructs him is a man—a young man, I realize when he looks up, probably younger than Percy and me. He's thin, with a library pallor and a bookish stoop; spectacles are jammed onto his forehead and his arms are full of what appear to be scrolls covered in pictorial glyphs. He nearly drops them all when he sees us.

"I'm so—I didn't—so sorry." He speaks French as well, with a bad stammer that bottlenecks his words.

"Dante, greet our guests," Helena says. She's behind us, one hand still on the doorknob, and the sensation of being trapped creeps up on me.

"You should have—I could have—Why'd you bring them here?" He thrusts the papyrus into an open desk drawer, like he's trying to tidy up before we can get a good view of the mess. Which seems a bit futile.

"They've brought Father's Baseggio Box," Helena says.

"What?" Dante knocks his spectacles down onto his nose—only partly on purpose, I suspect—and clambers around the desk, tripping over the headstone in his haste. "You—you got it back? I mean, you—you found it? You have it?"

I extend it to him, and he accepts, careful not to brush his fingers against mine, then holds it very close to his face.

"Dante," Helena says, sounding like a stern governess. He looks meekly to her. "I told them it's yours, as our father is dead."

His eyes go wide at her, then back at the box. Then he looks up again and seems to see us for the first time. "My—my God." He doesn't look entirely happy about his reunion with the box any longer—a bit more shocked, with a shade of panic I can't fathom, though that might be more due to our presence than to the delivery itself. "Thank you, I didn't think we'd—we'd see it . . . Thank you. Would you . . . ? Thank you! Can you sit down? Would you like to?" He kicks at a chair before the desk, and a stack of books topples off. They land with their spines cracked upward and pages spread, like birds shot from the sky.

There are two chairs, and I take one, Percy the other. Felicity has become distracted by a cabinet near the door; it contains seven ampoules in varying shades from basalt black to a pearled pink like the inside of an oyster shell.

"Don't touch those," Helena snaps, and Felicity drags her hand back.

"Sorry. I was interested in the compounds. Are they medicinal?"

"They're cure-alls," Dante says, then goes fantastically

red. He can't seem to keep his eyes on Felicity, even when she looks at him. "*Panaceas* being the most—the scientific term, though they're not—not entirely—"

My heart leaps—it couldn't possibly be this easy, could it, to be shown into the exact room and seated beside the substances we're looking for?—but then Helena adds, "They're antidotes that work for most poisons. Activated charcoal, magnesium oxide, tannic acid, elephant tree sap, ginseng, tar water, and *Atropa belladonna*."

Dante clambers over a stack of crates and swings himself into the chair behind the desk. It's so low and the desk so large it looks as though he could rather comfortably rest his chin upon the tabletop. He pushes his glasses up his forehead and they immediately slip back down and knock him on the nose. "They're our father's. He is—he was. He was an alchemist."

"Was he the author Mateu Robles?" Felicity asks. "I went to a lecture on one of his books."

"The same. He has—quite a following." Dante keeps his eyes on the floor and the box between his hands as we talk, all the while twisting the dials in an absent way that suggests it's a familiar habit. "Very sorry about the . . ." He waves his hand vaguely at the room. "It's all his."

Helena has edged around to stand behind her brother.

Her eyes keep flitting down to the dials of the box as he turns them. "Did you come from far to bring this?"

"From England," Percy says. "By way of France. We were on our Tour, but we diverted to return the box to you."

"And how did you come to be in possession of it?" she asks.

Felicity and Percy both look to me, like they're giving me the choice of how honest I'd like to be. "I stole it," I say, which comes out a bit blunter than it sounded in my head. "I didn't know it had any value," I add quickly when the Robles siblings both look strangely at me. "I was just looking for something to steal."

Which certainly makes me sound benevolent.

Then, to truly buttress the image I have painted of myself as gallant swain, I finish, "And we were coerced into returning it."

Percy—bless—comes to my rescue. "There are dangerous people looking for it. They were ready to kill us for its possession."

Neither Dante nor Helena looks particularly surprised by this news. "Likely the same men who stole it from us," Helena says.

"What's inside?" Felicity asks. "If you don't mind. We were told about its make, but that's all."

Dante sets the box on the desk, then immediately

picks it up again. He looks to his sister, and they seem to conduct a silent conversation using only their eyebrows. Then Dante says, "We don't know."

Which is rather disappointing.

"His work was panaceas, wasn't it?" I ask. "Is it anything to do with—"

"Our father had many theories," Helena interrupts.

"Could we ask you—" I start, and Dante looks ready to answer but Helena parries before he can.

"His work died with him," she says. "If you've read his book, you know as much as we do. We can't help you if you're looking for information."

My heart sinks, though her words are a bit too rehearsed for me to swallow them as sincere. And Dante's doing a shifty-eyed dance that would do him no favors at a card table.

"Can you open it?" Felicity asks. "There's a cipher—a word that unlocks it."

Dante shakes his head. "He never told us. But thank you—thank you for returning it—for bringing it back to us. It is—was—sorry, it's so . . ." He pinches the bridge of his nose between his fingers, and I'm afraid he might start to cry. Then he looks up and finishes, dry-eyed, "Important to our father. So it's important to us. He told us to protect it and we . . . But now you've brought it back." He looks at Felicity, and she smiles at him. He goes positively vermillion.

An uncomfortable silence falls between us. Dante kicks his legs against the chair like a boy, then says, "Well, it was very nice to meet you all."

"Oh, yes, we should leave you be." Felicity stands from her perch on the arm of my chair, and Percy picks up his fiddle case, and for a moment it seems that our arduous journey is going to end in a single afternoon and a dead end. I can hardly bear to look at Percy for fear I'll crumple up at the thought of failing him.

But then Helena says, "Don't be absurd. If you came all the way from France, you'll stay here, at least for tonight."

"Oh, they don't—" Dante looks up at her, but she ignores him.

"You've done us a great service." She taps a finger toward the box, of which Dante still hasn't let go. "It's the least we can do in return."

"I don't think—" he says at the same time Felicity protests, "We don't want to impose!"

"Just for the night," Helena interrupts, sort of to both of them. "We can feed you and get you into some clean things and at least give you a proper bed. Do stay, please."

Felicity still looks ready to refuse, so I make a verbal hurdle between them. "Yes, thank you, we'd love to stay."

Felicity deals me a murderous look from the corner

of her eye, just as Dante does the same to his sister. Helena and I both ignore our siblings. I'm not certain Helena's intentions toward us are entirely innocent, but I am certain mine aren't. I'm not convinced there's nothing in this house that might be of use to Percy, and if the sister won't tell us, the brother looks ready to collapse like poorly made furniture if pressed. And I'm keen to press.

Helena gives Dante a little encouragement with the tips of her fingers on his shoulder. "Dante, could you show them abovestairs?"

"Right. Yes." He clambers to his feet, trips over the drawer he opened earlier, and catches himself on the edge of the crystallophone. The glasses clink together. It's an eerie, haunted sound.

"Do you play?" Percy asks him.

Dante goes red again. "Oh, um, no. It was—"

"Your father's?" Percy fills in for him.

"Part of his collection," Dante mumbles.

"What's a crystallophone have to do with alchemy?" I ask.

"Not alchemy—death, and burial practices. Before he . . . died, he became . . . quite obsessed."

"Dante," Helena says quietly, her tone a bowstring drawing back a poison-tipped arrow.

Dante dips his hand into the bowl of water and runs his finger along the top of one of the glasses. It releases a wobbling note, more vibration than sound. "There's a song . . . If played on the crystallophone," he says, "it is believed to summon back the spirits of the dead."

The house is small in spite of its height, and with the three of us added, there aren't enough beds. Felicity takes the only spare, while Dante gives Percy and me his apartments to share, a second-floor chamber with meager furnishings and walls that may have once been red, but have faded to the coppery brown of blood dried into linen. He lends us each a set of nightclothes and a change for the morning so we can let the garments we've been living in for a fortnight have a good soak—they seem likely to stand on their own when we shuck them.

In spite of all the beds Percy and I have been sharing along the road, this is the first time we've slept alone together since we were home, and the first time I haven't had an excuse to not disrobe entirely for bed. I've never been shy about undressing in front of Percy, but suddenly the idea of it makes the entirety of my being blush, so I wait until he's occupied with the razor and the mirror before I strip quickly and put on my nightclothes. Dante's an average-sized fellow, so the sleeves of the dressing gown pool over my arms. I have to keep tossing them back, like I'm raising my hands to conduct an orchestra.

When Percy's finished, I take his place before the dressing table and tuck into my first proper wash in weeks, which is sincerely the most marvelous thing that's happened since those two ecstatic minutes of our kiss in Paris.

"Did you think that was strange?" he asks as I stand at the mirror with my back to him, shaving. I can hear him shuffling about the room, making ready for bed.

The light is very poor and the glass very spotted, and it's taking all my concentration not to accidentally slit my own throat with the razor, but I manage to reply, "What was strange?"

"I don't know. Helena and Dante. All of it."

"Think they've asked us to stay so they can smother us in our sleep because we know too much?" I scrape a rim of soap off the blade and onto the edge of the basin. "I think they're holding out."

"How are they holding out? They don't owe us anything."

"I think they know what's in the box. Or at least have an inkling. They both got shifty when I asked about the cure-alls. Whatever's inside it must have to do with their father's work."

"Perhaps he was trying to turn rocks into gold. That's alchemy too."

"But that's not what we came for."

"Perhaps that box is full of rock-gold." Behind me, there's a *flump* as Percy drops his clothes to the floor. I catch the edge of my chin with the blade, and a glassy bead of blood rises to the surface of my skin. I press my thumb to it.

"I'm going to ask Dante tomorrow, before we depart," I say.

"About what?"

"About the cure-alls. He seems like an agreeable-enough chap, if you get him on his own." I tip my head for a better view of my jawline, checking for patches I missed. "Can't decide about the sister, though. She's a bit . . ."

"Intense?"

"Well, yes, but she's gorgeous, which makes that intensity less repellent."

Behind me, Percy gives a laugh that's mostly a groan. "Henry Montague."

"What? She is."

"I swear, you would play the coquette with a well-upholstered sofa."

"First, I would not. And second, how handsome is

this sofa?" Now Percy groans in earnest. I scrub the rest of the soap off my face. "If you were half as pretty as me, darling, you might understand—"

I turn, and the words crumble into dust. Percy's sitting on the bed, fiddling with a tinderbox on the nightstand and wearing nothing but a long shirt, which has gotten bunched up around his hips, leaving very little to my imagination. The neck hangs open so that the dusky light slides over the smooth skin of his chest like oil on water.

It is perhaps the most unfair play in the history of unrequited love.

I take a step back without meaning to, knocking into the dressing table. The razor stone falls to the ground with a clatter.

Percy looks up. "I might understand what?"

"I . . ." And I can't stay here with him, let alone sleep next to him—very suddenly, it is all too much, to think of lying with him, chaste and distant but with the sheets warm from his skin and his drowsy breath against my ear. I think it might eat me alive. I'm halfway to the door, my back against the wall, before I even realize I've moved. My hands are strangling the ties of my dressing gown. "I'm not going to turn in yet."

"What? Aren't you tired?"

"No. I think I'm going to see if I can find something to drink."

"Drink tomorrow. I want to go to bed."

It is impossible to explain how you can love someone so much that it's difficult to be around him. And with Percy sitting there, half in shadow, his hair loose and his long legs and those eyes I could have lived and died in, it feels like there's a space inside me that is so bright it burns.

"I'll try not to wake you when I come in," I say as I unlatch the door behind my back, then slip out into the hall before he can say anything more.

The house is eerier at night, which I hadn't thought possible, but poor lighting and long shadows are masters of sinister ambiance. I think about going back into the study where we met Dante, until I remember all the dead things and cursed objects there, and instead shuffle to the front parlor and settle in before the fire, on a leather sofa which is just short enough that I can't stretch out all the way and just stiff enough that I can't get comfortable and I am just irritated enough to know I won't sleep. There's a decanter on the sideboard with a bottle-collar proclaiming it cognac, but no glasses, so I take a swig straight out of the neck. I haven't had a drink in a while, but it's not quite as soothing as I want it to be.

There are footsteps in the hallway, then a moment later a shadow blots the rug. "I thought I heard you wandering about."

I sit up as Felicity makes a very unladylike flop onto

the sofa where my legs just were. I offer her the cognac, and she shocks me by accepting it, then taking a delicate sip. Her nose wrinkles. "That's vile."

"It's not the best I've ever had, no."

"I don't think it's this particular vintage."

"It's an acquired taste."

"Why acquire a taste for something so horrid?"

Something flaps by the window, a black shape torn from the black sky, and Felicity and I both jump. Then we smile sheepishly at each other. "This house is strange," I say.

"Yes, but we're here, aren't we? They've been kind to let us stay. We haven't any other options." She takes another tight-lipped sip of the cognac, pulls a spectacular face, then passes it back to me. "Helena's very pretty."

"Yes. So?"

"So? So I thought you'd be slavering over that."

"Should I be?"

"Honestly, Monty, I've never quite understood who's really got a hold on you."

"Do you want to know if I'm a bugger?"

She winces at the crass word, but then says, "It seems a fair question, considering I've seen your hands all over Richard Peele *and* Theodosia Fitzroy."

"Oh, dear Theodosia, my girl." I collapse backward into the sofa cushions. "I remain inconsolable over losing her." I do not want to talk about this. Especially with my little sister. I came down here for the sole purpose of getting drunk enough to sleep and avoid venturing anywhere near this subject, but Felicity goes on staring at me like she's waiting for an answer. I take an uncivilized swipe at my mouth with my sleeve, which would have earned me a cuff from Father had we been at home. "Why does it matter who I run around with?"

"Well, one is illegal. And a sin. And the other is also a sin, if you aren't married to her."

"Are you going to give me the *fornication without the intention of procreation is of the devil and a crime* lecture? I believe I could recite it from memory by now."

"Monty—"

"Perhaps I am trying to procreate with all these lads and I'm just very misinformed about the whole process. If only Eton hadn't thrown me out."

"You're avoiding the question."

"What was the question?"

"Are you—"

"Oh yes, am I a sodomite. Well, I've been with lads, so . . . yes."

She purses her lips, and I wish I hadn't been so forthright. "If you'd stop, Father might not be so rough on you, you know."

"Oh my, thank you for that earth-shattering wisdom. Can't believe I didn't think of that myself."

"I'm simply suggesting—"

"Don't bother."

"—he might ease up."

"Well, I haven't much choice."

"Really?" She crosses her arms. "You haven't a choice in who you bed?"

"No, I mean I haven't much choice in who it is I *want* to bed."

"Of course you do. Sodomy's a vice—same as drinking or gambling."

"Not really. I mean, yes, I enjoy it. And I have certainly abstained from abstinence. But I'm also rather attracted to all the men I kiss. And the ladies as well."

She laughs, like I've made a joke. I don't. "Sodomy has nothing to do with attraction. It's an act. A sin."

"Not for me."

"But humans are made to be attracted to the opposite sex. Not the same one. That's how nature operates."

"Does that make me unnatural?" When she doesn't reply, I say, "Have you ever fancied anyone?"

"No. But I believe I understand the basic principles of it."

"I don't think you really can until it's happened to you."

"Have you?"

"Have I what?"

"Ever fancied someone?"

"Oh. Well, yes."

"Girls?"

"Yes."

"Lads?"

"Also yes."

"Percy?"

I had felt her winding up to that, but it still catches me on the chin. I don't say anything, which is answer enough, and she gives me a sideways glance. "Don't look so surprised. Neither of you is very subtle."

"Neither of us?"

"Well, yes, it does take two. Isn't Percy—"

"No," I interrupt. "Percy is not . . . No."

"You mean you've never—"

"No." I take another long drink. The bottle collar rattles against the neck.

"Oh. I suppose I assumed, as you lean toward lads and the two of you are always so familiar with each other."

"We are not."

"You *are*."

"Fine. But I'm like that with a lot of people."

"Not like you are with Percy. And he's certainly not. Percy's so stoic and polite with everyone but you. And I've never known him to be, you know, *involved* with anyone. Lad or lady."

He hasn't, it occurs to me suddenly. Or if he has, I've never been privy to that information. He's never mentioned being sweet on someone, or spoken of anyone fondly, and for all our junkets, I am the only person I've ever known Percy to kiss.

"Even if it isn't, you know, romantic," Felicity goes on, "it's hard not to see. You're the kind of pair that makes everyone around them feel as though they're missing out on a private joke." We sit still for a minute, neither speaking. The fire pops and flails, spitting out sap. Then she says, "It's a relief, actually. I wasn't certain you had it in you to truly care for anyone."

I slouch down a little farther and nearly slide right off the sofa. It's very slick upholstery. "It would have been good if it were someone who wasn't my best mate. Or someone I could actually be with. Or, you know. A woman."

"I thought you liked women too."

"I do, sometimes. But that doesn't mean I don't like Percy more than anyone else."

Felicity presses her fingers to her temples. "I'm sorry, Monty, I'm really trying to understand this and I . . . can't."

"It's fine. I don't understand it most of the time."

"What does Percy think?"

"Not a clue. Sometimes I think he knows I'm smitten and ignores it. Sometimes I think he's just thick. Either way, he doesn't seem to feel the same."

"It must be difficult," she says.

I want to throw my arms around her for acting as though this conversation is ordinary. But as hard as she's trying, any more honesty would likely burst her head open. Because Percy goes so deep inside me, like veins of gold grown into granite. I think again about our kiss in Paris. His hand on my knee in the carriage when the highwaymen ambushed us. Lying side by side on the roof of the livery stable. It makes me ache to line them up like that, each of those moments that fall just short of where I wish they would land. "Not very enjoyable, no."

"What are your expectations, exactly? If Percy did feel the same way about you, what would happen? You can't be together. Not like that—you could be killed for it if you were found out. They've been sentencing mollies by the score since the Clap Raid."

"Doesn't matter, does it? Percy's good and natural and probably only fancies women and I am . . . not."

Silence again. Then Felicity reaches out and puts a hand upon my shoulder. As far as physical affection goes, we're a fairly delinquent family, so coming from her, it's a momentous gesture. "I'm sorry," she says.

"What for?"

"You've had a rough go."

"Everyone has a rough go. I've had it far easier than most people."

"Maybe. But that doesn't mean your feelings matter less."

"Ugh. Feelings." I take a long drink, then pass her the bottle.

She has another delicate sip. "You were right—it's less horrid now."

It occurs to me then that perhaps getting my little sister drunk and explaining why I screw boys is not the most responsible move on my part. I almost snatch the bottle back, though it feels rather hypocritical to take a stand for sobriety. So instead I say, "I wish I could be better for you." She looks over at me, and I duck my head, shame sinking its teeth in. "I'm older and I know I'm supposed to be . . . an example, I don't know. At least someone you aren't embarrassed of."

"You do fine."

"I don't."

"You're right, you don't. But you're getting better. And that isn't nothing."

16

Felicity and I stay up much later than either of us intends. I finally go above—at her insistence, as she says kipping up in the library is rather dramatic—to find Percy long asleep. He's balled up in bed, arms curled into him and knees pulled to his chest, but when I crawl in beside him, he slides against me without waking, cheek to my shoulder, and I can't put any more space between us without going straight off the edge of the mattress. He shifts in his sleep, bare legs hooking around mine, and suddenly my body is very much out of my own control. *Calm yourself*, I instruct it firmly, and it doesn't really obey, so I pass the rest of the night with Percy nuzzled up to me and me trying to think of anything but that. I hardly do more than doze—we've been lodging in dodgy inns for weeks and yet *this* is the worst sleep I've had since Paris. When it finally seems an acceptable hour to rise, I'm exhausted and frustrated and sort of hard.

Which is just unfair.

I splash cold water on my face until my body seems to understand that a romp with Percy is not about to happen, then dress in my borrowed clothes and slip down the stairs before Percy stirs. If we are to quit this place today, I plan to at least have a word with Dante before and see what I can find out about his father's cure-alls. Perhaps play upon the tremendous debt he owes us, work the *remember the great personal risk at which we brought your father's precious box back to you so why not spill a bit of his alchemical secrets your sister was so keen on us not knowing yesterday?* angle.

A spacious kitchen with scuffed floors and high windows juts from the back of the house like a broken bone. Clusters of candles are stuck with wax along the table, and copper pots dangling above sway in the breeze filtering through the open window. It's not yet eight and already hot as yesterday afternoon.

Dante is crouched in the hearth, trying to coax chalky embers into flame, and I think for a moment I may have lucked into catching him on his own, but Helena is at the table, flipping through a stack of letters, her thumbnail between her teeth. A kettle filled with cold chocolate, waiting for the fire, sits beside her, alongside an amber cone of unnipped sugar and tongs. It's exceedingly odd to see the pair of them, lord and lady of the house, in the

243

kitchen preparing their own breakfast.

They both look up as I enter. Dante stands quickly, bangs his head on the lip of the hearth, then wipes his sooty hands on his breeches, leaving two black palm prints. "Mr.—Mr. Montague. Good morning. How did— Did you sleep well?"

"Um, yes," I lie. "Thank you, . . . sir." It's not a thing I'm accustomed to calling a man my own age, but he's got a house and likely his father's title on me, so I err on the side of awkward formality.

Dante holds one of the candles to the kindling and blows until it catches, then tosses a log overtop for the flames to curl their fingers around. "Is Mr. . . . Newton . . . ?"

"He's still asleep," I say, to save him the trouble of finishing the sentence.

He nods, and I nod, and Helena says nothing, and the sort of silence that makes a man want to talk about the weather falls between us. I take a spot at the table and help myself to a crusty bread roll off a tray in the center, just for something to do. It's staler than it looks.

Helena's eyes narrow at the letter she's reading, face pinched until she catches me watching her and composes herself. She refolds it and tosses it onto the stack on the table, then stands to hang the chocolate pot over the fire.

There's a noise in the hallway, and a moment later a tousled Percy makes his entrance, sleepy and oblivious to the distress he caused me all night. Dante greets him with the same puplike enthusiasm he offered me, though with less head bashing this time. Percy slides down the bench to my side, just far enough away so that he won't crack me in the eye with his elbow when he starts to wrangle his hair back into a queue. As he fastens it, one long ringlet escapes and settles around his ear. I think about tucking it back into place for him, but take another bite of my roll instead.

"Sorry that we haven't much to eat," Helena says, then gives me a wry smile across the table. "You don't expect a trio to show up on your doorstep looking like someone dragged them from the sea with nothing but stolen property and a violin."

"Oh!" Dante laughs. "The violin. I'd forgotten."

"Do you play?" Helena asks, looking between us.

"I do," Percy says.

"Well?"

"Well, what?"

"Do you play well?"

"Oh. That depends upon your standard."

"He plays very well," I interject. Beneath the table, Percy knocks his knee into mine.

Helena sets a jar of grape molasses between us, spoon clanking against the crystal. "Our father was a musician."

"I thought he was an alchemist," I say.

"A hobby musician," she qualifies.

"Mine as well," Percy says. "My fiddle was his."

Dante, still crouched at the hearth and poking at the flames like a boy, pipes up, "I have some of his music in the bedroom. My bedroom. The bedroom you're . . . I saved it. If you'd like—if you want—you might—"

"I'm sure he's not interested, Dante," Helena says. She's fetched mugs from a cabinet and is spreading them around the table before each place. When she bends over, the neckline of her dress dips so low I can see all the way to her navel. I was going for my bread but nearly take a bite of the candle instead.

Dante's face goes red, but Percy, bless him, says kindly, "I'll take a look at it. It'd be good to play some."

"He played mostly the—the glasses. So the songs, the music, I mean, it's meant to be performed on the crystallophone. But they might still—"

"If you're planning to depart this morning, there are diligences that will take you from the city center to the border," Helena interrupts. "And you can hire a coach from there." It seems she's really shoving us out the door, but then she tacks on, "Though if you're in no great rush, you're welcome to stay with us for a time."

Clearly there was no consult on this subject, for Dante drops the fire poker with a clatter. "Wh-what?"

Helena ignores him and instead says to Percy and me, "You've come so far, it seems a shame to leave so soon. And if you're touring, you should see Barcelona. Not many English tourists make it this far, and there's so much to do. The fort, and the citadel—"

"We should be moving on," Percy starts, but Helena cuts him off.

"We're going to the opera on Friday night—you should at least stay until then. I'm not sure we can compete with Paris, but it's grand to us." She gives me a smile that's rather too predatory to accompany such a benign invitation.

I can think of plenty of reasons to flee the house right then, ranging from that smile to *All those death objects in the study are damned unnerving* to *Dear Lord, don't make me share a platonic bed with Percy again.* But I'm not going anywhere until we have a chance to ask them about their father's cure-alls or whether there's anything they know that might help Percy, even if Helena seems as keen to keep an eye on us as I am on her. No secret so carefully guarded isn't worth knowing.

"We'll have to speak with Felicity," Percy says, at the same time I start, "Seeing the opera would be good," but we're both interrupted by Dante's squeak of "Boiling!"

We all look over as the kettle lid clatters, foam spilling over the sides. The fire spits. Helena curses under her breath, whipping her skirt over her hands so she can hoist the kettle from the fire. Percy leaps up too, lifting the lid off the serving pot. A thin line of chocolate splatters from the spout as Helena pours, leaving a dark splotch along the linen. A few drops make it as far as the letter she tossed down the table, and I feel compelled to assist in some way, so I scoop them into a pile, out of her way. "Should I—"

"There's a box on the study desk," Helena says, still focused upon the chocolate pot. "Dante, please don't sit there. Fetch plates and the cutlery."

I pad into the study, tripping yet again on that damned loose floorcloth. The room is dark after the bright kitchen, windowless and all light swallowed by those bookshelves and that dark papering. The death masks seem to stare at me, empty eye sockets sunken into shadows.

The tabletop is buried, same as the rest of the room, both with papers and with more of the paraphernalia, but there's a single box shuffled into one corner. I shift off a few layers of papyrus and a plaster casting to find a smattering of letters, the top one addressed to Mateu Robles. They must be quite piled up if they've still post for their dead father. I shift the top few aside, curiosity getting the better of me. A few down, there's a sheet of fine creamy stock with a green wax seal broken in one piece, the crest imprinted on it the fleur-de-lis in triplicate.

I nearly drop all the letters I'm holding. It's the crest of the Bourbons.

The House of Bourbon controls Spain, so perhaps it's a tax letter. Or news from friends in the court. Maybe that impression in the green wax did not come from the ring of the duke who stole the box from the Robles siblings and attacked us in the woods.

I toss the stack of mail onto the desk in a haphazard pile and snatch up the letter, unfolding it with fumbling fingers.

> *Condesa Robles,*
> *In regard to our arrangement pertaining to*
> *your father's Lazarus Key—*

"Did you get lost?"

I whip around. Helena is standing with one hand on the door frame, giving me a coy smile until she sees the letter in my hand. Then her eyes narrow. "What are you doing?"

"Just . . . making certain . . . this was the right place."

She's still staring at me, so vehemently that beads of sweat begin to congregate on the back of my neck. I almost thrust the letter behind my back, like that will somehow conceal my rather obvious treachery.

"Come for breakfast," she says.

"Oh. Yes." I'm not certain what to do with the letter, but that question is answered when she steps forward and snatches it from me, so hard that it rips and I'm left with a scrap pinched between my thumb and forefinger. As we pass into the kitchen, she tosses the letter into the fire.

I slide down to my spot at the table beside Percy, my hand on my lap still fisted around the scrap of the letter. As Helena turns her attention to breakfast, I smooth the paper out against my knee and glance down at the moniker upon it in blotted ink.

> *Louis Henri de Bourbon, Duke of Bourbon,*
> *Prince de Condé*

Percy and I leave the breakfast table together, nearly colliding with Felicity at the top of the stairs as she comes down from her room, her hair mussed and her eyes still drooping.

Before she can offer a good-morning, I pull her into our bedroom, Percy on our heels, and shut the door. "Look here, I found something." I unfold the torn scrap of the letter, kept tucked tight in my fist all through breakfast—which was quite a feat—and hold it for them to see. My sweating palm has smeared the ink, but the words are still legible. "I tore it from a letter in their study."

Felicity rubs at her eyes with her fists, like she's still trying to wake. "The Duke of Bourbon."

"The one I stole the box from."

"He's . . . writing to them?"

"Looks to be."

"Did you read the rest of the letter?" Percy asks.

"Just the first line, then Helena barged in. It was something about a Lazarus Key. He said it belonged to their father."

"Why's he writing to them if he's the one who stole the box?" Percy asks.

"Well, if he wanted it, perhaps he was trying to make a bargain first?" Felicity offers. "And they wouldn't comply, so he stole it?"

"We should find out what's in it," I say. "I think they're lying when they say they don't know."

"But it's theirs," Percy says. "What they do with it is their business, not ours."

"But we nearly died for it, and—in case you forgot—it might be something to help you. It's clearly some carefully guarded secret of Mateu Robles's, and his whole work was alchemical cures. It makes sense. We should stay here—just for a few days—and see what we can find."

"But if they're in contact with the duke—" Percy starts.

"I think Monty's right," Felicity interrupts him. "We have no money. And we're going to wear ourselves out if we travel again so soon. You especially"—she looks to

Percy—"should take care of yourself."

Percy blows a sigh from his nose. The single errant curl about his ear flutters. "I don't think it's a good idea to go courting trouble, is all."

"We're not courting trouble," I say. "Flirting with it, at most."

"I'm going to write to Lockwood," Felicity says, "through the bank in Marseilles. Tell him where we are and ask if he'll send funds to help restore us. Until then, if the Robleses will have us, we should stay here. And you"—and here she looks to me—"can do whatever sort of investigative work in that time that you'd like to, so long as you don't sour our hosts on us. Are we in agreement?"

"Yes," I say. It seems that, for the first time, my sister is enthusiastically on my side. Percy looks far dourer about it, but he nods.

"Until then," Felicity says, "perhaps we can learn about this Lazarus Key."

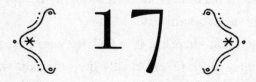

It's three days before we manage to set aside some time for quality snooping, a disoriented three days of being intensely aware that we are strangers in a stranger's home, but with nowhere else to go. The first two we spend mostly sleeping, as our last few weeks suddenly seem to fall upon us all like a sack of bricks dumped from above. The third, Helena insists on accompanying us out of doors to see the city.

Dante stays behind. He seems to live in the study—he takes up his post there every morning directly after breakfast and is still there when we turn in—which makes poking about for further correspondence with the duke or anything about Mateu Robles's work difficult. We've all looted our respective rooms and found nothing—though Percy was almost entirely unhelpful to me once he discovered the stack of the father's music and decided his time was better spent riffling through that. The study seems the place for answers, and Dante seems disinclined to leave it, preferring the safety of the stuffy mausoleum his father left behind for him to populate.

Investigative efforts foiled thoroughly by our exhaustion and his social anxiety.

To my great surprise, it is Felicity who first pounces upon Dante. She's taken to this investigation with considerably more enthusiasm than anticipated, considering how tight she usually keeps her corsets laced. Since we arrived, the pair of them have been keeping up an ongoing conversation about *chemistry* and *phrenology* and *electricism* and other words I don't know the meanings of, and he's quite a bit more keen on her than our initial interaction would have led me to believe was possible. Far more so than he seems to be toward Percy or me, though each time she attempts to nose anywhere near the subject of alchemy, he takes the conversational cul-de-sac back to safer ground. My initial hope that he might be inclined to spill secrets begins to slip.

We find Dante in the study, not so much tidying as shifting the mess about, but he stops to listen as Felicity asks if there's a university nearby with a library we might visit. "There's a bookshop," he says. "Down the corner. I mean around the corner. Down the street and around the corner." He flaps his hand for direction. "You may—might—might try that. Or we have books here. If you care to . . . stay in." His gaze scampers over Felicity, then he goes red from his neck to his hairline.

"Oh, that's kind, but I wanted to"—Felicity snatches a lie out of thin air with a speed that is frankly impressive—"I wanted to buy your father's book."

"We have copies around, I think."

"Yes, but I'd like my own, to take with me when we go." It's not an airtight lie by any means, considering we have almost no money and she first asked after a library. But before Dante can start to pick at the holes in it, she offers him a sweet smile. Not knee-weakening, per se, but perhaps charm is a bit more of a family attribute than I previously thought. "You can come with us, if you like."

The flush that had begun to fade from his cheeks flares again like a stoked fire. "No, no . . . I think I'll stay. Oh," he calls us back as we reach the door and says to Percy, "I heard you yesterday, practicing. My father's music. If you'd play some for me . . . I'd—I'd very much like that."

"When we return," Percy says, "I'd love to."

Dante beams.

The bookstore is not library-sized, which is disappointing, but it boasts a good selection. Crowded shelves are

255

packed into rambling rows, excess inventory stacked at random intervals along the floor. Behind the counter, a headmastery-looking man with majestic jowls glowers. He looks like a bit of a traditionalist, the sort that wouldn't take queries from a lady or a Negro boy, nor think either of them has any place in a bookshop, so I sally forth alone.

I opt for a daft-but-earnest approach—lead with a smile and a stumble and my shoulders pushed up to make me look smaller and less threatening. Though I'm not particularly large or threatening to begin with.

"Good morning," I say in French.

The bookseller tips his bridge specs from his nose and tucks them into his pocket. "May I help you?"

"Yes, actually I was wondering—it's a bit of a slim chance—but if you happened to know what a Lazarus Key is? Or if you have any books on it?"

The bookseller blinks. "Are you making a Biblical reference?"

"Am I?" I laugh. He does not. "I don't know."

"Lazarus is the man Christ raises from the dead, detailed in the eleventh chapter of John in the New Testament."

"Oh." That hadn't occurred to me. I've never been an attentive scholar of the Bible, my father being a deist and my mother being of an anxious disposition that manifests most prominently before disagreeable church services. "Yes, perhaps I am."

"Then I suggest you study the Bible."

He looks ready to tuck back into the demanding occupation of scowling, but I press on. "What about Baseggio puzzle boxes?" I show him the dimples. "Do you know about those?"

He is—tragically—immune. "No."

"Do you know what they are?"

"Young man, do I bear resemblance to an encyclopedia?"

"No. Sorry." I duck my head in surrender. "Thank you for your help."

I start to walk away, but then he calls, "We do have a small section on Venetian history."

I turn back. "Venetian history?"

"It's a Venetian name—Baseggio. A patronymic from a Venetian diminutive of the surname Basile. Perhaps you might begin your search there."

"A patronymic diminutive of . . . that, yes." I understand less than half the words in that sentence, but God bless the book people for their boundless knowledge absorbed from having words instead of friends. "Yes, thank you. I'll try that."

"Young man," he calls, and I turn back again. He gives me a nod, head bobbing though his jowls all hold their formation. "Good luck."

So perhaps not entirely immune to the dimples after all.

"Anything?" Percy asks as I return to where he and Felicity are waiting.

"Baseggio is a Venetian name," I reply. "And Lazarus might be from the Bible."

Felicity claps a hand to her forehead. "I should have thought of that."

"So I suppose we can each take one of those," I say. "Bible and Venice and then the alchemy book, and see what we can find."

"I've the alchemy," Felicity says.

"Venice," Percy says quickly.

I moan. "Please don't make me read the Bible."

Percy gives me a wide smile and touches one finger to the tip of my nose. "Should have spoken faster."

We spend the afternoon in our respective corners of the bookshop. I read John 11 twice, then do a skim of the surrounding pages to see if any further mention is given to that Lazarus character, though it devolves quickly into less of me reading and more me trying to stay awake— the bookstore is warm and the chair comfortable and exhaustion is a houseguest that has rather overstayed its welcome.

When a bell tower down the way chimes the hour, I stand, stretch my arms over my head, then go to find

Percy, first casting a quick glance around for the jowly book minder, who might be less than keen on the fact that I left my readings scattered across the floor instead of shelving them again, but he's still holding court behind the counter.

Percy's at a table by the window, bent over a book with his palms clamped over his ears, the green glass panes casting a jeweled sheen upon his face. He doesn't look up when I sit down across the table, until I nudge his shin with my foot and he starts rather spectacularly. "You scared me."

"Very engrossed in your reading. Did you find anything useful?"

"Abso-bloody-lutely nothing." He tips the cover shut with a dusty slap. "Not even a mention of the name or a family. Perhaps Baseggio isn't Venetian after all. You?"

"Nothing about a key, though there's quite a lot about that Lazarus chap. One of Christ's showier miracles, apparently."

Percy laughs. "Oh, please do tell me your version of this story."

I lean forward on my elbows, and Percy mirrors me, hands knotted before him. "So Jesus and Lazarus are chums, right? And while Jesus is off preaching, He gets a shout from Lazarus's two sisters, Mary and Martha, letting Him know that Lazarus is not long for this world—"

"Mary and Martha?" Percy repeats. "I don't remember that."

"Should have paid more attention in your Sunday services. So Jesus doesn't come, and Lazarus dies, and he's been decaying for days when the man Himself finally shows up at the tomb—"

"There's an island," Percy interrupts.

"No it's not, it's a tomb."

"Not in the Bible—in Venice. I read about it in one of the books—an island off the coast with a chapel on it called Sante Maria e Marta."

The room seems to hush around us, the soft flutter of pages suddenly shivering and ghostly. "Mary and Martha," I say.

"Lazarus's sisters."

"Probably a coincidence."

"Probably," he says, though neither of us sounds as though we really believe that.

We both let that seep into us for a moment like ink into blotting paper. Outside the window, the sun shifts behind a cloud, casting the room into shadow. Then, under the table, Percy nudges my shin with his foot. "So. Tell me the end."

"The end of what?"

"After Christ shows up at Lazarus's tomb."

"Oh! So the man Himself shows up at Lazarus's tomb, and the sisters and their friends are all wondering what He's doing there, for Lazarus is very dead by then. And Jesus asks the sisters if they believe in Him and God and life after death and all that and they say, 'Yes, fine, but it would have been brilliant if You'd come when we first called because then our brother might still be alive.' And then Jesus says, 'Well, watch this'—"

"Really? *Well, watch this*?"

"That's biblical language."

"If your Bible is written by Henry Montague." He's grinning at me, and I open my mouth to reply, but realize suddenly that beneath the table he's still got his foot on my leg—it's such a light touch I don't notice it until he shifts, toe hooking around the back of my calf, which knocks me straight off course, thoughts dashed to pieces against his touch.

"Ah, it's something like that." His foot slides down my leg, pulling my sock out of place and dear God it is stirring in me every sinful desire that I'm rather sure the Bible frowns upon. "It's 'Take away the stone' or something like that, but my version is a bit better."

"Did you say your version is *a bit better* than the Bible?"

"Well, the Bible's stale."

"Not sure what God's going to make of that assessment."

I swallow as his foot shifts against my leg again. I'm starting to sweat from the effort of keeping still. "I think

I'm going to have worse than revising scripture to answer for when He and I meet."

He laughs, closemouthed and breathy. "So Lazarus comes back from the dead? Is that how it ends?"

"Walks out of the tomb as though nothing was ever wrong."

We look at each other across the table. Our faces feel closer than they did when I first sat down, both of us with our hands clasped before us like we're praying over supper. Percy's got such fine hands—larger than mine, with thin, graceful fingers and round knuckles a bit too big for him, like a puppy still growing into its paws. For a delirious moment, I am possessed by the insanity the poets hath called *love*, and it makes me want to reach forward and take both those hands in mine—he has got his foot making its torturous ascent upward, after all, which feels like an invitation—but before I can, he frowns suddenly and peers under the table. "Has that been your leg all this while?"

"What?"

He unhooks his foot from around my calf. "I thought it was the chair. Sorry about that. Dear Lord, why didn't you say something?"

Before I can reply, there's a *flump* at the end of the table and we both start. Felicity has slammed her alchemy book down between us and is standing over it with her palms flat on the cover and her elbows straight.

"Did you finish already?" Percy asks her. In the second I looked away from him, he's gone and tucked those fine hands out of sight.

"I skimmed," she replies. "And I knew some from the lecture. It's scientifically sound, as far as I can tell, though I'd always heard alchemy was being disproved. Mostly his book is a summary of the principles—the purification of objects and returning them to their most perfect state. But then there's a chapter at the end—hardly even a real chapter, it's a practically a footnote—about artificial panaceas."

"What does that mean?" I ask.

"One of the pillars of alchemy is creating a single item or compound that heals all ailments and restores the body to its perfect state," she explains. "There's no universal one in existence—mostly they're plants and things that work as antidotes to a wide range of poisons."

"Like the chemicals in the study," Percy offers.

"Right. But it seems that when Mateu Robles died, his work was primarily focused upon the creation of a universal panacea that synthesized inside a human heart."

"How would that work?" I ask.

"Well, his theory is that the component missing from previous attempts to create a panacea was life. He believed that were the correct alchemical reaction to occur within it, a beating heart could be turned into a sort of philosopher's stone, and then the blood pumped

from that heart would take on the same healing properties."

I scrub my hands through my hair, tearing a few
strands from its queue. A beating heart and open veins
is an altogether different thing than the chemicals in a
vial I was expecting.

"What if he succeeded?" Percy asks. "Maybe whatever's in the box has something to do with finding the
person with that heart—or making it. Perhaps that's
what the duke is after."

"It seems ill-advised for one man to have access to
something like that—particularly one with his hands in
so many political pies." Felicity looks over at me and
scowls. "What's that face for?"

"What face?"

"You look put out."

"Just thinking about all that blood." I nearly shudder.
"Doesn't it make you a bit squeamish?"

"Ladies haven't the luxury of being squeamish about
blood," she replies, and Percy and I go fantastically red
in unison.

18

The opera is Friday evening—Helena reminds us over breakfast that morning. Dante nearly faints. I have a strong sense both that this is his first time out of the house in a long while, and that he's not going willingly.

We haven't clothes fit for the outing, so Dante lends Percy a wine-colored suit—noticeably too short in the sleeves, but they're built similar enough that it's pass-able. I get black silk breeches and an emerald coat that swallows me, but it's the only thing that fits in the tails and the cuffs, after I roll them. Twice. "It's my father's," Dante says, with seemingly no understanding of how dis-concerting it is to be wearing a dead man's clothes.

When I come into the bedroom, all attempts to con-vince my shoulders to fill out a smidge abandoned, Percy's perched upon the bed, still not dressed. He's got one leg pulled under him and his violin clenched between his chin and his shoulder. A set of weathered sheet music is spread before him.

"Is that the music Dante picked?" I ask.

He nods, the violin bobbing. "It doesn't translate as well as I hoped—it's all written for the glasses. Well old-fashioned, too."

"Let me hear."

He twists the end of his bow, arranges his fingers, then plays the first line of the song. It's got a formal sound to it, swallowed and courtly, until Percy confuses his fingering and the strings squeak. He whips the violin out from beneath his chin with a frown, then tries the measure again, plucking out the strings instead of bowing them, with no real mind for the timing.

"That was beautiful," I say.

Percy jabs me with his bow, right to the stomach, and I flinch with a laugh. "You are a menace."

"What's that one called?"

He squints at the title. "The 'Vanitas Vanitatum.' Oh." His brow creases. "This is the song."

"What song?"

"The one Dante mentioned. The summoning song, for the spirits of the dead."

"Trying to call the soul of Mateu Robles? He might be the only one in this damn house willing to tell us about his work."

Percy sets his violin on the bed, then reaches for the

clean shirt laid over the headboard, already pulling his arm through his own sleeve. "How soon are we leaving?"

"Ah, not sure," I reply, forcing myself to avert my eyes as he pulls the shirt over his head. "I'll meet you below, shall I?" I snatch up my shoes from beside the door and flee. I'll not torment myself with a half-naked Percy any more than is absolutely necessary. Entirely clothed Percy is almost more than I can bear.

Dante seemed to be hoping that if he sulked above-stairs for long enough, he might be accidentally left behind, and I can't imagine Helena is very quick in dressing without a maid, so I assume I'll be the first one down. The study door is shut, and I pause beside it, tempted to try the handle.

My fingers brush the latch when, from behind the door, I hear Dante's voice, pitched in a whine. I nearly jump out of my skin.

"Why does it matter if we keep them here?"

"We need to wait . . . ," I hear Helena say, but the rest of her sentence is drowned out by Percy starting up with the violin again from above. I wish dearly I could throw something at him through the floorboards. I lean in to the door, pressing my ear flat against it.

"Perhaps they can—they can be persuaded. Into silence. Or they aren't interested."

"They're obviously interested."

"But they seem so reasonable."

"Haven't you learned yet that many seemingly reasonable people are far from it?" There's a shuffling click, like pearls sliding against each other as a strand is tugged. "You'll see him *tonight*. We're running out of time."

"What if he isn't—"

"I'm certain he'll be there—he always goes to play with the magistrates."

"Then you—"

"He won't speak to me anymore. I've pestered him too often. It has to be you."

"But . . . I don't . . ."

"Please, Dante. If he could only come home . . ."

A shuffling. Dante mumbles something I can't make out.

"You'd let him rot away without trying everything?" Helena hisses. "We keep them here until—" The door opens suddenly and I about go face-first into Helena's breasts, an impropriety so grand it might distract from my being caught eavesdropping. I catch myself on the door frame and straighten, making a fruitless attempt at playing casual. Helena and Dante are both at the threshold of the study, Helena with one hand down the front of her dress, adjusting the tucker. Her sacque gown is pale pink, the color of rose quartz, with a pannier beneath and her waist pulled so narrow that everything else is pushed upward. Suddenly, nosing into her breasts doesn't seem like such a terrible fate.

"I thought you were above," she says.

"No, just . . . waiting." We stare at each other for a moment longer. I adopt my best *I was certainly not eaves-dropping* smile. Helena's eyes narrow.

"Coach," Dante murmurs, and darts down the hall-way. The front door slams so hard the vials in the study cabinet tremble.

Thank God Percy appears on the stairs behind me at that moment, his violin case under one arm. "I think I've—Oh, where's Dante gone? I thought I heard him."

"Hailing a coach," Helena replies, shouldering past me and into the hallway. "We need to go."

"Yes." Percy sets his violin inside the study door. "Felicity should be down soon."

Helena is still staring at me. "That coat," she says suddenly.

Fashion was the last thing I expected her to remark upon. I shift in the shoulders, and the whole thing settles upon me like a snowdrift. "Bit big."

"It's my father's."

"Oh, Dante said I could—"

"I know," she says, turning down the hallway before I can see her face. "Just a statement of fact."

We arrive at the opera too early to be fashionably late. The singing hasn't begun, but the footlights are being trimmed. The opera house is bright and chaotic, far less gaudy than the one in Paris but twice as loud. The chandeliers glimmer like sunlight on water. The footman's gallery is stuffed, aisles crowded with young men coasting up and down for company. In the boxes, women play cards and eat cream-filled pastries brought to them on silver trays. Men are discussing politics. When the singing begins, the noise is amplified as everyone raises their voices to be heard over it. The standing crowd on the stage kick their legs and shuffle from foot to foot, already weary.

Percy and I don't go to the Robleses' box—instead I drag him to the gambling hall attached to one of the upper galleries, looking down over the audience, so we can have a private chat about what I overheard and conspire on what to do.

Felicity put up a fuss at being left behind, mostly in whispers as we climbed the stairs with her hand on my arm, so Dante and Helena prancing ahead wouldn't overhear. "I want to come with you."

"Well, you can't. Ladies aren't allowed."

I nearly stepped on her train as she cut the corner of the landing in front of me. "If you are scheming about the alchemical cures, please do it where I can hear."

"We aren't scheming. We're . . ." I didn't get to a fib fast enough, and Felicity's eyes narrowed. She darted up the step in front of me, cutting off my progress.

"You *are* scheming!"

"Just stay in the box and keep an eye on Dante, won't you? See if he goes anywhere."

"Don't give me some nonsense task to make me feel included."

"It's not nonsense, just . . ." I didn't know how to finish, so I just flapped a hand at her.

Felicity tore her fingers from my arm, straightened her dress, then stuck her nose in the air. "Fine. Don't include me. Perhaps I'll scheme on my own, then."

"I look forward to it," I said, then grabbed Percy by the hand and dragged him away.

The gambling hall is gauzy with smoke and hotter than the summer air outside. It's a great effort not to loosen my cravat as soon as we enter. As we wait at the bar for whiskey, I recount to Percy what I overhead.

"From what I gather, they're meeting someone here tonight," I finish. "Do you think we could find out who it is? Maybe we should get back to the box and follow Dante if he goes anywhere. Bit conspicuous, though, I suppose. What if it's the duke he's rallying with? Maybe that letter I found was instructions for a meeting time. I'd bet it's the duke—what if he followed us here from Marseilles?" I resist the urge to look around, as though he might suddenly materialize at our side.

I look to Percy, hoping he might lend some shears to my intellectual hedgerow, but he's pulling at his coat, fanning the collar against his neck. "God, it's hot in here."

"Are you listening to me?"

"Course I am. But I think you're getting excited over nothing."

"Hardly nothing—"

"Just because you found one letter from Bourbon doesn't mean they're on familiar terms."

"Then who else would they be meeting?"

"Perhaps it's nothing to do with the alchemy. Or their father. Or us."

"Helena stopped awfully short when she realized I was listening."

"Well, you were being rude."

"I wasn't being rude!"

"You were eavesdropping."

"No eaves were dropped, I was just standing about. It's their fault they weren't speaking softer. And that's not the point! The point is, something is going on and I have a sense we're being conspired against. We need to find what we can about Mateu Robles's alchemical cures and then get away from here. Why aren't you as worked up about this as I am?"

The bartender delivers our shot glasses, and Percy slides one down to me with a smile. "Because I don't want to worry about that right now. I just want to be out with you. We're here, aren't we? In Barcelona. At the opera. Let's enjoy it." He traces the rim of his glass with a finger, and it hums at his touch. "We won't have many more nights like this."

"Don't say that."

"It's true."

"No, it's not, because we are going to find whatever secrets they have about alchemical cures and then you'll be well again." On the stage, the soprano starts in on a punishing first aria at a pitch that makes the air tremble. I wince. "Here then, let's play a game where we drink every time someone sings something in Spanish."

"Italian."

"What?"

He tips his head toward the stage. "This is Handel— it's in Italian."

"Is it?"

"Definitely Italian."

I decide not to mention how adorable I find it that he knows all that just by hearing a few bars. The soprano strikes another blistering note and I grimace. "Doesn't matter, I hate it." I tap the rim of my glass against his. "To beauty, youth, and happiness."

He laughs. "Do we qualify for any of those of late?"

"Well, we are indisputably young. And I am happy— at least right now, because I haven't had a proper drink in a fortnight and I'm quite excited about this. And you are . . ." I trail off, my neck starting to heat.

Percy turns to me quickly, his eyes catching the light and reflecting a mischievous glint. I'm suddenly aware of my body in a way I wasn't a moment before, every twitch and blink, the way my shoulders sit inside this too-big coat, the bob of my throat as I swallow hard, every point of my silhouette that his gaze touches. Love may be a grand thing, but goddamn if it doesn't take up more than its fair share of space inside a man.

I could tell him. Right here, right now, let it out in the light. *Percy*, I could say, *I think you are the most beautiful creature on God's green earth and I would very much like to find a hidden corner of this opera house and engage in some behavior that could only be termed* sinful.

Percy, I could say, *I am almost certain that I am in love with you.*

But then I think about that kiss in Paris, the way he pushed me away once I let slip a hint that it might mean something more than a random romp. He's been so fond with me since we reached Spain, in a way he hasn't since before I put my mouth on his that disastrous night, and that feels fragile as spun sugar, too sweet and precious to risk its collapsing.

"I'm what?" Percy asks, mouth curling upward.

The singer breaks off, the orchestra lapsing into an interlude. Percy's eyes flit away from me, toward the stage, and I slap him on the shoulder. "Yes, Percy, you're very handsome," I say as flippantly as I can muster, then toss back my whiskey in two quick swallows. It burns as it hits my throat.

When I turn back to him, that drowsy hint of a smile has vanished. He shifts so he's propped backward against the bar on his elbows, tugging again at his coat collar to ward off the heat. Then he leans suddenly in to me and says, "Here, there's something I've been wanting to talk to you about. When we were in Paris . . ."

He halts, and my stomach drops. When I look over at him, his eyes are fixed on a point across the room. "What about Paris?" I say, trying to be dead casual about it, but he doesn't seem to hear. "Percy?"

"Look, it's Dante."

"What?" I whip around and follow his gaze across the room. Amid the tables, there's Dante, hands in his coat pockets and shoulders pulled up, like a turtle drawing into its shell. He's talking to an older gent in a white wig and a fine gold coat, his fingers curled over a silver-handled cane. The man smiles kindly at Dante, who looks to be stuttering something, but then shakes his head.

Both Percy and I keep silent, though we're too far away to hear anything being said. The man bends down, forcing Dante to meet his eyes, says something that makes Dante go red, then makes to clap him on the shoulder, but Dante steps out of the way and instead he ends up swatting the air between them. The man smiles, then starts off toward the gambling tables while Dante flees the other direction, through the doors and back out to the boxes.

"Do you think that's—" Percy starts, but I'm ahead of him.

"We need to talk to him."

"Who, Dante?"

"No, whoever that is." I flail a hand at the white-wigged cove. He's already settled himself at a hazard table across the room—for a man with a cane, he's a speedy bastard. "Let's have a game, get him talking, ask about the Robleses, see if he'll tell us anything. Maybe he knows about their connection to the Bourbons or what their father was doing with his alchemy. Or *anything* about them."

I start toward the table, but Percy catches me by the back of my coat. "Hold on, they're not going to let you sit at a gambling table for a chat. We're going to have to bet."

"Oh . . ." I glance over—there are only three empty seats left at the man's table, and one gets snagged almost as soon as I look.

"I'll get chips," Percy says. "You corner him."

"Brilliant." I start away again, but then double back to him. "You all right?"

"Fine," he says, though he's plucking at his shirt. "It's so hot, is all."

"We'll make this the quickest card game of our lives. Meet at the table."

I sidle through the crowd, trying not to look like I'm making a charge for those two empty seats. A pair of swains are standing behind them, talking, one of them with his hand resting on a seat back, but I dive in before they can and fall, a little less gracefully than I had hoped, into the chair beside the man Dante was conversing with.

He glances up from his chips and gives me a smile. I offer a big one in return. "Not too late, am I?" I say in French.

"Not at all," he replies. "Welcome to Barcelona."

"Sorry?"

"You sound foreign."

"English. My friend and I are on our Tour—he's gone for chips."

"We don't get many English tourists here. How did you make your way so far south?"

Oh, this is going splendidly. "We're visiting friends. The Robles family."

His eyebrows meet in the center of his forehead. "Oh, are you?"

"Wagers, please, gentlemen," the caster interrupts. "We're ready to begin."

I resist the urge to glance around for Percy. "Do you know them? The Robleses."

"In a professional capacity. I spoke with Dante earlier tonight, actually."

I'm not what might be called accomplished at

subtlety, but asking forthrightly *And what did you two speak about?* seems excessively bold, so instead I say, "What's your profession?"

"I serve as warden of the city prison. Rather grim, I know." That was not what I was expecting. He shuffles his chips between his thumb and forefinger, then tosses a few on the table for the caster. "Good for those poor children to have some company after all they've been through with their parents."

I'd hardly call either of the Robleses a child, but I don't correct him.

There's a tap on the table in front of me, and I look up. The caster is frowning. "Your wager, sir."

"Ah, just a moment." I lean in to the warden. "I'm quite concerned about Dante, actually, I haven't seen him since his father died, and he's been so tight-lipped about it ever since—"

"Died?" the warden interrupts. "He hasn't died."

"But he's . . . What?"

"Sir," the caster says, "the wager."

I try to swat him away. "My friend's on his way—"

"Sir—"

"What do you mean, he isn't dead?" I demand.

The warden looks rather alarmed by my vehemence, but says, "Mateu Robles is a Hapsburg sympathizer, jailed for refusing to aid the House of Bourbon when they took the crown."

My heart is really going now. "You're certain?"

"I've been charged with his care by the king. He's housed in my prison."

"Do his children—"

"Sir," the caster says, "if you won't be wagering, I'll have to ask you to leave."

"Fine, I'll . . ." I stumble to my feet, searching for Percy. He's a hard fellow to miss, but the crowd is thick and the air smoky and I am more than a bit flustered. "I'll be right back," I say, partly to the caster, but mostly to the warden, then shoulder into the crowd. *He's alive* is thumping through me like a heartbeat, and I'm tripping myself trying to work out what this means. Mateu Robles is alive, though both Dante and Helena had assured us he was dead. Dead as Lazarus, and here he is, risen again.

I do two laps around the hall before the realization that I can't find Percy kicks its way through my discovery. He's not at the chips table, or at the bar where I left him. I can't think where else he would have gone, and I'm starting to get frantic.

Where are you, Percy?

And then I spot him, slumped on the ground beside the door, his head between his knees and his hands shoved into his hair. My heart stands still for a moment, then begins to pound again for a new reason entirely.

I shove through the crowd, with no care whatsoever for who I'm smashing into, and drop to my knees beside

Percy. I touch his arm and he starts more than I expected. When he looks up, his face is drawn, thin beads of sweat gathering along his hairline. "Sorry," he murmurs.

"What's wrong? Is it . . . ? Are you about to . . . ?"

He pushes his face into the crook of his elbow. "I don't know."

"Right. Well . . . right. How about, maybe . . . maybe . . ." I don't know what I'm supposed to do. I'm fishing bare-handed in my stream of consciousness for some way to take charge of this situation and be what he needs, and I'm coming up empty. *Do something, you imbecile.* "Let's go," I say, which seems like a good place to start, and I help Percy to his feet. He sways unsteadily, though that might just be the crowd jostling us. I slide his hand around my arm and lead him out of the hall, the truth about the Robleses taking second place to Percy.

Everything will always be second to Percy.

I'm not certain if he's about to fall into a fit, or how long we've got if he is, or if there's anything I can do to stop it. He's clutching my arm as I lead him down the stairs and through the lobby, into the courtyard, which— thank God—is cooler than inside and nearly deserted.

In one corner, a grove of lemon trees clings to the stone wall, branches bowing under the weight of ripe fruit. I walk Percy over, hoping there'll be a bench or at least a hefty rock, but he doesn't seem to give a whit about the seating, for he sits down on the grass, then falls backward with his knees up and his hands over his face. He's breathing rather fast.

"Please, not now," he murmurs, so soft I'm not certain he knows he spoke aloud.

I'm fighting the urge to go fetch Felicity because she's so much better at this than me—probably would have if it didn't mean leaving him on his own. I haven't a clue what to do, so I clamp onto the first idea that arrives before I have a chance to really consider it: I crouch down at his side and put a hand upon his elbow. It is perhaps the least comforting place upon which a comforting touch can be bestowed, but I'm committed to it now, so I don't move.

I am doing the wrong thing, I think. *I am doing the wrong thing and I am going to do the wrong thing and I am never going to be what he needs.*

For a time, we're both silent. Above us, the canary-yellow lemons sparkle among the leaves, their rinds swollen and slick with starlight. Interwoven with the glittering chatter from inside the opera house, sounds of the city play from the other side of the courtyard wall— the clack of carriages and the soft *shush* of fountains emptying their throats. The thin peal of a watchman's voice sings the hour. Barcelona is a handsome symphony all its own.

"Are people staring?" Percy asks. His breathing is evening out, but he still looks poorly.

"No." I glance around the courtyard. A lady and a gent perched near the wall are giving us a glare that plainly implies we interrupted what was about to be his hands up her skirt. "Want me to lie down as well? It's less strange if there's the pair of us."

"No, I think it's passed."

"Certain?"

"Yes. I just got a rather odd feeling and I thought it might be coming on." He sits up, closes his eyes for a moment, then opens them again, and I nearly collapse with relief. "You can go back inside."

"Absolutely not, we should go."

"I'm fine, I promise."

"Come on." I climb to my feet, brushing my hands off on my coattails. "Back to the house."

"What about the others? Shouldn't we tell them?"

"They'll work it out." I hold out a hand to him, and he lets me pull him to his feet, a little unsteady on the slippery grass.

We take a hired carriage back to the Robleses'. A few streets from the opera house, Percy nods off, his head slipping onto my shoulder, then down to my chest. When the hack stops, I sit for several minutes longer before I shrug, very lightly, so that he raises his head. "We're here."

Percy sits up, pushing his knuckles into his forehead. "Did I fall asleep?"

"A bit. Ah, look, you've gone and slobbered all over my jacket." I take a swipe at my lapel.

"Dear Lord. Sorry."

"You were only asleep five minutes. How'd you manage to drool that much?"

"Sorry!" He pulls his sleeve up over his thumb and tries to wipe it off and instead ends up smearing it into the silk. I bat him away and he covers his face with his hands, laughing. He doesn't seem quite himself yet—I'm still braced for the fit to come on—but he looks less flimsy than he did in the gambling hall, and when we climb out of the cab his step is steady.

The house is stifling, but a window is open in the parlor and the lamps are still lit, so it's there that I leave Percy curled up on the sofa, while I muck about in the kitchen—nearly lose a chunk of my hair and the skin off my palms trying to get water boiling and spill at least ten shillings' worth of leaves from the jar.

When I return to the parlor, I am victory personified with kettle and teacup in hand. Percy raises his head as I approach and regards my offering with a peery eye. "What's this?"

"Tea. I made you tea. I could get something else, if you want. There's wine around somewhere."

"What are you doing?"

"I dunno. Helping? Sorry, you don't have to drink it."

"No, that's . . . Thank you." He takes the cup from

me and has a cautious sip, then coughs once and claps a fist sharply to his chest. "This is . . . tea?"

"Did I ruin it?"

"No, no, it's—" He coughs again, which turns into a laugh, and then he's laughing with his head tipped back. I kick the sofa leg and he's nearly unseated. A bit of the vile tea sloshes onto the upholstery. I set the kettle on the side table and sink down on the other end of the sofa, mirroring his body so we are face-to-face, curled up like question marks with our feet off the floor and our knees together.

"You're hopeless," he says, and it is so strange and horrible and utterly lovely how the way that he's looking at me makes me want to both back away and throw myself upon him. It hurts like a sudden light striking your eyes in the dead of night.

He wraps his hands around his teacup again, his shoulders hunched. "I'm all right now."

"Oh." My voice cracks, and I clear my throat. "Good."

"Thank you."

"I didn't do anything."

"You stayed."

"That wasn't much."

"Monty, I have never once woken from a fit and found the people who were there when it began still with me. My aunt has quite literally run from the room when I said I was feeling unwell. And I know it didn't happen now, but . . . no one stays." He reaches out, almost as though he can't help himself, and puts his thumb to my jawline. The tips of his fingers brush the hollow of my throat, and I feel the touch so deep I half expect that when he moves, I'll be left with an imprint there, as though I am a thing fashioned from clay in a potter's hands.

Percy drops his arm suddenly and lifts his chin, nose wrinkling. "Something's burning."

"I set a fire in the kitchen grate."

"No, I think it's here. Oh, Monty—the kettle."

I look over at the side table. A thin strand of smoke is rising from where I set the kettle. I snatch it up, though the damage is done—a perfect circle in charred black on the wood. "Damnation."

"Let's not burn their father's house down while they're out," Percy remarks.

"Is there a way to hide—" *Their father's house.* I nearly drop the kettle. "Percy, their father isn't dead."

Percy looks up from fishing some floating thing out of his tea. "What?"

"Mateu Robles—their father. He isn't dead, he's a prisoner. The man Dante was talking to—he's the warden at the city prison and he told me Robles is locked up."

"He's jailed? Did he say why?"

"Something about politics. I think he was on the wrong side of the war that the Bourbon family won."

"Maybe that's something to do with the duke's letter—"

"The letters!" I leap to my feet and fly out of the parlor, still clutching the kettle. The study door is as we left it—propped and unlocked. I push it open, half expecting some trap to fall upon me from above.

"What are you doing?" Percy calls.

"The letters from the duke. There might be more." I dash to the desk, nearly tripping on Percy's fiddle case, which is still just inside the door, and begin to paw through the letters in the box, searching for any more with the Bourbon crest on the seal. Near the bottom, another fleur-de-lis winks up at me from green wax, and I snatch it up. "Here."

Percy joins me at the desk, sifting through the papers strewn atop it. "Lucky they don't seem to throw anything out."

With Percy going through the drawers that aren't locked and me working across the surface, we come up with almost a dozen letters with the Bourbon family crest set into the seal. "He's not just writing to them, *they're corresponding,*" I say, picking one at random and confirming the duke's signature at the bottom before I scan the page.

On the other side of the desk, Percy holds up another. "This one's dated nearly a year ago."

"They're all to Helena."

"Not all." He flaps one of the pages at me. "This one's for Mateu."

"'Upon the execution of our arrangement,'" I read, a phrase picked at random from the middle of one. "What arrangement have they got?"

When I look up at Percy, his face is grave. The shadows from the firelight mottle his skin. "Monty, I think we should leave here. Tonight. Or as soon as we can."

"And go where?"

"Anywhere. Back to Marseilles. Find Lockwood. At least find somewhere else to stay until he sends funds."

"But . . ." *But what about Holland and the asylum?* I want to say. *We came here to help you and instead we'd be leaving with nothing.*

Before I can reply, the front latch clacks from the hallway, followed by a *bang* as the door hits the wall and bounces back. Percy and I both freeze, eyes locked, then in unison begin shoving the letters back where we found them. Percy shuts one of the drawers too forcefully, and a glass beaker rolls to the floor and shatters. We both go still again, listening hard. There are the sounds of a scuffle outside the door, and a clatter, like something's been struck.

Then a voice that sounds distinctly like Felicity's gives a smothered cry.

Which is enough to kick into motion a strange mechanism inside of me that has never before been triggered. I snatch up the closest thing to a weapon I can find—the kettle of hot tea, which I imagine will do a fair bit of damage if tossed in someone's face. Percy, clearly of a similar mind, hefts a sword he finds wedged between two of the bookshelves, though it's too firmly attached to its plaque to be convinced to part, so the plaque goes with him. Together, we inch toward the door, weapons raised.

Something strikes the wall from the other side. The canopic jars on the shelf jump. I fling open the study door and fly into the hallway, Percy on my heels.

It is apparent at once that we have made a grievous mistake. Even in the dim light, I can clearly see Felicity and Dante collapsed into the wall with their arms and hands and mouths and abso-bloody-lutely everything all over each other. Neither of them appears to quite have a handle on what it is they're doing, but they're nonetheless enthusiastic about it.

I'm not certain if I want to make a hasty retreat back into the study and pretend we saw nothing or throw the hot tea in his face anyway, but then my foot catches that damned loose floorcloth and I pitch into the wall. The kettle leaves a crater in the wainscoting with a resonant *thud*. Dante shrieks and flails into one of the armless statues beside the door. It falls with a crash. Felicity whips around, a long strand of her hair that's collapsed from its arrangement whacking Dante in the face. "What are you doing?" she cries.

"What are *we* doing?" I return, my voice coming out at a much higher pitch than anticipated. "What are *you* doing?"

"What does it look like I'm doing?"

"We thought you were in danger!" I cry. Dante bolts for the stairs, but I thrust my kettle in his path. A few steaming drops spit onto the carpet. "Don't you go anywhere. I've got very acidic tea and Percy's got a sword with a stump, so keep your hands where I can see them."

Felicity throws her head back. "For the love of God."

"If I may—" Dante starts, but I cut him off.

"Oh no, you don't get to say a thing. You and Helena are liars and thieves and now you're trying to take advantage of us in every conceivable way."

"Monty—" Felicity interrupts, but I've got too much momentum to halt. I am Sisyphus's damned boulder rolling down that damned mountain and I intend to flatten the rogue Dante beneath me.

"You've got the duke who wants to kill us writing your sister letters, and your father, turns out, isn't dead, he's in prison, so thanks for that lie—"

"Monty—"

"And now you're, what, keeping us here until it's convenient to slit our throats? But not before you played a bit of Saint George with my sister."

"Jesus, Mary, and Joseph, Henry Montague, for once in your life, be quiet!" Felicity snaps. "This wasn't Dante's idea, it was mine."

Which is a bit of a cold slap to the face. The spout of my kettle droops. "Yours?" I repeat.

"Yes, mine. I thought we'd be alone here."

"So did we. We came home because Percy was feeling poorly."

Felicity looks to him. "Are you well?"

"I'm fine." He's got the sword hefted in both hands, but the tip is starting to sink. Blades are beastly heavy, with or without a dozen pounds of solid oak attached. "Where's Helena?"

"Still at the opera, presumably," Felicity replies. "Since we all four decided to flee without consulting the others."

"Perhaps we should discuss this in the morning." Dante has begun to creep again to the stairs, but I step in his path. Even if it was Felicity who dragged him here for a bit of tongue, I'd still like to slam him into the wall for going along with it.

"Stay where you are," I say. "None of this changes the fact that you've been corresponding with the duke who you claimed stole the Baseggio Box from you."

"You—you went through our things?" he stammers.

"It was right there on the desk!" I say, then remember

it is not me on trial here and add, "You lied to us!"

"My—my sister was right, you came here to spy on us."

"We weren't spying—" I say at the same time Percy says, "Why did you tell us your father was dead?" And Dante lets out a whimper, hands thrown up in a *Don't shoot!* gesture.

"All right, everyone into the study, *now!*" Felicity barks, in a tone that is essentially verbal castration, and not a one of us protests.

We shuffle in, single file, while she stands at the door like a headmistress, watching us with her arms folded and a glower in place. I set my kettle on the cold fireplace. Percy keeps the sword in hand, but Felicity snaps at him, "Put that down before you hurt yourself," and he lowers it beneath the desk. Dante lets out a visible sigh of relief. "Sit," she orders, and we three all sit, Dante and Percy in the matching chairs before the desk, me on the floor because Felicity's glare is making me afeard for my life if I delay. She shuts the study door with a snap, then whirls to face us. "Now." She points a finger at Dante. "You owe us some truth."

Dante seems to wither in his chair. In spite of the fact that I'm still ready to wring his scrawny neck, I can't help but feel a bit bad for the poor lad. One minute he's working himself up to put his lily-white hands down a girl's dress for likely the first time in his life, and the next he's facing down an inquisition from said girl whose dress he was about to reach down. "Yes. Yes, I suppose."

"Start with this," I say. "What's in the Baseggio Box?"

Dante does not look as though he was prepared to start there. "That's . . . a very large question."

"It's a very small box, so it can't be that large," I reply.

"Is it a Lazarus Key?" Percy asks.

Dante's head snaps up. "How do you know about that?"

"We saw it in"—Percy glances my way, a silent apology for coughing up the truth—"your sister's correspondence."

I snatch a letter off the desk and hold it up like evidence presented at trial. Felicity gives me a pronounced eye roll.

"The Lazarus Key is . . . I mean the . . . It's not . . ." Dante rubs his temples with his fingers, then says, "You read my father's book, so you know about his theories. Human panaceas—the beating heart as the only place in which a true cure-all can be created."

"He was trying to make one," Felicity says.

"Yes." Dante coughs, then casts an eye at the fireplace. "I'll take some of that tea, if you're offering."

"You don't want any," Percy says.

"Did it work?" Felicity asks.

"Um, it didn't quite . . . He performed the experiment,

but it didn't . . . It went wrong. It was tried upon"—
Dante swallows hard, his Adam's apple making a great
hurtle up his neck—"my mother. Our mother. She volun-
teered," he adds. "They were both alchemists, and they
wrote the book—it was hers, too. But she couldn't put
her name on it, as she's . . . well, a woman." He trips on
that word, his eyes darting to Felicity, and I wonder if
he's considering whether or not bringing this deception
into the light is going to ruin his chances of getting his
tongue in her mouth again. I nearly upend the kettle over
his head. "But the compound they created . . . it stopped
her heart."

"So she died?" Felicity asks.

"No," he replies. "But she didn't—she didn't *not* die,
either. She's . . . stuck. Not living, not dead, with an
alchemical panacea for a heart."

Hope leaps like a flame inside me. "It worked?" I
interrupt, a bit too keenly, for Felicity gives me a frown
that suggests I have rather missed the point.

Dante nods. "The panacea was created, so . . . Well,
yes."

"So, why hasn't it been used?" I ask. "Why didn't he
make more?"

"Because she had to give her life for it," Dante replies,
looking a bit shocked I had to ask. "It's—it's a horrid
cost."

"Where is she now?" Percy asks.

"She's buried . . . or entombed, rather. My father, before he was arrested—he knew they were coming for him and he wouldn't be able to protect her any longer. So he had her locked up where no one could get to the heart. The key . . ." He picks up the puzzle box from the desk and shakes it. The sound of something fly-light rattling around inside it whispers through the room. "It opens her vault."

This is, without question, the spookiest thing I've ever heard. It sounds like the sort of scary story Percy and I used to tell each other when we were lads, just to see who could get the other worked up first.

"And where's the vault?" I ask. I'm ready to leap to my feet and sprint to some cemetery on the other side of the city as soon as he names the place, even though it's the dead of night and we don't actually have the key we need to open her tomb. I'd pry the damn thing open with nothing but my bare hands and sheer determination.

"Is it in Venice?" Percy asks. "There's an island called Mary and Martha. Lazarus's sisters in the Bible."

Dante nods. "My father apprenticed with an alchemist there, as a boy. His teacher is long dead, but the men at the sanctuary . . . they still knew him. And they said they would hide her. That's why he called it the Lazarus Key. It all seemed rather poetical at the time."

"So his plan is to—what? Leave her there for the rest of time and waste his cure-all?" I ask. Felicity shoots me another *think before you say inappropriate things* look.

"Well, there's a complication of late." Dante reaches for his spectacles, remembers he's not wearing them, and instead rubs his eyes. "The island is sinking."

"It's what?" Felicity and I say in unison.

"The tunnels under the sanctuary are collapsing. It's all flooding. No one's allowed there anymore. There isn't much time left before the whole thing . . . it's going to be at the bottom of the Lagoon."

"So the one item on earth that can cure anything will be underwater in a few months if you don't go fetch it?" I say. I want to smack my head against the hearth in frustration, because of course this couldn't be as easy as it seemed for a brief, bright moment.

"That's—that's why the duke—why he came for us," Dante says. "Collecting her has . . . it's become more urgent."

"So where does the duke come in, exactly?" Felicity asks. She's taken one of his letters up from the desk and is examining it.

Dante rubs his hands together. "We had . . . When the experiment went wrong, my father destroyed his research before anyone could replicate it. But the duke— he wanted the panacea. He wanted the method more, but my father wouldn't give it up—not any of it, not my mother or the work—so Bourbon had him locked up for his Hapsburg loyalty and came to Helena and me instead. So many people have come—come calling. Men who read my father's book. They want the secrets to his work. That's why—why we began to tell people he was dead and the work gone. Just so we'd be left alone." He scrapes at his bottom lip with his teeth. "One Duke of Bourbon is—is bad enough."

"Why didn't your father destroy the heart, then?" Percy asks. "If he was so desperate to keep people from getting it."

Dante shrugs. "I don't know."

"Why does the duke need the panacea?" Felicity asks. "Is he ill?"

"The French king is," I say, remembering suddenly a few scraps of information I was tossed at Versailles. They all look to me, and I scramble for more. "And the duke's been dismissed as his prime minister."

"Why would he want to give it to the king if they've parted ways?" Felicity asks.

I press at my temples with the tips of my fingers. "Maybe if he brought this cure-all to the king and kept him alive, he could get his position back. He could ask for anything he wanted, really."

"Which secures the Bourbon family's control of the French throne," Percy finishes.

"And the Spanish," Dante says.

"And Poland," Felicity adds. "They're everywhere."

"So he's going to blackmail the king in exchange for his health," I say.

"Or, what if he took the heart and then found a way to duplicate it after a study?" Felicity says. "If the Bourbon family had that sort of knowledge—if *anyone* did . . ." She trails off, leaving each of us to spin his own end to that sentence.

Dante nods, looking suddenly miserable. "We know Bourbon has alchemists in the French court. They haven't been able to copy my father's work, but they've been trying, and if they had—had the heart to study . . ." He lapses into silence.

Felicity rounds on him, looking cross again. "So, why did you give him the box?"

"If he gets the heart, he'll let our father out of prison. But it doesn't matter." He makes an attempt to laugh, but he's so nervous it sounds a bit maniacal. "We don't know the cipher. The duke took the box with him to Paris in hopes cryptographers in the court could crack it, but our father's the only one who knows. And if he knew what we'd done . . ." He looks around at all of us, like he doesn't quite know what the right course of action is and is hoping someone will offer it up for him. "He told us not to. Made us swear we wouldn't hand her over."

"And he won't tell you the cipher?" I ask.

Dante shakes his head. "No, not Helena or me since she—she gave up the location of the tomb. To the duke. Father knows Helena would trade it for his freedom—I think that's why he put the key in the box to begin with, to protect—to keep it from her. She's devoted to—she and Mother fought, constantly, for . . . But Father was always her defender. And I think . . . now she wants to be his." He rubs the back of his neck, then knits his fingers behind it, mouth pulling into a frown. "After our mother died, Father became obsessed—obsessed with trying to bring her back . . . or let her die. For good. Hence . . ." He waves a hand at the museum of funerary rites that decorates the walls. "Helena said . . . it was like losing both our parents to his obsession. And she—she blamed our mother for that . . . that too."

"Well, if he won't tell you," I say, "do you think he'd tell me?"

Felicity actually laughs aloud at that pronouncement, which is rather hard not take personally. "Why would he tell *you*?"

"Because we could help him," I say. "The island is sinking—if he doesn't get her out soon, she'll be gone forever, whether or not someone uses the panacea. If we can convince him of that, perhaps he'll tell us the cipher and then you can fetch it." It's a great fight to keep my voice steady when all I'm spouting is rubbish—if we get the box open and get to that alchemical cure-all, there is only one thing I am going to do with it, but I can't imagine Dante would be too keen if he knew our idea.

Or rather, *my* idea. Both Felicity and Percy are giving me a look that clearly conveys it is I alone taking a machete to this jungle.

Dante, in contrast, lights like a struck flint. "We—do you think—would he? What about Helena?"

"You needn't tell her," I say. "She can't hand it over if she doesn't know you've got it."

Dante taps the tips of his fingers together. He's practically bouncing in his chair. "We'd have to get you into the prison. They won't let him have visitors. But—but he's here, in Barcelona. They've all their political prisoners in one hold. Would you—could you do that? For me?"

"So we get the cipher and then we leave *here*," Felicity interrupts. "At once. This is getting dangerous."

"Yes," Percy says, and I nod. If there's an alchemical treatment in Venice—or better still, an honest-to-God *cure* that can rid him of this forever and knock Holland permanently off the docket—I want to be out of here and on the road as quick as possible.

From the street outside, there's the clatter of a carriage pulling up to the walk. Felicity twitches the drapes open and peers out. "Helena," she says.

Dante scrambles, his foot catching a pewter cross hanging from one of the drawers and wrenching it out of place. "You mustn't tell her what I've said, or that we're—that we're going to see—see my father. She'd murder me." I'm not sure if that's literal murder or figurative; he looks terrified enough that it could be either.

The front door opens, and a moment later the study follows. Helena appears, a silhouette blacker than the hallway darkness, like ink poured into oil. There is just enough light on her face to see that the first thing her eyes go to is the Baseggio Box on the desk before she looks at each of us in turn. "You're all here," she says.

None of us seems keen to offer an explanation, so Percy steps up. "I was feeling ill," he says, and I expect he'll launch into a good lie as to why this mysterious affliction required the entirety of our party except for Helena to accompany him home, but that's all he says. That straight-edged silence settles back into place.

"Did you enjoy the opera?" Felicity pipes up.

"Operas tire me," Helena replies. She looks to the box again, then says, "Dante, may I have a word before bed?"

Which is our cue to depart. Dante gives me a pleading look as we shuffle by him, and I return a raised eyebrow that I hope is a vehement reminder not to spill our plot to Helena. As dedicated as he might be to seeing his mother's heart stay out of the hands of the Bourbons, he's already proved he's not the sort to hold up well under pressure.

Percy goes straight into our bedroom, but Felicity calls me back before I can follow. She glances down the stairs to be certain Helena and Dante are still in the study, then says, "Tell me what you're plotting."

"Me? I never plot."

"All you've been doing since we arrived is plot! Why did you offer to get the cipher from Mateu Robles? That was uncharacteristically benevolent."

"How dare you. I'm the most benevolent person I know."

"Monty."

"The benevolentest."

"Don't play thick—you don't fool me."

Now it's my turn to check for the Robles siblings approaching before I speak. "If we can get that box open and get the key, we can go to Venice and use the panacea for Percy so he can be cured of his falling sickness and then he won't have to go into an asylum."

"There are far better solutions for avoiding institutionalization than this. And solutions no one had to die for. And incidentally, none of them have to do with you." She pokes me in the chest. "In fact, none of this has to do with you, it's to do with Percy. Perhaps he doesn't want this."

"Why wouldn't he want it? He'd be well. It'll make his life . . ."

Felicity quirks an eyebrow at me. "Make his life what? *Worth living*? Is that what you were going to say?"

"Not exactly in those words."

"Asylum aside, I think he seems quite fine as he is."

"But he's not—"

"*But he is.* He's been ill for two years and you didn't know because life goes on. He's found a way."

"But . . ." I'm floundering. *But he's going to Holland, but I don't know how to help him if not for this, but perhaps he can handle it but I don't think I can.* "We should still speak to Mateu Robles. Even if we can't . . . for Percy . . . I think . . . we could help. Someone."

"Yes, *someone*."

"So we'll go see him tomorrow."

"And then we need to leave here—whether to Venice or back to Marseilles to find our company, we need to go. We're getting in too deep."

She starts up the stairs, but I call after her, "So. You and Dante."

She pivots back to me, and I give her what I know from experience is my most annoying smile. I expect her to flush, but instead she performs one of her spectacular eye rolls. "There is no *me and Dante*. Particularly if you're being grammatical about it."

"Do I sound like I'm interested in the grammar of the situation?"

"Whatever the case, you're wrong. There is only *Dante*, full stop. And *me*, full stop."

"So it wasn't you who rubbed your foot up his leg in the box and got him to sneak away from the opera for a bit of a romp?"

"I would have stopped it long before any romping began. I had a plan until you burst in."

"Plan? What plan?"

"Well, they both knew more than they were letting on—that was apparent—and Dante seemed more likely to crack. And since my usual strategies weren't working, and he clearly seemed rather sweet on me—"

"Clearly, was he?"

"Oh, please. Men are so easy to read."

"And here I thought you were a paragon of frail English womanhood. Turns out you're a temptress."

She tugs at a loose thread on her cuff and lets out such a violent sigh that it raises the fine hairs trailing down around her ears. "I was rather bad at it."

"Seemed like you were doing fine to me."

"I think I chipped his tooth."

"Well, as with any fine art, practice is required. Rome wasn't built in a day." I hope that might make her laugh, but instead she frowns down at the floor. "Was it good, at least?"

"It was . . . wet."

"Yes, it's not the driest of activities."

"And uncomfortable. I don't think I'll be trying it again."

"Information by way of seduction? Or kissing in general?"

"Both."

"Kissing gets better."

"I don't think it's for me. Even if it's better someday."

"Perhaps not. But I think you've more in your favor than your skills as a jezebel." I nudge my toe against hers until she consents to look up at me, then give her a smile—of the less-annoying variety this time. "Far, far better things."

19

I hardly sleep that night in anticipation of our planned felony. I'm up beastly early, though we don't leave until midafternoon, when Helena goes out to pay calls and we can slip away undetected.

We walk for nearly an hour in the oppressive heat, our clothes suctioned to us with sweat before we've left the yard. Dante leads the way, through the Barri Gòtic and down the tree-lined mall that saws the city in half. As the church bells announce the half hour, we reach a square, lined in market stalls selling produce wilting in the heat, grains to be scooped from barrels, and boxes of autumn-colored spices. Along one edge, sows with their stomachs split are hung from hooks by their feet. The butchers' boys run beneath them with buckets to catch the innards, their fronts smeared with blood. Beggars kneel between the paths, their hands cupped before them and their faces pressed into the dust. The light is giddy and loud, and the air crowded with flies. Everything reeks of mud and fruit too long in the sun.

Dante stops in the shade of a Roman tower abutting the square and points to two men strolling the stalls with swords dangling at their sides, their gazes far too predatory for them to be casual shoppers. "There. Thieftakers. They'll be quick." Dante wipes his sweating hands upon his breeches, then looks over his shoulder at me. "Father looks quite a lot like Helena. Dark haired and slim."

"You told me," I reply.

"And he's only three fingers on his left hand."

"I know."

"Are you . . . still certain you want to do this?"

"Of course." It's strange to be reassuring him when it's me doing the deed, but in that moment, I am feeling damn heroic. "What's the worst that could happen? They're not going to cut off my hands for theft, are they?"

"No," Dante says, with just a bit too much of a pause. A tremor of nerves cracks through that damned heroism.

"We'll give you an hour," Felicity says. "Then we'll come."

"And you're certain they'll let me out without my standing before a court?"

"The jailers aren't compensated," Dante replies. "They'll—they'll take a bribe." He reaches into his pocket—the same artificial gesture he's been repeating every few seconds, as if to check that his money hasn't disintegrated.

"And you're certain they'll take me to the same place as your father?" I ask.

"It's hard to . . . yes?" Dante twists his hands before him. "They'll take you close by and it's—it's the nearest to here."

"And if he isn't there, you'll know soon enough," Felicity interrupts. "Now, if you don't move quick, those men are going to be occupied by an *actual* crime. Get along, Monty."

Stoic Felicity is nearly as irritating as anxious Dante. I look to Percy, hoping he'll offer a comfortable middle ground of confident concern, but his face is unreadable as he watches the thief-takers prowl the square. One of them stops to nudge the tin cup of a beggar with his toe.

"Well. I'll see you all on the other side." I tug on the edges of my coat, then start toward the nearest market stall.

"Wait." Percy's hand closes around my wrist, and when I turn back, his face is very serious. Felicity makes a rather obnoxious show of looking away from us. "Please be careful."

"I'm always careful, my darling."

"No, Monty, I mean it. Don't do anything stupid."

"I'll try my best."

Percy leans in suddenly, and I think he's going to tell me something in confidence, but instead he touches his lips to my cheek, so light and fast I doubt it happened as soon as he steps back.

"Go on," Felicity hisses at me. "They're moving."

Percy nods me forward, his hand falling from around my wrist, and as much as I'd rather cling to him and demand he kiss my cheek again so I can turn my head and he'll meet my mouth instead, I trot over to the stall at the end of the row. The lad manning it looks a few years younger than me, with spots and a bit of puppy fat clinging to his cheeks. He seems thoroughly occupied with throwing rocks at the pigeons picking at the dirt, but he glances up when I approach. I give him a smile.

And then begin loading my pockets with potatoes.

It is a bizarre sort of inverse thievery, as the primary goal of a thief is to avoid detection and I'm putting rather a lot of effort into the opposite. But that mutton-headed shop boy's entire being is held in rapture by those damnable pigeons—he hasn't so much as looked up by the time my pockets are heavy with fingerlings, each the size of my thumb and all a livid purple. I let a few fall to the ground for maximum effect, but even that doesn't commandeer his attention.

I'm getting short on room for more—going to have to start dropping them down my trousers soon—so I make a dramatic decision and kick over the entire crate. It upends with a crash, and finally, *finally*, the daftie looks up. I grab a last handful of potatoes for good measure and bolt.

"Stop him! Thief!" I hear him shout as I sprint away, directly to where the two thief-takers are standing. I pretend to spot then, try to spin around and get away, but one of them hooks me around the neck and jerks me back. The collar of my shirt nearly tears off in his hands.

The shop boy catches us up, his face bright red and his hands in fists. "He stole my potatoes!"

The thief-taker that hasn't got his arm around my neck grabs the hem of my coat and turns the pockets inside out with two good shakes. The potatoes fall to the ground in a gentle violet rain.

The swain yanks at my collar again, nearly lifting me off my feet. "What have you to say for yourself, prig?"

I fold my hands in dramatic penance and adopt my best waifish eyes. "Sorry, sir, I couldn't help it. It's just, they're such a pretty color."

"My master will have him locked up!" the shop boy shrieks. "If you don't take him, I'll fetch my master. He's tossed cutpurses in prison himself before—he'll do it again, he knows the bailiff!"

"Oh, no, please, sir, not the bailiff!" I cry in a mocking tone. Anything to rile them—I'm rather concerned they're going to let me go with nothing but a wrist slap, and then what will have been the point of this? "Your master must be a very important man to know *the bailiff.*"

"Keep quiet," the second gent growls at me. He's still collecting potatoes from the pavement.

"He's taunting me!" the shop boy cries. He's nearly stamping his feet in rage.

"Come to that conclusion all by your lonesome, did you?" I say with a wide smile. The boy throws one of the potatoes at me. It sails straight over my head and knocks the thief-taker holding me in the ear. His grip loosens, and I start to wriggle away, like I might be trying to escape, but his fellow snags me before I can get far, sacrificing his armful of potatoes to grab me by the front of my coat. I give him a wink. "Easy, darling, we've only just met."

He cracks me before I even realize he's raised his hand, a backhand that catches me under the jaw so hard I nearly lose my footing. My own hand flies up and clamps over the spot, same as where Percy put his lips to my skin just minutes ago.

"Pervert," he mutters.

A familiar tremor rumbles through me beneath the surface, like a ripple resonating from my heart as it starts to climb. All at once, this feels real, in a way it didn't before—it's not playacting, it's *real* prison and *real* constables and very real pain spiraling into panic inside me. I'm suddenly desperate for this man's hands to be off me, but I'm too afraid to move in case he thinks I'm trying to run and cracks me again. My muscles tremble for wanting it, wanting to pull away, be out of his reach. When I try to take a breath, it sticks in my chest like a knife.

Don't fall apart, I scold myself desperately, even as I can feel myself caving. *Not here, not now, do not fall apart. Don't you dare.*

I raise my head, and across the street I can see Percy, Dante, and Felicity. Dante's got both hands over his eyes, and Percy's standing a bit ahead of them, looking like he might sprint to my rescue if Felicity didn't have a hold of his arm. Our eyes meet, but then the gent drags me around, yanking my arms behind my back and clapping a set of manacles around them. The shop boy gives me a smug smile, his triumph bolstered by the stunned silence I've collapsed into. When I'm dragged away, he spits at the back of my head.

Hold yourself together, I tell myself, over and over in time to our footsteps down the street. *Hold yourself together and don't fall apart. And do. Not. Panic.*

And do. Not. Think about Father.

The march to the prison blurs. I'm shaking and sick—shakier with every step and every second longer this officer has a hold on me—and crawling with the shame of being bowled over by something as small as a knock across the cheek. My breathing is short and sharp, and I can't seem to get enough of it. My lungs feel as though they're popping against my heart.

The next thing I know, I'm standing in the foul-smelling courtyard of the prison, the clerk taking down my name, which it takes me three tries to stammer out, and informing me I'll be held until the next meeting of the general council, where I'll stand for sentencing. I'm freed from the manacles, at least, though it's the thief-taker who cracked me that removes them, and it's hard to let him touch me. He must sense the way my muscles all coil up when he draws near, because he raises his hand again, prelude to another slap, and I flinch so enormously I stumble backward and slam into the wall. As the jailer leads me away, I hear the thief-taker laugh.

A single room houses all the male prisoners. It's cramped and crowded and reeking of gents who've been unwashed for far too long. There are at least twenty of them, all looking like skeletons dug up from soft clay. Most are curled up on heaps of matted straw. A small knot are cross-legged in the center around a set of dice that look like they were carved by fingernails and teeth. The walls are damp wood, sweating from the heat—it's so hot it's hard to breathe. Everything smells of piss and rot—one man is standing in the corner, top-heavy and weaving as he relieves himself against the wall.

A few men turn in my direction when I'm shoved in. Someone wolf-whistles. I stand by the door for what is probably at least a full minute, trying to remember how to breathe, and far more of a wreck than I'd hoped to be at the pinnacle of a plan of my own devising. I am so far from heroic it's pitiful. I'm not gentlemanly or brave. I feel small and cowardly, frozen near the door and shaking like mad because I got slapped.

Pathetic, says a voice in my head that sounds like my father's.

Find Mateu Robles. I shove that thought to the forefront of my mind and focus on it. *You're running out of time.*

I force myself to raise my head and look around, taking an inventory of the men. Most of them are thickly bearded, but a good number look too young to be father to the Robles siblings, and they're mostly five-fingered, except for one of the dice players with half a pinky, and another man asleep on his back who has no arms.

Then I notice the man sitting on a ratty blanket in the corner, his thin clothes swallowing him and a gaunt, clemming look about his face. And two missing fingers—he's got his hands knotted in his lap, like a gentleman, and I can see the gaps.

Courage, I tell myself, and I think of Percy. Then I go sit beside the man. He looks up when I approach, and I'm about to ask him if he's who I hope he is, but he speaks first. "Your nose is bleeding."

Which scrambles up the speech I had planned for him. "I . . . Is it?" I swipe at it with the back of my hand

and return with a stripe of blood across my knuckles. "Damnation." I give a rather fantastic snuffle that does me no favors.

"Your jaw as well." He raises his hand—the one with two empty spaces where his ring and pinkie fingers should be—and I throw my arms up over my face before I can stop myself—such a violent motion it must have looked as though he'd drawn a knife on me. A few of the men nearby glance at us.

His arm drops. "They hurt you."

"Not much."

"Someone did, then." He stays very still, like he's worried I might spook again, then asks, "What have you been arrested for?"

"Just a theft."

"Keep your head down—you'll be fined and freed before the week is out. The guards here are devils, all of them." He speaks with the same cadence as Helena, words sifting and sliding into each other like cream swirled into coffee. He gives me a slow up-and-down, taking in the odd combination of finery and filth I have become. His eyes linger upon my lapels, and I almost look down to see if I've dripped blood upon them. "You know," he says slowly, "that looks very much like a coat I used to own."

Which is about as good a lead-in as I'm going to get. "You're Mateu Robles," I blurt.

His eyes fly to my face. "Who are you?"

I had planned this moment in my head—rehearsed it all morning, even practiced aloud to Percy, Felicity, and Dante on our walk to the market, my convincing, friendly argument that would win him over into surrendering his cipher. But instead it all tumbles out of me in a glob. "I'm Henry Montague. I mean, I'm a friend of Dante's. My name's Henry Montague. Well, not a friend, we just met him last week. I'm touring—myself and a friend—and my sister, because—not important. We're touring, and I did something daft and stole something— not the thing that got me here, some other stealing—and that something was your box with your Lazarus Key and now we're wrapped up in the mess that came with it."

Mateu blinks at me, like he's a few words behind. "You stole the Lazarus Key . . . from Dante?"

"Oh, no, we returned it to Dante. I stole it from the Duke of Bourbon."

"Why did he have it?"

"Your children gave it to him."

His face hardens, then he tips his head backward against the stone wall and lets out a long sigh. "Goddammit, Helena."

"Yes, I get the sense it was mostly her."

"Never have strong-willed children, Montague. Or at least don't allow them to adore you. Don't turn them against their mother because you think you need an ally."

"I'll remember that, sir."

"*Sir*? You're a gentleman."

"Not always." I snuffle again—I can taste blood all up and down the back of my throat. "Helena made a deal with the Duke of Bourbon."

"My release for the box, is that right?" I nod. "So if they gave it to him, why aren't I free to chastise them myself?"

"Well, I think your freedom was contingent upon the duke having access to the key. So take heart in that—he doesn't have it yet."

"Are you making a joke?"

"What?"

"*Take heart*?"

"Oh. No. Not intentionally."

"Your nose is bleeding again." I swipe at it. Mateu stares down at the blood across the back of my hand. "Did Dante tell you about his mother?"

"She's the panacea. In the tomb."

Pain darts across his features, clear as glass and sharp as flint. "I was not good to my wife, Montague. We were not good to each other."

"Then why does it matter what happens to her now? You could give the duke her heart and be free."

"If I give that heart to a man who did not count the cost, it would not be long before yet another business would spring up in this world around the barter and sale of human life."

"What do you mean?"

"Well, tell me this: Who would decide which life was worth taking so that someone else could be cured? The duke and his men want political leverage—keep their people alive, keep them in power, keep their hold on that power. And if one house has it, how long before the others want it too? With this heart in the wrong hands, imagine how many men will have to die for their kings."

"So, why didn't you destroy it? If you knew it was a dangerous thing."

"I was foolish to shut her away rather than be through with it. But it was my wife and my work, and she existed, even though she didn't really exist any longer. I can't give her to any man—noble-hearted or not—because she's my wife. That's her life." He rubs the bridge of his nose with his fingers. "Now there's nothing I can do about it." He laughs, humorless.

"But it worked?" I ask. "Her heart is truly a panacea? It will cure anything?"

"If it's consumed."

"You mean you have to *eat* it?" That's a sour thought, though I suppose one unsavory meal for a lifetime of health isn't a bad trade.

Mateu cocks his head at me. "What is your intention

with my Lazarus Key, Montague? If you're just a thief doing a good turn, why are you here?"

Which seems as good a time as any to make my offer. "If you tell me how to open the box, we'll go to Venice for you."

His eyes narrow in a very Helena-like way. "So they've sent you to work on me."

"No, I swear to it."

"Was it Helena, or the duke himself? Or has Dante been dragged in now as well?"

"Neither. None of them, I swear to it. We want to help you. The island where you've kept her—it's sinking."

He blinks. "It's what?"

"The whole thing is collapsing. If you don't get to her soon, she's going to be sleeping at the bottom of the sea forever. You're not going anywhere for a while, but we could bring her to Barcelona, if you want. Or at least take her somewhere else where she'd be protected until you could get to her. Or destroy the panacea. Whatever you want, but you're running out of time to make peace with this."

He must not have known about the sinking, for his face settles into a different sort of frown. A thinking one. "How do I know you aren't lying?"

"Look, I know what it's like," I say, "to feel you've

failed someone completely, and that you need to make penance or peace or something for that but you can't because you made a choice and now all that's left is feeling guilty for it. And if I could make it right—even in a way that didn't make it right at all—I'd take it. In a moment. And if I can do that for you, I would. I will. Please. Let us help you."

That soliloquy was not part of my rehearsed script, and I'm not entirely certain where it came from or whether it makes any difference. Mateu is drawing in the dusty prison floor with his fingers, not looking at me. "That key," he says, "and that heart, is a tremendous thing for any man to possess."

"And we know the duke will use it for ill—"

"I'm not speaking of the duke," he says. He's still scratching at the dust, but then he looks up at me, and it's a hard thing to hold his gaze. I'm feeling guiltier than I expected, because here I am clamped onto his weaknesses and twisting them up for my own intentions. But I don't let go.

I pull the cuffs of the coat over my hands, then take it off entirely and extend it to him. "Here."

He doesn't take it. "What's this for?"

"It's your coat. Sorry if I got . . . I don't think there's any blood on it." When he still doesn't move, I set it on the floor between us.

He stares at it for a moment, then smiles. "I wore that coat to both my children's christenings. It was in much better shape then." He takes the sleeve between his fingers, running them over a patch where the ribbing has frayed to nothing. "Helena would always hold my hand in one of hers and my sleeve in the other, just here. Dante—you couldn't make that child hold on to you. Never wanted to be touched or held or stood too close to. But Helena wanted to be as close to me as she could—if my hands were full, she'd clutch at my legs. Didn't want to be alone. And she was always so afraid we'd leave her. She'd wake us in the middle of the night to be certain we hadn't gone. Made her mother furious."

It is hard to imagine this Helena, with big eyes and baby teeth, weeping and lonely and sick with fear she might be left behind. But then I think of the way she's handed her mother over to the duke—perhaps handed him the lives of hundreds of men, the fate of nations—all to have her father sleeping in the next room over again.

So perhaps not hard to imagine at all.

"We used to run a string," Mateu says, fingers walking the stitchery upon the hem, "between her room and ours, one end knotted to her finger, and the other to mine. And in the night, she could give that string a tug, and I would tug back. And then she'd know I was still there."

Across the room, the prison door suddenly bangs

open, and from the hallway a jailer barks, "Henry Montague."

Dear God, my time is already up. Felicity is nothing if not aggressively punctual.

"Please," I say to Mateu. "We can help you."

"Montague!" the jailer shouts again. He's looking around for me. "Your bail has been posted."

Mateu looks up at me. "So help me," he says, and when I look down, he's drawn out six letters in the dust.

A G C D A F

"That's it? That's the cipher? It's random." I almost laugh. "It's not even a word."

"It's not random," he says. "It's notes."

"Notes?"

"Musical notes—it's a song. The first few notes of a melody to be played on the crystallophone. It's the song to summon back the dead."

"The 'Vanitas Vanitatum,'" I say.

"Henry Montague!" the jailer shouts a third time.

"I'll be Henry Montague," shouts one of the men over the dice, and someone else laughs.

"They're calling you," Mateu says. As I stand up to go, he smudges out the letters on the floor with the heel of his hand, and they're brushed back into dirt like they never existed at all.

In the courtyard of the prison, Felicity is making a good show of exasperation, very little of which is likely put-on—I assume she's channeling some of the sincere exasperation she always has for me in reserve. Dante and Percy are hovering nearby, Dante with his head down and Percy watching me approach with his face drawn. His eyes flit to my jaw, which feels tight and enormous.

"He's such a rakehell," Felicity is saying to the clerk. "Ever since we were children, he's always doing things like this. I've had to bail him out of jail more times since we arrived on the Continent— Henry, you imbecile, get along. We've a coach waiting. Thank you so much, gentleman, I'm so sorry for the trouble. You won't hear from us again." As I follow them out of the courtyard, the clerk's eyes boring into our backs, Felicity says under her breath, "Well, that's much more to my taste than seduction."

As soon as we're out of the courtyard, Dante steps in front of me, blocking my path. "Did you meet him?" he asks, and I nod. I see the questions fly across his face, shuffled like the dials of the Baseggio Box. *Was he well? Was he hurt? Did he mention me? Is he hungry? Is he sleeping? Is he thinner? Is he older?*

But instead he asks, "Did he tell you the cipher?"

I'm not certain what I feel in that moment, but it isn't the ironclad certainty I was nursing before I stepped into the prison that Percy needed to be made well and the heart was the way to do it, consequences be damned. My footing is starting to slide in my own foundations, perhaps because of the way Mateu Robles spoke of his wife, or because Helena was once a small girl with a string tied to her finger, or maybe because he trusted me with those six letters scraped into the dust and now I don't have a clue what I'm meant to do with them. He gambled all he had on me—the slowest pony in the race.

Perhaps none of us needs it. Perhaps none of us deserves to know.

But it's me—hopeless, pathetic me—who does.

"Sorry," I say, "but he didn't."

20

None of us speaks much on the walk home. Percy stays close to my side, his pinched gaze darting to my face too often to be subtle.

We arrive home late. Helena is in the kitchen, and Felicity stalks in to present her rehearsed story almost before she's been asked. *Monty was arrested, we'd better not stay, no, really, what a stunt, he's such a child, it's time for us to be moving along, so in the morning we'll be off.*

A light touch brushes my elbow. "You want some supper?" It's a moment before I realize it's Percy speaking to me, though it's just the two of us in the hallway—Dante's already slunk away.

For an odd moment, it feels like I'm standing beside myself, watching, divorced entirely from my own being. I see my arms pull up and around me. Percy's hand falls away. "No, I'm going to bed," I hear myself say.

"You haven't eaten all day. Come have something with me, you'll feel better."

"Who says I'm feeling badly?" I snap, then turn on my heel and head up the stairs.

Percy follows me into our room, closing the door behind him as I turn to the glass for a look at the damage done to my jaw. There's a thin crust of blood dried around my nose, and a bruise starting to build to the left of my chin—red and swollen for now, but I know from experience that when I wake tomorrow morning, it'll be a sunrise. The pain is a low, persistent throb like the rhythm of a song.

"Are you all right?" Percy asks. I can see him reflected behind me, no more than a shadow beneath the gauzy layer time has left splattered across the glass.

I scoop up a handful of water from the basin and scrub at the blood, leaving a faint trail through the water when it splashes back that turns from brown to red to pink before diffusing like a fist opening. "I'm fine."

"Let me see your face."

"No, don't—"

"I can't believe how hard he hit you."

"Mmm."

"It scared me."

"I'm fine, Perce."

"Let me see it—" He reaches out, and I snap, "Don't touch me." I yank away from him so hard my wrist

325

catches the basin and it rattles in the stand. Percy's hand stays raised for a moment before he draws it to his chest and holds it in a loose fold over his heart. We stare at each other in the glass, and suddenly it feels like we're at my dressing table back home, me smearing talc over a black eye to mask it and Percy trying to coax me into telling him where it had come from.

We've been here before. This is a silence we've shared.

My hands are starting to shake, so I crumple them into fists at my sides before I face him. "Don't you want to know?"

"Know what?"

"If Mateu Robles told me how to open the box."

"I don't care."

"What do you mean, you don't care? You damn well better care, because I'm doing this for you. We're here for *you*, Percy, and we're going to get to that damn tomb for you because you're the one of us that needs a panacea, so maybe be a bit grateful for that." My voice is rising and my jaw is throbbing, and I clap my hand over it, like that might stop it. "Goddamn, this *hurts.*"

Silence. Then Percy says, "I care that you're all right."

"Of course I'm all right. Why wouldn't I be all right?" I slap another handful of water across my face, then wipe it on my sleeve, trying not to wince as the material scrapes at my raw skin. "I'm going to bed. Stay if you want or go have supper. *I don't care.*" I kick my shoes off, letting them bounce at random across the floor and lie where they land before I slump down on the bed and curl onto my side, my face away from him.

Part of me wants him to be stubborn and stay. More than a part of me—I want him to come lie down with me, fit his body around mine like spoons in a drawer and not ask a thing and not be bothered by the silence. I want him to know what I need him to do, even if I'm too proud to say it.

But I hear Percy cross the room; then the door opens and latches softly behind him.

I lie still for a long time, feeling scrambled and tense. The only thing that nearly gets me out of bed again is the idea of finding something to drink, but even that isn't enough. After a time, I hear Dante's and Percy's voices drift up from the study; then Percy's fiddle starts. I recite the cipher again in my head, same as I was doing the whole way home: *A G C D A F.*

I should feel worse for lying to Mateu Robles. But if it's a choice between preserving his wife and saving Percy, it's not a choice, not for me. Someone deserves to make good use of what he's wrought, and it's certainly not the damned duke. It's me and Percy. We've as much a right as anyone. More so, perhaps, because we aren't extorting kings or selling souls or philosopher's stones. We're trying to stay together. *I'm* trying to keep us together.

I rebuild my surety of that, one shaky brick at a time, as I lie there in the blood-colored room, which grows darker as the night ages.

You're right, you're right, you're doing the right thing for the person you love.

A sliver of moon is visible between the chimneys when Percy comes up and starts shuffling about, dressing for bed. He must think me asleep, for I can tell he's making a good effort to be as silent as possible. *Say something*, I tell myself. *Apologize.* But instead I lie still, pretending to be sleeping, until he gets into bed beside me, our backs to each other with a canyon between us.

I wait until his breathing evens out into soft snores. Then I get up, put on my shoes, and go belowstairs.

There are still cinders popping in the study grate, and by their light I spot Percy's violin case beneath one of the chairs, a wad of loose music bundled beside it. The Baseggio Box is there too, on the desk. The moonlight pearls along the dials. I pick it up and spin the first dial into place. The engraved A is worn down and slick, like it's been touched often.

Robles could have lied. He had no real reason to put his trust in me. But he had no one else to turn to, and desperation is a strange soil. It turns up reason like intruding weeds.

I slide the rest of the dials into place, the first six notes of a song to summon the souls of the dead.

And then I hear a very soft click.

The drawer of the box pops out of place and inside, on a bed of dusty silk, is a small brown bone cut to the shape of a key.

I touch the tip of my finger to the bow, stroking the coarse grain of the bone. A shiver goes through me, like a winter breeze through a window. Somehow, it feels more real with my finger on the key: the gravitas of an alchemical heart that can heal all and the woman who died but not all the way for it. It feels humming, like the moment after the last notes of a song have been played.

Above me, the floorboards creak.

We have to leave for Venice—tomorrow. And we have to take this key with us or Percy's last hope will be gone. If I take it now, in the rush of next morning and the send-off they might not have time to notice. We may have quit Spain entirely before they come calling.

I can hear footsteps on the stairs, and I know that if I'm going to walk out of the house with the key, I'm going to have to hide it *now*, so I toss the box onto the desk, then snatch up Percy's violin case from under the chair and stash the key in the rosin drawer beneath the scroll. I slam the lid shut and slide the case under the desk with my foot as the study door opens.

I can't say I'm surprised when Helena appears. I do feel significantly more trapped than I expected to. She's not very large, but she's tall, and I am neither of those things. One step over the threshold and she seems to fill the whole room. She's wrapped in a dressing gown the color of heated bronze. The neckline is gaping, and her hair is down and mussed. And there must be something wrong with me, because my brain briefly flirts with the notion of how gorgeous she is.

"Mr. Newton said you went to bed," she says, her voice a smooth purr like a shuffled deck of cards.

"Came to fetch his violin." I nudge it with my foot for emphasis.

She takes a step toward me, the lapels of that open wound of a dressing gown sliding a little farther apart. She's clearly got nothing under it. "And you dressed to fetch it?"

"Well . . . didn't want to be caught wandering about the house in my underthings." It takes a Herculean effort not to look straight down the neck of her dressing gown when I say that. The lapels give her breasts narrow hand-holds with which to keep themselves out of sight.

She's very close to me now. I can see the brittle shadows her eyelashes cast against her cheeks. I take a step back, and my heels knock into the desk. "I heard you had a bit of trouble with the law earlier."

"Something like that."

"Did you find what you were after?"

"I wasn't after anything. Just stole some potatoes. It was daft."

"I mean in prison."

My heart stutters. "How did you . . . ? I wasn't after anything."

She tips her head, arms folded and one finger tapping her elbow like she's keeping time to a melody. "The problem with trusting Dante," she says, "is that he doesn't know whose side he's on."

I start to back away from her again, though there's nowhere for me to go except straight into the desk. I nearly sit atop it just to put more space between us. "I don't know what you mean."

"I know you saw my father. Did he tell you how to open the box?"

"We didn't see your father."

"Did you promise to save my mother from the sinking island in exchange for the cipher?"

"Your mother's trapped," I say. I can't help myself. "Doesn't that matter to you?"

Her eyes flash with triumph, and I know I'm caught. "So is my father. Tell me how to open the box."

"I don't know."

"You're lying. Open it for me." She reaches for the box, and the moment before her fingers fasten around it, I realize that in my haste to hide the key, I didn't shut it all the way. When she picks it up, the drawer slides out of place and clatters to the floor, empty.

We both stare down at it, like it's a firecracker

dropped between us. Then Helena says, "Where is it?"

I swallow. Lying is pointless at this juncture, but I'm clinging to ignorance with everything in me. "Where's what?"

"Where is the key, the damned key that was in here!" She flings the box against the wall and it rebounds with a *thunk*. I flinch. "What have you done with it?"

"Nothing!"

"Where is it?" She makes a snatch for my pocket, and I twist out of the way. "Give it back to me."

"Get out of my way."

I start for the door, but she shoves me before I get far. My foot catches the edge of the chair and I trip, sitting down hard enough that my teeth clack together. Helena is tearing apart the top of the desk, flinging papers and inkwells and pens to the floor as she searches for the key. Then she moves to the cabinet, wrenching it open so hard that the legs all jump.

I don't wait about for her to realize I've got it. I snatch up the fiddle case and stagger to my feet, setting a course for the hallway. "Stay where you are," Helena growls, but that's not a directive I feel I need obey. I'm not sure where I'm going to go—it's their house, after all, but at least putting a locked door between us is necessary. I dodge the chair and make a vault for the door. "I said stay—" She grabs me by the arm, dragging me backward and jamming her fist into my shoulder. It pricks like she's stabbed me with something.

She *has* stabbed me with something, I realize as I look down, though not a knife. It's too fat to be a needle and too thick to be an actual blade, and it's black and opaque as obsidian, though the color is draining out of it and into me, leaving behind crystal glass. "What are you doing?" I try to wrench it out, but she's got a beastly good grip, and shoves it deeper into my arm. I feel a shudder through my muscle, and a warm bubble of blood oozes up to the surface of my skin.

We wrestle for a minute over the needle, and she seems to be getting stronger because it's she who ends up wrenching the damn thing out of my arm. I stagger backward into the desk. The legs screech. "What was that?"

She doesn't reply. I twist around, trying to get a better sense of the wound, but it's barely a nick, shadow thin. It's hardly even bleeding, though I swear I felt it go bone deep. I seem to be victim of the least effective stabbing of all time.

Helena doesn't make to stop me, so I start for the door again, but my body doesn't seem to understand what I'm telling it to do. The fiddle case falls from my hand, and when I reach for it, I miss the handle entirely but my arm carries me into the chair. There's a crash and suddenly the chair and the fiddle case and I are all on the ground in a broken sprawl. I make another snatch at the case, but in spite of how much mental energy I'm putting into the movement, my arms hardly work. Neither do my legs, I realize, when I try to stand.

The world starts to ripple like the center of a flame, time turning stretched and distorted. And while I have, admittedly, been this high before, there's no fun in this. There wasn't a lot of fun in it before either, but at least then I knew what was happening. Now this insane woman has stuck some sort of poisoned pen in me and I'm fairly certain that my body is losing its ability to perform basic functions at the behest of whatever was inside it.

Helena is suddenly right overtop of me, her face ghoulish and frightening. With the firelight on her cheekbones, it looks like she's burning. She's tearing at my clothes, trying to find the key she seems convinced I've hidden there.

"Stop," I manage to get out.

"Oh, sweetheart." She pats my cheek and it rattles through me. "You should be long gone by now."

My throat is feeling very closed up and my sight slides into a thin black line. "Oh, for God's sake," I hear Helena growl; then she slaps me across the face and everything comes crashing back. The blow turns the world into a splintered looking glass. I can see her face three times above me. "Come on, wake up. Tell me where it is."

"You . . . stole it," I murmur.

"No, *you* stole it. It's mine to begin with—it belongs to *us,* and I'm going to do what needs to be done with it to save my father. Now, where is it?" When I don't answer, she hits me again, so hard my neck wrenches. "Tell me. Where—"

And I can't fight back or defend myself and suddenly I can hear my father's voice in my head—*Put your hands down*—and I'm not sure whether it's now or one of so many times that I tried to protect myself and wasn't permitted to.

She slaps me again. "—is it?"

Get up and stop crying and put your hands down and look at me when I'm talking to you.

"What about your mopsy little sister?" Helena grabs my face and forces me to look at her. My vision is falling in and out of focus. "Has she got it? She was lurking here earlier. I'll find her next."

She rolls off me and clambers to her feet, heel snagging in the hem of her dressing gown as she makes for the door. She's reaching for the handle when suddenly the door bangs open, and she staggers backward. I think for a moment it must have struck her. Then there's a *clang* and Helena drops like a stone, collapsing to the floor in a boneless heap. And there on the threshold is Percy, wielding the brass bed warmer with which he's just clubbed Helena. "God, Monty." There's another

335

clang as he tosses it to the ground and drops to his knees beside me.

The world is making less and less sense. Percy's trying to shake me awake, and I can hear him calling for Felicity, and the entirety of my strength is devoted to not losing consciousness. "Monty, can you hear me? Monty!"

I turn my head and vomit. It's a struggle to breathe, but I don't know if that's because I'm choking on my own sick or because part of dying is not breathing so it's got to happen sometime soon.

Percy pulls me up into a sitting position, and I start to cough hard. He slaps me on the back, and then suddenly I'm breathing again.

"Stay awake," Percy is saying. "Stay awake, stay awake," and then it sounds like he's saying, "Stay alive."

Put your goddamn hands down, Henry.

The next thing I know I'm lying on my side on hot, slick cobblestones. Or maybe it's me that's hot and slick—my skin feels damp, like I'm drying off from a swim. But my head is on something soft, and I realize it's Percy's lap. I've got my head in Percy's lap and he has his fingers on my forehead and he's smoothing my hair. And the worst part is I'm in such miserable shape I can't even enjoy it.

"He's coming round," I hear Felicity say. Then, "Monty, can you hear me?"

My stomach turns over, and I realize what's about to

happen the moment before it does. I wrench away from Percy—my limbs are weak but praise God they at least somewhat obey me—and lurch sideways on my elbows, into what is thankfully a gutter, before I vomit. And then again. And again. And there's nothing left in me and I'm still on my hands and knees, retching.

My arms give out, and I nearly go face-first into the cobblestones, but Percy catches me. He holds on to me while I gag, pulling my hair back and rubbing my shoulders until my stomach finally settles, and then he draws me to him, his fingers massaging my skin. I'm sick and shaking and clutching Percy and suddenly I'm thinking of him ill and helpless in Marseilles and how poorly I'd been able to deal with that, and now here he is, knowing just what to do. Perhaps everyone is born with this caring knack in them but me.

Felicity crouches down in front of me. "Monty?"

I'm still clinging to Percy like a leech. Felicity reaches out like she's going to touch my face, but all I can feel is Helena slapping me and the thief-taker raising his hand just to see me flinch and then it's my father, and all the while me with no power to fight back or protect myself against any of them.

And I begin to cry.

Though *cry* seems far too gentle a word. I begin to abso-bloody-lutely sob.

Felicity is kind enough to look away. Percy is kind

enough not to. He puts his arms around me and lets me turn my face in to his shoulder because I'm trying to stop and that's making it worse, so stifling it is second-best. "It's all right," he says, his hand working in soft circles on my back, which just makes me cry harder. "You're safe, you're all right." And I go on crying, great rolling sobs that rip through my whole body, and I can't seem to stop. I can hardly breathe. I cry and I cry—it's years' worth of it, and it's years overdue.

I don't realize I've stopped until I wake up again—I fell asleep or insensible or whatever happens to you when you're sobbing and trying to rid yourself of a drug. Percy is still holding me, though he's shifted so that it's my head on his shoulder, my body curled into his, and one of his arms around the small of my back. My face feels swollen and tight, a shameful reminder of completely losing my mind when I thought about Helena striking me and somehow it turned into my father.

I sit up, and Percy starts beside me. He must have been dozing. "You're awake," he says. "How are you feeling?"

"Better," I say, which is the truth. I feel exquisitely more myself than I did before, though still rattled to my core, and my stomach isn't yet sitting well. A foul taste shakes loose in my throat, and I cough.

Percy pushes my hair out of my eyes, his thumb lingering upon my temple. I still feel right up against the verge of tears, so I press my face into the crook of my elbow, like there's anything subtle about that. "What happened?"

"We ran." He offers a small smile. "Only a few hours earlier than we were planning to anyway."

"What about Helena? And Dante?"

"We were gone before Helena came to. And Felicity stuck a chair under the handle of Dante's bedroom door, though I don't think he would have done anything to stop us. She's very dastardly, your sister."

"Did you get your fiddle?" I ask.

"What?"

"Your fiddle. Have you got it?"

"It's only a fiddle, it doesn't matter."

"Did you?"

"Yes." He shifts so I can see where it's sitting on his other side.

Warm relief floods me—the first pleasant sensation I've enjoyed in days. "Where's Felicity?" I scrub my hands hard against my eyes, then peer down the street in either direction. We're under a long, cobbled bridge, a canal lapping at the gutter in front of us. The smell is rancid—rotted fruit and piss and sewage stewing in the heat. "Where are we?"

"Somewhere near the docks. Felicity's gone to see about a boat back to France."

"We're going back?"

"Where else would we go?"

339

We're interrupted by the slap of wooden heels on cobblestones, and a moment later Felicity sinks down on my other side. "You're awake."

"So are you."

"I think your case is a bit more noteworthy." She puts the back of her hand against my cheek, the movement a bit stuttered, likes she's afraid I might start to cry again. "Your color's much better. And you're not so cold."

"We're going to get cut up and sold back to Father in pieces down here."

"Oh, Monty, you're so dramatic." She tests my pulse with two fingers, then asks, "Do you remember what happened?"

"Helena poisoned me."

Felicity gives a little sigh through her nose. "She did not poison you."

"She stabbed me with something." I pull up my sleeve to show her, but the mark from the needle is gone. "And then everything went wrong."

"It was the *Atropa belladonna*."

"The what?"

"Sleeping nightshade—one of the alchemical cure-alls they had in their cabinent. It's not a poison, it's an anesthetic that sends the body into a temporary coma-tose state to heal. It made you look . . . quite dead."

"Well, I'm not."

"Obviously," Felicity says, at the same time Percy

murmurs, "Thank God."

I sit up straight, pulling my legs up to my chest with a wince. "We need to get away from here, before the Robleses find us."

"Why would they care what happens to us?" Felicity says. "It's not good that we know about their mother's alchemical heart, but I imagine they'll have other things on their mind now that they've got their box back."

"About the box." I tip my chin toward Percy's fiddle case. Percy and Felicity are wearing twin expressions of dread as he flips it open.

"What were you thinking?" Felicity cries as Percy lifts the lid on the rosin drawer to reveal the Lazarus Key. "We're trying to get rid of it! That's why we brought it to them."

"I couldn't leave it—Mateu Robles told me how to open the box." I fish the key from the drawer—my hands are still so shaky it takes three tries to get a grip—then hold it flat on my palm. We all three bend our heads together to examine it. It's well small, I realize now that I have it in the light. The teeth look like nothing more than the feathered ends left after a bone is snapped. On one side of the bow is inscribed the Lion of Saint Mark, the patron saint of Venice.

When I look up from the key, Felicity is glaring at me. "So. What precisely are you planning to do with this now that you've stolen it again?"

"I think we should go to Venice and collect the heart," I say.

"What for?"

"For Percy."

I look over at him. He lifts the key from my palm and holds it upon his own. "Did you find a boat?" he asks Felicity.

"Several," she replies. "There's a fleet of xebecs that go between Genoa, Barcelona, and Marseilles—the next one leaves in an hour or so. They're not meant to carry passengers, but they'll take us on." She pauses, then adds, "If we can pay."

"Unless you two had a windfall while I was mostly dead, we're short in that department," I say.

"Well, yes, that's where my plan collapses. I think first we need to decide where it is that we're going."

"We can't go back to Marseilles," I say. "Not yet. We should sail to Genoa and from there find a way to Venice."

"But that heart is not ours to use," Felicity protests. "A woman died for it."

"But we need it," I say. "And if she's already dead, then what's the difference if it's used or not?"

Felicity's eyebrow hitches. "*We* need it, do we?"

"Percy needs it," I amend. It seems a trifle not worth addressing. It's not as though any of us don't know what I'm speaking of.

"What say you, Percy?" Felicity asks.

Percy closes his fist softly around the key. "I don't want to take her life."

"Why not?" I ask.

He looks up at me, a bit surprised, like he didn't think he was going to have to argue this point. "God, Monty, I couldn't live with that. Knowing I stole this woman's life from her so I could be well."

"But she's already dead. Someone should use it and it shouldn't be the duke and you need to be well."

"I don't *need*—"

"What about Holland? If you were well, you could come home. You wouldn't have to leave. And you and I, we could . . ." I've no notion how I was meaning to finish that sentence, so I trail off and let him fill it in however he wants. I'm certain Felicity's filling it in as well, which is mortifying considering she seems to know more than Percy about my feelings toward him, but I don't look at her.

"Or, what if we . . . ?" Percy trails off, staring down at the key again. He turns it over with his thumb, his other hand working on the back of his neck. A small crease appears between his eyebrows.

"Whatever we do, we're the only ones who can get to her now," I say. "We've got to do something with that."

"You don't have to—" Felicity says to Percy, but he abruptly returns the key to its resting place in his violin case.

"Fine," he says, eyes still downcast. "Let's go to Venice."

Relief funnels through me, though it's followed by a bitter aftertaste I can't account for. Percy looks more stricken than I feel he ought to, and Felicity's still watching him, like she's seeing something that I'm not.

"Do we have time to catch the next ship?" I ask. I start to climb to my feet, but a wave of nausea lurches through me, everything left inside of me demanding to be outside of me, and I collapse backward before I've gotten far.

Percy's hand grazes my back. "Steady on."

"I'm fine." I try to stand again, and stagger into Percy. He grabs me under the arms and eases me back down onto the stones. "We have to go," I protest, though it's pitifully feeble this time.

"We can wait a few days," Felicity says. She's looking rather concerned as well.

"But the island is sinking and the Robleses are looking for us," I murmur.

"Both excellent reasons, but I don't think you'd get far in this state." Felicity stands up, brushing off her hands on her skirt. "I'm going to go see if I can find something for us to eat."

I raise my head. "I don't want—"

"I was thinking for Percy and me—not *all* sacrifices being made are on your behalf, you know." She revels in that telling-off for a moment, then adds, "Though you should try to eat something. It might help."

"Do you want me to go?" Percy asks, but Felicity shakes her head.

"I'm much more waifish-looking than you—and Monty still looks like he's recently risen from the dead. Stay here, I'll be back soon."

As soon as she's gone, I slump against the wall, pressing my cheek against it. My hair snags on the stone.

"What if we can't find it?" Percy asks suddenly.

"Find what?"

"The tomb. The heart. Or what if we get there and it's already sunk?"

"It won't be."

"But what if it is? Or if it isn't real, or it doesn't make any difference? If I'm still ill at the end of all this, what do we do then?"

"It's going to work."

"But if it doesn't." A ragged note of frustration punctures his tone. "What if there was another way?"

"Another way to what? Make you well?"

"No, to keep me from being put away."

"Stop worrying, darling. It's going to work." A chill goes through me and I shudder hard. "It's cold."

"It's not. You've just got belladonna in you." Percy shucks off his coat and wraps it around me, rubbing his hands up and down my arms. He smiles at me, and

I slump forward into him, head against his chest. He laughs. "Want to sleep?"

"Desperately." I think he means to let me lie down on the cobblestones, but instead he pulls me in to him, folded into his arms like we together are a single thing. It is not, strictly speaking, the most comfortable position I've ever been in. The bruise on my jaw is throbbing where it's pressed against his shoulder, and my knees are curled up at an awkward angle that starts them aching straightaway. A strand of his hair keeps fluttering against my nose, threatening to bring on a sneeze, but I don't move.

"What can I do for you?" he asks, and I think suddenly of Mateu and Helena, a string tying them together so she knew they'd never be apart. Two hearts, knotted.

"Don't go anywhere, all right?"

"I won't." I can feel him breathing, low and even, and I focus on that rise and fall until my own falls into time with it, a stumbling vibrato like the notes from his violin.

At Sea

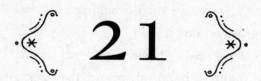

21

There is a single merchant xebec departing the following day that will dock first in Marseilles, then in Genoa, before moving to the open waters of the Mediterranean. The boatswain, a stocky cove with wiry hair and pox scars spat across his cheeks like holes in a cribbage board, lets himself be sweet-talked by Felicity and agrees to take us on so long as we pay in France. We don't elaborate on the particulars of how that payment will occur—I hardly think we can pop in on Lockwood, collect some coinage, then dash out the door again, nor do I expect he's been twiddling his thumbs in Marseilles all this while waiting for us to turn up.

Or rather, the boatswain's willing until he realizes it's Percy and me who will be traveling with her.

"Who's this?" he demands, pointing a finger at Percy that halts us as we start up the gangplank.

"Your passengers," Felicity replies. "I did say there were three of us."

"Is he yours?"

"He's his own."

"No." The boatswain is shaking his head. "I'll not have Negroes on our ship."

"You have colored men on your crew!" Felicity replies, flinging a hand up toward the deck where two dark-skinned men are hauling cargo.

"Don't like Negroes we don't own," he replies. "Can't control them. Free Africans get big ideas about their own grandeur. I don't want him on my ship."

Percy looks horrified. Felicity looks as though she'd like to skin the boatswain alive, but she puts on at least a pretense of politeness and attempts to elicit some sympathy. "He's not African, he's English, same as we are. We're from highborn families, all. Our father"—and here she scribbles a hand between herself and me—"is a peer of the realm. He's an earl. We can pay you whatever you ask. We're stranded here without means, sirrah, please, have a bit of compassion."

The boatswain is maddeningly unmoved. "No free colored men on board."

So Felicity abandons compassion and whips out the law. "Slavery is illegal in this kingdom, sir."

"And we make berth in the Virginia colony, madam," he replies, then mutters under his breath, just loud enough for her to hear, "Bitch."

For a moment, it seems a real possibility that Felicity is about to shove him off the gangplank and into the sea. Good luck for the boatswain that he chooses that moment to spit into the brown water, then stalk past her and down the dock. Felicity gives his back a murderous look.

"I'm sorry," Percy says, his voice hoarse.

"It's fine," Felicity says, though she's clearly mourning the collapse of her plan.

"I'm *so* sorry," he says again.

"Nothing to be done about it." Felicity's attention has been commandeered by two men shuffling up the gangplank past her, dressed so gentlemanly that they must be passengers. She watches them go, her fingers drumming against her folded arms, then starts to follow.

"What are you doing?" I hiss at her, making a snatch for her sleeve and missing so spectacularly I almost pitch into the water.

She halts midway up the gangplank and turns back. "We have to get there somehow. And he did agree to take us."

"So we're going to, what—stow away?"

"The next ship to Genoa doesn't leave for a fortnight. So unless you have an alternative, this is our only choice."

Neither Percy nor I follow her, but, undeterred, she

continues upward. "Felicity," I hiss after her, casting around to see where the boatswain's gone. "What if they catch us?" I'm keen on getting to Venice, but the risk affixed to this stratagem seems far too high. If we're caught, that would put a knot in our itinerary that could take a long while to untangle. Our beloved island would likely be a sunken thing by the time we reached it.

She turns back yet again, looking rather vexed, which is unfair since she's the one being unreasonable here. "What will they do? Throw us into the ocean? Maroon us in a dinghy for African pirates to scoop up?"

"What if he catches *me*?" Percy asks.

She considers that for a moment, then says, "We won't get caught. Now step lively."

As she stalks up the gangplank, walking with such confidence that I half believe she belongs there, I take Percy by the arm. "We don't have to," I tell him. "We can wait for the next boat."

"It's fine," he says, casting another glance over his shoulder for the boatswain. "Let's just go quick before he comes back."

Felicity doesn't bother to try blending in with the few passengers skirting about—we're far too vagabond-looking to shuffle unnoticed among the half-dozen gentlemen in their wool traveling suits, and she seems to be the only lady on board. Instead she goes straight below—a few of the sailors deal her curious looks, but no one stops us—all the way down to the nether regions of the ship where the cargo is stored, haphazard shelves of wooden crates protected from the pitching sea by the grip of rope netting. Most of it has already been loaded. The air is thick and stifling, hazy with the smell of packed goods and rotted wood. The only light comes from the sunbeams filtering down from the deck two levels above us, and a lonely tin lantern wavering on its hook. From somewhere in the rigging, the ship's bell is tolling in warning of departure.

Felicity squeezes herself into a hollow space between rows of barrels stamped with the tangled "VOC" of the Dutch East India Company, her back against the wall. Percy and I follow, Percy with a bit more discomfort due in part to his beastly long legs. He drags his fiddle case after us.

"Not quite the view I was hoping for," I say once we're all wedged tight.

"Oh, don't be so dramatic," she replies, with an eye roll that's far more dramatic than I was being. "It'll be a quick jaunt to France—seven days, depending upon the weather—then another week to Genoa, after a few days docked."

"That's near two weeks," I say, "and then there's the time overland to get to Venice, which will be another five days at least. The duke is going to be waiting there if he decides to give chase."

"Do you think they'll follow us?" Percy asks.

"They must know where we're going," I reply. "Now that we've got the key, there's only one conceivable place. I can't imagine Helena is the sort to sit back and let—"

"Hush," Percy hisses, and I fall silent. There are heavy footfalls on the stairs, then the *thwack* of a load being dropped. The floor trembles. None of us makes a sound, and a moment later the footsteps retreat up the stairs again, the lantern going with them, and we fall into a darkness filigreed by the dust motes and faraway snatches of sunlight.

Felicity shifts her weight and her foot slams hard into one of the barrels. It might be my imagination, but I'm almost certain I hear her curse under her breath. "Comfortable?" I ask.

She scowls at me. "Once we're out to sea, we'll be able to move around a bit more."

"You mean walk all the far distance to the other side of this hold?"

"We can still disembark, if you're inclined to be moaning all the way."

I look from her to Percy. He's got his elbows on his fiddle case and his chin resting upon his hands. "No," I say. "We've got to get to Venice somehow."

We spend what I imagine is close to five days in the cargo hold of the xebec, and though we aren't wedged quite so tight all the while as we were those first few hours, we can't risk much movement. We've barely left Barcelona before my knees begin to feel as though they're going to snap like brittle sticks. My stomach still isn't quite back to its good-natured, gin-swilling self yet and I spend a not-insignificant portion of the time feverish and nauseous, trying not to be sick as the ship rolls, since there's nowhere to do so conveniently. It's uncomfortable enough already, the three of us in such close quarters with nowhere to go for privacy. The farthest we can venture is the other side of the hold, which is hardly any distance at all.

I have little interest in food, but Felicity and Percy are both maddeningly unmoved by the pitching, so we crack into a few of the crates in search of provisions. They're mostly raw Dutch wares—Holland linens, blocks of nutmeg and black tea leaves and tobacco, crumbly sugarcane in amber cones, and cacao nibs that are so bitter and sharp they make us all gag when we chew them. The barrels yield little-better spoils—the first two we open are syrupy molasses, another flax oil, which sloshes over the rim when the ship rolls and soaks through all our shoes, leaving us skating the planking. The final barrel we try is a cask of dark wine, and we drink it from cupped hands like the philistines we have become.

We rest in staggered shifts, with one of us always on watch in case crewmen decide to make a spontaneous visit to the hold. The lingering effects of the belladonna have me sleeping more than is my fair share, but Felicity and Percy are kind enough not to chastise me for it. Felicity still looks at me like she's petrified I might start sobbing again with no warning, and Percy's sharp attention to my every movement is making me feel like an invalid.

It's several days before I take my first proper watch, nestled into a nook where I can see the stairs, but just out of sight and wishing there was something stronger than wine in the barrels sheltering me. The last drink I had was at the opera house, and I'm feeling the want of it like an itch in my lungs. Gray light creeps down the stairs from the upper decks, fogged by the dust that hovers in the air. On the deck above me, the sailors are shouting to each other. A bell begins to toll.

There's a shuffle on the other side of the hold, and when I raise my head, Percy is picking his way through the crates toward me, his hair wound into a knot with a scrap of sailing rope and his bare shirtsleeves drooping around his elbows.

"Hallo, darling," I say as he slides down against the wall beside me. The lacquer pulls at his shirt and drags it up so that I catch a flash of his bare stomach. I look away quickly, though I'd prefer to openly ogle. There's not a thing on God's green earth that has the power to disarm me quite like two inches of Percy's skin. "You're meant to be sleeping, you know. Don't waste my time."

"Can't sleep. Got tired of lying in the dark. Do you want to? I'll stay up."

"No, I think I need to start pulling my weight as a watchman."

"Mind if I sit up with you, then?" He leans down to rest his head upon my shoulder, but sits up again before I can get excited that we're cuddling up. "You smell terrible."

I laugh, and Percy shushes me with a meaningful look in Felicity's direction. "Thank you, darling." It is, by conservative estimate, several thousand degrees, stuffed up here in the hold. We've both shed our duds nearly down to our stockings and I'm still soaked through.

"How are you feeling?" he asks.

"Better. Didn't throw up my supper, so I suppose that's progress."

"How's your chin?" He takes my face in his hand and tips it into the dawn light tumbling down the stairway.

"Not the worst hit I've ever taken." I smile at him, but he doesn't return it.

His thumb brushes the bruise. "I wish I could do something."

"Well, stop rubbing it, for a start."

"I mean about your father."

"Oh." I drop my eyes, heart suddenly feeling heavy and swollen inside me. "Me too."

"What are you going to do about him?"

What was I going to do? I had been doing my best to avoid looking head-on at my future, with my father breathing down my neck for the next few years. Even when I took over the estate in earnest, he'd still find ways to creep into my life like spiders rising up through the floorboards—I'd be living in his house, sleeping in his bed and sitting at his desk, and married off to a woman he'd chosen for me. That last one cankered inside me. I'd spend the rest of my life lonely, cruising Mulberry Garden for purchasable companionship and pining for the boy with dark freckles beneath his eyes. I can see them now, in that sliver of moonlight, as he tips his head.

"I suppose I'll learn all about estate management and try to guard my face." I scrub my hands through my hair, then add with more levity, "And then perhaps I'll pay a sly call to Sinjon Westfall from my Eton days and see if he remembers me." I look over for Percy's smile, but instead his nose wrinkles. "What's that for?"

"What's what for?"

"That face."

"I didn't make a face."

"You did, just now when I mentioned Sinjon. There, you did it again."

He claps his hands over his eyes. "Stop mentioning him, then."

"Why are you sour on poor Sinjon? You didn't know him."

"Felt like I did—you wrote me all those letters with him prominently featured."

"Not *that* many."

"Every week—"

"For a fortnight, maybe—"

"No, it was longer. *Far* longer."

"Was not."

"'Dear Percy, I saw this boy across the dining hall with a dimple in his chin.' 'Dear Percy, his name is Sinjon and he has eyes so big and blue you could drown in them.' 'Dear Percy, blue-eyed Sinjon put his hand on my knee in the library and I thought I might lose consciousness.'"

"Well, that's not at all what happened. *I* was the one who made the first approach, and it was certainly not his knee I put my hand on. Why waste time on the knees when he had far, far better—"

"Please stop."

I glance over at him. He's looking rather sincerely distressed, his face pulled up and his gaze pained. "What's the matter?"

"Nothing."

"It's not nothing. Tell me."

"There's nothing to tell!"

"I'm going to pester you until you tell me."

"How much longer do you think we've got before we reach France?"

"That was the worst attempt at a subject change I've ever heard."

"Worth a try."

"A poor one."

"Your hair looks nice."

"Better, but a lie."

"No, I like it long and scraggly like this."

"*Long and scraggly.* What a charmer you are."

"I just meant the rugged look suits you."

"You're avoiding the question." He groans, and I nudge his shoulder with my nose. "Go on, tell me."

"Fine." He rubs his temples, a bit of a sheepish smile starting about his mouth. "Those letters . . . wrecked me."

That was not what I had been expecting. *Too long* or *too mushy* or *Dear God, Monty, use less descriptors, how many shades of blue can be contained in a lad's dreamy eyes?* perhaps. But not that. "What?"

"Completely lost my mind. Half the time I couldn't read them, just tossed them in the fire."

"They weren't *that* gooey."

"Oh, they were plenty. You were *moony.*"

"So maybe I was. Why did that bother you?"

"Why do you think?" Percy looks at me quick, like he didn't mean to say it and is checking for my reaction, then away just as fast. A slow flush crawls up his neck, and he scrubs a hand over the back, like it might be wiped away. When he speaks again, his tone is nearer to reverence, a voice for saints and sacred places. "Go on, you must know by now."

My heart makes a reckless vault, flinging itself against the base of my throat so that it's suddenly hard to breathe around it. I'm desperate not to let all my stupid hope fill the silence between us but it's filtering in anyway, like water running through the canyons that longing has spent years carving. "I don't . . . I don't think I dare."

"I kissed you in the music hall."

"*I* kissed *you*."

"You were drunk."

"So were you. And *you* stopped it."

"*You* told me it didn't mean anything to you. *That's* why I stopped it."

When our eyes meet, his mouth rises into a smile, almost as though he can't help himself, and then I'm smiling too, and then his goes wider, and it seems we might be caught in an infinite loop of beaming at each other like fools. And I wouldn't mind it a bit.

"What are we arguing about?" I ask.

"I don't know."

My heart is sending tremors through me, a frantic flail like a bird landing on water. I can feel the ripples all the way to my fingertips. *Maybe . . . maybe . . . maybe.* It makes me brave, the sudden chance of it tying stones to the fear and loneliness of one-sided wanting until they sink out of sight. So I take a breath and say, "It meant something to me—that kiss. That's what I should have said. I didn't, because I was stupid and afraid. But it did. It does."

He stares forward into the darkness for a long while, or perhaps it's not long at all, but I swear those few silent seconds seem to last half my lifetime. In the end, he doesn't say a thing. Just reaches over and puts his hand upon my knee. A burst goes through me, like teeth breaking through the skin of a summer fruit in its prime.

Knees, as it turns out, can be rather grand.

I put my hand overtop, fingers fitted between his. His heart is beating so hard I can feel it in every point where our skin meets. Or perhaps that's mine. We're slamming, both of us. Percy stares down at our stacked hands, a deep breath trembling in his shoulders. "I'm not going to be the most convenient mouth around when you're drunk and lonely and missing blue-eyed Sinjon," he says. "That's not what I want."

"I don't want Sinjon. I don't want anyone else."

"You mean that?"

"I do," I say. "I swear to it." I touch my nose to his, a fawn-soft brush, and his breath presses against my mouth as he exhales. "What do you want?"

Percy hooks his bottom lip with his teeth, eyes flitting down to my mouth. The space between us—what little is left—grows charged and restless, like a lightning strike gathering. I'm not certain which of us is going to do it—close those last, longest inches between us. I touch my nose to his again, and his lips part. Breath catches. I close my eyes.

And then, on the deck above us, a cannon goes off.

22

The recoil trembles through the whole boat. I lurch into Percy, my chin catching hard on his shoulder, and he grabs me, one hand fisted around my shirt and his other around my wrist. The bell is really going—somehow I'd failed to hear it—and the sailors are shouting, orders and "all hands" alike. There's a holler of "Fire!" and another cannon blasts. We hear the *bang* at the discharge, then again as the frame slams into the planks, straight over our heads. The smell of gunpowder kicks through the rot. My heart begins to pound for a different reason.

On the other side of the hold, Felicity's dark silhouette tears itself away from the shadows. "What's going on?" she calls, and Percy's hands slide away from my waist.

"They're firing—" I start, but then a cannonball tears through the wall above our heads.

I throw my hands up over my face as the air rips apart around us. Percy yanks me to him, his head over mine as we both hit the deck. A shower of dust and splinters speckles the back of my neck. There's a second splintering from above, another cannonball breaching our hull. My ears are ringing, and when I take a breath, I gag on the dust and gunpowder—the air is hazy and sparkling with it. On the other side of the hold, Felicity starts to cough.

"Are you all right?" Percy takes my face between his hands and raises it to his. He's kneeling before me, his dark skin powdered and his hair sprinkled with flakes of wood. Above us, a stream of water sluices in through the hole left by the cannonball and dribbles down in a thin waterfall. The knees of my breeches go damp.

"Fine," I say, though the word comes out as more of a gasp. "Fine, I'm fine. Felicity?"

"I'm fine," she replies, though her voice sounds too tight. She's hunched over between the crates, one hand clamped against her arm. A thin line of crimson leaks between her fingers and spills down her knuckles.

"You're bleeding!" I scramble to my feet, Percy crawling after me. "Fire!" is called again, and the guns buck, pitching us sideways into the cargo.

"I'm fine," she says, and I almost believe her—beyond a clenched jaw, she hardly looks like she's pained. "Just a graze from the splinters."

"Can you—do you need to bandage it? Or can I—what do we—should we do something? What do we do?"

"Calm yourself, Monty, it's not *your* arm." She crooks her finger at me. "Give me your cravat."

It's Percy who hands his over first, and Felicity peels her fingers from the slash above her elbow and wraps it so fast I hardly get a look at it. She pulls the cloth tight with her teeth before either of us can offer assistance, then wipes a bloody palm print upon her skirt. The sight of it makes me a bit woozier than is admirable.

There's another blast and the ship gives a spectacular cant, so violent that one of the rope nets around a stack of crates breaks and they go flying free. From high above us—higher than the top deck, even—there's a creak like a tree falling, then the long, low wail of wood splitting. We all three duck, pressing closer to each other, though we can't see what it is that's coming down. The ship gives its greatest heave yet. A barrel tips and breaks, flooding the hold with violet wine. Another swell of seawater pours in through the hole.

Then, silence, a long, eerie stretch of it. None of us say a thing to each other. Up on the top deck, a few sailors yell. There's a single gunshot, like the bark of a seagull.

After a long while, there's a hard slam on the deck above our heads and we all jump. A chorus of shouted surprise follows, then a man calls in French, "Everyone above!" A whole chorus of gunshots. Loud voices in a language I don't recognize.

"What's going on?" I ask quietly.

"We need to get out of sight," Felicity replies. She's watching the stairs, her face drawn in a way that is nothing like pain.

"Why?"

"Because I think we're being boarded by pirates."

For a moment, there seems to be no conceivable way that our ship is truly under siege by actual, godforsaken Mediterranean pirates. Not a chance. We already did our time with the highwaymen, and I am certain that no tourists—not even those in possession of an alchemical key—should have to endure both.

There's a commotion above, heavy footfalls and then another shot and a scream of pain. Felicity scrambles into the trench between the rows of VOC barrels, with Percy and me close behind her. We collapse in a heap between the barrels, our heads ducked low and backs pressed into their divots, all of us breathing like we've been sprinting. Between the near-kiss with Percy and now goddamned pirates, my heart is certainly being put through its paces today.

For a time, all we can hear are indistinguishable noises from above. Shouting and cursing and the *chink* of hobnailed boots and axe heads ripping into wood. The bell tolling like mad. Then, the first certain sound in a long while, thundering footsteps on the stairs leading down to the hold, accompanied by men's voices in that foreign tongue. Between us, Percy's hand fumbles for mine.

Then three men who are most certainly not members of the xebec crew come bounding into view, a lantern thrust aloft by the one in the lead. He's dark-skinned, with a thick black beard and a tar's garb. His fellows are all similarly skinned and outfitted, and they've all got pistols and wicked axes strapped to their hips, belts weighted with pouches of grapeshot and musket balls. I can hear the lead chatter with itself as they move.

They spread themselves across the hold, prying the tops off crates to get a look at what's inside and riffling through. One of the men cracks a barrel open like an egg—graceless, with the head of his axe—and his mate gives him a reprimand.

The first man comes near to our hiding spot and all three of us shrink backward. A cloud of splintery dust from the cannon blast blooms from the material of my shirt.

And Percy sneezes.

The pirates freeze. We freeze too, except for Percy, who claps a hand over his mouth. Behind his fingers, he's wearing the same look of horror Felicity and I are both giving him.

And then he goddamn sneezes again. His hand isn't near enough to stifle it.

The pirate nearest us disappears from our view, calling out to his mates in his dialect. I think for a moment we might miraculously be unnoticed, but then the barrel shielding us is kicked out of the way and there they are, looking as shocked to see us as we are to see them. For a minute, we all regard each other in stunned silence. Then one grabs me by the front of my shirt, dragging me to my feet. "We said everyone on deck," he says in French, his face very close to mine. His breath could strip paint.

Before I can protest, I'm shoved into the arms of the biggest of the three men, which seems unfair because I'm nearly as small as Felicity. Before the men can grab Percy, he snatches up his fiddle case and swings it at one of them like there's some hope of escape if we resist, but they are impervious to the stunt that felled the Duke of Bourbon in the forest. The pirate, a man with a bacon face and a glass eye, catches the fiddle case and wrenches it out of Percy's hand, then hauls him to his feet and pins his arms to his sides.

The man with the lantern holds out a hand to Felicity to help her to her feet, but, proud thing that she is, she doesn't take it. The makeshift bandage done up around her arm is beginning to blush as the blood seeps through it.

The man laughs. "Let's report," he calls, then bows Felicity up the stairs. "After you, miss."

They march us out of the hold—not a one of us is fully dressed or wearing shoes, and we leave purple foot-prints from the spilled wine on the stairs—and up to the top deck, where chaos reigns. One of the yards has come down—that must have been the final tremendous ruckus—and is caught on sails around it, dragging them all out of alignment. The mast itself looks unsteady, wob-bling in the wind as though it might tip at any moment. The sailors and the handful of passengers—most of them still in their nightclothes—have been herded like sheep onto the quarterdeck, more of the Moorish pirates roaming between them with swords and axes drawn. Everyone's been made to kneel and put their hands upon their heads. Spread at their feet are what must be their luggage, trunks and cases looted and their contents scat-tered. No one seems injured, but those hangers and axes and steel-toothed marlinspikes in the pirates' hands look ready to reverse that with little effort. It's the early hours of the morning—the horizon is the color of a tarnished ha'penny with a few stars left fading into its blush. Against the rust-colored burn of the sunrise, I can make out the pirates' ship, a gaunt, three-masted silhouette. From the top yard, they fly a black pennant.

The xebec's captain is nowhere to be seen, but there is a pirate standing guard before a cabin door and the latch is rattling like someone's shaking it from the other side. The first mate and the boatswain are being held at gunpoint by a fellow who seems to be in charge of the corsairs, since he's the one with the biggest hat, and the only cove watching everyone do something rather than doing something himself. He's got a lanky build, with a black beard and a long coat fastened by a sash with frayed edges. "Who did you find?" he calls to his men as they approach with me and Percy pinned and Felicity trailing them like a martyr.

"They were belowdecks," the big one holding me calls.

The boatswain must be truly furious we snuck past him, because as soon as he spots us he goes from looking as though he's fearing for his own life to looking as though we should be fearing for ours. "You," he hisses at Felicity.

The captain of the pirates tips his pistol toward us. "Friends of yours?" he asks the boatswain.

"Stowaways," the boatswain replies, like it's an oath.

"What's below?" the captain calls to the big man with his arm around me.

"Dutch East India goods," he replies. "Spices, fabrics, and sugarcane. It's all dead cargo."

"Rudder chain's disabled, Scipio," comes a call from the quarterdeck.

The captain's—Scipio's—jaw tightens. "Bring up the Dutch goods and consolidate the passengers' trunks." He stows his pistol but keeps his hand on it as he says to the officers, "And then we'll be away. I was in earnest when I said we meant you no harm."

"Is this some kind of trick?" the boatswain demands.

"Not at all."

"You aren't going to kill us?"

"Would you like me to?"

"Then you're selling us into slavery. I know how you Barbarians operate. You'll torch our ship or claim it for your fleet, then trade us innocents to be Muslim slaves in Africa! We'll be forced to convert to your godless ways or else be slaughtered. You'll make our women your whores."

Scipio lets out a tight sigh through his teeth. He still has a hand on his pistol and looks tempted to use it.

"We won't be enslaved to heathens," the boatswain says, clearly believing himself to be making some sort of impassioned speech that will save his crew from a fate worse than death. "We would rather be slaughtered by your blade than made your prisoners."

"Not all of us," I pipe up.

The boatswain growls at me like a feral dog, then points to Percy. "Take him with you," he says to the pirate captain. "He's your breed of African filth."

"He's not African," I call, my French slipping into English as my temper rises. I'm not sure how we are in the middle of a pirate siege and I'm arguing with this bigot about Percy's nationality. "He's English."

372

The boatswain laughs. "I believe that like I believe you're an earl's son."

"I *am* an earl's son!"

Scipio pivots in my direction, his hand slipping off his pistol, and I realize suddenly what a grievous error I've made. Blame it upon the lack of sleep or the lack of food or simply the deliriousness brought on by pirate-induced panic.

"You're an earl's son?" he asks.

I swallow. "No. Yes."

He stares at me for a moment, then says to the boatswain, "We'll take them."

"Well done, Monty," Felicity says under her breath.

I've hardly time to get a hold on what's happening before the big man shoves me forward, down the rope ladder they've strung up along the side of the ship and into a longboat waiting in the choppy water below. Percy and Felicity are shoved after me.

And so it is that we come to be hostages to pirates.

23

In the longboats, we three are bound at the wrists, which is a new experience for me. I've never been tied up before—neckwear to a headboard hardly counts. The pirates wedge us on the floor, between oars and the plunder, our stiff knees folded under our chins and hands curled like claws before us to keep the ropes from digging in. The yawning stretch of sea between the xebec and the pirates' schooner is rough and gray, and more than once, as we're rowed forward, I'm certain we're going to be pitched from the longboat into the unforgiving waves. Which might be a fate preferable to whatever waits for us on the other side.

The longboats are hauled up onto the deck of the ship, where I'm expecting to find a whole mess of corsairs waiting, but there's only two men and a greenhorn, all wide-eyed when they see us curled between the feet of their crewmen. They're a sundry bunch, all—dark skinned and dressed in the rough ticking favored by tars. They're also a far smaller and skinnier number than I expected from the size of the schooner. There's only three and ten of them in total. I'm not certain how they crew it—the tall ships I've seen back in England are manned by legions of sharp-dressed navy men. No wonder the pirates disabled the xebec instead of taking it—they've hardly crew for a single vessel, let alone a fleet.

We're left to stand on the deck, barefoot and bound and guarded by one of the corsairs, while the longboats make the journey back and forth between the two ships, dragging over more loot. There's a frantic energy to the crew, like lions after the kill, bounding and preening and obnoxiously proud of themselves. They almost seem surprised by how well the seizure went.

At last, the captain climbs aboard and calls for all-hands, and I watch our chance of reaching Venice shrink into the horizon, growing smaller and smaller until it's out of sight entirely. My heart sinks.

The man guarding us calls to his captain in English, which is an astonishing language to hear after so many weeks in foreign lands, "Who are these?" He tips his head in our direction.

"Hostages," Scipio replies.

"We agreed we wouldn't take hostages," the man says. I realize suddenly that a few of the others have abandoned their work as well and are standing in defiance against their captain. It seems we might be witness to some sort of mutiny.

"We won't deal with the slavers," another man calls, his arms folded. "Cargo only. That was the agreement."

Scipio, to his credit, looks unmoved. "You think I'd put us in that business?"

"When we first mustered, we agreed—"

"We'll take the goods to Iantos in Santorini," Scipio interrupts. "The trunks can be sold on the island."

"And what about them?" One of the men jerks his head at us, but Scipio snaps at him.

"Shut your mouth and do as you're told. Get the plunder below," he instructs, which seems a rather generous word for what they took—a smattering of passenger trunks and a few crates of Dutch linen are hardly the spoils of a successful pirate raid. The men consider him for a moment, then begin to shuffle off, murmuring to each other and eyeing us sideways as though we are to blame for our current situation as hostages.

The greenhorn bobs at the captain's elbow, his eyes wide as shillings. "No slavers, Scip," he whimpers.

As Scipio looks down at him, the ruthless pirate captain seems to vanish, just for a moment, like he was a put-on act. He gives the greenhorn an affectionate scruff on the head. "Trust me, Georgie-boy."

While it's good news we're not to be enslaved, I'm not

keen on what the ulterior motives behind our kidnapping might be. Fates worse than slavery begin to dance before my eyes.

As the men begin to haul the stolen goods into a cabin beneath the quarterdeck, Scipio calls to the big man, "What have you?" The man holds up Percy's fiddle case. A wash of relief goes through me that he brought it—I had lost track of it in our transport, but thank God we are still on the same ship as our Lazarus Key.

"It's his." He nods toward Percy, who is frozen at my side with his bound hands clasped before him like the cathedral likeness of a saint.

"Please, it's only a fiddle," he says.

"I have no doubt," Scipio replies, then peers at Percy like he hadn't seen him before. "You really are English?"

"Yes."

"But not the earl's son. That would be . . . you." Scipio swivels his attention my direction. He has a strange way about him that keeps tricking me into believing he's not going to slit our throats, but then his eyes will flash in a distinctly nefarious way and I am reminded both of the pistol at his hip and his post as pirate captain. I take a step backward and smash into the big man, scraping my heel on the rough leather of his boot. He collars me, like he's afraid I was about to dive over the side for freedom. Scipio folds his arms, surveying me. "You are very far from home, sirrah."

I don't know what to say in return and haven't a notion what pitch my voice will be if I do speak, so I settle for defiant silence. Or rather, silence that I hope comes off as defiant.

Felicity takes a different approach—defiant speech. "I don't believe you're pirates," she says. She is standing ahead of Percy and me and in a stance considerably bolder than ours. She's got her chin stuck out, her dark hair whipping around her face like she's floating underwater. Even with her hands bound and that bloody bandage upon her arm, she looks nearly as threatening as some of the men.

Scipio runs a hand over his beard as he surveys her. He seems to be already regretting taking such petulant prisoners. "And what makes you believe we aren't pirates?"

"A pirate ship survives by outrunning and outgunning its enemies and victims alike," Felicity says. "This doesn't appear to be an overly fast ship, nor one in possession of enough guns for speed to not be a concern. You've hardly more weaponry than the merchant vessel we were on. And all pirates from the Barbary Coast deal with the slavers, especially if there's so little taken, and you have walked away with hardly any get, for you haven't crew to manage it, and you would have taken no hostages if Monty had kept his mouth shut. If you truly are pirates, you're very bad at it."

One of the men whistles. Scipio stares at her for a moment, then calls to the man behind me, "Bring the English lord to my cabin to select which of his limbs we'll be cutting off to send to his father in demand for ransom payment. Let's see if that makes us piratical enough for milady."

The big man hooks his arm around my neck and drags me forward before I've got a chance to do anything more than shoot Felicity a look that is mostly panic. Behind us, I hear her shout, "Wait, stop—" at the same time Percy shouts, "No!" and makes a bolt for me. One of the men catches him round the waist before he gets far, and he doubles over with a gasp. That's the last glimpse I get of them before the big man pushes me across the deck after Scipio, shoves me into his cabin, and slams the door behind the three of us, so hard the amber panes that are set into it rattle in their frames.

Scipio crosses behind a battered desk, pushes a set of charts and a sextant out of the way, then reaches into his boot and withdraws a bloody great knife with a serrated edge. "Now," he says to me, "which of your fingers do you think your father will best recognize if we send it along with a letter demanding payment for your safe return?"

"So we're to be ransomed, is that it?" I'm not keen on being hostage to pirates in any capacity, but ransom is by far the most savory of our distinctly unsavory possible fates.

"Would you like to protest that?"

"No," I reply. "But I think Felicity's right."

Scipio looks up. "Excuse me?"

I swallow hard. I've little ammunition against him, but I'll use it until I'm dry. "You're rotten pirates."

"Does that matter? We needn't be the best raiders in the Mediterranean to be worth fearing."

"I'm not afraid of you."

"Then put your hand on the table and tell me which finger is your least favorite."

He reaches for me and I pull back, smacking hard into the big man still planted like an oak behind me. It's akin to running into a wall.

"I thought you weren't afraid of me," Scipio says.

I'm breathing properly hard now, and that *not afraid* bit was definitely a lie. I'm afeard down to my bones. Out on the deck, I can hear Percy still hollering after me.

I put my bound hands on the table, fingers spread like I am brave enough to let him choose, though if he truly comes at me with that knife, I intend to make certain he also walks out of this cabin with at least one finger less.

Scipio makes a study of my hands that's so deliberate it feels put-on. His whole pirate persona feels strangely like an act, that of a man who chooses to be threatening simply to avoid others' threatening him. "Why not chop off my head?" I ask. "He'll recognize that even better."

To my surprise, he laughs. "What's your name?"

"Lord Henry Montague, Viscount of Disley."

"So very grand. How old are you?"

"Eight and ten years."

"Tell me, Lord Henry Montague, Viscount of Disley, if you truly are an earl's son, why were you stowed away upon a merchant ship and why do you look as though you've been several days without the sort of luxuries usually afforded to a viscount? If you're honest about who you are, you might save your finger yet."

"I'm not lying. We're touring, from England, but we've lost our company."

"Well then, let Ebrahim tourniquet your arm so you don't bleed out on my desk." Scipio jams the knife into the table. I flinch more than I wish I had. "How much do you think your father would pay for the return of you, your lady, and your man?"

"My sister," I say, tripping over the words in my haste to get that clarifying point out. "And my friend."

"Friend? Is he a lord as well? I thought you English were particular about your coloring."

I'm not sure why an African pirate might have reason to know this—or why words like *earl* and *viscount* would mean anything to him unless he's been studying the peerage on the off chance a hostage situation such as this arose—but I say, "He's not a lord, but we've all people who will come looking for us."

"People who will pay for you?"

"So long as we've still got all our limbs when we're returned. We've been separated from our company and we're trying to get to Venice to meet up with them but we haven't any money. So you can cut off my finger, but know that decreases my value considerably."

"How much do you think your father has authorized your cicerone to pay in the event of kidnapping?"

I am, first, not certain those terms were ever written into my father's agreement with Lockwood, and, second, not certain my father would give a ha'penny to have me back. And we have absolutely no company to speak of in Venice—that's entirely a rook—unless you count the duke and Helena, who may very well be waiting for us there. This lie is going to fall apart like wet newsprint if he actually takes to it.

I'm spared answering by a frantic slapping on the door. Scipio nods to Ebrahim, who opens it, revealing their greenhorn with a spyglass clutched in his hands. "Ship to the north, Scip," he says, panic pitching his voice.

"Well then." Scipio jerks his knife out of the table and stashes it in his belt. "Let's see the men to stations. Roll out the guns—"

"It's not a merchantman," the lad interrupts. "It's the French Royal Navy."

"What?" Scipio makes a break for the deck. I follow, but Ebrahim seizes me by the arm, making certain that if I'm going anywhere, it's with one of his hamlike hands locked around me.

The men are gathered at the starboard rail, staring out to the water and murmuring to each other. Felicity and Percy are nowhere to be seen, and I have a sudden, horrid vision of them being tossed overboard while I was conferencing with the captain.

Scipio takes the steps up to the quarterdeck two at a time, then whips an agate spyglass from his coat and raises it to his eye.

"Is it truly the French?" one of his men calls to him.

Scipio adjusts his glass. "It's a navy frigate—French pennant," he says. "Twenty-six twelve-pound long guns, six of the twelvers." It's clear from his tone that's more guns than we've got on board.

My first thought is that we're saved.

My second is that we are now in a whole different variety of trouble.

"Do you think they've spotted us?" Ebrahim calls. "They're far out still."

"They're angling this way." Scipio lowers the glass and looks up into the rigging. "Strip the colors! We'll not be running a black pennant if we're to be seized by the navy. Get a French flag up—anything, get anything up. Roll out the guns—"

"We can't fire, there's still a chance we might fly," one of the men argues.

"Then fly. Hoist all sails, and run out the sweeps if you won't roll the guns. Get him out of the way," he snaps at Ebrahim, and I'm again seized from behind, and then tossed into the second cabin below the quarterdeck.

Percy and Felicity are seated on the cabin floor with their backs to the row of looted luggage from the xebec. Their wrists are still bound, and, dear God, they really are waifish looking. Felicity's hair has gotten lank with grease, the tail of her plait crusted pale gray with seawater, and she's still in the same Jesuit as when we were robbed by the duke and his men. The taffeta has shifted from golden to dirt brown, and the embroidered blossoms along the skirt are beginning to unravel.

Percy flies to his feet when he sees me. "Monty! What happened? Are you hurt? Did he hurt you?" He's speaking so fast his sentences step on each other.

"I'm fine, Perce."

"He said he was going to—"

"He didn't." He grabs each of my hands in both of his and examines them, like he doesn't quite believe me. I wiggle my fingers for emphasis. "All still attached. Would you like to have a count?"

His shoulders slump. "Dear God, Monty. I really thought—"

"Yes, I heard you shrieking." I press my palms flat against his. "Much appreciated."

"What's happening on the deck?" Felicity asks. She's on her feet now too, standing with her face to the rippled glass panes set into the door. She's not looking quite as concerned about me keeping all my appendages as I would like.

"There's a ship coming our way," I reply. "French Royal Navy. The pirates are going to make a run."

"The navy will outrun this ship with little effort," she says. "And we'll be victims of the shortest kidnapping in the history of piracy."

"We can't let them know who we are," I say.

"Who? The pirates? I think you already did a bang-up job of announcing us."

"No, the navy. If they find us, we'll be in trouble."

"What are you talking about?" she replies. "We're already *in* trouble. That ship could be our rescue."

"If we're taken by those navy men, they'll send us back to Lockwood or Father. They might even hand us over to the duke if he's got some sort of notice out to be on watch for us, and then we'll never get to Venice."

"So, which is worse?" Percy asks. "The duke or pirates?"

The worst thing would be never making it to Venice for Percy—particularly now that I've had his hand on my knee and his mouth that close to mine. I'll not give up on getting to the sinking island for him, even if it's by pirate ship we have to travel. "I think I have a plan."

"Would you care to air it for the rest of us before you act?" Felicity asks. But before I can, the cabin door is thrown open and we're greeted by Scipio and two more of the pirates in silhouette against the dawn.

"We need this out of sight if we're boarded." Scipio pushes past us to hoist one of the trunks onto his shoulder. No one is stopping me, so when he goes out onto the deck, I chase after, Felicity and Percy at my heels.

"We can help you escape the navy," I call.

"Get back in the cabin," Scipio replies, barely looking at me.

"No, listen." I step between him and the stairs leading to the lower deck. I think he's going to shove me out of the way, and I flinch, but he stops, trunk still balanced upon his shoulder. I swallow. "You know that ship will catch you, and you know you'll be outgunned if you stand and fight—even running from them makes you look guilty. You'll be either slaughtered or taken back to Marseilles and hanged for piracy. But we can help you get away."

"Why would you want to help us?" he asks.

"Because we are good Christians who extend charity to those who have done us wrong?" I try not to make that a question but the little bastard peaks at the end.

The lie doesn't stick for long. "Are you running

from the navy?" Scipio asks.

"We might be. Look, we've as much need to avoid being caught by them as you do. But if you trust me, and if you let them board, I think we can get away from here."

"Why should I trust you?"

"Because you've got no other choice."

Above us, one of the high sails drops with a muted *crack*.

"You can still ransom us at the end of this," I say. "But you're not going to be free enough to do said ransoming if you run now."

Scipio looks from me to Percy and Felicity, his face unreadable. Then abruptly he tosses down the trunk and calls across the deck. "Bring her around. We wait for the navy."

"Scip—" someone calls down from the rigging, but Scipio interrupts.

"Montague's right—we'll be outgunned and outmanned, and standing to fight will condemn us. Pull in the sails and drop the anchor, now!" Then to me he asks, softer and more anxious, "What is it you're planning?"

"Well," I reply, keenly aware that everyone is paying me attention, "could I have a look in that trunk?"

24

The French have, indeed, spotted us and they do, indeed, fly a flag of parlay, which we ignore so that they're forced to drop their longboats and come to us. We extend only the barest accommodation in throwing down a ladder for them to haul themselves aboard.

A few of the lower ranks come up first—presumably to absorb any bullets we might be waiting to rain upon them—before their commanding officer appears. He's a man about my father's age, with skin as sea-whipped as the pirates' but with considerably more polish about him. The tails of his coat flap against his legs as the wind rips at them, tangling around the scabbard dangling from his belt. He swings himself aboard, then struts across the deck to where the crew is assembled, his hand behind his back and his chin thrust in the air—it doesn't seem a far distance until you watch a cove really make a meal of walking it. Behind him, more navy men are swarming onto the deck. Our pirate hosts are outnumbered at least three to one.

Scipio steps forward to meet the commander, his hat in his hands. "Sir."

The officer pulls up short like he's spotted a rat underfoot. "How dare you address me."

Even across the deck, I swear I can hear Scipio's teeth grinding. "I'm the captain of this vessel."

"That seems unlikely, unless this is some kind of pirate operation." The officer wrinkles his nose. "Where is your commanding officer?"

His gaze moves to the crew—he's clearly looking for someone else to present himself. Then his eyes fall upon Felicity and me, standing in the fine clothes we plundered from the trunks of the xebec. It was damn near impossible to find a coat that fit me in the sleeves—I'm hoping the fact that I've cuffed them twice and am still swimming won't give away our ruse. But in a miracle worthy of the New Testament, amid all the men's wear in the trunks was a fine silk dress wrapped in thin paper—probably a gift for someone's sweetheart back home. It's scooped far lower than Felicity's usual necklines, and as the officer's eyes sweep us, her hands twitch at her sides, like she's desperate to hold them over her chest. She's one strong breeze away from creating a diversion of an entirely different variety.

"Who the devil are you?" he demands of us.

"We could ask you the same question," I reply, as cheerful as I can muster considering my not-unsubstantial distress. "What cause have you to be boarding our ship?"

"*Your* ship?" the man repeats.

"Well, my father's ship," I amend.

The officer's eyebrows seem to be climbing to his hairline. "Your . . . father's?"

"I certainly wouldn't be sailing a ship belonging to my mother." I flash him a bit of the dimples posthaste. He frowns.

"You fly no colors."

"Beastly storm winds whipped them right out from over us. Thought about running up my most English-looking coat as a stand-in to avoid precisely this sort of brush, but didn't want to sacrifice one of my fine jackets. I had them all tailored in Paris and they're positively macaroni." I step forward—nearly straight out of my shoes, which are as large on me as the coat—and hand him the leather skin dug up from the selfsame trunk from which Felicity's dress was plundered. It's full of travel documents, much like the ones my father bestowed upon Lockwood for the three of us before we departed. It was a gamble, hoping the luggage would yield such, but Luck apparently realized she owed us a good turn after sticking us with these son-of-a-bitch pirates.

The French officer takes the papers from me and

shuffles through them. "James Boswell, ninth Laird of Auchinleck," he reads.

I spread my hands. "That would be me."

"You're Scottish."

"Do I not sound it? Must be all these months in France."

"And this is . . . ?" His eyes drift to Felicity.

I had been hoping he wouldn't ask, so I say "Miss Boswell" in a tone that reeks of *of course*.

"And this is a ship of . . . your father's?"

"Not entirely—he chartered it for our travel across the Mediterranean. We're touring, see, and I put up a fuss about being made to travel on a common ferry between Dover and Calais—all those people, you know, utterly filthy and so cramped you can't breathe, I was positively gasping the whole way and I had no intention of tolerating those circumstances again for *weeks* on our way to Italy." *Keep talking*, I think as he stares at me, his gaze glazing. *Keep talking and tell him so much that perhaps he won't notice it's all a crock.* "So I wrote to Da and positively begged him to charter me my own vessel and as I'm the eldest and he's never been able to say no to me—I could ask that man for anything, honestly, there was a rug in the king's palace in Paris and I swear to God I told my father to write to the king himself—"

"That's enough," the officer snaps, bundling up my papers and thrusting them back at me. "We will be searching the ship." He signals to his men, but I step in his way.

"On what grounds, sir? We are a legitimate operation."

"These waters are thick with Barbary pirates. By order of the French king, we have a right to make certain that you are not among them."

"You have no such right. We are not French citizens, and most certainly not pirates, and we have provided you with the necessary travel papers to verify our identities. You hold no jurisdiction over us."

"Have you something to hide?" he challenges.

A good deal of stolen cargo, no papers verifying our charter, and also there's Percy lurking back there with the crew, I think, but I raise my chin and play the small-minded tourist. "My father told me before I left I was not to bow to the whims of foreigners who would endeavor to take advantage of me because I was a young man far from my homeland. Of Scotland."

The Frenchies haven't moved. They're all looking to their commander, and he's still looking to me like he can't quite work out this nonsensical tableau. The silence stretches like taut, fraying rope. "And tell me, Mr. Boswell," the officer says at last, "when your father charters you a ship, does he always enlist such a filthy colored crew?"

That gets a chortle from his men. At my side, Scipio

seems to rise a few inches taller, hands clasped behind his back.

"Please apologize to my captain, sir," I say.

Now it's the officer's turn to laugh. "I won't apologize to a colored man."

"Then you'll leave my ship, please."

"Don't be absurd. We're servants of the crown."

"And I'm an Englishman—Scotsman—and have no obligation to comply with French seizure. You board my ship with weapons drawn, accuse me of piracy, and insult my upstanding crew. I'd like you to apologize, or leave this ship at once."

The officer makes a rather grand sniff, then extends a gloved hand to Scipio. "My apologies . . . sir."

Scipio doesn't take it. "Thank you. Now please leave my ship."

The officer looks like he's ready to give Scipio a telling-off, but then he remembers we are not his men. His mouth curls; then he gives us both a curt bow. "Apologies for the trouble, Mr. Boswell. Thank you for your cooperation."

I don't dare believe we've gotten away with our ruse until the navy frigate is nearly as far away as it was when first spotted. Scipio keeps his spyglass trained upon it until it's out of sight, then at last calls all hands to stations.

I expect a word of thanks from him, or at the least

some sort of manly, approving nod, but instead he calls to Ebrahim, "Stow our prisoners below."

"Prisoners?" I repeat, but Scipio doesn't hear me. Ebrahim reaches for my arm, but I pull away from him and shout after Scipio as he pulls himself up onto the ratlines. "A bit of thanks would be good."

He stops and looks down at me. "For what?"

"For saving your skins."

"You were saving yourselves, not us."

"You'd be captives of the navy if it weren't for my sister and me—" I start, but Scipio jumps back to the deck and faces me.

"There is nothing good about watching another man claim your ship because your skin is too dark to do it yourself," he says, each word a glancing wound. "So in future, you needn't demand apologies on my behalf. Now, you're underfoot."

Before I can speak, Ebrahim grabs me with one hand and Felicity with the other—she gives a bit of a yelp when his fist fastens around her wounded arm, and he lets go, then grabs Percy instead—and drags us away from the captain.

Prisoners once more.

It's clear solely from the absence of a proper prison on board that these men are not pirates. We three are taken to the gun deck and ineptly knotted at the feet to one of the long-nosed cannons, which seems like a bad choice for several reasons. Ebrahim doesn't even stand guard—he stays just long enough to toss a leather skin of surgical tools at our feet with a grunt of "For your arm" at Felicity.

And then he leaves us to our own devices beside a store of gunpowder and flint and a cannon, thereby solidifying our captors' reputation as the worst pirates in the history of the Mediterranean.

Felicity falls upon the surgical kit, withdrawing a curved needle and a skein of black thread. "That was a rather good plan, Monty," she says, and I'm about to swell with pride, but then she adds, "Except we're still hostages."

"Well, now it's your turn to come up with something, darling. I've rather pulled my weight for the day." I tug at the ropes keeping Percy's feet bound to the cannon and they loosen. The tar-dip on the ends is sticky from the heat. "That prick of a captain would be on his way to the noose if it weren't for me."

"He's been rather decent to us, considering the situation," Percy says. "He trusted you."

"And then told me off for it. It was good of me to help him!"

"Maybe so," he replies. "But that doesn't mean it wasn't hard for him to witness."

"What's hard about it?"

"Well, do you think I enjoy being mistaken for your manservant everywhere we go?"

"But you're not my man, so what does it matter?"

"If he doesn't understand it, don't explain it to him," Felicity mutters. I glower at her, though she's focused upon getting her needle threaded and doesn't notice.

But Percy says, "It's good of you to stand up for me when I can't do it for myself. But it's difficult that you have to. And I'd expect the captain feels the same. Especially when it's his prisoners who have to come to his rescue."

Which still doesn't entirely make sense to me—perhaps it can't. I tug at the knot again, and it comes undone with little fight. Percy kicks his feet free, then gives me a weak smile. "Nowhere to run."

"We could lead a mutiny."

"Against pirates?"

"We're quite piratical ourselves, Captain Two Tooth. And now we have a cannon."

"And some length of rope."

"And with your brains and my brute strength and Felicity's— Dear God, Felicity Montague, are you *sewing yourself shut*?"

Felicity looks up, innocent as a schoolgirl. She's got the bloody cravat unwrapped from her arm, sleeve pushed up, and that wicked needle buried in her own arm around the gash left by the splinter—already sewn

396

half shut while Percy and I were distracted. "What? It needs to be done and neither of you knows how." She dips the needle out and pulls tight so that the ripped edges of her skin meet. I slump backward against the cannon to keep from keeling over in earnest. "See if you can find Henry a couch before he's overcome," she says to Percy, though he's looking nearly as horrified.

After two more neat stitches, she knots off the thread and cuts it with her teeth, then gives her embroidery an examination, looking pleased as Punch. "I've never actually done that on a person before." She glances up at us—Percy looking very obviously away and me swooning against the artillery.

And rolls her eyes. "Men are such babies."

{ 25 }

After some time alone with the guns, the sound of boots on the stairs announces our benevolent captain's approach. We all three look up as he halts a few feet away and gives us a peery up-and-down. None of us stands. It's a gesture that passes for defiance but is mostly exhaustion.

To my surprise, he sinks down too, elbows resting upon his knees so our faces are level. He looks very young in that moment, though he's got at least a decade on Percy and me—perhaps more. He looks, also, profoundly weary. Ferocious pirate gone again in an instant.

The first thing he says is, "Thank you. For helping us get away."

After the snappy retort I received on this subject before, this feels like a trap, so I just nod.

"Perhaps we can come to an agreement," he goes on.

"Explain why you're running, and I'll tell you about us."

"You first," Felicity interrupts, though I was ready to spill. "Every book I've ever read has taught me not to trust a pirate to hold his word."

Scipio's eyes flit to her, and her chin rises. "That logic would be sound," he says, "except you were right—we're not pirates. We're privateers. Or we were, until recently. My crew and I were employed by an English merchant during the war with Spain. He had us issued letters of marque so we were legally permitted to seize Spanish vessels that attacked his ships in the Caribbean."

"What happened?" I ask.

"The English crown withdrew all letters once the war ended, though we didn't know that until we were arrested for piracy when we tried to make port in Charleston. Our employer wouldn't pay for us—he freed his captain and the other officers, and left the rest of us to rot. We were there for a year when pirates raided the town and we were able to escape. We took a ship. *This* ship. And since we had no letters of marque and needed funds and had a difficult time finding legitimate work for . . . obvious reasons, we thought we might take up the piracy we'd been accused of. We're . . ." He scrubs a hand over the back of his neck. "New at it."

"Was ours the first ship you'd ever seized?" Felicity asks.

"Piratically? Yes."

"Why not return to your employer and get the letters reissued?" I ask. "He doesn't need to bail you from prison any longer."

Scipio doesn't say anything to that.

"You weren't employed, were you?" Percy asks softly.

"No," Scipio replies. "We were enslaved. Even though he wouldn't pay for our return, we still belong to him. And I'd take a noose as a pirate before I'd go back to living a slave." He rubs his hands together before him, then looks up at us. "So, where is it that you run from?"

"There's a French duke who is after us," Percy replies.

"Have you offended him?"

"We've stolen from him," I say.

"One of us has stolen from him," Felicity amends.

"Well, that one of you sounds as piratical as us. Why were you stowed away upon the xebec?"

"We need to get to Venice—truly," I say. "We've something to be done there."

"Do you expect us to take you?" he asks. "If you aren't to be ransomed, Venice is off our route."

"We could compensate you," I say.

"Your ransom would similarly compensate us."

"My uncle," Percy says suddenly.

I look over at him. "What about your uncle?"

He's sat up straight, brow furrowed in thought. "He could issue you letters of marque, as payment for your taking us to Venice. That's far more valuable than ransom."

"Who's your uncle?" Scipio asks.

"Thomas Powell. He serves on the Admiralty Court in Cheshire."

"No. Thomas Powell? Are you in earnest?" Scipio laughs—a deep, resonant rumble. "You look nothing like him."

"There's a reason for that," Percy replies with a small smile. "Do you know him?"

"Our first ship made berth in Liverpool and he was one of the magistrates that oversaw our charters. He was always good to us, your uncle. Some of those admiralty men are bastards to Negro sailors, but he was kind. Makes more sense why now. Damnation, Thomas Powell's ward. What are the chances?"

"He wouldn't care that you were a colored crew—he'd get you the letters of marque," Percy says. "Valid ones, in exchange for transporting us."

"Don't you think he'd be less inclined if it was asked as ransom for his nephew's return? He'd withdraw them as soon as we'd left the harbor."

"What if we offer it as a reward instead of a ransom?" I suggest, and Percy nods. "If you get us to Venice, we'll write to our families and tell them how you rescued us. From pirates, even, if you really want to go for the drama. They'll be so grateful they'll offer you anything, and all you need ask for is letters of marque to sail as privateers under the protection of the English crown."

Scipio runs a hand over his beard, looking at each of us in turn like he is searching for a definitive reason to either trust us or strap us to a cannon and fling us over the rail.

"You could get a ransom for us," Felicity pipes up. "But they won't issue letters of marque to our kidnappers. And that's far more valuable."

"I'm sure we could console ourselves with a good deal of money. And I'll be much less moved to compassion if I find out this is all a con."

"We're not lying," I say, though it sounds feeble.

"I'll have to consult my crew—"

"Aren't you the captain?" Felicity interrupts.

"We're more of a democracy. Though if none of them protest, and if you—" He scratches a hand through his beard. "You really think you can get us letters issued?" he asks, and Percy nods. "Well, then we'll take you to Venice. We can facilitate your return to your families from there."

I'm about to extend a hand of accord to him, but Felicity has a few more terms. "You're not to mistreat us on this voyage," she says. "We're not to be kept as captives."

"Then, in return, you'll stay out of my crew's way, give them your respect, and cause no havoc," Scipio counters. "Any whiff of ill intentions toward any of us from any of you and I'll shackle you to the masthead. Do you agree to that?"

"Agreed," we three chorus.

Scipio helps us unwrap from our imitation bindings, then leads the way up from the gun deck so we can make our proposals to the crew. Felicity follows close behind him, her surgical kit rewrapped and clutched close to her chest the way some girls might cling to a favorite doll. Percy and I bring up the rear.

As we climb the steps, Percy nudges me with his elbow. "You're daft, you know."

"Am I?"

"James Boswell. Rooking the navy. Making deals with pirates."

"Well, they're not pirates. And"—I poke him in return—"the deal was mostly your doing."

"You're still daft."

"Are you complaining?"

"No," he says, giving a quick tug on my sleeve that turns into his fingers pressed into my palm in a way that makes me weak in the knees. "I sort of love it."

26

It will be weeks before we make port in Venice, weeks that I assume will be filled with hard labor and abuse from our captors, but instead consist of a strange calm and a stranger camaraderie.

We're given hammocks on the lower deck alongside the crew (Scipio surrenders his captain's cabin to Felicity for the sake of her modesty), and we take meals with them—*meals* being a loose term, as they mostly eat hardtack softened in coffee or warm rum. Ebrahim teaches us that the biscuits need a good soak so that the maggots burrowed into them drown and float to the top, which is a positively scrummy thing to consider every time you tuck in.

The crew keep their distance from us at first and we from them, though the ship is small and there is only so much space in which one can avoid the other. The standoff breaks when Percy and I, starved for entertainment, play a game of dice with a handful of the men, which feels at first like conspiring with the enemy and ends up being a better night than many we've had with the blades back in Cheshire. They don't cheat half as much as Richard Peele and his lot.

They are not what I expected of pirates, nor really of tars at all. They're not bloodthirsty, drunken rogues passing round-robins and black spots and ready to knock the man in charge on the back of the head with a belaying pin. Rather, they are a small, tight-knit crew, who trade jokes and stories and songs mostly in jack-tar lingo, and we become their strange, temporary crewmates, assigned small tasks with no irreparable consequences if bungled.

They all take to Percy right away—their greenhorn, who they all call King George, follows him around like a puppy, not saying much, just always staring with his enormous eyes at Percy, like he's a rare orchid brought aboard.

"Is he truly a lord?" King George asks me one night, as he, Ebrahim, and I sit on the deck tying monkey's fists.

"Who, Percy? Not a lord, no, but he's from a high-born family."

"And they raised him well?" Ebrahim asks. "Even though he's colored?"

"I don't think he was allowed to take supper with

them when they had company, but, with some exceptions of that sort, they've been first-rate to him."

Ebrahim tosses his monkey's fist between his enormous hands, his mouth pulling down. "So it's not the same at all, then, is it?"

It occurs to me suddenly, as I look down the deck to where Percy's sitting with his fiddle and two of the men, who are singing a tune for him in hopes he can pick up the melody, that this must be the first time in his life he's around men who look like him. Men who don't assume he's worth less than them just because of the color of his skin. Among the pirates, he has nothing to prove.

"Maybe *I'm* a lord," King George says.

"Maybe, Georgie," Ebrahim replies, with no conviction.

We round the tip of Italy—the heel of the boot, as Scipio calls it—and enter the narrow straits between the Neapolitan state and Corfu, where Archaic temples sit like bulwarks along the cliffs. The water shifts from turquoise to emerald as the light billows across it. Percy and I spend long stretches of these days standing together at the prow, marveling at the way the whole world around us seems to be made of raw cerulean pigment and playing a silent and absolutely maddening game of who can get his hand closest to the other's without actually touching it.

We haven't yet had a moment alone since the

unfinished one in the hold of the xebec, though we both keep finding increasingly creative ways to touch each other without anyone noticing. I think I quite deserve some medal for the restraint I have thus far shown in regard to Percy now that I know he and I seem to be reading from the same book on the subject of our romantic sentiments, until Felicity mutters one night at supper, "Be a bit more obvious, won't you?" Though, in fairness, I had just hooked my foot around Percy's ankle and he had nearly choked on a mouthful of salt pork.

The *almostness* of it is driving me mad—nearly as mad as Percy's fingertips brushing mine between us and not being permitted any more of him than that—coupled with a desperation bordering on panic to not be parted from him at the end of this Tour. I have lost years of my life loving him from afar and I'll be damned if I'm robbed of him as soon as we realize we've both been admiring each other from a distance all this while. I'd fight Death himself one-handed to get the panacea for him.

Scipio has been tight-lipped about asking us what our business is in Venice, but considering our brush with the French navy, he's likely deduced it's not particularly savory. He might prefer ignorance to sharing the weight of a secret, but I cough up the truth with no prompting, while he and I are together on deck slopping a new coat of paint over the sun-weathered rail. Partly because I expect we're going to need further assistance from our piratical allies in getting to the island itself, but mostly because I'm starting to get twitchy about reaching Venice before the duke and hope the captain might have some sort of hidden sails he will offer to roll out for increased speed.

I expect he'll contest it—alchemical compounds and sinking islands and coded puzzle boxes are rather fantastic when said aloud—but all he says is, "You're very impressive, you know that?"

"Who, me?" I laugh. "I'm the deadweight. It's mostly thanks to Percy and Felicity that we're all still alive."

"Do you truly not see it?"

"See what?"

He drags his brush along the rail. "You're worth far more than you seem to think. You have value."

"I've no value. None at all. My best attribute is getting into scrapes I need to be bailed out of." As though to prove my point, a string of paint drops off my brush and splashes across the canvas we've laid. "And the dimples."

"Be kinder to yourself. You saved us from the navy. You saved yourselves from the navy. And you've clearly had some hand in defending your crew." He points his brush at my jaw. "You've the scars to prove it."

I scrub a thumb up over the spot where the thief-taker struck me. It's still sore to the touch. "Thought my cheeks needed a bit of color is all."

"Didn't you fight back?"

"I'm not well practiced at fighting back. I'm far less gallant than you seem to want to believe me." I give the rail a zealous *thwack* with my brush. Paint sprays from its bristles like the powder from a cannon shot. "Has she a name?"

"Who?"

"Your pirate ship." I knock my fist against the rail.

A glop of paint drips onto his bare foot, and he scrubs it against the back of his leg. "The *Eleftheria*."

"What does it mean?"

"It's Greek," he replies. "The word for *freedom*."

"Did you name her?"

"When we stole her, yes. The men who've agreed to buy the VOC goods from us are all in Oia, so a Greek name helps us there. And we all needed a new start. It seemed fitting."

"How long have you had her?"

"You're changing the subject, your lordship."

I flick a bit of paint at him as I bend to load my brush. When I straighten, he taps me upon the cheek with the back of his hand in retaliation. It's hardly a glance, and all in fun, but I flinch so badly I drop my brush. It falls to the deck with a clatter, leaving an ivory stamp on the wood between my feet.

"Dammit. Sorry." I go to scoop up the brush, trying to wipe the paint off the deck with my foot and instead smearing it. I expect he'll chastise me for it, but when I look up, he's watching me, his face sober.

Then he sets his own brush across the rail and climbs to his feet. "Come here."

I don't move. "Why? What are we doing?"

"I'm going to teach you something. Stand up."

I toss my brush into the trough, wipe my hands on my trousers, then stand and face him.

"Put your hands up," Scipio instructs, holding his own forward with the palms flat toward me.

I don't move. "Why?"

"I'm going to show you how to swing at the next man who strikes you." He pushes his sleeves up, then raises an expectant eyebrow at me. "I mean it, put your hands up."

"I don't think—"

"Hands up, my lord. Even a gentleman should know how to defend himself. *Especially* a gentleman."

It feels futile, but I shake out my shoulders, then pull my fists up close to my chest. It's so unnatural that I drop them straightaway. "I can't."

"Course you can. Get your hands up."

"Isn't there a way I'm meant to stand first?"

"When you're in a proper fight, you'll be lucky if you're standing at all. But put a foot forward. Your right one, if that's the arm you swing with. Come now, square up. I know you're taller than that."

"I'm not."

"Get your arm back. And cock your knee there." He

hooks his foot around my back leg and tugs until I sink into it. "It comes from the knees. And keep your other hand up, to protect your face. Come on now, give me a swing."

I swat at his hand with my fist, flimsy and loose like a wet cloth flicked through the air. I give it a few more tries, too self-aware to ever get much power behind it.

"Like you mean it," Scipio says. "Like you mean to protect yourself."

I think of my father—not of him swinging at me, but of all the times he's told me how pathetic I am. How useless and hopeless and embarrassing I am, *good for nothing* and *will amount to nothing* and *nothing, nothing, nothing*—reason after reason until I had begun to believe it wasn't worth putting up my hands.

And here's Scipio, telling me I'm worth defending.

I pull back and swing harder this time—it's still not a good punch, but there's a bit more enthusiasm behind it. Less of a defense or an apology. It feels like my bones crack in half when I make contact, and I double over. "Son of a bitch."

Scipio laughs. "Get your thumb out of your fist. That'll help. That was a good swing, though. You meant that one."

He sits down on the step, flicking the sweat off his brow, then takes a flask from his pocket and offers it to me. I can smell the vinegar tang of gin, and I want nothing more than to snatch it from his hand and down it. But I shake my head. "No, thanks."

Scipio takes a drink, then picks up his paintbrush. I think he's going to start in on our chore again, but instead he turns, looks me straight in the eye, and says, very seriously, "Now, next time someone takes a swing at you, you swing straight back at him, all right? Promise me that, Henry."

We've both started back into the painting before I realize it's been a long while since someone's called me Henry and it didn't make me flinch.

Venice

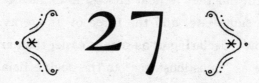

27

From my first sighting, I fall in immediate and passionate love with Venice.

It is, to be fair, a spectacular first sighting—that
white-and-russet skyline surrounded by a lagoon of
bright teal water. Flocks of ships and striped mooring
posts jut from the waves like resting cormorants, black
gondolas flitting between them. Against the amber burn
of the sunset, domes and bell towers peak, the columned
facade of the Doge's Palace and the capped point of Saint
Mark's Basilica along the Grand Canal flanked by pal-
aces with checkered fronts, their balconies hanging over
the canal. The glassy water clasps the light and reflects it
back, like there's a second city beneath the sea.

The only sobering greeting is the gibbets dangling
from a row of scaffolds where the Grand Canal opens to
the Adriatic, each stuffed with a half-moldered corpse,

jagged bones jutting through dimpled gray flesh. Ravens and seagulls swarm them, turning in the sky like Catherine wheels before they break ranks into a dive. Scipio and his men may not be pirates in the strictest sense of the word, but they're near enough to be afeard of meeting the same fate, and the three of us are as good as crew now—declaring us as such is easier than explaining our role as "quasi-hostages" to the dock officials. Percy and I have even swapped our impractical dandies for wide-legged linen trousers and knit Monmouth caps on loan from the crew, along with rough shirts made from striped ticking, and leather boots worn soft by the sea. We're proper tars now. Felicity, bless, keeps her lady's garb in place.

Ebrahim and Scipio stay with the ship and see to customs and port taxes, while the three of us are sent into the city to cash some of the long-suffering Mr. Boswell's letters of credit, as I'm the only one who can pass for him, then to find lodgings. A fine mist of rain is falling, soft and steamy as it flutters against the canals. The heat is sultry and fragrant, and the rain clears the stink of sewage from the air.

The city is a splintered labyrinth, with canals running like veins between the narrow streets. We find a public house in Cannaregio, near the Jewish Ghetto. Our crew fills a corner of the barroom to enjoy the first hot and hardtack-less meal in weeks, punctuated with posset and fruit pastes and some very fine wine that the bar-keeper is overly willing to supply. As darkness settles, the noise in the barroom rises until we're all shouting at each other to be heard—or perhaps that's the drink as well. Everything's louder when you're in your altitudes, and I'm the tipsiest I've been since France.

Felicity goes up to bed as soon as supper is finished, leaving Percy and me to our own devices with the crew. We keep losing each other in the crowd, then coming together for just long enough to comment on how we lost each other, before we're pulled apart again. He finally leaves me sitting in corner booth with instructions to stay put, then fights his way to the bar for drinks.

Almost as soon as he's gone, he's replaced by Scipio, who places his hat upon the table as he slides down the bench to my side. "I think I found your island."

"Hmm? Has there found . . . ? Have you found . . . ?" By the time I've sorted out my conjugations, I can't recall how I was intending to finish. I nearly slap myself across the face. "What did you find?"

Scipio frowns at me. "Are you drunk?"

"No."

"You sound drunk."

I shake my head, trying to make my eyes as wide and innocent as possible. My *no spirits have touched these lips* face that my mother is fond of.

Scipio's frown holds formation, but he goes on. "One

of the dockhands knew it. It's been quarantined, like you thought, but it's not sunk yet. There were too many catacomb tunnels built beneath it and they're collapsing, which is why it's going under."

I say a silent but sincere prayer to the God who raised Lazarus from the dead that one of those collapsed tunnels isn't the one we need, because at last—*at last*—something about this absurd journey seems beautifully simple. "But you found it. It's still standing, so we can go straightaway."

"There are officers patrolling the waters around it to keep people away. Apparently there have been problems with looting."

"So we go tomorrow night, when it's dark. We knew there would be guards, what's the trouble?"

"Look here." He fishes a piece of jaundiced vellum from his coat and unfolds it on the table. "This was given to me by the dock officials."

It's a crude drawing of our Lazarus Key, with the inscription below:

STOLEN FROM THE HOME OF MATEU
ROBLES BY A TRIO OF YOUNG ENGLISH
RASCALS, TWO GENTLEMEN—ONE SMALL
AND TALKATIVE, THE OTHER OF A NEGRO
COMPLEXION—AND A LADY, BELIEVED
TO BE HARBORED IN VENICE. UPON THE

RETURN OF THE KEY AND THE CAPTURE
OF THE BLAGGARD THIEVES, THE REWARD
AND ALL REASONABLE CHARGES WILL BE
PAID BY THE FAMILY.

I suppose I could do worse than *small and talkative*, though the notice sobers me too much to comment upon that. The duke must have beaten us here—we were delayed enough that I'm not surprised, but it still makes me anxious, knowing we're in the same city as him. He might very well be skulking about the island, waiting for us to arrive. I wrap my hand around the key, now snug in my pocket. "So tomorrow. Straightaway, at dawn before anyone's out, let's take the ship to the island."

"We're not sailing the *Eleftheria* to your sinking island."

"Why not? We'll plow straight over the soldiers in their gondolas."

"Not much subtlety in that. We'll take the longboats."

On the street, someone shrieks, followed by a chorus of boisterous laughter. I can't help myself—I glance out the window. The rain has stopped, leaving the glass speckled with water droplets that shine like pearls against the darkness. "What's going on out of doors?"

"It's the Festa del Redentore. Feast of the Redeemer. Everyone's drunk and masked and rowdy."

The candlelight on the table flickers, and Scipio and

I both look up as Percy slides into the booth beside me, two mugs in hand. "I didn't see you come in," he says to Scipio. "I would have gotten you something."

"No need." Scipio stands, pulling his hat on. "I'll have some of my men watch the patrols tonight and see if we can anticipate any chance to slip through. I'll fetch you from here when we're ready to sail."

"Where are we sailing?" Percy asks.

"Out to the island." I nudge the vellum in his direction. His eyes scan the page.

"We'll go in the morning, as quick as we can," Scipio says. "Is that a problem?"

"No, that's . . . soon," Percy says.

A band takes up on the street outside, a whole slew of voices joining it in drunken song. Scipio sighs through his nose. "The sooner we can quit this place, the better."

"What about our ransom?" I ask.

"We'll have to do the exchange elsewhere. Once we have your spoils from the island, we'll move to Santorini, in the Aegean. Our buyers there will harbor us while you write to your families. I'm not staying here for months waiting for them to send someone for you if there are posters everywhere advertising a reward for your capture. Stay out of sight tonight."

"We will," Percy says, but Scipio swats his hat at him as he departs.

"Not you I'm worried about."

I make a face at his back, then take one of the mugs from Percy—the one he didn't half finish between the bar and the booth—and down most of it in four swallows. Percy is still staring at the notice, folding and unfolding its corner with his thumb. A black crinoline crushes up against the other side of the window beside our table like the wings of a raven as a woman stumbles, the crowd pushing her from all sides. His gaze flits up. "Sounds like a gay occasion on the street."

"Sounds like the sounds of . . ." I give up halfway through that sentence—too many versions of the same word and not enough of a preliminary idea where I was going with it—and instead put my forehead against his shoulder.

Percy laughs. "How much have you had to drink?"

"Mmm. Some."

"Some?"

"Some of the drink."

"Well, there's my answer." He slides the glass he just brought me out of my reach.

"Ha, I already finished that. Wait, where are you going?"

"*We* are going up to bed. You're bashed and I'm shattered."

"No, come here." I grab his hand as he stands and pull him back down onto the bench beside me. He nearly lands in my lap. He laughs, but doesn't let go of my hand, instead tucking his thumb against my palm and giving my fingers a soft squeeze. Recklessness rises suddenly inside me, like flotsam disrupted from the seafloor, at the feeling of his skin against mine and that terribly fond smile flirting with his lips. "I want to go out."

"That is a terrible idea. We are being hunted, remember?" He pokes at the notice.

"It's a large city. And a party."

"Are those meant to hide us, or are you listing things you enjoy?"

"What's the use of temptations if we don't yield to them?"

"That'll be chiseled upon your tombstone." He presses his shoulder to mine. "Come on, bed. Scipio told you to stay in."

"No, he said *stay out of sight*. They're entirely unrelated. And we're not sailing until the morning, so he'll never know. *And* we shall wear masks like everyone else and be out of sight entirely." I blow at a strand of hair that has come loose over his ear. "Please come. I feel like we haven't been together in a long while and I want to be out. With you. Specifically. Out with *you*." I bring our still-clasped hands up to my mouth and deal a quick kiss to his knuckles.

Even before he speaks, I know what his answer will be—it's written in the way his whole being melts like tallow when my lips touch his skin. He lets out a dramatic sigh, then says, "You are an enormously stubborn pain in the arse when you want to be, you know that?"

"Is that a yes?"

"Yes, I'll come out."

"Really? No, don't answer—I shan't give you a chance to change your mind. Let's away!" Our hands fall apart when I stand, but he keeps his fingers upon the small of my back as I lead him from the booth, across the packed barroom, and out into the steaming, raucous night.

The rain has taken a recess, though the clouds are still coffered and low. Percy and I follow the masses to the square of Saint Mark's, which is a riot of people. Everyone's drinking—a creative array of libations are being sold from carts, and we taste some fine wine from silver tastevins and then some less-fine wine from less-fine cups, sharing a glass between us like we've done our whole lives, though suddenly it feels strangely intimate to put my mouth where his was just a moment before. Someone hands us masks made from stretched animal skin and dyed black-and-white, and Percy ties mine for me, his hands twining in my hair before he draws me back for a look with his fingers linked behind my neck. I laugh at his mask, and with a wide smile he flicks at the long nose of mine. As we shoulder our way down the street, we walk close enough that our hands sometimes knock.

The air is full of colored smoke, drifting from fire-crackers and bottle rockets set off from the bridges and over the water. Music is playing from so many different places that all the notes tangle into a strange, dissonant symphony. People are dancing. They are standing and singing and arguing and laughing. They are lounging on the bridges, packed into gondolas and hanging off the prows, shrouded in the light from lanterns and firecrackers and torches, on balconies and in doorways, touching each other like the whole city is familiar. I see a ginger-haired man lean over the rail of a bridge and lift his mask so he can deliver a quick kiss to another man with a thick beard, and, zounds, I never want to leave this place.

I glance over to check if Percy saw that, but beneath the mask I can't tell. It's hard for me to think of anything other than what he might be thinking, and what this night means to him, and if it's the same as for me. Here, in the bellow of this music and the torchlight dyed as it flickers through the Murano glass that lines the shop windows, it's easy to pretend we're sweethearts, ordinary as anything, out for a night together in a brilliant city we have never known. Though I could have done without any of it—the drinking and the partying and the revelers in a whirlpool around us—so long as Percy and I were together. The world could have been a blank canvas and I still would have been exactly this livid with happiness, just to be with him.

The crowds thin as we wander from the Grand Canal and the square of Saint Mark's. Revelers stumble in pairs and small knots, their faces still covered, and most heading for the basilica square. When we cross the next bridge into an empty alley, I make a snatch for Percy's hand, and he laces his fingers with mine and gives them a squeeze.

Fetch me a couch, for I nearly swoon.

"Aren't you glad we came out?" I say, swinging our hands between us. "It's like being back home."

"Except not at all and so much better."

"Better because the gin doesn't taste like piss."

"And no one wants to play bleeding billiards."

"And there's no Richard Peele."

"*WE HATE RICHARD PEELE!*" he shouts, which gets me laughing so good I have to stop walking.

"See, *this* is what our Tour was meant to be like," I say as he drags me after him down the street. "There have been far more thrilling heroics than advertised."

"Thrilling heroics suit you, though."

"You know what suits you?"

"Hm?"

"That bit of a beard."

I snatch his mask off so I can get a better look, and he laughs, one hand flitting to the scruff along his jaw-line like he might wipe it away. "Go on, mock me all you want."

"No—I mean it. I like it. You look good."

"So do you." He tugs the mask off my face, that fond

smile again curling about his mouth, though it slips as he qualifies, "I mean, you always look good. But now you look . . . not good. Wait. I mean *yes*, good, you always look good, but you don't look good so much as you look . . . better? Dear Lord. Ignore me."

Under that handsome scruff, his face is rather red. I smile, and Percy laughs again, then swings his arm around my neck and pulls me against him, pressing his lips to my forehead.

The street is still shiny with the afternoon rain, and the canals are jumping as the first soft drops of a new rainstorm strike them. The lantern light shafts across the black water in cords and whorls. And Percy is right there beside me on that beautiful, glowing street and he is just as beautiful and glowing as it is. The stars dust gold leafing on his skin. And we are looking at each other, just looking, and I swear there are whole lifetimes lived in those small, shared seconds.

It takes a moment—an embarrassingly long moment—of resting in his gaze and mentally encouraging myself before I lay my hand upon his cheek and bring my face up to his. It is remarkable how much courage it takes to kiss someone, even when you are almost certain that person would very much like to be kissed by you. Doubt will knock you from the sky every time.

I nearly start to cry when his lips touch mine in return. Pain and ecstasy live tight-knit in my heart. It's a very gentle kiss at first—closemouthed and chaste, one of his hands rising to cradle my chin, as if each of us wants to be certain the other is in earnest. Then his lips part a smidge, and I nearly lose my head. I grab him by the front of his shirt and pull him against me, so forcefully that I hear the seam at the neck pop. He takes a deep breath as his hands go under my coat, his mouth firm for a moment before it softens and then opens against mine. His tongue snakes between my teeth.

We're so wrapped up in each other that we stumble a bit, and he presses me backward against the alley wall, bending down so I don't have to stand quite as high on my toes to reach his mouth. The bricks tear at my coat like briars as I pull his hips to mine so I can feel him going stiff. We're so close that there's not a thing between us but the rain, each drop feeling like it might sizzle and spark on my skin—a spitting quench against molten metal.

He's fiddling with the waistband of my trousers, and a shock goes through me when his cold fingers meet the bare skin along my stomach. "Do you want to . . . ?" His voice comes out ragged and breathless, and he doesn't finish, just hooks his finger in my waistband and tugs.

"Yes," I reply.

"Yes?"

"Yes, yes, absolutely, yes."

I'm already fumbling with the buttons along the flap,

cursing everything I drank that's now making my fingers fat and awkward, but Percy stops me. "Not here, you tomcat. There are people about."

"There are no people about."

As though prompted, someone calls to his mate from the other end of the street. A few dark silhouettes run through a barrel of lamplight. I reach for the buttons anyway, but Percy threads his fingers between mine and pulls my hand away. "Stop. I won't let you take your trousers off in the middle of the street. That is a terrible idea."

"Right. Well. Shall we keep kissing until we think of a better one?"

He brushes his mouth against the corner of mine, and Jesus, Mary, and Joseph, it takes every ounce of the not-inconsiderable restraint I've spent years exercising around Percy not to rip all my clothes off right then, passersby be damned. But I am nothing if not a gentleman, and a gentleman does not take his trousers off in a public place, particularly if the great love of his life is asking him to refrain.

"What if we went away together?" he says.

"Back to the inn? Because I could certainly take my trousers off there."

"No, I mean after this is over."

"What's over?"

"This Tour. This year." He kisses me on the

forehead—a soft, breathy peck. His face is bright. "What if you didn't go home and I didn't go to Holland and instead we went somewhere together?"

"Where somewhere?"

"London. Paris. Jakarta, Constantinople, anywhere—I don't care."

"And what would we do there?"

"Make a life together."

"You mean leave forever? We can't."

"Why not?"

"Because we'd have nothing."

"We'd have each other. Isn't that enough?"

"It's not." I don't mean for it to come out so abrupt, but it slaps that dreamy excitement off Percy's face. His brow furrows.

"But if we left together, I wouldn't have to be put away. If I was with you . . ."

I can't quite wrap my head around this strange reversal between us, because it is always Percy who is the sensible one and me with the feverish notions. But here he is, proposing we run away together with nothing but each other like some sort of star-crossed pair in a broadside ballad, and while my heart is ready to burst for loving him, love is not a thing you survive upon. You can't eat love.

"Think it through, Perce. We'd have no money. No livelihood. I'd lose my title, I'd lose my inheritance. We'd ruin our reputations—we could never go back."

"I can't go back, no matter what." When I don't say anything to that, he takes a step away from me, our hands falling apart. "And what about your father? You'd go back—to him, and that estate work, English society—before you'd go away with me? God, Monty, what are you more afraid of—him or not having all the privilege his money buys you?"

Now it's my turn to step away. I'm not certain how we've slid from his hands down my trousers to the sharpest Percy's ever spoken to me. It makes my head spin. "Come on, Perce, be sensible."

"*Sensible*? I'm being put away in a madhouse at the end of this year and you're telling me to be sensible?"

"Or—" I almost reach for his hand, like touching him will somehow tamp the anger and panic puncturing his words. "*Or* we find the panacea and it works and you can come home with me because you've been cured."

"I don't want it."

"What?"

"I don't want the cure-all. If we find it, I'm not going to use it."

"Why not?"

"Because I'm not going to take this woman's life so I can be well again. And I don't think I have to be well to be happy. God." He takes another step away from me, head tipped back to the sky. "I should have said that ages ago."

"Ages? How long have you been thinking this?"

"Since Dante told us about his mother—before that, even. Monty, I've never wanted it."

"Never?"

"Not never—at first, the idea of finding Mateu Robles and him having something that could make these fits easier to manage was appealing, because epilepsy is *hard*. It is *so hard* to be ill. But I'm not going to take someone else's life—it's not worth that."

"So, why did you let us come all this way?"

"*Let* you?" he repeats, the words feathered by an astonished laugh. "I didn't let you—you never gave me a choice. You never gave me a choice about anything— about speaking to Mateu Robles or taking the key or going with the pirates. You never think what anyone else might want but you! And now you're only interested in being together if it doesn't require any sacrifices on your part."

"And you using the panacea is—what, a sacrifice for you to be well again? Are you *sacrificing* your illness for me?"

"What do you want me to say? Yes, I'm ill. I'm an epileptic—that's my lot. It isn't easy and it isn't very enjoyable but this is what I've got to live with. *This* is who I am, and I don't think I'm insane. I don't think I should be locked up and I don't think I need to be cured of it for my life to be good. But no one seems to agree with me on that, and I was hoping you'd be different, but apparently you think just the same as my family and my doctors and everyone else."

I am losing ground. It's giving out from under me, all the certainty I'd nursed over the past few weeks since learning of the key and the heart, certainty about him and me and us and how all that needed to happen to go back to the way we were was for Percy to be cured, but I'm realizing suddenly that this has always been Percy. It was never a barrier until I knew, so it's not something wrong with him. It's just me who's driven this wedge between us. "But we'd have the panacea! If we ran away together now, you'd still be ill—nothing would change."

He folds his arms. "So which is it—do you want me to be well to keep me from an asylum, or so you don't have to deal with me being ill?"

"Does it matter?"

"Yes."

"Then it's both, all right? I don't want to lose you to an asylum, but this . . . It would be so much easier on both of us if you were well. God, Perce, we've got enough in our way, why this too?"

"Whatever things we have standing in our way, this isn't one."

"Fine." I wrench the key out of my pocket and throw it to him—perhaps a bit more *at* him than *to* him. "There. Now it's yours. Do whatever you want. Make yourself well or run away or toss it in the goddamn sea for all I care."

I expect him to keep arguing, but he doesn't. All he says is, "All right."

Shout at me, I want to tell him. *Fight back, because I deserve it.* I deserve to be fed all the ways I've made him feel unwanted, slapped with my own selfishness. But he's Percy, so he doesn't say another cruel word. Even at his worst, he's so much better than me. His shoulders slump, and he swipes a hand under his eyes. "I'm going to go to bed," he says, "and tomorrow morning, I'm going have a word with Scipio about getting away from here. And I don't think you and I should see each other for a while."

"Wait, Percy—"

"No, Monty. I'm sorry." He starts to walk away, stops and raises his hand like he might say something more, then shakes his head and leaves me.

I don't know what to do. I stand there, silent and stupid and absolutely in pieces as Percy walks away. I watch him until he's gone and I'm certain he won't come back. The hour strikes—church bells around the city all begin to clamor. The air quakes. It starts to rain again, very softly.

I don't want to think about it. Can't think about it.

Got to shut up that voice in my head telling me that I've just lost the only good thing I had because I couldn't get out of my own self. All this while I'd spent thinking we could never be together because we're both lads, but it's not—it's because of *me*.

He asked, and I couldn't give it up.

Can't think about it. Will do absolutely anything not to think about it.

I follow the revelers back toward the piazza—my mask lost somewhere back in the alley and my face bare—and I know what I am going to do, which is drink until I can't even remember this night happened.

Back along the Grand Canal, it's easy to find cheap, virulent gin, easier to drink it until everything smudges and I start to feel like I can leave myself behind. I take four shots of it in quick succession, chased by ambiguous ale and clear spirit straight from a bottle I have to reach behind a bar for. The skyline slants. The moon turns black. It feels like everyone around me is screaming and I am not thinking about Percy.

"Monty. Hey, Monty. *Henry Montague*."

I raise my head and there's Scipio, one hand on my shoulder and his face a bit distorted like he's standing behind glass. I've that mostly empty spirit bottle clenched in one fist and also I cannot remember where I am—sitting on the edge of a bridge overlooking a canal, which narrows down possible locations not at all. A gondola passes beneath me, a woman in a blood-colored dress perched on the prow with her train dragging behind her in the silver water.

"Monty, look at me." Scipio crouches down so our faces are level. "You all right, mate?"

"I am spexcellent. Mmm. No, that's not a word. See, I was going to say *excellent*, and then instead I went with—"

"Monty."

"How are you?" I stand up, roll my ankle on the cobbles, and nearly fall over.

Scipio flies to his feet and catches me. "Let's get you to bed."

"No, no, I can drink more."

"I'm sure you can."

I hold out the bottle. "Have some."

"No, it's too late for me."

"Right. Tit's late. *It's* late." I laugh. Scipio doesn't. He pries the bottle out of my hand and empties it into the canal. I try to snatch it back and miss so spectacularly I would have pitched into the water if he hadn't had a hold on me. "What'd you do that for?"

"Because you're bashed. Come on, to bed."

"Mmm, no, can't."

"Why not?"

"Bed is where Percy is and Percy doesn't want to see me again."

"He mentioned something about that when he came in. You two got each other quite worked up." Scipio tosses the bottle into the canal, then claps me on the back. "He'll calm down."

"Don't think so."

"Why not? You're friends. Friends quarrel."

"I ruined everything. I always ruin everything." I let my forehead fall against his shoulder, and I can tell from his awkward grip on me that neither of us is quite certain what it is that I'm doing, but we don't move. "Goddamn Percy."

Scipio pats me on the shoulder, flat-handed, then pries my forehead off him like he's pulling up a floor-board. "You can sleep on the ship if you're so keen not to see Percy. I told you not to go out—people are after you, remember? You're going to get us all strung up." He wraps an arm around my shoulders and I fall a bit more into him than I mean to and let him pull me back through the crowd.

I trust Scipio to lead the way—either to the docks or the inn, wherever he feels it best to take me. The first landmark I recognize is the Campanile in Saint Mark's Square—a needle poking at the moon. Percy and I stood here together just hours ago, in the shadow of the bell tower, and goddamn Percy, I'm so angry at him I want to punch something, but it's just me and Scipio and crowds of strangers, and none of those seem like good options. Someone slams shoulders with me, and someone else screams right near my ear, and I pull up short, suddenly drowning in the night.

Scipio stops as well. "Come on, Monty, we're turning in."

"I need to . . . I can't . . ."

I'm breathing too fast, and he must notice it, for he steps closer to me. "What's the matter?" I press my hands into my cheeks, regret rancid inside me, and I want to cry so badly, like that might flush it all out. Scipio steps behind me and puts his hands upon my shoulders. "You need to sleep. See how you feel in the morning."

"Percy doesn't want me anymore," I murmur.

Scipio's hand flexes, and I'm not certain if he knows what I mean and ignores it, or simply interprets that sentence in the holiest way. "He'll come around."

He starts to push me forward, and I let myself be pushed, but someone plants himself in our path. My feet aren't as quick as my brain, though that isn't performing at top speed either, and I crash into him. Scipio toes the back of my boot and I step out of it.

"*Scusi.*" Scipio keeps ahold of me as he tries to go around the man, who I realize is dressed in the livery of the Doge's soldiers. The man steps into Scipio's path again, a deliberate move this time, and Scipio halts. I'm still standing on one foot, trying to get my boot back on, and he nearly pulls me over.

The soldier asks us something in Venetian, and we both stare back blankly. Scipio answers in French, "Excuse us."

The soldier steps in his path again. Scipio's grip on my arm goes tighter. "Do you speak English?" the soldier asks, the words fumbled like he doesn't understand the phrase, just the sounds individually.

Scipio's still sizing him up, then says, in English as well, "Yes."

"You English?" The soldier says it more to me, and I nod before I realize I am.

Someone grabs me from behind and I'm wrenched away from Scipio. My muscles seize up. It's another soldier, this one square-jawed and hugely tall, with missing front teeth and the same livery. I'm starting to catch up to what it is that's happening, panic hot on its heels, and I try to yank away from him but I'm too tipsy and he's a good deal bigger than me, and he takes my feeble resistance as a reason to twist my arms behind my back like they're made of cloth. I yelp in pain. Scipio is putting up a much more successful fight than I am, enough that two more soldiers are called over from where they were lurking unnoticed in the shadow of the cathedral.

The soldiers are speaking to each other in Venetian, and Scipio is trying to argue with them, first in French, then English, which none of them seem to understand. I don't know what anyone is saying, so I try to get free again, this time taking the boneless approach in the hope that a sudden collapse will twist my arms free. But the officer hauls me up by the back of my shirt, saying something right in my ear, and I'm flailing to get away when Scipio suddenly says, "Monty, stop!"

The fear in his voice stills me, and when I look over, one of the soldiers has drawn his knife, the blade so thin it's almost invisible until the moonlight catches it. He has the tip of it held to Scipio's throat. I stop fighting and the soldier wrenches my hands behind me again; then the four of them begin to march us across the square, a soldier on either side and the fourth bringing up the rear with that wicked dagger drawn.

They don't take us far. We shove through the crowd—pressed from all sides by feathers and crinoline and baize, strings of pearls whacking at us as they're tossed over shoulders—until we're before the Doge's Palace on the edge of the canal. The soldiers at the door, same uniforms as our escorts, let us pass without a question, and we're prodded across a courtyard rimmed in white stone colonnades, then up two flights of stairs and through a set of large ebony doors.

The room beyond is dominated by a massive four-posted bed. Dark wood panels fringed in gold scrollwork run all the way to the ceiling, where the winged Lion of

Saint Mark looks down from the frescoes. A white-glass chandelier drips wax onto the carpeting. The light of it nearly blinds me and I throw my hands up, face curling in protest. I hear the door shut behind us.

The soldier holding me finally lets go and says in French, his words whistling from his missing front teeth, "Are these the gentlemen you were looking for, my lord?"

"One of them," a sickeningly familiar voice replies. "I've no notion who *that* cove is."

I lower my hands. The Duke of Bourbon is rising from an emerald chaise, Helena with him, perched forward on a window seat across the room. Her plaited hair swings over her shoulder as she squints at Scipio. "Who the devil is that?"

"One of the corsairs that brought them into port, I'd wager," Bourbon replies. "I was informed of their arrival this morning by the dock officials. Was there anyone else with them?" he asks the soldiers.

"No, my lord. Just the pair."

"Where are your friends, Montague?" Bourbon calls to me. "I was hoping you would all be in attendance this evening."

My heart is really going now. *Sober up*, I think. *Sober up, sober up, get your head on straight and sober up and get out of here.* The soldier has sheathed his knife, so I try to make a break for the door but misjudge where I'm standing and slam shoulders with Scipio. One of the soldiers grabs me by the collar and shoves me into the bed. The backs of my legs hit the footboard and I topple over it, landing on the mattress with a dusty *flump*. The metallic tang of blood bursts in my mouth.

"What have you done to him?" Helena asks.

"He's drunk," the duke replies, nose wrinkling. Then, to the soldiers again, he says, "Thank you, gentlemen, you may leave us. The fee will be arranged through your patron."

As soon as the Doge's men are gone, Bourbon seizes me by the arm. He's got a massive pistol with an engraved barrel jammed into his belt, and the grip rams me in the stomach as he drags me back to my feet. "Hand it over, Montague," he says, one hand resting upon his belt, perchance I failed to notice what is essentially a small cannon beneath his coat.

When I speak, my words run together, partly from the drinking but more from the fear. "I haven't got it."

"What do you mean, you haven't got it?" The duke paws at the pockets of my coat, overturning them, then wringing them between his hands like I might have sewn the key into the lining.

"He has it, I know he does," Helena says from behind him.

"Keep quiet," he growls at her.

"They took it from the house."

"I said keep quiet." Bourbon grabs me by the chin,

jerking my face close to his so that a thin mist of spittle freckles my cheeks. "Where's the key?" He shakes me hard, and my head slams backward into one of the bedposts. "Where. Is. It."

"Let him alone." Scipio grabs the duke by the arm and tries to pull him off me, but Bourbon takes a swipe in his direction. The blow lands with a wet *crack*, and Scipio stumbles backward, trips over a footstool, then slams into the wall.

"Stay away, sirrah," Bourbon snaps at him. "You'll stand at the gallows when I'm finished with you."

Scipio stays doubled over, his face pressed into the crook of his elbow and his shoulders heaving. *Swing back*, I think desperately to him and hopelessly to myself. But neither of us does. Fighting back against everyone who cracks you is a luxury we both stopped believing in long ago.

Helena is on her feet now, back to the wall with her hands flat against the paneling. "What do we do?" she says, so quiet she must be speaking to herself.

Bourbon pivots to me again, the soles of his boots making a soft *shush* upon the rug. "Where's the damned key, Montague?"

"I haven't got it," I stammer. I can feel a thin line of blood running down my chin from where I bit my lip, but I'm too stuck with fear to wipe it away.

"Then who does? Tell me. Where is it?" When I don't reply, he shoves me backward onto the bed again and I collapse without protest.

There's a moment of cacophonous silence. Outside the window, the revelers in the square make themselves heard, a pretty and oblivious sound. I can feel the duke staring at me, like he's still waiting for my reply, but I'm not sending this man after Percy and Felicity—I'd rather die now at his hand with the hope they get away.

"Fine," Bourbon snaps. Then his voice shifts as he turns. "You, pirate, stand up. Stand. Up." I raise my head as Scipio straightens. The skin on one side of his face has been scraped raw by the encrusted rings Bourbon wears, and thin tracks of blood are beginning to rise, jewel-colored against his dark skin. "You will deliver yourself to Montague's two companions, who are undoubtedly in your care," Bourbon instructs. He's speaking slowly, like Scipio's a simpleton. "You will inform them they are to meet us on the island of Maria e Marta at dawn, alone, with the Lazarus Key and none of you pirates in accompaniment. If they fail on any of these accounts, I will shoot Mr. Montague and dump his body in the Lagoon."

He pulls his pistol from his belt and pantomimes it for fullest effect. *Bang.*

I let my head fall back against the bed.

Another moment of silence, then he cocks the

pistol—a sound like a snapping bone. "If you don't get along," Bourbon says, "I'll shoot him now."

A moment later, the hobnails in Scipio's boots complain against the floorboards; then the door shuts, and I'm alone.

As soon as he's gone, Helena cries, like she's been holding it in, "Don't shoot him!"

"Keep your head, Condesa." There's a clatter, something heavy tossed onto a wooden surface so hard it rattles everything upon it. "Christ, women are volatile."

She's standing between us, I realize suddenly, as though she doesn't trust him to keep that pistol away. "No one else is dying for this."

"And he shan't, so long as that key of yours is in my possession tomorrow morning."

I'm starting to drift away. My senses are each becoming unfamiliar things in turn, my vision graying, then my hearing slipping out to sea like a message tucked into a bottle. This bed is going to swallow me whole. A shadow falls across me and I push my face deeper into the mattress.

"Let him sleep until we depart," Helena says. "He'll be no good to us until he's sobered up."

Outside the windows, the sky explodes—a fireworks show is beginning. The storm clouds flush, each raindrop a colorful lantern, and the crooked finger of a moon hanging low over the palace turns blood-colored.

I want to be home.

No, not home. I want to be not here. I want to be somewhere safe. Somewhere I know.

I want to be with Percy.

"Sleep well, my lord," I hear Helena say, and I surrender.

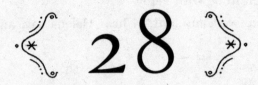

{ 28 }

When I wake, I'm still curled up at the end of the bed, my knees aching and my shirt stuck to my back. My head throbs. I haven't a clue what time it is—it's too colorless to tell. Outside the window, the sky is gray and frothy, though it blushes suddenly white with a tongue of lightning. The water of the Grand Canal bounces as the rain peppers it.

"Are you going to be sick?"

I raise my head. The duke is gone, but Helena is on the window seat, twisting her necklace around her fingers. I don't answer, because I don't believe a prisoner owes his captors any sort of report on his health. That, and if I'm going to be sick, I'd prefer to do it all over her, and I'd prefer it to be a stealth attack.

Helena retrieves a porcelain basin from the washing

table and brings it over to me. I expect her to toss it onto the blankets and then go back to her sentry post, but instead she sits down at the head of the bed, one leg pulled under her and the basin between us. We examine each other for a moment—me with considerably more squinting and wincing. She's different here, away from her father's house and her own terrain. She seems more human, with less armor around her emotions, and for a moment I believe she simply wants this finished.

Then she says, "How did my father look?"

I hadn't been expecting that—not the subject, nor the gentleness of her tone. "How did . . . what?"

"When you saw him in prison. Was he unwell? Did he look as though he'd been mistreated?"

"He was . . ." I'm not certain how to answer, so I choose "Emphatic."

"Emphatic about what?"

"That his children not turn over their mother's heart to the Duke of Bourbon or any man who would use it wrongly."

Her face sets. "You mean a man such as you? You want to use it as well, don't you? That's why you stole the key once Dante told you about our father's work."

"We wouldn't use it wrongly."

"And who decides what is wrong and what is good?"

"Your father said—"

447

"I love my father," she says, each word ironclad. "That is the only thing that matters to me in this world, and I don't care what has to happen for him to be free again." She smashes the wrinkles from her skirt with the heel of her hand, eyes away from me. "So, who was it for?"

"Percy."

"Your friend?" She presses her fist into the mattress, her shoulders never losing their graceful slant but her head drooping in something like penitence. "I'm sorry."

"For what?"

"I don't know," she says. "I'm just sorry."

Before I can reply, the door bangs open and Bourbon sweeps in, the shoulders of his cloak speckled with the rain. Helena flies to her feet, so fast the porcelain basin is almost knocked to the floor. Bourbon tosses his hat upon the chaise. "Am I interrupting something?"

"Did you find a boat?" Helena asks.

"A gondola," he replies. "We'll get past the patrols easier in something small. Get up, Montague," he barks at me, sweeping back the tails of his coat so I can see he's still keeping company with that pistol the size of his forearm. I stumble to my feet, nearly pitching into one of the bedposts.

"Dawn approaches." Bourbon scoops up his hat from the chaise, then bows me out the door. "We're going sailing."

The Doge's Palace sits with its back to the canal, thin docks jutting over the waves like limbs. A sharp black gondola is tied off at the end of one, bobbing in the choppy water. The duke shepherds us into the boat, Helena ahead of me. She hangs a lantern at the prow and takes up the pole without consult, leaving Bourbon and me sitting face-to-face, regarding each other, his pistol resting loosely in his lap.

Helena steers us down Saint Mark's, between the tall ships and the ferries, until we are spat into the Lagoon. We float alone in the water between the city proper and the surrounding islands. As we pass the harbor where we docked the day before, I scan the sails, searching for the *Eleftheria* among them, but she isn't there. The gondola strikes a wave, and a gulp of frigid water soaks my knees.

After what must be near an hour, the silhouette of Maria e Marta blots the horizon. It's a small spit of lonely land—before the water invaded the churchyard, it could likely have been walked end to end in a half of an hour. The only piece still above the waterline is the chapel built upon a hill, its spire a compass to the sky.

"Here they come," Helena says quietly.

Two catboats are gliding toward us, a few men in uniforms of the Doge's soldiers standing at their prows. Bourbon raises a hand to them, tucking his pistol under

449

his cloak but careful to keep it pointed at me.

"Good morning," he calls.

"You're out early, my lord," one of them returns.

"We came to see the island. My nephew, here"—he claps me upon the knee and I flinch more than I think a nephew believably would when clapped by his uncle— "is on his Tour, and I promised him a close view before it goes into the Lagoon."

"It's quite unstable," the guard calls.

"We won't get too near."

Look at me, I think as the soldier's gaze drifts across the three of us, though he seems far more occupied by Helena, who's perched at the back of our gondola like an inverse figurehead. *Look at me and sense that something is wrong. Make us turn back. Arrest him before he shoots me. Tell us to have a good look from here and then go home.*

"Keep your distance," the soldier says. "One of the walls collapsed this past week. Wouldn't want your nephew to be crushed."

Bourbon gives a good-natured laugh. "We'll stay far away, sir."

The catboats go their way, and we ours. My heart sinks to the bottom of the Lagoon as we draw ever nearer to the jagged ruins of the remaining sanctuary walls, their silhouette a gap-toothed smile against the sky.

We approach the chapel from the east, above what used to be the graveyard before it was submerged.

Through the sudsy water, the silhouettes of gravestones ripple and distort. The wings of Saint Mark's Lions jut out of the water like dorsal fins, marking the gateposts every few feet. The chapel facade is ghostly in the corpse-gray light of dawn. Flecks of quartz in the walls sparkle.

We disembark on a submerged dock, ours the only boat in sight. The loneliness of it makes my heart heave. The water hits me above the knee, funneling around my legs as we hike to the chapel, and the rain picks at me from above. The whole damn world seems made of water.

The sanctuary seems more fragile and precarious from the inside, like one good sneeze might topple the whole thing. The doors creak as the water sluices against them, a crusty line of scum marking the level. Beneath the waves, the floor is slick marble set in a chessboard pattern, so every other step feels like a hole I might tumble into. The silence is absolute but for the occasional splash as mortar drops from the ceiling, and the haunted trembling of the waves crawling into corners and scraping against the bottom of the pews.

Bourbon strides up the aisle, lifting his feet high so that each step splashes. "Where are we going, Condesa?" he calls to Helena, and his voice echoes like the sound of the ocean in a shell. A shard of the cracked rose window falls.

"Down," is all Helena replies. The waves carry her skirts behind her like ink spilled from a pot.

Helena leads us to a chapel off the altar; it's higher than the rest of the sanctuary, so the flooding is no more than puddles collecting between the tile. A single tomb sits in the center, two figures carved prostrate upon it. They're both women, one with her hands steepled in prayer, the other with two fingers held to her thumb. Above the tomb, a few lines of scripture are painted.

It was a cave, and a stone lay upon it.
Jesus said, Take ye away the stone.

Helena sets her lantern upon the ground, then works her fingers beneath the lid. "Help me," she says to me.

I don't move. "I'm not overturning a saint's tomb."

"They're biblical women," she says, like that's an explanation. "Their bodies aren't here—only their relics."

"So?"

"So this isn't a real tomb." She jerks at her end of the lid and it slides out of place with a screech. A gasp of hot air escapes, smelling of earth and bone and a long, deep dive. Beneath the lid, a spiral staircase sinks into the darkness.

"Help me," she says again, and I take the other end. Together, we heave the lid off the tomb.

With the stone taken away, Bourbon joins us, all three staring downward. That air billowing up feels freakish, both for its temperature and for its steady rhythm, like the thump of a heartbeat. I'm swallowing fear in short, sharp gasps.

Bourbon draws out his pistol, then jerks his chin at Helena. "You first."

Suddenly I'm not certain which of us is more his prisoner—she or I.

Helena takes up her lantern again and lights a votive candle at the head of the tomb, the glass holder filled with floodwater but the wick dry enough to catch. I think, for a moment, she's going to pray before we descend, but then I realize she's leaving a calling card for Percy and Felicity, so they know where to go if they come. As the flaxen light curls across her skin from below, her face looks empty, any emotion wiped away like rain-fog from a windowpane. For a moment I think she must be too far gone for the gravity of this moment to take root inside her, our shared moment earlier no more than a play act. Then I realize it's the sort of empty that presses out everything else, like if she isn't vacant it will fill her up and soak in like a stain. I recognize it because I've worn it before. Hollow yourself or the fear eats you alive.

Helena is not afraid—she's terrified.

I follow her down the stairs without prompting, the duke bringing up the rear with his pistol at my back. The stairs are built in a tight spiral, so round and narrow we have to go single file with our hands on the wall for balance. The air gets hotter the deeper we go, which seems to be the opposite of what's natural.

At the base of the stairs, Helena raises her lantern so we can all see the corridor ahead. The sallow light doesn't reach far, but in its glow I can see the walls are pocked, their surface raised and rippled like they're made from paper that has been soaked, then dried in waves. We've gone a few meters in silence when the lantern light glances off a bend, and I suddenly realize what it is that's forming those swollen patterns upon the walls.

Bones.

The whole corridor is fashioned from bones, rows and rows of them stacked as high as the ceiling, browning and polished by the drafts of hot air billowing over them. Skulls are hung at intervals between them like sconces, brittle spiderwebs threading them together. Where the corridor bends again, there's a whole skeleton assembled, dressed in dusty Capuchin robes and wired upright with a sign hung around its neck.

Helena leans forward so her lantern illuminates the inscription.

Eramus quod estis. Sumus quod eritis.

I haven't used Latin since my Eton days, and I wasn't what could be called attentive in my study of it, but she translates. *"What we once were, that you are now. What we are now, soon you shall be."*

Another gust of the hot air breathes over us.

We go on, down the gallery of bones, quiet but for the occasional rumbling, like a great giant shifting in his sleep. The ground beneath our feet is a mosaic, grooves worn into the glossy tesserae by funeral processions bringing down their bodies. I imagine Mateu Robles here, carrying down his dead-but-not wife, his conscience heavy as her alchemical heart.

The hall ends in a vaulted ceiling and three columns of skulls, a doorway behind them framed in what seem to be femurs—I try not to look too closely for fear it might send me into a dead faint if I do. Helena doesn't move any farther. Bourbon tips his pistol at me, so I reach for the latch, only to find that it's not a latch at all but a skeletal hand, reconstructed and sitting in its place so that it has to be held for the door to open. A shudder goes through me, head to toe, and I give a fast tug. The door creaks open with a shower of dust. The tunnel gives a moan.

I step into the tomb.

29

The tomb is small and dusty, one wall lined with rows of vaults built into the stone. The highest one is just above my eye level. Each drawer is made of polished black stone with a mother-of-pearl inlay, a family name inscribed upon each beneath the handle. *Robles* is carved upon the center drawer, a prominent keyhole built into a slick silver frame just beneath the *b*. On either side of the vaults, two iron bowls are suspended upon crossed legs, and when Helena touches her lantern to them, the dry kindling inside writhes to life, smoky fingers scratching the darkness in chorus with the hot air that seems to gasp from the walls.

Bourbon does a quick sweep around the room, his cloak tossing up dust from the corners. Helena hangs her lantern on a hook beside the door, then walks up to the drawers, fingers tracing her family name before she presses her palm flat to the polished stone, head bowed.

His lap finished, Bourbon leans back against the vaults, heel scuffing the black stone. "Now," he says, one finger fiddling with his pistol, "we wait for your friends to bring me my key, Montague."

"It isn't yours," Helena says, so quiet I almost don't hear her.

"Then whose is it, Condesa?" Bourbon barks, but she doesn't say anything. Her forehead is nearly touching the stone vaults. "Yours? Your brother's? Mr. Montague's? Your mother will have died for naught if none of us use it." He knocks on the drawers. The ceiling groans, a geyser of dust misting down upon us. "Your father is a cowardly, wasteful fool for hiding her this way."

"He isn't," I say, my voice breaking on the last word, but I feel suddenly obliged to stand up for Helena, or perhaps not so much her as her father, the man whose coat I wore to the opera and who spoke about his daughter when she was small enough to tie a string from her finger to his. Perhaps that means I'm defending her as well. She used to be that small girl, after all. Perhaps she still is, the girl who loved her father so much she'd give anything to again be close enough to have that string between them.

Bourbon shifts his gaze from Helena to me. "Would you like to discuss cowardly fathers, Mr. Montague? You'd school us all."

"What?"

"I assumed you robbed me on his instructions, or in some sort of desperate play to aid him. He's been looking to knock me out of favor for years."

"My father wouldn't instruct me to steal from any man." As much as I might loathe him, I'm certain of that—he's far too stiff-collared. "He may not care for you, but he's a gentleman."

"Your father's a rake." Bourbon spits the word. "About as filthy a man as I've ever had occasion to meet."

"What are you talking about?"

"Don't you know?" A slow smile stretches over his lips. "Since we're *waiting*, let me ask you this, Montague: Do you know what your father likes?" A pause. I'm not certain if this is a rhetorical question and I should keep silent, or if he's using my father's favorite strategy of a rhetorical question I'm still meant to answer so I'll look stupid. But before I can work it out, Bourbon supplies, "Your father loves nothing so much in this world as slow ponies and other men's wives."

A jolt goes through me, like a missed stair. "You're lying."

He flicks his thumb at the handle built into the Robleses' tomb. Helena's shoulders rise. "I knew him, when he was young and living in the French court. He was a bastard even then, squandering his father's money on horses and cards and always screwing someone else's

458

woman. The wives and intendeds of his friends, those were always his favorites. And then he got himself a wife of his own." I have a brief moment of wondering if, all these years, my father's been unfaithful and if Mother knows, but then he goes on, "Some French girl in the country. He ruined her and then tried to run, but her father badgered him into marriage."

A ripple of that hot air nearly knocks me off my feet. I almost grab Helena. "He had it . . . He must have annulled it."

"Too late for that," Bourbon says. "When he refused to stay and accept the consequences, he called for me to rescue him. He couldn't tell his family—they'd have turned him out—and all his friends hated him by then. I got him back to Paris and helped get him married off the Continent. The country wench probably couldn't have found him if she'd tried, but better not to take the chance. His family never knew. I suspect your mother doesn't either, that her union to him is invalid, as he had one already when it was formed. It's only he and I that know the truth. And you. So tell me, Montague." He leers at me, a toothy grin that the firelight licks. "What do you think of your father now?"

My head is pitching in a way that has nothing to do with the drinking from the night before. It's hard to take it all in in this single heaping dose, but what I think at once is that my father—my Reformation of Manners

Society father—the man I've lost years of my life ducking my head before, racked up debts and ruined women and then ran from it all rather than claim the consequences. I am thinking that my father lies, and maybe the foul things he's fed me about myself for my whole bleeding life were just as untrue. That my father cheats. That my father has no pedestal from which to hand down judgment on me for my sins.

He's not a gentleman, any way you might unravel the word.

He's a scoundrel. And a cowardly one at that.

"Running out of time," Bourbon says suddenly, as though there's any way he can gauge the hour in this pit. "Perhaps your friends don't care for you after all."

He hefts the pistol from his belt and I flinch, but Helena steps between us. "Don't you dare shoot him."

"I'll shoot him if I goddamn like. This island is sinking around our heads and my key has been taken by pirates and children. If your mother's bewitched heart isn't in my hand by the end of this day, Condesa, your father will rot for the rest of his life, I'll see to it."

Bourbon lifts his pistol, but Helena doesn't move. Neither do I, though that's a far less gallant thing to be noting. There's something quite ungentlemanly about cowering for your life behind a lady, but if Helena wants to put herself between Bourbon and me, I'll not refuse that gift.

But the duke freezes suddenly, pistol still leveled, with his head cocked toward the door. I can hear it too—a dry slapping echo coming down the corridor of bones behind us. Footsteps.

Bourbon looks to the door of the tomb, but Helena looks to me. Our eyes meet—a strange, solemn hush in the middle of a storm.

Then she steps back, leaving nothing between me and Bourbon, but before he can make good on his promise to shoot me, someone shouts, "Stop!"

I've only got a second to get a good look at Percy standing in the doorway, Felicity at his side—both of them panting like they've been running, and both dripping wet from the floodwater—before Bourbon grabs me from behind and drags me in front of him like a shield. The cold press of his pistol noses my temple. "Where's my key?" he calls.

Percy fumbles in the pocket of his coat, his other hand raised above his head, until he comes up with the toothy Lazarus Key and holds it up to the light. It casts a frail shadow across the vaults. "It's here. Take it. Please. Take it and let Monty go."

"That's it?" Bourbon says, his head tipped toward Helena for an answer. "That's all?" Helena nods. "Unlock it for me, then," Bourbon calls to Percy.

Percy blanches. "What?"

"You heard me, unlock the drawer. I'm sure you can

work out which one. Quickly, please." The pistol jerks against my skin and I let out a soft whimper without meaning to. Percy winces. The duke still has one arm clamped around my chest, so tight it's hard to breathe. Or maybe that's just the fear stopping me up.

Percy steps forward slowly, hands still raised, and then slides the key into the hole in the Robleses' drawer. As he turns it, there's a series of clicks, like a stick's being dragged up a stack of vertebrae. The drawer pops open. Percy stumbles backward to where Felicity is frozen, looking as frightened as I've ever seen her—raw, naked fear, no battlements to hide it.

Helena and Bourbon both advance, and I'm still wedged before the duke, so when they cozy up to the drawer and peer in, I'm forced to as well.

For one strange moment, I think it's Helena in the vault. But the woman lying there, pale and naked, is older, her nose thinner and chin rounder. Her hair covers her bare shoulders in shimmering waves, and I can smell the perfume off it. Her skin too looks newly oiled, like the funerary rights were done just before we arrived. Her eyes are open, and the whole of them is black, as though they've been filled with nightshade. Stitching runs up the center of her torso from her navel to her collarbone, a scarlet sheen pressing against her skin from the other side, like a lantern tossed beneath a sheet.

Neither dead nor alive.

I understand suddenly, in a way I hadn't before. No one but me had had to see her to realize this would be taking a life.

"That's my mother," Helena says, soft as a prayer, and I look up at her. She's staring down at the woman, two fingers pressed to her lips and a look about her that feels as though she might come untethered at a breeze.

Bourbon lets me go just long enough to get his pistol against my spine and take a step back from the vault. I can hear him rooting around in his coat; then his arm enters my eye line. He's clutching a great knife, which he extends to Helena. "Do it, then."

She doesn't take it. "You have the key. I'm finished."

"Our agreement is complete once I've the heart. Your father can stay in prison if you retreat now."

"I won't."

Bourbon taps the blade of the knife flat against the rim of the drawer. It rings like a tuning fork. "Consider your actions, Condesa, before you cross me."

"That's my mother." Her voice tears on the last word, a ragged note of grief like ripped paper. She stumbles back from the tomb, one hand pressed over her mouth.

Bourbon's pistol nudges me in the back. "Fine. You do it, Montague."

"Oh dear God, no. No, thank you."

"Go on."

"No, please, I can't—"

"Here." He reaches in with the butt of his pistol and cracks the woman across the chest so that her rib cage collapses with a sound like dropping a stone on a sheet of ice. Helena flinches like it's she who's been broken open, both her hands flying up to press against her own heart. "Let me start things off for you," he says.

I'm shaking like mad at just the thought, but it isn't really a choice, with that pistol again to my back and both Percy and Felicity standing there. My fear is less that he's going to shoot me and more that he'll turn it on them. All my soft spots are exposed.

Another gust of the hot air hits me—hot air that's rising off her, I realize, pulsing from that glowing heart as it beats. My breath sticks in my chest.

Then Felicity says, "I'll do it." Bourbon regards her as she extends a steady hand. "I can," she says. "Better than Monty. Give it here and I'll do it for you."

Pistol still pressed into my back, Bourbon hands the knife over and she steps up to the drawer, right across from me. Her gaze flits up to mine. "Help me," she says quietly, then presses the tip of the blade into the hollow of Helena's mother's throat.

The skin peels away with little resistance, like paper off a wrapped package. I hold the flaps in place while Felicity wedges her fingers into the sternum, a jagged crack like a lightning strike down the center from Bourbon's blow, and gives a sharp wrench with more strength than I knew she had in her. There's another *crack* as the ribs snap from the spine. Helena lets out a soft sob.

And there is the heart, raw and red, not so much beating as pulsing, like it's a throbbing wound. As I hold the skin in place, Felicity makes quick work peeling back the withered husks of the lungs and severing the veins. Each one breaks from the heart with a sound like delicate glass, and with each, the rest of the mother's body seems to grow less and less alive, as though her whole being is distilled and packed inside her heart.

Felicity forces her hands between the ribs and lifts the heart out, careful as if handling a newborn kitten. I can feel the heat radiating off it, and Felicity's arms bow against its weight, like it's a precious stone or the anchor of a ship.

Felicity holds it out to Bourbon, but he steps back, dragging me with him, like he's white-livered at the thought of being too near it. "Give it to Condesa Robles," he says. "She'll carry it from here."

Helena steps up to meet Felicity, in the empty space between Bourbon and me, and Percy. Helena takes the heart between her cupped hands, so very carefully, like it's fragile and alive. Her fingers curl around the edges, and a transparent bead of something that is half blood, half light slides from the surface and down the back of her hand.

Helena starts to say something, but Bourbon grabs

me from behind and yanks me to him as a shield again. Percy has been inching forward, reaching out like he might pull me to his side as soon as the exchange was made, but he freezes, hand still raised. Felicity darts back to his side, arms wrapped around herself. She leaves fingerprints of the strange, shimmering residue from the heart along her sleeves.

"You've what you want," Percy calls. "Please, let Monty go." Then, once more for good measure, "Please."

"No, I'm afraid there was never a chance the three of you would leave this place alive—surely you knew that when you came."

"This was my fault," I say. I feel like I'm sagging into him, my strength waning and all my fight to survive eaten up. "Let them go; I stole the box."

His arm tightens around my throat, choking out my words. "Sorry, my lord. Condesa, back out in the tunnel. Since you're so keen to keep blood off your hands, we'll seal them in and they can sink with the island."

Helena hasn't taken her eyes off the heart, still cradled between her hands. It casts a faint sheen upon her face from below.

"Condesa," Bourbon snaps.

Helena raises her face, though it's not the duke she looks to—it's Percy. "Do you want this?" she asks him softly.

"Condesa," the duke says again.

"Do you?" she asks.

"No," Percy replies.

Bourbon seems to realize what she's about to do the moment before she moves. As Helena holds the heart toward one of the bowls of flame, he lunges forward, ready to snatch it from her, but finds I'm rather in his way. Our legs tangle up, and he slams into me, sending us both to the ground. My shoulder strikes the stone with a *thwack*, the pain from impact doubled when he lands atop me.

Bourbon tries to wrestle himself free, his foot ramming me so hard in the stomach I lose my breath, and makes a scramble forward on his hands and knees. He's clawing toward Helena, and she's reaching for the flames, the heart between her hands. He's going to grab her—or it—before she can destroy it, and part of me wants to as well. Reach out and catch that precious thing between my hands and claim it.

But instead, I do the only thing I can think of to stop the duke: I make a fist and wind up, then, at the last second, untuck my thumb from inside my palm and punch him straight in the nose.

And it still bloody well hurts, but it's loads more effective this time—I feel cartilage crumple beneath my fingers. Bourbon howls with pain as blood pours down his face and splatters the stone, and Helena seizes her moment with maximum panache—she doesn't just toss, she *flings* her mother's heart into the fire.

It catches at once, like it's been soaked in alcohol. A column of flame jets upward, so searing we all put up our hands, except the duke. He's still got blood pouring over his lips and dribbling down his chin, but he's clawing his way forward, like he might pull the remnant from the flames and salvage it. The heat from it blisters his forehead.

I grab him by the coat, trying to yank him backward, and he growls in frustration, taking a blind swipe in my direction with his pistol. The barrel knocks me above the ear, and then he fires, right up against my face. There's a fantastic *bang* and I'm slammed into the floor, my head burning. For a moment, I can't hear a thing but a metallic hum.

A torrent of sparks rises from the fire where Helena dropped the heart, like a weld struck when nearly molten; then another blast of hot air explodes through the room, full of ash and spark and a glittering dust that smells of bone and chemicals. The walls begin to tremble, pebbles sifting from the ceiling and showering us. The lights dance. One of the iron bowls topples, spilling lit kindling. The sound starts to return, though it's smothered. A low rumble begins to underscore the whistling in my ear.

Felicity's lips are moving, and I hear her cry, "The tunnel!"

I'm trying to get to my feet and finding it a great deal more difficult than it should be. Percy grabs me by the arm and hauls me up, pulling me after him, one arm wrapped around my waist and Felicity ahead. She wrenches the door open and the three of us clamber through, just as a pillar on the other side tumbles like a felled tree, bones cascading. Percy yanks me out of the way before I'm struck by them.

Helena is close behind us, but in the doorway she turns and screams, "Come on!" I don't know who she's talking to until I turn and there's Bourbon, still on his knees before the fire, clawing at the flames and trying to pry free any fragment of the heart that might be left. Flames are climbing up his sleeves, leaping to his hair, and he's screaming, but he doesn't stop.

"Come on!" Helena shouts again. "It's gone, come *now*!"

But he isn't coming—he's burying himself in this tomb. The doorway crumbles, and Felicity—bless, for I've not an ounce of Christian charity left in me for the pair of them—grabs Helena and drags her away.

The four of us hurtle down the passageway, the walls buckling around us. Even the air seems to be vibrating, split by the sound of all those bones cracking and folding and collapsing into splinters and sand. The tunnel is growing so thick with dust it's getting hard to breathe. At the bend, the wired Capuchin leers at us as we pass.

Soon you shall be flashes before the sign hits the ground and snaps in half.

At the base of the tunnel, Helena pulls ahead of us, flinging herself up the stairs and out of sight. By the time we emerge into the chapel, she's already splashing down the dock, where our gondola was tied off. Another boat is moored beside it.

Helena shoves the gondola off from the dock, burying her pole in the water and riding the current away. As we follow her, there's a crack like thunder behind us, and a piece of the chapel wall collapses. The dusty wind of it strikes our backs, and we all stagger. The floodwater pitches into waves.

The vibrations of the stones tumbling into the Lagoon are raising ripples around our legs, the deck tipping badly enough that I tip with it, sideways into Percy so that the water soaks me up to my waist. He somehow manages to stay on his feet. Perhaps, I realize, because it's only me that's tipping. I am amazed to discover my limbs have almost entirely ceased to function—the only reason I'm still upright seems to be that Percy's holding me—and my head is feeling strange, like it's filling up with thick water. My ears are ringing.

Percy hoists me into the boat after Felicity, then gives us a good shove-off from the dock before he leaps in after. The island rumbles again, and a shower of stones scratches at my face as another wall of the chapel goes into the Lagoon.

"Monty." Percy grabs my shoulder, and I have a sense he's said my name a few times without a response. He's leaning over me, his face smeared with soot and dust, and a faint shine left by the alchemical heart. "Monty, talk to me. Say something."

I raise one hand to the side of my face to find it hot and damp. "I think I've been shot."

"You have not been shot." Felicity pulls the oars into the boat long enough to peel my fingers away from my head. Her face goes pale, then she presses my hand back where it was. "Fine, you've been shot."

Of course this would be the one time I'm right about my injuries.

"It isn't bad," she says, but she sounds as though she's working so hard to be calm about it that I know she's lying. That, and I can feel my heartbeat all the way through my skull, which is alarming. It's like swallowing my pulse. "Keep your hand on it," Felicity cries as my hand slips. "Tight, Monty. Press it tight."

Percy grabs my hand and presses both our palms, overtop of each other, to the side of my head. Blood is bubbling up against my palm and running in thin rivulets between my fingers and down my arm. It's pathetic how dizzy the sight of my own blood makes me. Or perhaps that's got to do with the fact that it seems to be abandoning me en masse. I'm starting to breathe faster without meaning to. The air is feeling very thin.

Then Felicity shouts, "There they are!"

And through the gray mist, the *Eleftheria* looms like the silhouette of a cathedral against the sunrise, two cat-boats chasing lamely behind.

Felicity drops the oars and steers us up against the prow until two ropes unfurl from the deck. She takes one and Percy the other, his hands slick with blood as he ties us off. The ropes turn scarlet between his palms.

"Heave!" comes a shout from above, and the boat jerks upward until we are spat out onto the deck, which is looking more underwater than the chapel.

I'm trying to stay awake, but my head keeps sinking, like I'm dozing. Someone's pressing something against the side of my face and, holy Mary, it's really hurting.

The sailors are all clustered around us. Every boot on the planking rattles me to my teeth.

"Christ—"

"—a lot of blood."

"—on his side."

"Is he breathing? I don't think he's—"

"Let Miss Montague through!" Scipio's voice roars over them.

"Monty." Percy is shaking me. It sounds like he's speaking from the bottom of a well. He's right beside me, holding me steady on my side. "Monty, look at me. Try to stay awake. Keep your eyes open—come on, darling, look at me. Please."

He's got blood all over his shirt, the wet material clinging to his chest. "You're hurt," I murmur, raising a hand to pluck at it.

"No, I'm not."

Oh, so that's *my* blood. Fantastic. A pathetic whimper escapes me.

"It's all right," he says softly, his other hand twining with mine. "Breathe. You're going to be fine. Please, breathe."

And then the next thing I know, I'm flat on my back on the bunk in Scipio's cabin, the lantern overhead swinging as the ship cants. Percy is on the floor beside me with his legs drawn to his chest, asleep with his forehead against his knees and his hand in mine. The angle of it twists my wrist up, but I don't move.

My vision is cloudy, and one of my ears is still filled with that metallic ringing. The entirety of my face is throbbing, and when I shift, pain rips through my head and cracks behind my eyes like the gunshot all over again. I cry out without meaning to, and Percy bolts upright. "Monty."

"Hallo, darling." My voice is rusty, and the skin along the right side of my face pulls when I speak.

"You're awake." He hoists himself into a crouch

beside me and touches his thumb to my chin. His voice is muffled, like I'm hearing him with a pillow over my head. If I wasn't looking straight at him, watching his lips form the words, I couldn't be certain where they were coming from.

"You look worried," I murmur.

"Yes, well, that's your fault, you know." I laugh weakly, but it turns into rather more of a wince. "I think I was shot."

"You very nearly were."

"*Very nearly*? That's less harrowing than I hoped."

I raise my hand—which is heavier than it should be—and touch my head. There's a tight wrap of bandages all the way around it, and the spot over my ear is damp. "Does it look bad?"

"It . . . doesn't look very good," he says carefully. "It's burned and swollen, but that'll fade. Though the ear is a bit . . ." He tugs on his own lobe.

"A bit what?"

"Gone. It's a bit . . . gone."

"You mean I've only got—"

"Don't touch it." Percy catches my hand before I can rip the bandages off.

"I've only one ear left?"

"Most of it got blown off and the rest was sort of . . . mangled. Felicity took it off cleanly. You're lucky the powder didn't wreck your eyes as well."

"Where is Felicity?"

"She's fine."

"No, where is she? I'll rip *her* ear off and see how she likes it."

"I should tell her you're awake. She's been going mad over you. Didn't know Felicity liked you so much until you nearly kicked it."

"Nothing brings a pair closer than a near-death experience, I suppose."

Percy rubs his temples. I can tell he's trying to play this off as casual, though I must have been right bad off if it's sitting this heavy on him. "When Scipio told us Bourbon had you, and then you were shot—"

"*Very nearly* shot."

"Zounds, Monty, what if the last thing we ever did was fight?"

"Do you have better last words to me that you'd like to deliver? You could share them now, in case things go south again."

He puts his hand atop my knee, the blanket between us, and I suddenly feel like I'm tempting fate with this question. But then he says, "I'm sorry."

"Oh, darling," I return, stacking my hand over his, "you haven't a thing to be sorry for."

I'm still not hearing right, and it's beginning to shift from irritating to worrisome. Percy's voice is stifled, and my own is echoing backward in my head, like I'm speaking in a vast, empty hall. Maybe it's the bandages that have everything muted, but when I snap my fingers next to my right ear—the one that is apparently no longer with me—it sounds like it's coming from the other side of the room.

Which is when I realize.

I try to sit up and the room tips—it nearly knocks me straight back out. Percy grabs me before I keel over. "Easy."

I manage to get one hand pressed over the ear I've got left, closing it up, and then snap again beside the missing one.

And it's . . . nothing. No sound at all.

Percy is watching me, his eyebrows knit. "Is it gone?" he asks.

My throat's feeling a bit wobbly, so I just nod.

It's hitting me a lot harder than I feel it should. I'm quite lucky to be alive—shouldn't be crying over losing the hearing in one ear. Percy seems to understand it, though—he slides an arm around my waist and lets me press the side of my face that isn't minced meat against his chest.

"I'm sorry," he says.

"S'all right," I murmur, trying to sound mild as milk about it and failing spectacularly. "Could have been worse."

"Yes. Could have been so much worse." He laughs,

the way Percy always does when something's got him properly spooked. I can feel his heart beating through his chest, right up against mine. "I'm just so, so glad you're alive." His voice breaks a little on the last word, and he touches his lips to the top of my head, so soft it's almost imaginary.

And I'm not certain what that is. But it isn't nothing.

Oia, Santorini

After seven days at sea, the *Eleftheria* makes port in the small, mountainous island of Santorini in the Aegean Sea. Its cliffsides are canvased in cave houses burrowed into the volcanic stone and whitewashed buildings domed in cobalt blue. Thatch-roofed windmills jut between them, their blades like rays of the sun. The sun itself is a vivid thing, brighter in this crook of the Continent. The whole world looks somehow brighter.

Scipio and his men stay with their ship, but he helps Felicity, Percy, and me find a flat on the cliffs above the sea, with its own cobalt dome and stone floors and a landlord friendly with the captain and willing to take our Italian lire. The rooms are sun warmed and clear, the courtyard crowded with fig trees around a small, laughing fountain. The sea seems everywhere.

The first few days feel packed and frantic, full of

learning the land and selling the cargo and arranging supplies and repairs for the ship and looking for a proper doctor who speaks at least one of the languages we do and who can take a look at my face. It's mostly been Felicity tending to me while we sailed from Venice—my hearing seems to have no inclination to return, and along with the bullet clipping my ear, I caught the discharge from the gun, which left thick speckled burns in random patches from my hairline to my collarbone. I haven't seen myself in a glass yet, but I have a suspicion that the right half of my face will be off-colored and scarred for the remainder of my life.

My best feature, ruined.

"I don't think you can claim your entire face as your best feature," Felicity tells me. "You're meant to be a bit more discerning."

We're at the table in the courtyard, Felicity unwrapping the bandages from my head so she can get a look at how everything is healing. When the Greek doctor came, every instruction he gave was met by a "Yes, I know" from Felicity, though Scipio didn't translate those for him. He also complimented Felicity on her stitching, which she's been crowing over ever since.

"Well, it's difficult to choose when you have so many good options." I swipe my hand at my right side, forgetting momentarily that the empty buzz that has replaced all other sound isn't an insect I can swat away.

"Fortunately my right ear was the less handsome of the pair."

"Fortunately, or else you'd be devastated."

A few months ago, I might have been. I'd be lying if I said I wasn't mourning the loss a wee bit. But we're all still alive, and still together, so instead it feels strangely like luck.

Felicity lets the bandages fall into her lap atop her surgical kit, then does a careful inventory of my disfigurement. "It looks . . . better."

"Your telling pause disagrees."

"It does! The swelling's gone down, though we need to watch for infection. Let's leave the bandages off for a bit so it can breathe." She squints for a moment longer, then says, with a bit of a smug smile, "That stitching of mine is rather impressive."

"I'd say you're quite good at this physician business as a whole."

She looks up from packing her kit, eyes narrowing. "What are you doing? Oh no, are you trying to get along with me? Do we have to get along now?"

"What? No. Of course not."

"Thank God."

"*Get along.* Don't be absurd."

There's a rap on the courtyard gate and Scipio steps into the garden, a coat thrown over his seaman's duds though the heat is livid. "Good morning," Felicity calls, sliding down the bench to make room for him. "We were just about to breakfast."

"Where's Mr. Newton?" Scipio asks as he joins us.

"Still abed," I say. "How's your darling ship and your cutthroat crew?"

"The crew and the ship are both anxious to be off," Scipio says. He takes a mug from the spot waiting for Percy and pours himself lime-flower tea from the jug.

"You want to leave?" I ask as Felicity looks up.

"And we'd like you to be with us," he says. "We'll take you home, to England, and if Thomas Powell can indeed be persuaded to exercise his influence, collect our letters of marque. We'd like to sail with some legitimacy."

"Home?" I ask, unable to keep my voice from pinching the word like a creased napkin. Here I was beginning to grow accustomed to this optimistic sunlight and exile-in-Eden business, and now we're packing it in yet again, this time Britain bound. Back to Father. "How long before you go?"

He shrugs. "Four days. Before the week's out, at the latest."

"Can't we stay a bit longer?" I ask. "I've just suffered a grievous injury, after all."

Felicity's eyes flick to mine. "Oh, you're fine. I cleaned you up so well that not only will it heal, but the missing ear will do wonders for taming your ego."

"Ho, there—" I must be sufficiently recovered,

because Felicity has begun to feel it appropriate to begin needling me again.

Scipio surveys Felicity over the rim of his mug, then asks suddenly, "You want a job? We could use a surgeon on board. Gangrene got our last one at the end of the winter."

"Hard not to see the irony in that," I remark.

Felicity laughs, though he looks earnest. "Good jape."

"None intended," Scipio replies.

"Your men would take a woman among them? That's hardly appropriate for either party."

"Plenty of women take to sea. My mother sailed the African coast with her father when she was young. Have you heard of Grace O'Malley? Or Calico Jack? He had two ladies aboard with him."

"And they both would have swung with him if they hadn't pled their bellies," Felicity finishes. "Yes, I've heard that story."

"Difference being, if you all make good on your bargain, we won't be pirates long. You wouldn't swing."

She laughs again. "I can't be a surgeon! I've had no training."

"You'd learn."

"On you and your men."

"We'll all have to strive to injure ourselves often for your educational benefit."

She looks astonished—an expression Felicity so rarely

wears that it's rather alarming. "I will . . ." she starts, but instead of finishing, she says as she stands, "I was going to make breakfast."

Scipio stands too, trailing her into the kitchen. "Just think it over, Miss Montague," I hear him say as they go. "You needn't decide until we reach England. The boys are useless, but I'd take you on."

I would have done a dramatic drop of my face into my hands at the news that we're going home, had I not recently parted ways with a good piece of that selfsame face. I don't know what I was expecting to happen at the end of all this, but somehow it wasn't a return home. Or at least not so soon. I don't know what Percy's going to do—if he'll come with us, or if he's still going to Holland. In spite of how much we've been together since we quit Venice, I haven't been well enough or alone with him long enough to have a proper talk.

Scipio and Felicity make busy in the kitchen as I sit on the terra-cotta step into the courtyard—truly the only benefit of my near-death experience is that it has temporarily disqualified me from all chores. Soft conversation floats through the open window, first just Scipio and Felicity trading light japes about women aboard a pirate ship, then Percy's voice as he joins them. Scipio relays the same message to him as he did to us—the leaving news. My heart kicks.

There are footsteps on the walk behind me, and I

shuffle out of the way, but it's Percy, half dressed and still wild-haired from bed.

"Good morning, darling," I say as he sinks down at my side, his bare toes curling around the scrubbed fingers of grass growing up between the stones. "Ack, don't sit on that side of me. Can't hear anything." It pricks a strange vein of grief inside me to say it aloud. I wonder if it will ever stop being strange, that empty whistling on one side of my head, or the way anything but conversation had face-to-face is near impossible to decipher. Felicity says I'll grow accustomed to it in time, though she also keeps sneaking up on my deaf side and scaring the shit out of me.

"Forgot. Sorry." Percy slides from the step so that he's sitting in front of me instead, knees pulled up to his chest and arms looped around them.

I resist the urge to scratch at the torn-up side of my face. Burns, as it turns out, get beastly itchy once the pain retreats.

"Don't touch it," he says suddenly.

"I'm not!"

"You were thinking about it."

I sit on my hands. Consider wrinkling my nose at him as well, though I'm afraid it might fell me. "This is going to significantly hinder my future romantic prospects."

"Not necessarily."

"It will certainly discourage initial approach. I'm

going to have to start relying on nothing but my personality. Thank God my dimples survived."

"Thank God. Because you've nothing else in your favor. And how do you know what it looks like? You can't see it."

"I have a sense, as it's my head, and I can tell it's going to be a great ugly scar no one will ever be able to look away from."

"It's not."

"Not what?"

"Not ugly." He catches my chin in his hand as I turn away from him and tips my face up. I can feel the sun upon my skin like a second set of fingers looped with his. He traces my jawline with his thumb, then smiles widely, his head canting to the side. "You're still gorgeous, you know."

There's a clatter from the kitchen, a tin plate dropped on stone, and Percy and I both jump. His hand falls from my face.

"Are you steady enough to go walking?" he asks.

I've been rather shaky on my feet since I parted ways with my hearing—apparently those two things are related in a way only Felicity understands. "If we go slowly. Anywhere in particular you care to walk to?"

"I've an idea, if you'll trust me."

"I trust you," I say, and he pulls me to my feet, my hand in his.

Percy leads me on through town to the edge of the cliffs, where we take the steep, snaking path down to the beach. We don't say much beyond the occasional good-natured moan about what a son of a bitch this mountain is going to be to climb back up. I stay on his right side, and he keeps one hand at my elbow, resting there but not quite touching, and ready to grab me if I pitch over.

From a level eye with the sea, the Aegean is almost too radiant to be real, the vivid turquoise of the speckles on a robin's egg. There's not a soul about this stretch of sand but us—no one else daft enough to make the trek down the cliffs, I suppose—so Percy and I both take off our jackets and waistcoats and leave them to crease in a heap on the beach. I make a show of kicking off my shoes in a high arc and letting them lie where they land, which makes Percy laugh. He's much more civilized about pulling his off and then bundling the socks into the toes before he walks into the sea. I follow, skirting the edges of the waves and dancing out of the way each time one gets too near.

"Come into the water," Percy calls from where he's standing up to his knees in the sea.

"No, thanks. I'm wounded, remember?"

"Come on, you coward. I'm not going to make you swim."

He stumbles back up the beach toward me, sand

caving under his feet as the waves take it, and makes a snatch for my arm. I dodge, so he gets the back of my shirt instead and drags me after him until the sea and I meet and I am forced to wet my toes. I make to wriggle from his grasp, but a wave of dizziness knocks me asunder. I stumble, but Percy catches me, his hands suddenly harboring my waist while I grab a handful of his shirt. Our faces swoop close.

"Steady on," he says.

I blink hard a few times, trying to clear my head. "I'm ready for these spells to be over so I can get on with being partly deaf."

"Perhaps you can buy a handsome ear trumpet once you get home."

"And then this time next year, everyone will be carrying one."

"As goes Henry Montague, so goes the nation."

Now that I'm steady, I think he's going to pull away, because the last time we toppled into each other it ended in shouting. But instead he puts his arms around my neck, and though my vision has settled, we sway together as a wave strikes us, soaking the knees of our breeches. It's something like dancing.

When I can't think of anything else, I say, "It's gorgeous here." Then immediately wince because, oh God, have we reached such a barren spit of land in our relationship that I'm reduced to making observations about the surroundings just for conversation? And if so, I'll have to find a sharp shell upon the beach and slit my wrists right here.

But Percy just smiles. "The Cyclades weren't really on our itinerary."

"Oh, I think we're well off track now. We've had an adventure novel instead of a Tour."

He reaches up and pushes a loose thread of my hair behind my ear. "What will everyone say, do you think? We'll be the shame of our families."

"Oh, I think my father holds that title. Turns out, I'm rather a bastard." When Percy gives me a quizzical look, I supply the details of my father's abandoned French bride. "If anyone knew, he'd lose everything," I finish. "The estate, the title, the money, his standing. Probably be jailed as well. Even a rumor of it would wreck him."

"So, what will you do?" Percy asks.

A flock of seagulls take flight from the beach and settle upon the sea, bobbing like sailboats upon the current as they complain to each other. I've been thinking about it a good deal in the space between Venice and Santorini, this question of what might happen if I turned up the bodies my father has buried in our garden. The damage I could do to him, fitting retribution for the years he's spent beating me down.

"Nothing," I say, because I'm not the only one who'd have to live with those overturned graves.

"So, you're just going home? Like nothing's changed?"

"Well, I was thinking . . ." I swallow hard. "I was thinking about not going back. At all. And maybe you and I could go somewhere together instead."

His eyes drop from mine. "You don't have to say that."

"I want to—"

"Wait, listen. I shouldn't have asked that of you—running away together. That was too much. Asking you to throw away your whole life on a whim like that. I just got excited that we might have similar . . . sentiments about each other and there might be a chance for me to not be put away and see if perhaps those sentiments might play out into something. But it's all right. I promise. I know it's too much to walk away from. It's your whole life."

"But I would. For you."

"You don't have to—"

"I want to. I mean it. Let's run away."

He smiles, though I'm not certain he believes I'm in earnest. "All right. Where will we go, then?"

"London, maybe. Or move to the country. Live like bachelors."

"Drive the local girls wild?"

"Something like that." The wind catches the strand of my hair Percy pushed away and pulls it over my forehead again, right across my burns. It stings faintly. "Though I think first I should sober up a bit. Stop mucking around so much and get my head on straight."

"That'd be good."

Percy smiles again, and I turn my face away from his, toward the sea and the spotty fishing boats gathered at the horizon. A few tall ships with their bowsprits pointed to the Aegean cant in the cradle of the waves. "Why've you stuck by me?" I ask. "I've been such a mess for a while now and . . . Holy Christ, Perce, I could hardly stand to be around myself. It's still really hard some days."

"Because that's what you do when you . . . for your friends." He flinches a little, a crease appearing between his eyebrows, then amends, "When you love someone. That's what I meant to say. When you love someone, you stand by him. Even when he's being a bit of a rake."

"More than a bit."

"Not all the time."

"For the better part of the last few years—"

"Perhaps, but you had—"

"I would have left me long ago. Kicked me into a ditch and been done."

"Monty—"

"Stopped answering the door, at the very least—"

"Shut it, will you?" He nudges the side of my head with his nose. "Just take it."

I put my cheek to his shoulder, and he rests his chin

against the top of my head. We stay like that for a while, neither of us speaking. The Aegean presses us together, the water sun-warmed and soft as court velvet.

"You don't have to come with me," he says quietly. "If you think you have some obligation to me because—"

"It's not an obligation. Perce, I love you." It trips out of me, and I can feel my neck start to burn, but I'm in this thick now, so onward I press. "I love you, but I don't know how to help you. I still don't! I'm an emotional delinquent and I say wrong things all the time, but I want to be better for you. I promise that. It doesn't matter to me that you're ill and it doesn't matter if I have to give up everything, because you're worth it. You're worth it all because you are magnificent, you are. Magnificent and gorgeous and brilliant and kind and good and I just . . . love you, Percy. I love you so damn much."

He looks down into the water, then back up at me, and it lifts my heart like a rising tide. His gaze makes me feel brave.

"And I need to know," I go on. "I need to know where your head's at. I don't care what the answer is—if you want me to walk away now and leave you be, I can do that. Or if you want a bachelor flat together with separate bedrooms, or if you want . . . more than that. I know it would be hard—because we're both lads and we'd be starting with bleeding nothing—but if you'll run away with me, let's run. I'm ready."

494

He doesn't say anything for what is likely only a minute but seems to drag across several years. His hands slide from their loop around my neck and down my arms before they finally settle upon my wrists, and it feels suddenly like he's edging away, the waves pushing us apart. Dread begins to snake through me like smoke between floorboards, because this determined avoidance of my eyes is looking like the prelude to a very kind *no, thanks.* I missed my chance in that rain-slick alley in Venice.

I brace for my heart to be shot from the sky, but then he says, "Monty, I will always care for you. I hope you know that. Perhaps if we had been more forthright with each other, or perhaps if we had trusted each other more, it could have been something sooner. But we weren't. So now we're here."

Good Lord, I think he's trying to let me down gently and instead it's like he's starting my execution by pulling out my fingernails. I'd take the bullet again over this. I'd catch that bullet with my teeth a dozen times over this.

He's still not looking at me. He's staring at the ground, winding up to break my heart, and I can't stick it any longer, so I interrupt, "Just say it, Perce. Please don't drag it out, just say that you don't want me. It's all right."

"What?" He looks up. "No. No! That's not what I . . . I'm trying to tell you I love you, you sod."

My heart takes a wild vault. "You . . . what?"

"Dammit." Percy tips his face to the sky with a moan. "I've had this whole speech worked out in my head—I've been planning it for weeks, waiting for a moment on our own—"

"Oh no, did I wreck it?"

"You completely wrecked it."

"I'm sorry!"

"And it was *so good*!"

"I'm so sorry!"

"Couldn't keep your fat gob shut for two minutes. Dear Lord."

"Well, that was a rubbish way to start it! I thought you were angling in the other direction and I panicked."

"Yes, well, I wasn't."

"Yes, well, I know that *now*." We're both red faced, both of us laughing, though we sober at the same time and trade a look that feels like silk against my skin. I tap his side with my elbow. "Say it anyway."

"In its entirety?"

"At least the important bit."

"The important bit was that if you go behind my back, I swear to God, I'll skin you alive—"

"I won't—"

"—murder you, then alchemically raise you from the dead so I can murder you again—"

"I won't, Percy. I won't, I won't, I promise you, I

won't." I put my hands upon either side of his face and pull him to me, standing on my toes so we are a breath apart. "Now say the rest."

His face goes shy, eyes flitting down, then back up to mine. "Yes, Monty," he says, and he smiles on my name. "I love you. And I want to be with you."

"And you, Percy," I return, touching my nose to his, "are the great love of my life. Whatever happens from here, I hope that's the one thing that never changes."

My hands are upon his face, mirror to the spot where I'll carry red, puckered scars for the rest of my life. In his gaze, they seem to matter less. We are not broken things, neither of us. We are cracked pottery mended with lacquer and flakes of gold, whole as we are, complete unto each other. Complete and worthy and so very loved.

"May I kiss you?" I ask.

"Abso-bloody-lutely you may," he says.

And so I do.

Dear Father,

As I write these words, I am sitting at the window of a small flat on a small island that is decidedly off the route you planned for me, having been dropped here by a group of pirates (though this lot are more aptly termed aspiring privateers) after fleeing Venice as a fugitive. I am not certain which of those will most horrify you.

If you desire to be further scandalized, proceed.

In the courtyard below me is Felicity, and she is looking rather happy—and here I was starting to believe her brow was permanently furrowed—and beside me is Percy, and were I not entirely occupied with this missive and he with his indestructible fiddle, I would be holding his hand. Perhaps even a bit more than hand-holding. I will absolutely be scratching that part out before I send this, but I needed to put it down in writing. I still can't believe it's real.

I have become the Grand Tour horror story, the cautionary tale for parents before they send their boys off to the Continent. I have lost my bear-leader. I have been kidnapped by pirates and attacked by highwaymen. I have humiliated your good name before the French court, run naked through the gardens at Versailles, turned up corpses, and sunk an island—a whole bloody island. You must be at least somewhat impressed by all that. Also I'm now short one ear (I'm certain it will grow back, though Felicity seems less confident).

But at least I didn't gamble away my fortune, run away with a French girl, and then abandon her. Now, that *would be scandalous*.

You would hardly recognize me if I returned home. Which I don't intend to do. Not now, anyway. Perhaps not ever. Percy and I will be staying in the Cyclades for the time being, and who knows where we'll go from here or what sort of life we will make, but we will make it together, on our own terms. Both of us. The first step will be unlearning all the things you've taught me for my entire life. It took several thousand miles for me to begin believing that I am better than the worst things I've done. But I'm starting.

Our pirate friends depart shortly, and I need to hand this letter off before they do. I'll send word once we're settled, and perhaps you and I will someday see each other again, but for now, know that we are safe, and well, and know that I am happy. For perhaps the first time in my life. Everything before is all shriveled and pale in *comparison to this. And I don't care what you say or what you think or what I am giving up—the Goblin can have it all. From here on out, I intend to have a damn good life. It will not be easy, but it will be good.*

And now Percy has his arms around me and Santorini and the sea are spread like a feast before us and there is sky all the way to the horizon.

And what a sky it is.

Henry Montague

Author's Note

I first learned about the Grand Tour of Europe while working as a teaching assistant for a humanities survey course in undergrad. I became fascinated by the concept because I had just come off my own Tour of sorts—a year abroad doing research for a thesis I would eventually write, interspersed with frequent jaunts to whatever European city Ryanair was running a deal on. The idea of young people left to their own devices on the Continent in the eighteenth century seemed fertile ground for the sort of tropey adventure novel I had always wanted to write.

But historical fiction is always a blend of real and imagined. So here I will attempt to separate fact from fantasy and lend context to Monty, Percy, and Felicity's escapades.

Bear with me as we take this last leg of the journey together.

The Grand Tour

In its simplest definition, the Grand Tour was a journey through the prominent cities of Europe, undertaken by upper-middle- and upper-class young men, usually after completing their formal education. The tradition flourished from the 1660s to the 1840s, and is often credited as the birth of modern tourism.

The purpose of the Tour was twofold: partly to expand yourself culturally through activities like perfecting language skills, observing art, architecture, and historic landmarks, and mingling with the upper echelons of society, and partly to sow those wild oats, and get the drinking, partying, and gambling out of your system before returning home to become a functioning member of society. Travelers toured under the eye of a guide, called a *cicerone* or *bear-leader* (a term that stemmed from the unsavory practice of leading leashed bears around the ring in a bearbaiting), and their Tour could last anywhere from several months to several years, depending on financial resources. The Grand Tour was a luxury limited to rich men, or those who could find a sponsor, and was dominated by the English, though in the 1800s some young women also toured, and the nationalities of Grand Tourists multiplied. Some Americans even traversed the ocean to make the journey.

The locations most commonly visited were the cities considered the most culturally important—Paris and Rome being the two must-sees. Those visits were interspersed with other significant cities such as Venice, Turin, Geneva, Milan, Florence, Vienna, Amsterdam, and Berlin. Few Grand Tourists went to Greece or

Spain, which were considered rough, inhospitable country compared to the well-trod northern routes. The wealth of most Grand Tourists allowed them to travel in style (including being carried across the Alps in sedan chairs), though the journey was not without its difficulties and dangers. The complications Monty, Percy, and Felicity encounter are all accurate to the period—Mediterranean pirates and highwaymen included. Few Grand Tourists, though, were unlucky enough to encounter both.

For more information on the Grand Tour, I would recommend *The British Abroad: The Grand Tour in the Eighteenth Century*, by Jeremy Black; *The Age of the Grand Tour*, by Anthony Burgess and Francis Haskell; and, one of the most thorough primary accounts of the life of a young man on his Grand Tour, the journals of James Boswell (who Monty anachronistically impersonates—the real James Boswell wasn't born until 1740, but I couldn't resist paying homage to my favorite source).

Politics

In the 1720s, the French crown was held by Louis XV, a young, sickly boy king controlled by a circle of powerful advisers, including Louis Henri, Duke of Bourbon and head of the French House of Bourbon. The duke wanted to prevent the family of the previous regent, Philippe,

Duke of Orléans, from ascending the throne should the king die. He was looking to secure both his own position and his family's, as the Bourbons had their fingers in the courts of many European powers. He broke off the marriage arranged by his predecessor between King Louis and the Spanish infanta, Marianna Victoria, because she was eight years younger than Louis and thus unable to bear children in a timely fashion. Shortly afterward, the duke was dismissed from his position as prime minister.

Beyond the engagement, politics in the French and Spanish courts were inextricably intertwined. The War of the Spanish Succession, which lasted from 1701 to 1714, resulted when King Charles II of Spain died childless, and the French House of Bourbon and the Austrian Hapsburgs each made a claim to the throne. On his deathbed, Charles II fixed the entire Spanish inheritance on Philip, Duke of Anjou, the grandson of King Louis XIV of France, putting the Spanish crown in the hands of the House of Bourbon. Many politicians saw the House of Bourbon as a threat to European stability, jeopardizing the balance of power, and the Bourbons had many enemies.

Power was a fragile thing in eighteenth-century Europe, and I have done my best to represent the political climate as it was in the early 1700s—though some timelines have been adjusted and condensed, because history rarely obeys novelistic structure.

Epilepsy

Epilepsy, or "the falling sickness" (the most common of many names used in the 1700s), is a disease that humans have been aware of and studying since ancient times, but in the eighteenth century it was still hugely misunderstood. The idea that epilepsy was a spiritual disorder and seizures were caused by demonic possession, popularized during the Middle Ages, fell out of fashion, but there was still no true understanding of its cause, or what part of the body it affected. Even the word *seizure* in this sense did not yet exist. All the treatments mentioned in the novel are true treatments of epilepsy from the 1700s—including healing spas, blood cleansers, vegetarianism, and drilling holes in the head, a practice known as *trephination*—as are the speculated causes. (One of the most common beliefs was that epileptic seizures were brought on by masturbation. Yay, history.)

Until the twentieth century, most epileptics were social outcasts, shunned by society, and the disease was classified alongside insanity. Many were confined to asylums, often kept in separate wings, away from other patients, because epilepsy was thought to be contagious.

In the second half of the nineteenth century, there were institutions created specifically for epileptics. Laws against epileptics' marrying at all persisted in both the United States and Great Britain into the 1970s.

This social stigma and isolation persists today, though our understanding and treatment of epilepsy has progressed significantly. Thanks to modern medicine, many epileptics are able to control their seizures, but most of the general population still has very limited understanding of the condition. Harmful myths such as the idea that a person can swallow his or her tongue while seizing remain prevalent. There are many different types of seizures beyond those depicted in the novel, and resources for seizure first aid and more information about epilepsy can be found through the Epilepsy Foundation at www.epilepsy.com.

Race Relations in Eighteenth-Century Europe

Black people have lived in Britain for centuries, though their circumstances have varied greatly depending on the time period, the location, and their economic station. Percy's situation as a biracial young man raised among the upper classes of eighteenth-century England would have been rare but not unheard-of. While sexual relationships (both consensual and nonconsensual) often occurred between white aristocrats and their black servants and slaves, intermarriage was rare in high society. It was much more common among the working classes, and eighteenth-century England had a rising generation of biracial people as a result. Black and mixed-race communities sprang up around the country, particularly in metropolitan areas such as London and Liverpool.

Black and biracial people had few employment opportunities beyond servitude—though slavery had no legal basis in England, the law did not prevent people from keeping enslaved Africans and it was not officially abolished until 1833. Britain also played a large role in the triangular slave trade, and slave labor propped up the economy of the British colonies. Black and biracial people were banned from many employment situations, and servants who ran away from their masters often had rewards offered for their capture. However, safety and unity could be found among the lower classes, and not only in black communities, but also among many poor white people. The racial divide tended to grow wider the higher up you moved in society.

However, many well-respected members of the upper classes had African ancestry or were biracial, among them Olaudah Equiano, a writer and abolitionist who helped eliminate the slave trade in England; Ignatius Sancho, a literary celebrity of Georgian England; and Dido Elizabeth Belle, upon whom Percy's situation as a biracial child in a white aristocratic home is loosely based. There are also many prominent historical figures of the time period that the history books often fail to mention were biracial, such as Alexander Hamilton and Alexandre Dumas.

Scipio and his band of pirates are inspired by a real crew of African men taken as slaves and forced to work as sailors, who revolted against their white masters and became pirates. The eighteenth century was the golden age of piracy, and pirates from the Barbary Coast— modern-day Morocco, Algeria, Tunisia, and Libya—made the Mediterranean treacherous waters for travelers (though their reach extended along the Atlantic African coast and in some places as far as South America). Ships that wanted to trade there had to pay a fee to the pirates for protection, or else risk seizure. Most of these pirates dealt not only in stolen goods, but also in human cargo, and either took their captured passengers as slaves to be sold in Africa, or held them to be ransomed back to their families for grand sums. From the sixteenth to the nineteenth century, between 1 and 1.25 million Europeans were captured by pirates and sold as slaves. The problem became so rampant that the United States declared war against the Barbary States twice over this issue in the early 1800s.

Queer Culture

The history of sexuality is tricky to study and trickier to write about, because the concept of sexuality itself is a modern one. In the eighteenth century, the general population would have had no vocabulary or understanding of any identity beyond cisgender and heterosexual, and even those were unacknowledged (and unnamed) because they were of an assumed universality. *Sodomy*—the most formal term for homosexuality at the time, drawn from the Bible—was a reference to the act of homosexual sex itself rather than attraction or identity. Every country had its own laws, but in most of Europe, homosexuality was both sinful and illegal, and punishable by fines, imprisonment, or sometimes death. Under the Buggery Act of 1533—which was not repealed until 1828—sodomy was a capital offense in England.

But in spite of the illegality, many European cities had flourishing queer subcultures, particularly for men (relationships between women at the time were largely undocumented and less commonly prosecuted). London in particular claimed more gay pubs and clubs in the 1720s than the 1950s. "Molly houses," the eighteenth-century equivalent of gay bars (*molly* being one of many slang terms that preceded *gay*), were spaces where queer men could meet, have relationships, cross-dress, and playact marriages to each other. The most famous was Mother Clap's, in London, which was raided in 1726. Some queer couples found a way to make a life together beyond the underground, and a few were even acknowledged as romantic partners by their community. (For further reading on this subject, I'd suggest *Charity and Sylvia: A Same-Sex Marriage in Early America*, by Rachel Hope Cleves, and the essays of Rictor Norton, a historian whose work focuses primarily on queer men in history.)

In the eighteenth century, the concept of the *romantic friendship*—a close, nonsexual relationship between two friends of the same gender that often involved holding hands, cuddling, kissing, and sharing a bed—flourished. Though the term wasn't coined until the twentieth century, it is used by modern historians to express close same-gender relationships before homosexuality existed as a recognized identity. There's no way to know how many of these romantic friendships were truly nonsexual, and how many were those of queer couples covering their relationship with the guise of friendship—though the concept is distinct from homosexuality, the two may have overlapped. Close physical relationships between friends of the same gender like Monty and Percy were common, though taking it further than friendship would have required secrecy and discretion, and in most places would have been unacceptable.

Which begs the question—would a long-term romantic

relationship between two upper-class English men during the eighteenth century have been a real possibility? I don't know. They likely would not have been able to be open about it. But the optimist in me likes to believe that the twenty-first century is not the first time in history that queer people have been able to live full romantic and sexual lives with the people they love.

And if that makes me anachronistic, so be it.

Turn the page for

MONTY'S GUIDE TO LONDON

Henry Montague's Guide to London

Hallo, my darling! So you've come to visit jolly old London, have you? You've probably been fed all sorts of nonsense about all the cultural sights here that will widen the horizons of your mind. Don't worry—that's all tosh. London is, above all else, a gorgeous and grotesque den of hedonism, and with my expert guidance, you'll have a smashing time (though you may not be able to remember it).

First, make sure you look the part. . . .

English Fashion Tips for Ladies

For the most fashionably pale skin possible, might I suggest a lead-based powder? It may poison you, but beauty is pain.

And don't forget your *mouches*! What is a *mouche*? You're very behind the times—they've been in fashion since the 1600s! A *mouche*, or a pox patch, is a tiny piece of fabric that ladies attach to their faces, sometimes to hide the scars from a pox and sometimes just for vanity. They can also be used to send a message to a gentleman, so careful where you place it! Some women even signal their political affiliation with the placement of their patches—right side for the Whigs, left for the Tories! I prefer a patch worn just above the lip—it means you're ready for a good flirt.

Nowhere to put your lady things? Just tie free-hanging pockets beneath your skirt and voilà! You can access them through slits in your petticoat, and whenever another lady compliments your taste in garments, you can reply, "Why, thank you. It has pockets." And then they will *ooh* and *ah* appropriately.

English Fashion Tips for the Gents

There's nothing like a pair of high-heeled shoes to elevate an outfit. Louis XIV made a rule about only members of the royal court wearing red heels, and suddenly they were all the rage everywhere. You still might see them around. Also there is no such thing as too many ruffles about the collar or cuff. Remember, ruffles are the sign of a rich man.

Wigs—nearly every gent wears one! Because nearly everyone has syphilis. We eighteenth-century lads are obsessed with hair—long and luxurious that would rival Samson himself. So as syphilis began to spread, like, well, syphilis, and scads of the population afflicted with the disease went bald as a result, hair loss was a source of great shame . . . until good old Louis XIV decided to make a fashion trend out of those lemons. Soon wigs were all the rage and became a way not just to get the long, luscious hair of your dreams, but also to show off how wealthy you are by how much hair you could afford. Ever been referred to as a "bigwig"? That term comes from the men who showed off their wealth by the size of their wig.

How to Get About London

Should you not have a private carriage at your disposal and do not wish to ride a diligence with peasants, you may hire a sedan, which is a wooden box you would be carried in by several strapping young gentlemen. To hire a sedan, send your footman into the street to shout, "Chair! Chair!" and several will come running.

Should you travel at night, don't forget to also hire a linkboy to light the lamps as you go or you'll find yourself stumbling around in the dark. And London isn't a kind city to strangers. You'll be lucky if it's only your pockets that get picked.

Learn the Language

Below, for your reference, are all the most important terms you'll need to get up to the best kind of trouble in the city.

Uphill gardener—A gent who enjoys the company of other gents.
Chirping-merry—One drink deep when the whole world is warm and wonderful.
In the gun—Two drinks in, just a bit tipsy.
Clip the King's English—Full-on plastered.
Swill-belly—A well-drunk gentleman.
Cast up one's accounts—When you've had a bit too much to drink and it all comes back up.
Pump ship—To take a good piss.

Milk the pigeon—To do the impossible. For example: Our travel to Barcelona seemed like an attempt to milk the pigeon.

Grope for a trout in a peculiar river—A particular form of horizontal amusement between two people, generally married but not to the other, who either love each other or like each other (or two people who find each other a bit pretty or at least available).

Eve's custom house—A lady's bits beneath the skirt.

Tickletail and Thingumbobs—The equipment a gentleman's got to work with. I'll let you ask your mother which is which.

Left-handed wife—The married gent's bit on the side.

Roast meat clothes—Your finest outfit.

Macaroni—The young gents who travel to the continent on their Tour and bring back all sorts of smashing fashion and trends that England has not yet caught on to.

The Best Places to Spend an Evening

Visit a coffeehouse, where men debate and discuss current events, fashion, politics, commerce, business, and gossip over disappointingly nonalcoholic beverages. Only a penny for coffee and admission. But no ladies, please.

The Gentleman's Club—Perfect for a night of spirits, gambling, and passing judgment on other aristocratic men. You'll find the best over in St. James.

Bare Knuckle Boxing—You'll find the best fights at the Royal Theatre but most barrooms hold matches as well. Each boxer will hold half-a-crown in each hand, and the first to drop their money loses.

Brothels—Throw a stone and you'll hit a den of ill repute in London. Then the brothel bully will emerge and throw you into the street on your arse for throwing rocks at their house. Covent Garden and Drury Lane are lousy with women plying their trade. (And it isn't a bad way to make a living—some make about four hundred pounds a year!) They're right near the theaters—you can get two kinds of entertainment in one square!

(If you're feeling shy about your own sexual prowess, read *Aristotle's Masterpiece*. It's got everything you need to know about anatomy and the finer points of how to use it. And should you fear venereal pox or impregnation, there's a marvelous invention known by many different names, but my favorite is the English overcoat. They're made from sheep intestines, completely reusable, and can be fastened on with a handsome little bow.)

Love and London

Are you touring with someone you fancy, or have you taken a lover abroad and are now looking for a romantic outing away from the eye of your bear-leader? Take it from someone who found love on the road—there are plenty of places to inspire a bit of a snog around the city.

The Tower Menagerie—Since King John II, the Tower of London has been a spot for exotic animals, but it's only lately been opened to the public. Admission is only three pence—or if you can't afford that, bring a feral dog or street cat to feed to the lions. In addition to the lions, there are bears, ostriches, big cats, and even an elephant (who drinks wine). It's the perfect opportunity to let your date clutch your arm in fear, and put on an act of swaggering bravery in the face of fearsome creatures. Just don't actually get too close—the creatures have escaped their enclosures and mauled tourists more than once.

The Theater—Take your darling to see the *Beggar's Opera*, the satire everyone's talking about. Pay a little extra and you can sit on the stage, or get a box and watch the fops cruise the gallery aisles for company. Or perhaps you're in the mood for something a bit more somber? Alexander Pope has just premiered his newly rewritten version of *King Lear* at the Theatre Royal—don't worry, the ending is much happier than Shakespeare wrote it!

Molly House—Perhaps you and your paramour have a relationship of a more elicit nature. Molly Houses are a safe place for lads of a certain persuasion to meet up and play backgammon, if you take my meaning. You can dance, dress, get a room—some of them will even get you married. But do remember to be discreet—wouldn't want to end up in the pillory, or what you might know better as the stocks, surrounded by a mob ready to hurl everything from rotten cabbages to insults to rocks at your head. Even worse, a few sods have found themselves taking a short drop with a quick stop at Tyburn. Sodomy may be a well-worn vice in London, but it's still illegal!

Do remember . . .

Whatever you do, don't drink the water! It usually comes straight from the sewers. Best to stick to gin—it's cheap and it's everywhere.

Careful to spend within your means! Wouldn't want to end up in the Marshalsea, a debtor's prison where they make you pay for your own confinement.

Keep your eyes up! Chamber pots are often dumped from upper-story windows, so you never know what's going to land upon your head when you're out for a stroll.

London is a cesspool of vice, villainy, violence, and some other word that starts with a V, but it escapes me now. I may have topped off my drink while I finished writing this guide. But if you mind where you step, keep your eye on your valuables, and don't eat anything you found in the street, you'll have a smashing time. Remember, darling, it's your Tour! Don't waste a moment of it on something so maudlin as virtue.

Read on for a sneak peek at
THE LADY'S GUIDE
TO PETTICOATS AND PIRACY

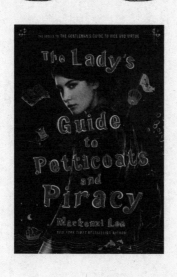

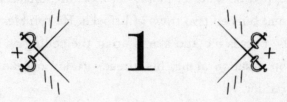

I have just taken an overly large bite of iced bun when Callum slices his finger off.

We are in the middle of our usual nightly routine, after the bakery is shut and the lamps along the Cowgate are lit, their syrupy glow creating halos against the twilight. I wash the day's dishes and Callum dries. Since I am always finished first, I get to dip into whatever baked goods are left over from the day while I wait for him to count the till. There are three iced buns still on their cake stand I have been eyeing all day, the sort Callum piles with sticky, translucent frosting to make up for all the years his father, who had the shop before him, skimped on it. Their domes are beginning to collapse from a long day unpurchased, the cherries that top them slipping down the sides. Fortunately, I have never been a girl overbothered with aesthetics. I would have happily tucked in to buns far uglier than these.

Callum is always a bit of a hand wringer who doesn't enjoy eye contact, but he's jumpier than usual tonight. He stepped on a butter mold that morning, cracking it in half, and burned two trays of brioche. He fumbles every dish he passes me and stares up at the ceiling as I prod the conversation along, his already ruddy cheeks going even redder.

I do not particularly mind being the foremost conversationalist out of the pair of us. Even on his chattiest days, I usually am. Or he lets me be. As he finishes drying the cutlery, I am telling him about the time that has elapsed since the last letter I sent to the Royal Infirmary about my admission to their teaching hospital and the private physician who last week responded to my request to sit in on one of his dissections with a three-word missive—*no, thank you.*

"Maybe I need a different approach," I say, pinching the top off an iced bun and bringing it up to my lips, though I know full well it's too large for a single bite.

Callum looks up from the knife he's wiping and cries, "Wait, don't eat that!" with such vehemence that I startle, and he startles, and the knife pops through the towel and straight through the tip of his finger. There's a small *plop* as the severed tip lands in the dishwater.

The blood starts at once, dripping from his hand and into the soapy water, where it blossoms through the suds like poppies bursting from their buds. All the color leaves his face as he stares down at his hand, then says, "Oh dear."

It is, I must confess, the most excited I have ever been in Callum's presence. I can't remember the last time I was so excited. Here I am with an actual medical emergency and no male physicians to push me out of the way to handle it. With a chunk of his finger missing, Callum is the most interesting he has ever been to me.

I leaf through the mental compendium of medical knowledge I have compiled over years of study, and I land, as I almost always do, on Dr. Alexander Platt's *Treaties on Human Blood and Its Movement through the Body*. Hands are complex instruments: each contains twenty-seven bones, four tendons, three main nerves, two arteries, two major muscle groups, and a complex network of veins that I am still trying to memorize, all wrapped up in tissue and skin and capped with a fingernail. There are sensory components and motor functions—affecting everything from the ability to take a pinch of salt to bending at the elbow—that begin in the hand and run all the way into the arm, any of which can be mucked up by a misplaced knife.

Callum is staring wide-eyed at his finger, still as a rabbit dazed by the snap of a snare and making no attempt to staunch the blood. I snatch the towel from his hand and swaddle the tip of his finger in it, for the priority when dealing with a wound spouting excessive blood is to remind that blood that it will do far more good inside the body than out. It soaks through the cloth almost immediately, leaving my palms red and sticky where I squeeze it.

My hands are steady, I notice with a blush of pride, even after the good jolt my heart was given when the actual severing occurred. I have read the books. I have studied anatomical drawings. I once cut open my own foot in a horribly misguided attempt to understand what the blue veins I can see through my skin look like up close. And though comparing books about medicine to the actual practice is like comparing a garden puddle to the ocean, I am as prepared for this as I could possibly be.

This is not how I envisioned attending to my first true medical patient in Edinburgh—in the backroom of the tiny bakeshop I've been toiling in to keep myself afloat between failed petition after failed petition to the university and a whole slew of private surgeons, begging for permission to study. But after the year I've had, I'll take whatever opportunities to put my knowledge into practice that are presented. Gift horses and mouths and all that.

"Here, sit down." I guide Callum to the stool behind the counter, where I take coins from his customers, for I can make change faster than Mr. Brown, the second clerk. "Hand over your head," I say, for, if nothing else, gravity will work in my favor in keeping his blood inside his body. He obeys. I then fish the wayward fingertip from the washbasin, coming up with several chunks of slimy dough before I finally find it.

I return to Callum, who still has both hands over his head so that it looks as though he's surrendering. He's pale as flour, or perhaps that is actually flour dusting his cheeks. He's not a clean sort. "Is it bad?" he croaks.

"Well, it's not good, but it certainly could have been worse. Here, let me have a look." He starts to unwrap the towel, and I qualify, "No, lower your arms. I can't look at it all the way up there."

The bleeding has not stopped, but it has slowed enough that I can remove the towel long for a look. The finger is less severed than I expected. While he sliced off a good piece of his fingerprint and a wicked crescent of the nail, the bone is untouched. If one must lose a part of one's finger, this is the best that can be hoped for.

I pull the skin on either side of the wound up over it. I have a sewing kit in my bag, as I have three times lost the button from my cloak this winter and grew tired of walking around with the ghastly wind of the Nor Loch flapping its tails. All it takes is three stitches—in a style I learned not from *A General System of Surgery* but rather from a hideous pillow cover my mother pestered me into embroidering a daft-looking dog upon—to hold the flap

5

in place. A few drops of blood still ooze up between the stitches, and I frown down at them. Had they truly been upon a pillowcase, I would have ripped them out and tried again.

But considering how little practice I've had with sealing an amputation—particularly one so small and delicate—and how much it slowed the bleeding, I allow myself a moment of pride before I move on to the second priority of Dr. Platt's treaty on wounds of the flesh: holding infection at bay.

"Stay here," I say, as though he has any inclination to move. "I'll be right back."

Go on a hilarious and heartwarming romp through 18th century Europe!

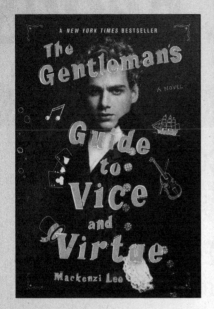

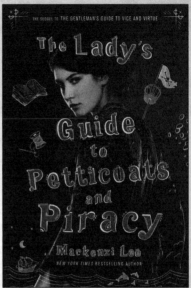

More from Mackenzi Lee

KATHERINE TEGEN BOOKS
An Imprint of HarperCollins Publishers

www.epicreads.com